AF348828

Praise for Timothy S. Johnston

The Furnace

"... a Crichtonesque thriller..."—Kirkus Reviews

"The action was tense, the mystery convoluted and interesting and the gore properly gruesome. Johnston held no punches while delivering his tale..."—SFcrowsnest

The Freezer

"The exciting tale will keep readers rapt, desperate to find out what happens next."—4 stars from RT Book Reviews

The Void

"This engrossing and exciting SF thriller is Johnston's third Tanner Sequence adventure (after *The Freezer*), but it stands well on its own... SF and mystery fans will be impressed with Johnston's tightly written deep-space whodunit."—Publishers Weekly Starred Review

The War Beneath

"If you're looking for a techno-thriller combining Ian Fleming, Tom Clancy and John Le Carré, The War Beneath will satisfy... I really enjoyed reading this book. It's what I call a ripping good yarn, a genuine page-turner. If you like action spy thrillers with lots of high tech in a science fiction setting this book will definitely please. It's loads of fun. And fast-paced. Did I mention fast-paced? 'Cause it is."—Amazing Stories

"*The War Beneath* is a thrill ride from beginning to end, with several heart-stopping scenes that clearly illustrate the boundaries of underwater living and warfare . . . Sometimes I couldn't turn the pages fast enough as I waited for Mac and his team to figure out how to live through their next quandary. The environment is well-described to the point where I nearly had to hold my breath for the entire book, something I find myself doing in underwater scenes in movies. The politics are sharp and twisty. What I really enjoyed about the story, though, was the evolution of Mac, himself. The plot challenges his past, present and future and he has to decide not only who he is, but who he wants to be. He has to balance his wish for a safe future for his city against the future of all the underwater cities and he has the legacy of his father and his relationship with his sister to consider as well. All in all, I really enjoyed The War Beneath. This novel is everything I've come to expect from Timothy S. Johnston and a promising start to a new series and one I look forward to following."—SFcrowsnest

"... sit back, start reading and enjoy a deep sea dive into the future . . . One very riveting, intelligent read!"—Five Stars at Readers' Favorite

The Savage Deeps

"*The Savage Deeps* delivers on every level. The action is perilous, but not an exact repeat of what we've seen before. New technology abounds, all detailed with exhaustive research. Once again, Mac is the star of the production, a wonderfully complicated character written with delicacy. There is a point when you can push a character too far. Mac is nudged up against the edge and held there until you think he might break. These scenes, for me, are just as thrilling as watching Mac perform daring underwater maneuvers. The emotional impact of this book is just as compelling as in the first one."—SFcrowsnest

"*The Savage Deeps* is like a futuristic *Das Boot* with a lot of intense action and some interesting technology . . . I give *The Savage Deeps* a five star rating."—A-Thrill-A-Week

"Reading *The Savage Deeps* is like watching a movie. The visual imagery of folks living and working in enclosed domes beneath the oceans, of zipping through the deep waters to visit other colonies using high-tech, high-speed subs is mesmerizing . . . In no time, the savage deeps explode with war. Torpedoes, mines, imploded subs, and bodies litter the ocean floor. With spies and traitors everywhere, will McClusky survive? Will Trieste realize independence? Twists, turns and the unexpected carry the exciting plot to its conclusion. You close the book and re-enter your own real world, feeling anything but certain that what you just read could never really happen . . . Johnston is an author skilled in bringing life to his characters through dialogue, engaging readers' emotions by their behaviors and thinking, and creating brilliant settings, all of which play out like scenes in a movie. Thinking of that, dare I suggest these two books are just ripe for becoming the next blockbuster movie? Food for thought!"— Five Stars at Readers' Favorite

Fatal Depth

"Timothy S. Johnston has the knack of getting the genre formula absolutely right in terms of balance. No one aspect hinders the others in any way. Plot, action, characterization, tech info, and originality are combined seamlessly into a tale that flows as rapidly as a river in flood. Some books are impossible to finish reading. This book is impossible to put down . . . In particular, the *Rise of Oceania* series by Timothy S. Johnston is sparklingly addictive, stimulating, entertaining, and truly "the pause that refreshes." In other words, a pleasant and exciting way to ignore your mundane real world problems. Escapist literature? You bet! In the best possible way. Action adventure techno-thriller done exactly right. Perfection, I'd say. Doesn't get better than this."—Amazing Stories

"The excitement factor in 'Fatal Depth' is no joke. You could almost compare it to a tsunami plow. The threads in the story culminate in an almighty push that will carry you all the way to the end in a dizzying rush. I read the second half of the book in one sitting . . . "—SFcrowsnest

"... heart-stopping action! Timothy S. Johnston is an incredible writer, word perfect, and so imaginatively creative one has to read his books to truly experience the cinematic aspects of his beloved underwater world.

He builds tension with every chapter as his plot twists and turns throughout, and even the last page jolts us with an unexpected shock. Yet, somehow in the midst of all the dangerous excitement, his readers find themselves caught up in the emotional pasts and presents of his characters, but
never at the loss of momentum or suspense. There's a reason Johnston
was the winner of the 2018 Global Thriller Award. Discover that reason
for yourself when you read his entire *Rise of Oceania* series of books."—
Five Stars at Readers' Favorite

"*Fatal Depth: The Rise of Oceania* is nautical thriller cli-fi reading at its best,
and joins two others in navigating a flooded, collapsed world in the 2100s
in which political clashes take place at sea . . .Exquisite in its combination
of futuristic vision, military maneuvering on all sides, conundrums facing survivors who keep encountering new situations, and political struggles that affect all communities above and below the tides of change, *Fatal
Depth: The Rise of Oceania* is both a powerful addition to the series and
a fine stand-alone read accessible to newcomers who may not have pri-
or experience with this setting. Maps, a timeline, and succinct description paint all the background necessary to thoroughly enjoy this thriller,
which should be on the shelves of any library strong in nautical cli-fi or
science fiction powered by political and military clashes."—Midwest Book
Review, D. Donovan, Senior Reviewer

An Island of Light

"From one of the most talented authors I've discovered in the past 2
years, Timothy S. Johnston, comes the fourth book in his series about
the new world beneath our oceans, *An Island of Light*. I've had the pleasure
of reading all three of Johnston's previous novels about Trieste City and
the hair-raising challenges faced by its gutsy mayor, Truman McClusky.
Johnston has consistently dazzled me with his cinematic descriptions of
this world in the deeps, a world created and populated in the hopes of
surviving the ravages of climate change on our planet's surface . . . The
result is a most satisfying and substantial read, especially for me, as who
we are is significantly more important than what we do. While the technology and science behind this undersea world are fascinating, as is the

ever-evolving and twisty plot, in the end, it's the characters who bring the story home. In conclusion, I have to say that of the four books in the series, *An Island of Light* is my favorite. That's because this time the emphasis is more on what makes people tick than on what is ticking inside the subs, the SCAVs, and the bombs. Readers are as riveted, maybe even more so, by what people say and do than by the ongoing battles for underwater supremacy. Is this a new direction that Johnston will pursue in his stories about Trieste and the underwater colonies? I look forward to finding out. Brilliant, stylistically flawless writing again, Mr. Johnston. It's a pleasure to read your books for so many different reasons!"—Five Stars at Readers' Favorite

"Readers of Timothy S. Johnston's *The Rise of Oceania* series will find plenty to appreciate here. Indeed, Johnston achieves the remarkable, not only exceeding the action and suspense of his previous books, but maintaining a pace that keeps the pages turning and the heart pounding, start to finish. Combine this with Johnston's command of leading-edge science and technology, and you've got one of the finest thriller writers working today. Prepare to be blown away, literally and figuratively."—Michael Libling, author of *Hollywood North: A Novel in Six Reels*

"Take a murder mystery, combine it with a futuristic setting, and add elements of psychological and social reflection for a sense of the action and focus of *An Island of Light*, which requires no prior familiarity with its predecessors in order to prove thoroughly engrossing on many different levels.

"Thriller, sci-fi and mystery audiences alike will find it crosses these genres with high-octane action and appeal."—Midwest Book Review, D. Donovan, Senior Reviewer

"*An Island Of Light*, the fourth book in Timothy S. Johnston's *The Rise Of Oceania* series, is perhaps the darkest chapter in the saga yet . . . Megan did it, no question. She also didn't have a plan beyond simple revenge, so when the USSF comes looking for their missing admiral, Mac and the rest of the team scramble to hide the evidence, to no avail. When the USSF leaves Trieste with Megan and Mac's chief of security in their custody, Mac has to gather the shreds of his current plans and tie them off to the dangling threads of what comes next: rescue his sister while interrupting the USSF occupation of a neighbouring colony . . .

"As author Johnston explores the morality of torture, murder, and retribution, he manages to keep Mac's moral compass pointing north but only just. It's this aspect of the book that will stay with the reader. Mac has always been a very real character. One the reader can empathise with and one we're willing to follow into the depths. So it's very fitting that he should struggle so mightily before pulling off the most inventive and daring rescue yet.

"*An Island Of Light* is a worthy instalment in the *Rise Of Oceania* series and I look forward to the next book."—SFcrowsnest

THE SHADOW OF WAR

Text © 2022 Timothy S. Johnston

All rights reserved. No part of this book may be reproduced in any manner without the express written consent of Fitzhenry & Whiteside, except in the case of brief excerpts in critical reviews and articles. All inquiries should be addressed to Fitzhenry & Whiteside.

Published in Canada by Fitzhenry & Whiteside Limited
209 Wicksteed Avenue, Unit 51, East York, ON M4G 0BB1

Published in the United States by Fitzhenry & Whiteside Limited
60 Leo M Birmingham Pkwy Ste 107, Brighton, MA 02135

Fitzhenry & Whiteside acknowledges with thanks the Canada Council for the Arts and the Ontario Arts Council for their support of our publishing program. We acknowledge the financial support of the Government of Canada through the Canada Book Fund (BF) for our publishing activities.

Library and Archives Canada Cataloguing in Publication

Title: The shadow of war : the rise of Oceania / Timothy S. Johnston.
Names: Johnston, Timothy S., 1970- author.
Identifiers: Canadiana 20220436177 | ISBN 9781554556007 (softcover)
Classification: LCC PS8619.O488 S43 2022 | DDC C813/.6—dc23

Publisher Cataloging-in-Publishing Data (U.S.)

Names: Johnston, Timothy S. 1970-, author.
Title: The Shadow of War ; the rise of Oceania / by Timothy S. Johnston.
Description: Toronto, Ontario : Fitzhenry & Whiteside, 2022. | Series: Rise of Oceania.
| Summary: "In the world's undersea realms the superpowers are pressing. Climate change is ravaging the surface nations and their militaries are surging into the oceans to seek out new resources to sustain their exploding populations. Now Truman McClusky, mayor of the underwater city, Trieste, must gather a team of operatives and travel to the world to steal the most unique and deadly weapon ever invented for use underwater. War is looming, and in order to win a war, one must do whatever it takes, even if it means embracing your darker side"-- Provided by publisher.
Identifiers: ISBN 978-1-55455-600-7 (paperback)
Subjects: LCSH: Military weapons -- Fiction. | Climate changes -- Fiction. | Undersea colonies – Fiction. | Science fiction. | Fantasy fiction.
| BISAC: FICTION / Science Fiction / Action & Adventure. | FICTION / Thrillers / Military.
Classification: LCC PZ7.J646Sh | DDC 813.6 – dc23

Image Credits:
© [ZinetroN] / Adobe Stock
© [NikolaM] / Adobe Stock
© [SergeyBitos] / Adobe Stock

Cover and text design by Ken Geniza
Interior schematics by Cheyney Steadman
Printed in Canada by Copywell

fitzhenry.ca

TIMOTHY S. JOHNSTON

THE SHADOW OF WAR

THE RISE OF OCEANIA

Books by Timothy S. Johnston

Fitzhenry & Whiteside Limited

The War Beneath
The Savage Deeps
Fatal Depth
An Island of Light
The Shadow of War
A Blanket of Steel (Forthcoming)

Carina Press

The Furnace
The Freezer
The Void

Timeline of Events

2020

Despite the fact that global warming is the primary concern for the majority of the planet's population, still little is being done.

2055

Shipping begins to experience interruptions due to flooded docks and crane facilities. World markets fluctuate wildly.

2061

Rising ocean levels swamp Manhattan shore defenses and disrupt Gulf Coast oil shipping; financial markets in North America become increasingly unstable due to flooding.

2062-2065

Encroaching water pounds major cities such as Mumbai, London, Miami, Jakarta, Tokyo, and Shanghai. The Marshall Islands, Tuvalu, and the Maldives disappear. Refugee problem escalates in Bangladesh; millions die.

2069

Shore defenses everywhere are abandoned; massive numbers of people move inland. Inundated coastal cities become major disaster areas.

2071-2072

Market crash affects entire world; economic depression looms. Famine and desertification intensifies.

2073

Led by China, governments begin establishing settlements on

continental shelves. The shallow water environment proves ideal for displaced populations, aquaculture, and as jump-off sites for mining ventures on the deep ocean abyssal plains.

2080

The number of people living on the ocean floor reaches 100,000.

2088

Flooding continues on land; the pressure to establish undersea colonies increases.

2090

Continental shelves are now home to twenty-three major cities and hundreds of deep-sea mining and research facilities. Resources harvested by the ocean inhabitants are now integral to national economies.

2093

Led by the American undersea cities of Trieste, Seascape, and Ballard, an independence movement begins.

2099

The CIA crushes the independence movement.

2128

Over ten million now populate the ocean floor in twenty-nine cities.

2129

Tensions between China and the United States, fueled by competition over The Iron Plains and a new Triestrian submarine propulsion system, skyrockets. The USSF occupies Trieste following The Second Battle of Trieste.

Winter, 2130

Trieste Mayor Truman McClusky begins a new fight for independence against the United States. With new deep-diving technology, he defeats French and US warsubs in battle in the Mid-Atlantic ridge, killing Captain Franklin P. Heller.

Spring, 2130

Russia launches dreadnought *Dragon*, a new terror in the oceans. She is 414 meters long, can travel 467 kph underwater, and possesses a new weapon: The Tsunami Plow. *Dragon* sinks many vessels and destroys the Australian underwater colony, Blue Downs. McClusky leads a raid to infiltrate and destroy the submarine.

June - August, 2130

Meagan McClusky, captured for murdering a USSF Admiral, is imprisoned at Seascape, the Fleet's new HQ. Truman McClusky, Mayor of Trieste, embarks on a perilous journey to rescue her using stolen German Submarine Fleet warsubs to draw Germany into the conflict. Seascape is destroyed with a new category of weapon, the Isomer Bomb.

January, 2131

Present Day.

"To light a candle is to cast a shadow."
—Ursula K. Le Guin

"I like my shadow; it reminds me that I exist."
—Mehmet Murat Ildan

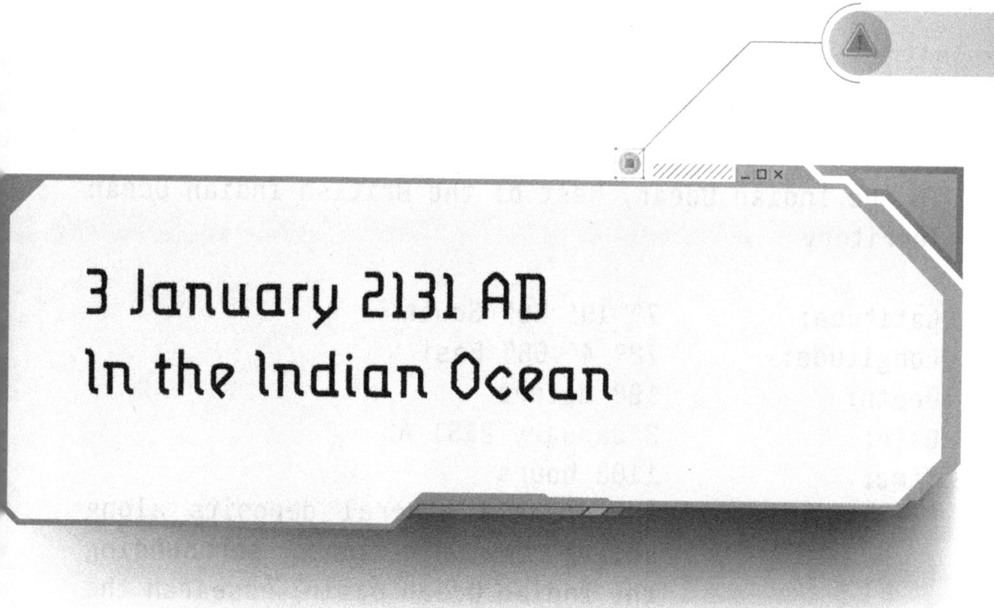

3 January 2131 AD
In the Indian Ocean

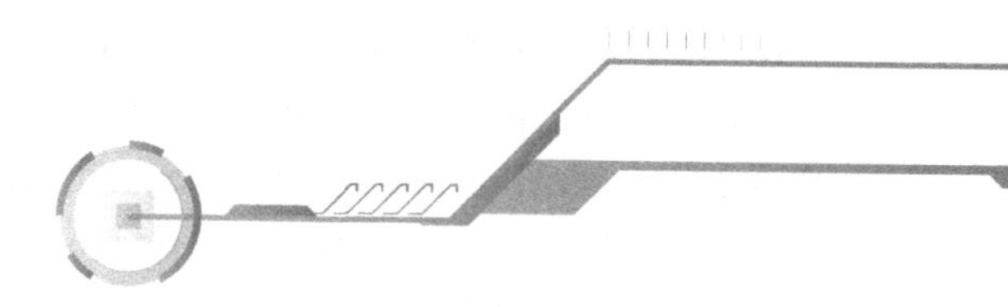

In the Indian Ocean, West of the British Indian Ocean Territory

Latitude: 7º 19′ 56″ South
Longitude: 72º 4′ 08″ East
Depth: 198 meters
Date: 3 January 2131 AD
Time: 1108 hours
Mission: Investigate mineral deposits along active tectonic zones surrounding the Indian Ocean basin; research the geology of the region.

THE GEOLOGIST'S HAND DISSOLVED INTO a gory mess before their eyes.

One second it had been completely normal. The next . . .

The skin bubbled and frothed, the upper layer peeled back and exposed the lower layer of fat, which then also began to liquify and drip to the steel deck. Blood boiled in an instant and wisps of vapor rose from the quivering mass of meat.

Mahiransh yanked his hand back from the hull, which he had just touched, and his eyes widened in horror as he watched white bone emerge. He clutched his forearm with his other hand, stumbled backward and opened his mouth to scream.

The shriek peeled through the seacar's living space, and Chalam Kaashif, the other geologist on board, watched his brother in stunned disbelief. "Manse, what the—" His words cut off in strangled horror at the sight before him.

Skin and fat and bone were melting from his brother's right hand and puddling at his feet.

What the fuck?

Just ten minutes earlier, things had been normal on board the seacar, though a tense eeriness had begun to settle on the small crew.

Chalam and Mahiransh Kaashif were both geologists in their early thirties. Born only thirteen months apart, in adulthood they resembled each other so much that many assumed they were twins. They were English, born on the mainland to two loving Indian parents, educated in science and technology in secondary school, following which both moved to Churchill Sands, the underwater colony in the English Channel, to study geology. Their lives had intertwined since birth, so much so that they not only looked alike, but they dressed alike, acted alike, and followed the same path toward the same career. Both wanted to live in the undersea cities, and had adopted a livelihood that could best make that a reality: geology, particularly undersea resource exploitation.

Now, in their doctorate years, they were in the Indian Ocean in a rented seacar loaded with sensing gear intending to study the Chagos Trench near Diego Garcia, the now-flooded island home to a United States Submarine Fleet and a British Submarine Fleet base. They had investigated the trench zone, an area unique in global tectonics, for it contained Subduction, Slip, *and* Ridge-Axis Boundaries—*three* different types, all in one location. It was highly geologic, not well understood, and the general area had hosted multiple major earthquake events in the past two hundred years, some of which had generated massive tsunamis and hundreds of thousands of deaths. Now that ocean levels were so elevated due to Global Warming—Diego Garcia was now a submerged submarine base!—tsunami study was more important than ever. Shores lined with concrete barriers only inches above the current ocean levels were vulnerable to the slightest geologic events.

The USSF bases at Norfolk and San Diego were proof of that; both facilities were now gone following the Russian attacks the previous year.

But the brothers' real purpose was to locate ocean floor resources for Churchill Sands. Wealth. Riches. Supplies to keep their undersea colony prospering.

Manse's girlfriend was piloting the seacar. They weren't deep—only about two hundred meters—and they weren't moving quickly. They were slicing through the water easily enough though; it sighed past the hull and the constant white noise was peaceful and calming. The sound of the single screw was pervasive, and the hum of ventilation and life support blended in with the background noise, eventually disappearing entirely into the mix. The seacar was at the limits of light penetration from the surface, so outside their ports it was a permanent twilight. The odd fish flashed by quickly, but before they could study it to determine the species, it was gone and in their baffles, lost to the buffeting and turbulence of their propulsion.

They'd all been enjoying the trip, even in the cramped confines of the seacar. Chalam had brought a friend as well—not yet a girlfriend, but he was hopeful—and so far the four had enjoyed the month-long trip. Evenings were for dinner and games. The days were for research and study of the undersea geology. The nights were for love, although Chalam was still working on Preet. She was receptive to minor things, like some kissing and mild petting on New Year's Eve, though things hadn't progressed past that.

Manse, on the other hand, and his girl Kalinda, were a different story. Their cries and moans echoed through the seacar on a nightly basis.

It was driving Chalam mad, though he felt happy for his brother, of course.

Preet often smiled when the topic came up, but she was too shy to speak openly about it.

Kalinda, however, was more liberal for an Indian girl, and she laughed about the sex and often joked about her nightly escapades with Mahiransh.

"You need to keep up with me!" she'd chided him one night over dinner while the brothers laughed. "Your libido is not manly enough for me!"

"I'm trying!" Manse cried back. "I'm working on my stamina!"

Meanwhile, Preet chuckled softly but said nothing, and Chalam stole sideways glances at her, hoping that she would open herself to their mutual needs soon. But she was a nice girl, he knew, and he could wait.

There was drink as well; the trip was an extension of university life: work, research, parties, studying, fun. Long periods of extreme stress, followed by short moments of release and pleasure.

The voyage in the Indian Ocean had been uneventful up until the strange sonar alarm had triggered its warning.

Kalinda was in the control cabin in the pilot's chair. "There's a weird ringing," she called back into the living cabin.

Chalam was studying the bathymetric readout of the ocean floor on a holoscreen, watching the peaks and valleys and searching the magnetometer for a cluster readout indicating iron nodules. The world was desperate for supplies—The Iron Plains dispute in the Pacific was proof of that—and if they could locate a deposit, it would make the trip more than worthwhile. "What does the sonar say?" he asked.

"Fish farms."

He looked away from his equipment and considered that. "Here?"

"Yes."

"Where are we, exactly?"

"West of the bases. We're not in USSF or BSF submarine port territory." The sub ports were located where Diego Garcia had formally poked above the ocean's surface—nowhere near their current location.

"We're not within their boundary?" he asked.

"Nope. I made sure to stay well away."

Chalam glanced at his brother, who was in the living space with him. Preet was still sleeping, hidden away in one of the narrow bunks recessed into the bulkhead. "What do you make of it?"

Manse shrugged. "Can't be a fish farm." He gestured outside, through a viewport. "Too deep. The bubbles would scatter and fish would escape."

Chalam nodded. His brother was right. Fish farms had to be shallow enough that the bubble walls maintained integrity. "Then why is it saying fish farms? The seafloor depth is—" he studied the readout "—five hundred meters."

"Doesn't make sense."

"What else causes bubbles like that?"

His brother considered the question. "Cavitation. Supercavitation. A hull leaking air." He shrugged. "A whale, maybe?"

Chalam yelled toward the pilot's cabin, "Are there any vessels near us? Any sounds of screws?"

"No," Kalinda responded.

"Any surface ships?"

"No."

"Weird," Manse said.

—••—

FIVE MINUTES PASSED. KALINDA REPORTED that the alarms were continuing, although there was no obvious source. Chalam checked with her in the pilot's cabin, and confirmed that the alarm was still saying *fish farms* as the source of the nearby noise.

He looked closer at the display to determine a range, and was shocked to find that it was within a hundred meters. "This can't be right," he murmured.

"What should we do?" Kalinda asked.

"Stop the ship, I guess. Maybe it's a mechanical flaw."

Kalinda's usually joyful expression grew concerned. "You think it's coming from us? From this ship?"

"It's possible." Chalam checked the depth again. They could survive a plunge to the bottom at that location, but whether anyone would know where they were was another story. They could call to the nearby BSF base for assistance, if need be. The two brothers and the women were British citizens, after all.

"If there's a rupture in our hull, wouldn't water be flooding in?" Kalinda's tone was now more anxious than usual. Her voice was quavering.

"Yes," Chalam said. "We'd have noticed." He gestured at the panel. "There are no red lights."

"This is just a rental. We wouldn't know."

"Is the ballast system functioning okay?"

"Yes."

Chalam considered it. "Maybe we should change to positive buoyancy and bring us toward Diego Garcia. Keep us level with a downward bow plane."

That way, if the engine failed and they lost forward momentum, they'd float upward and not sink.

The chances of rescue would be better.

Kalinda stared at him. "Will they be upset with us?"

"No. We're geologists. We're not doing anything wrong."

—••—

ANOTHER FEW MINUTES PASSED. KALINDA had made the navigational changes and had turned the seacar.

Manse, at Chalam's side, said, "That's odd."

The alarm was still sounding from the sonar, and it was still saying fish farms. Sonars were always listening to exterior noises; they could detect seacar screws, surface vessels, even various sea creatures.

"What?" Chalam said. He was staring at the image on the projection. There was some sort of structure on the seafloor that was not on the charts. The magnetometer reading indicating steel or iron was off the charts. What could it—

"The hull. Right there."

Chalam tore his eyes from the seafloor modules and stared at his brother. "What do you mean?"

Manse was pointing at the bulkhead just beside a couch in the living area. "It's changed color."

He frowned. What the hell did his brother mean? How could the hull—

But sure enough, Chalam could see what Manse was pointing to. A section of the hull was . . . *brighter?* The surrounding steel was a dull gray. But this area, about a meter in diameter, was shimmering. Giving off a strange flickering glow. Scintillating.

"What the fuck?" Chalam muttered.

Manse stood up and marched toward the bulkhead.

In the control cabin, the alarm was blaring.

—••—

"HEY BRO, BE CAREFUL," CHALAM warned.

"Why? What harm could there possibly be?"

He reached toward the exterior bulkhead.

"Is anyone around us now?" Chalam called to Kalinda.

"No, we're still all alone here."

He watched his brother step toward the bulkhead, his hand still outstretched. "Be careful," he repeated.

"It looks so weird," Manse muttered. "Seems like a glow, but it's . . . I don't know, *pulsating* maybe? And it's cold here."

It was indeed pulsing now. Flickering and glowing and rapidly shifting through the darker color spectrum. "Manse . . ."

And then Mahiransh's hand made contact.

———

HE YANKED IT BACK IN an instant.

The flesh was *steaming*.

Then his hand's *shape* suddenly distorted and grew bulbous. It lost its ridges and knuckles and even texture.

It just abruptly turned to . . . *glop*?

A memory suddenly occurred to Chalam. He and Manse used to attend a school where they had to eat hot meals at lunch. Had to sit with the entire school in a large cafeteria and eat in silence. If they didn't finish their plates, they got strapped. Corporal punishment in English schools had made a return in the 2100s. It was a result of escalating societal poor behavior, and parents willingly—and eagerly—signed on for it.

At those meals, the students always received custard for dessert. It had little form. It was supple, globular, shapeless.

As Manse's fist now appeared.

Within seconds, the underlying skeletal structure was visible, fat and skin were pooling around his wrist and dripping to the deck. Blood welled to the surface, mixing with the darker skin tones as his flesh peeled rapidly away.

Manse screamed.

"What is it?" Kalinda yelled from forward.

Chalam leaped to his brother's side and grabbed him around the shoulders. "Hold on—just hold on—" He struggled to lead his brother to the couch. Manse had grown suddenly limp, his knees had buckled, and Chalam was struggling with the weight.

A chuffing, creaking sound emanated from the hull.

"What was that?" Kalinda called again.

Manse had stopped screaming but was now wheezing in agony as he stared at his stump. The hand was now completely gone, melted away, dissolved right to the wrist. It wasn't burned . . . it hadn't been hot . . . it was just . . . *gone*.

Blood spurted from the stump, squirting with each thud of Manse's terrified heart.

"What the fuck?" Chalam said, for the second time. His eyes darted to the hull, and it was now bubbling where previously it had been flickering.

The steel was bubbling!

At the same time, an intense *cold* radiated from it. It caused a disconnect in Chalam's mind, for the bubbling made it seem like heat—as did the appearance of his brother's hand—but the temperature in the living space was plummeting, and mist had even started blowing outward from his exhalations.

And at that area on the hull, frost was forming, its tendrils stretching out like tentacles grasping at the steel . . .

There was another creak, this one long and sustained—almost a *moan*—from the hull.

The structure was giving in to the surrounding pressures at their depth.

"Oh, *shit!*" He darted to his feet. His brother had slumped to the couch, the whites of his eyes glowing behind half-closed lids as he passed out from pain and shock.

A survival instinct suddenly overcame Chalam.

He knew they were all on the verge of death.

The hull was about to wrench open.

Water would burst in, killing them in a crushing instant, or they would drown as the seacar plunged to the ocean floor.

The reason why was not important. He'd stopped thinking about the weird flickering and his brother's hand. All that mattered now was *survival*.

He thought frantically.

The alarm was still sounding.

Fish farms.

Fish farms.

Fish farms.

He bolted to the airlock and scrabbled at the locker. He needed scuba gear, and he needed it *now*.

He thought of Preet, currently asleep in the bunk, though that scream must have woken her. "Get ready!" he bellowed. "We're about to—"

The hull suddenly broke wide open, and the ocean surged in.

He saw a flash of blue lights—pressure warnings—and then—

Images of death flooded his mind.

And bubbles.

Fish farms.

Fish farms.

Fish farms.

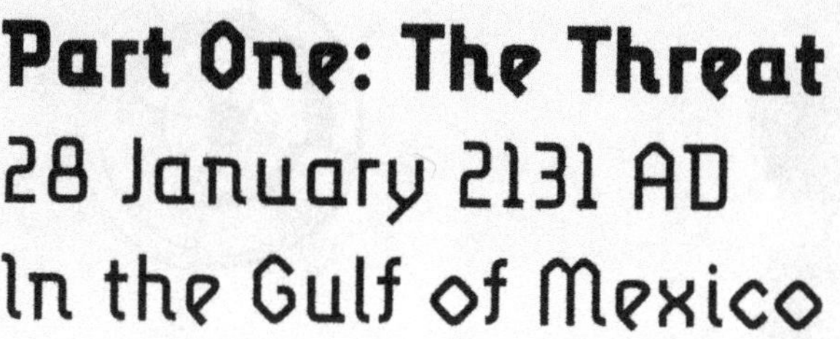

Part One: The Threat
28 January 2131 AD
In the Gulf of Mexico

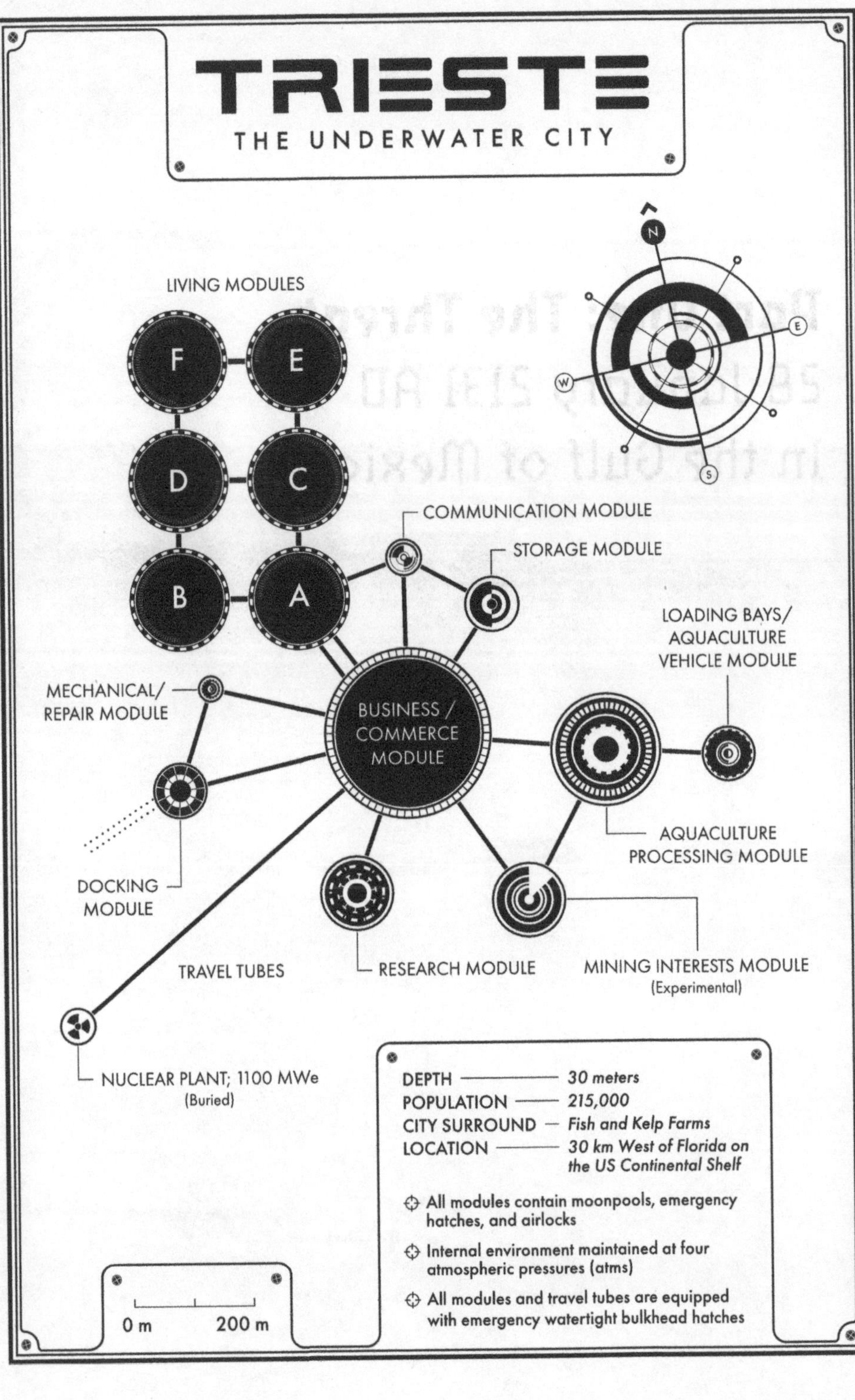

TRIESTE
THE UNDERWATER CITY

LIVING MODULES
F
E
D
C
B
A

COMMUNICATION MODULE
STORAGE MODULE

LOADING BAYS/
AQUACULTURE
VEHICLE MODULE

MECHANICAL/
REPAIR MODULE

BUSINESS /
COMMERCE
MODULE

AQUACULTURE
PROCESSING MODULE

DOCKING
MODULE

TRAVEL TUBES

RESEARCH MODULE

MINING INTERESTS MODULE
(Experimental)

NUCLEAR PLANT; 1100 MWe
(Buried)

N
E
W
S

DEPTH — 30 meters
POPULATION — 215,000
CITY SURROUND — Fish and Kelp Farms
LOCATION — 30 km West of Florida on
the US Continental Shelf

All modules contain moonpools, emergency
hatches, and airlocks

Internal environment maintained at four
atmospheric pressures (atms)

All modules and travel tubes are equipped
with emergency watertight bulkhead hatches

0 m   200 m

Chapter One

THE FIRST ATTACK OCCURRED ON 28 January. There would be three more before I deciphered the clues and figured out what was happening.

And when I did . . .

I needed to kill.

I'd never felt revenge that hot, that intense. It would turn into a fire burning within me, impossible to extinguish, impossible to quench. I'd learned that even murder didn't put out flames that angry—it only made the trauma burrow deeper within, where it festered and boiled, only to emerge later in some other toxic form.

I'd learned that from my own experiences, from my sister, Meg, and from my friend Rico Ruiz, now dead from his own need to achieve vengeance.

But that didn't stop me this time. Not when I finally realized the truth.

—••—

I WAS IN MY OFFICE in Trieste. It was cramped, plain, and mostly steel with chairs and papers scattered about, the remnants of multiple strategy meetings that never seemed to end but always seemed to start. Just a flood of people coming and going, one meeting merging into the next. There were always decisions to make, paths to choose, people to placate, and questions to answer. That was my life as Mayor in the underwater city of Trieste.

It was also my role as Director of Intelligence, a position I'd held for two years. TCI was covert—very few people knew of its existence, just those in my inner circle and the few agents we had still alive—and its mission was to fight to improve our position in the world's oceans. To always have the upper hand. We needed the best technology, the best military, the most knowledge of what the others were doing. In this case, that meant mostly the superpowers like the United States, China, and Russia. We needed to stay ahead of them, always. Sometimes it meant death, but it was what we did. My father had held my role before me, many years before, until the CIA and USSF killed him when I was only fourteen. It had caused a shadow across my entire family, one that had stretched on now for years, but I'd learned to endure. I had learned from the mistakes of others, and come to terms with the people who'd orchestrated the attack.

Now I kept my eyes on the other underwater cities and watched them carefully. Watched the various submarine fleets of the superpowers. My cabinet kept me abreast of new technologies, to make sure we were always at the forefront of the race to locate and extract resources. I sent my agents out to do our *business*—a euphemism, most definitely—and watched carefully.

Always kept my eyes on current events, to make sure we were ready for the coming war.

My role as Mayor, on the other hand, was vastly different. It was administrative in nature. I had to keep the kelp and fish farming going. Had to make sure crews monitored the city modules and keep the many citizens safe and happy. I kept the mining division extracting valuable minerals, the kelp farmers harvesting, and the repair people maintaining all the equipment, especially life support. I visited the schools and read to the children whose families were forging their lives in this underwater world.

The climate chaos on the surface was taking over. Global Warming had shattered shore defences and scorched farmland. Rising water had overwhelmed many island nations. Citizens had abandoned the low-lying ones, like the Maldives. The worst example on the mainland was Bangladesh. Tens of millions of people now had no homes. The humanitarian disaster there was indescribable. And, in the developed nations, even at higher elevations, economies suffered. Climate chaos had disrupted shipping when crane facilities on the shores became inundated.

And the topside nations were looking to us for resources. Fish, kelp, minerals, whatever we could locate and mine profitably. We used kelp to eat and shipped much out for further processing to methane. It grew half a meter a day at our location west of Florida, and was the purpose of Trieste, supposedly.

I glanced at Richard Lancombe, who was with me in my office. He was older, his hair long since white, and he'd lived most of his adult life in the underwater world. Despite his age, he was fit and agile. He swam each day—a five-kilometer route that many Triestrians seemed to enjoy lately—and he hadn't yet begun to hunch from age. His senses were still sharp. He was my confidante and most senior advisor, and we met daily to stay up to date on TCI and our activities.

"What are you thinking, Mac?" he asked, looking up from his notepad.

My name is Truman McClusky, though most people shortened it to *Mac*. "Wondering why you want to go to Churchill Sands."

"It's a logical choice."

"Why, again?"

He grinned. "Look, Mac. You've just brought New Berlin into our movement."

"And the six Chinese cities. Don't forget them."

"You've done better than I thought possible. Oceania now has fourteen cities! All working together to achieve independence."

That was TCI's ultimate goal, with me at the helm. My dad had failed, but now I'd taken over. The most recent addition—the German city—had been the result of an elaborate plan involving the commandeering of a GSF sub, an attack on the United States Submarine Fleet's HQ in the Gulf—Seascape—and its ultimate destruction with an Isomer Bomb. The US had assumed Germany was the culprit, and ongoing diplomatic discussions were threatening to explode into outright war.

Meanwhile, we sat out and watched the argument escalate.

It had worked brilliantly.

There was a tiny viewport in the bulkhead, and outside, in the sunlit warmth of the Gulf waters, my girlfriend Renée was checking the countermeasure stations and torpedo launchers that surrounded the city. I could just see her on her scooter approaching a launcher in the east quadrant—the side a Russian attack was most likely to come from in the coming weeks. I had been on the schedule to go out with her that morning, but had decided to stay in the office and take care of city business instead.

I was beginning to regret it.

"Thanks," I muttered.

"I'm not joking," Richard said. "The number of cities—"

"Russia destroyed Blue Downs in the fighting. We destroyed Seascape."

"Blue Downs has been rebuilt."

"Thousands died!"

"And Seascape," he said, ignoring me, "was the USSF base here. They were too close for comfort."

"I killed many people." My voice was gravel, but too quiet for him to hear.

"The US is rebuilding Seascape too. It'll be finished soon."

I sighed and tried to ignore the thoughts boiling in my head. Blue Downs was the Australian city. Already its population had surged into the tens of thousands. The world needed our resources, and the destruction of a city was not going to stop the topside nations. They needed food, iron, manganese, kelp . . . and whatever else we could provide.

It was why I wanted independence for us. They were practically stealing our produce, when they should be purchasing it and letting us develop our own economies. We were not their slaves.

I glanced outside again at Renée. As if on cue, my comm crackled. "Just finishing up here, Mac. The torpedoes look great. No corrosion. The equipment is fine."

"Acknowledged," I responded in a crisp tone. I wished I could have made it softer and more romantic, but business was business, and I wanted to be professional.

There were sometimes crews at the torpedo launchers, watching for potential attacks, but we could also fire remotely from City Control, from the console just outside my office. Renée usually operated it, but part of her duties included maintenance. She loved being outside. I could see her in scuba gear, mounting the scooter, and getting ready to power away to the next launcher.

"So why Churchill Sands?" I asked Richard again, keeping my eye on the scene outside. Kelp swayed in the currents and fish flitted about. Citizens were swimming and the surface light thirty meters above lit the entire scene. Beams of sunlight shimmered through the waves from far above; it sparkled and dazzled in the warm waters.

"The British city could be our next target."

"Target?"

"The population is ready to turn. They have an exciting Mayor there. I think we might convince her."

I searched my memory. "Sahar Noor."

"Yes, she's galvanizing the population to work for the benefit of their colony, not for the United Kingdom. It is a perfect precursor to what we want."

"You mean Oceania."

"Yes, of course." He frowned at me. "Are you okay, Mac?"

I started a response, then stopped. The truth was, I wasn't sure. There was just a lot going on. Meg, for one. My sister was still recovering from the recent episode at Seascape, before we'd blown it up.

"What else is there?" I turned and studied his expression. The wrinkles made him seem wise, but the eyes were dark and hard to decipher.

"What do you mean?"

"At Churchill Sands." I clenched a fist. "Come on, Richard. I know you. There's more going on there than a Mayor who might be receptive to us. What is it?"

His face was ice for a moment before a smile spread slowly across it. "You're good."

"I just know you."

"Well, a scientist has contacted me. About a new weapon."

—••—

THAT GOT MY ATTENTION. "WHAT type?"

"I'm not entirely sure, but—"

There was flash of light from the viewport and a moment later a dull thud rumbled past the city. I snapped a look out to Renée—

And saw an expanding fireball where the torpedo launcher had been a moment earlier. A surge of water was moving toward Trieste's modules, the kelp pressed nearly flat to the sand by the shockwave.

There was no sign of Renée.

I lunged to my feet and put my face to the port. "Renée!" I screamed. My spittle spattered the glass.

There was no response.

———••———

BARELY TWENTY MINUTES LATER, I was in the clinic staring at Renée, her body limp on a procedures table. I clutched her hand, desperately hoping for a sign of life. Richard had accompanied me, as well as Meg, and my Chief Security Officer, Cliff Sim. The doctor was working on Renée, staring at the readouts as she placed sensors on Renée's chest and arm.

The clinic was in the same module as City Control, but just a few decks down. We'd sprinted through the corridors and down the steep ladders to get there in less than a minute. Five minutes following that, a crew had brought Renée in, still in her wetsuit. Her scuba tanks were gone, however, blown apart in the blast. Her full facemask had remained on, luckily, and might have given her a precious minute or two of survival.

I desperately hoped for good luck.

I can't go through this again, I thought.

"She's alive," Doctor Stacy Reynolds said to me. "Still breathing, O2 levels are fine. The mask saved her life."

My breath blew out in a rush; I hadn't even known I'd been holding it in. "Why isn't she awake?"

"Concussed maybe. She's just unconscious. I'll give her something . . . just wait a second . . ."

I turned to my CSO. "Cliff, what the hell happened?"

"No idea, Boss. She'd been checking the torpedo launchers and the countermeasure stations. In fact . . ." He trailed off and stared at me.

I met his eyes. He was a mountain of a man, all muscle, bald, and tough as titanium. He was former USSF, but now worked for me. He still had a limp from the leg break he'd suffered at Seascape the previous summer, but otherwise he was back to his usual self. "What is it?"

"Weren't you supposed to be on that detail?"

I nodded. "Don't say it."

"Why not?"

Because it's yet another reason for me to feel guilt, I wanted to say. I settled on, "I can't stomach losing someone else, Cliff."

"I hear you." He gestured at her. "But she's alive. She was far enough away when it detonated."

"So it was a torpedo?"

"I have a crew headed there now. They'll report back when they know."

"That's the likely reason, isn't it?" Richard said. "Torpedo detonated during the inspection."

Meagan cleared her throat. "Makes sense. I don't think the rest of them blew, though. How many are at each station? Ten? Twelve? That couldn't have been more than one that went."

I studied her. She was blonde with blue eyes and freckles. Men generally found her irresistible, but our family past kept her from enjoying it too much. The anger from our dad's assassination in 2099 had consumed her to the point of committing murder. Since then, however, she had recovered physically, though there were still scars on her legs and a weight to her presence. She wasn't the jovial, happy self I'd known as a teen. But things had improved dramatically since she'd killed Admiral Benning and we'd rescued her from Seascape.

I turned back to Renée. She was breathing normally, and the color was returning to her face. Her dark hair was short, as most Triestrians kept theirs, and I could see her eyes moving under her lids.

"That's a good sign," Stacy said.

"Her eyes?"

"Yes. She's just unconscious, but aware. I'm bringing her out of it now." She adjusted the IV and the response was instantaneous.

Renée gasped. Her eyes snapped open, then she immediately groaned. "Oh, my head."

"Pain?" Stacy asked.

"Headache. Like a knife." It was all she could get out; her eyes were now squinted shut against the light in the ceiling.

Stacy gestured for the light to dim and administered a painkiller via the IV.

Almost immediately, Renée said, "Better. Thanks. Whatever that was, I want more."

"Morphine," Stacy said.

"I like it."

"What happened?" I asked. I gripped her hand tighter, if that was at all possible.

Renée sighed. Then she turned her head and looked at me. Her lips stretched into a lopsided smile. "You're here." Her lids were now half-closed as she slurred her words; the drugs had made an immediate impact.

"I am."

"Thank you."

"No other place I'd be."

"I'm happy."

I didn't want to say what I was really thinking at that point. "Any sign that a torpedo was about to go?"

"No. They seemed perfect. The crew has maintained them well."

It was as she'd reported earlier. *No corrosion, equipment is fine.*

Cliff had moved against a bulkhead and was in a discussion with his team out at the detonation site.

Meg stepped in and grabbed Renée's other hand. "Glad you're still around, Frenchie."

Renée smiled. "Glad I am too. I am not through with you two yet."

Meg had accepted my relationship with Renée and had practically already adopted her into the family. It had been difficult for all of us, since my previous girlfriend, Katherine Wells, had died in the fighting in the Mid-Atlantic Ridge a year earlier. At one point, Renée had wanted me dead. She had tried to kill me multiple times, but I'd convinced her to join our movement, and now she was living at Trieste and fighting by our side against the world's superpowers.

"I'm glad you weren't with me," she sighed.

"I wish I had been."

"Why? You think you could have prevented the explosion? You really are crazy."

"It's possible." I shrugged. "I might have protected you."

"I'm alive. I was far enough away I guess."

"Tell me what happened."

She squinted again as she tried to recall the events. Her voice was soft, her words still slurred slightly. "I had just checked the torpedoes. They're underground in a concrete bunker. There's an airtight cabin there too, where we sometimes have people to control them manually."

"No one was there though, right?"

"Yeah. It was on full remote."

"Did anyone touch the console in City Control?" I asked. I realized I'd have to ask Cliff to check the video surveillance to find out if someone had detonated a weapon from the command center. That chilled me to the bone; it was only a few meters outside my office, where I'd been with Richard. I didn't want to entertain the possibility that someone could have done this from someplace so near.

"No idea," she said. "I'd just reported back to you, got on the scooter and was jetting away. The next one is only a hundred meters farther to the east. I had descended a bit; there's a rock outcropping on that side. I was just behind it when all hell broke loose."

"That rock likely saved your life. Protected you from the blast."

"Yes."

I kissed her forehead, which was still wet with salty water. Her hair was still saturated, but I brushed the water aside and kissed her again.

"I have a headache tonight," she muttered.

It made me laugh. It was something she never said to me. In fact, she was one of the most sexually aggressive women I'd ever known. "I forgive you. A torpedo explosion is good reason to reject me."

"But only for tonight."

"Yes." I smiled. "Just one night's reprieve for you. That's all."

"I'll be all over you tomorrow. I promise."

I brushed her cheek with the back of my hand. "No pressure," I joked.

"Mac," Cliff called from the edge of the clinic. He was holding his PCD and staring at me.

I turned back to Renée. "One minute. I'll be back in a sec."

She closed her eyes. "Take your time."

I marched over to Cliff and let Meg take my place at the bedside. Cliff's eyes were darker, if that was at all possible.

"What is it? The report?"

"My team is there, and it's not good."

"The torpedoes are all gone?"

"Worse than that."

I grunted and stared at him, processing. "Say again?" I was stalling, trying to decipher what he meant.

"The torpedoes are still there. Twisted, damaged, ruined, yes. But my people accounted for all of them. None of them went up in the explosion."

I stopped and considered that. "So they didn't blow?"

"None of them did. Right."

I turned my back to Renée so she couldn't see the rage on my face. "So it was meant for me."

"That's right." His face was hard; the lines in his forehead deep.

"So what exploded?"

"That's the problem, Boss. It was a bomb. Planted somewhere nearby. Whoever did it likely thought all the torpedoes would also explode, maybe to conceal evidence, but—"

"They weren't armed."

"Right."

"So someone remotely detonated it."

"To kill, yes." He paused, then said in a soft but deadly hard tone, "To kill *you*, Boss. It was an assassination attempt, Mac."

Chapter Two

Two days later, we were on our way to the British undersea colony, Churchill Sands, in the English Channel. The bombing investigation was continuing, but I couldn't hang around Trieste anymore and sit on my hands waiting. I was driving Cliff crazy, for one. He had a team of people working on the issue, but the extensive damage to the torpedo launcher was hampering his efforts and the forensics took time. He had reviewed the surveillance video of City Control at the moment of detonation; no one had been near the console. And surveillance of the actual site was a challenge, because the perpetrator could have planted the bomb at any point during the previous weeks.

So I gave up waiting, gathered my team, and departed for the North Atlantic.

Richard was the principal operative on this assignment, so he led the mission and had researched all the important players. I still wasn't a hundred percent aware of who we were to meet or what the mysterious weapon he spoke of was, but he was a senior member of TCI and I trusted his instincts. He'd worked with my dad in the early days of Trieste's espionage activities, attempting to keep the city on top of the underwater food chain in terms of technology and resource extraction, and had been working for independence for the undersea colonies since before I'd been born. I trusted him implicitly.

Meg was also with us on the mission; Renée was staying back at Trieste to recover.

The true reason for my visit was Sahar Noor, Mayor of Churchill Sands. She had quite a reputation in the undersea colonies already— and probably topside as well—because of her status as not only a young, captivating leader, but also as a woman and a practicing Muslim living in the undersea world. I was curious, I had to admit. I'd seen videos of her at cabinet meetings, at political rallies, and giving speeches.

Colonists were rough people. We were hard, you could say. Determined. Many of us worked for our colonies to see our city prosper. We rarely took time off. We were often outside, in the water, working the fields or extracting resources. On off-time, we usually volunteered at other jobs around the city. And when we weren't doing that, we were sleeping in our tiny living spaces. It was not relaxing, it was not luxurious. We had families and raised our kids in the underwater cities, but they were a different breed as well. They all lived the same drive as the rest of us: the need to work hard and make sure our lives underwater continued. We wanted to make our colony efforts profitable and *necessary* to the topsiders, so they couldn't try to pull the plug on us.

We also wanted to make sure they didn't control us too much, but that was another story . . . one that involved war and suffering and death and subterfuge.

But Sahar was not just surviving in this situation; she was enormously popular and seemed to be thriving. She had become a bit of a celebrity in recent months. I was anxious to meet her.

Johnny Chang, another crucial member of my team and my Deputy Mayor, would stay at Trieste and keep things moving. We had several projects on the go: the shelters for our citizens under the modules were largely completed—carved into bedrock—but there were still some finishing touches to complete. Richard had been in charge of the construction. The remote launchers needed constant monitoring and upkeep, not to mention repairs to the one that had just exploded. There were countermeasure stations to add, as well as more sensitive listening posts to plant. Incursions—by warsubs or even individual troops—in our waters was something we always needed to be prepared for. It had happened to us numerous times in our recent history, most notably the Chinese theft of the SCAV technology in 2129, and the attempt on my life by German special forces during the previous summer, in 2130.

We boarded my ship, *SC-1*, powered out of the Docking Module and into the Gulf, banked to the east, and accelerated away from the city.

—••—

WITHIN MINUTES I'D ACTIVATED THE autopilot and leaned back in the pilot chair and stared at the clear waters surging past the cabin viewport.

I loved the oceans, and always had. The mystery, the depths, and even the danger—it all appealed to me. It seemed as though I'd never lived topside, though of course I had as a child before my dad had moved us to Trieste. I had a few memories of living on land. I remembered the blue skies, the dirt under my shoes, the heat, the sun.

The blistering sun . . .

I preferred the relatively cooler waters where I was now. Even the pervasive danger didn't bother me.

I glanced around at the ship's interior. *SC-1* was the size of small recreational vehicle topside. The control cabin had two pilot chairs; the console between them was for ballast to manipulate our depth and trim. Directly behind were the bunks, recessed into the bulkheads, then a living space with comfortable couches, the moonpool hatch in the deck to exit from the underside of the seacar—but only if our interior pressure of four atms matched the exterior, meaning thirty meters—and then the airlock, engineering, and behind that, the SCAV machinery.

The supercavitating drive.

It was the greatest innovation in undersea living since Cousteau's aqualung. Invented by the Soviets in the 1970s, the concept was simple: the seacar's blunt bow caused gases to churn from seawater as we plowed forward. Cavitation is a common issue around the blades of screws; it could cause bubbles and noise, which most stealthy warsubs want to avoid. But with supercavitation, the gases built into a bubble that eventually enveloped the entire vessel. At that point, friction lowered to almost nothing. Our fusion reactor flash boiled seawater and ejected the steam from the aft thruster, propelling the vessel forward. It was loud—there was no hiding from sonar while using it—but it was *fast*.

—••—

WE WERE MOVING AT FULL speed, northward, through the Atlantic and toward the English Channel. It was still difficult to wrap my head around the concept, even having lived it for the past two years, but the journey would take less than a day. It was simple math calculated by the onboard navigation system: 8,200 kilometers at 450 kph. That meant the journey would be only eighteen hours. We travelled at a 200-meter depth to take advantage of the northward Gulf Stream/Atlantic Drift current, which would give us an added boost of speed.

The comm beeped and I moved to answer it.

"Mac, it's Cliff, back at Trieste." His face appeared on the console screen.

"How are things?"

"Just running this investigation."

"Find anything?"

"I've finished monitoring the video surveillance of that launcher. Nothing out of the ordinary. A few swimmers out for regular exercise. Some sightseers. We're investigating them too, but they're lifelong Triestrians."

He stopped talking and I frowned. "That's it?"

"About possible suspects at the scene, yes."

I stared out the viewport. The bubble surrounding the seacar distorted things; it was shimmering and out of focus, like looking the wrong way through a telescope or wide-angle lens. The thrum of the fusion reactor vibrated the deck and chairs, and its loud, pervasive noise blanketed us in cold comfort.

Beside me, Richard watched the exchange in silence.

"But there must be more," I finally managed, trying to urge him to give me important information that just wasn't there.

"There's nothing. I'm sorry, Mac. We'll keep looking, of course."

"Is Renée helping?"

"She doesn't remember much of the actual event. She's concussed, and dealing with that right now. I'll talk to her again when I can."

I knew she was still in the clinic, recovering, and had insisted that I continue on my original plan to go to Churchill with Meg and Richard.

"What about the actual explosive?" I asked.

"I have the mining division looking into it."

I frowned. "Why?"

"I think it was a mining explosive. Used in underwater blasting."

"Why?"

On the vid screen, Cliff paused and glanced at something on his desk, probably his notes. "It's relatively common. It's stable and easy to handle. Plus it wasn't a massive detonation."

"Meaning it was a small amount?"

"Yes, the perpetrator didn't want to create a shock wave that would have damaged a city module."

I considered that. "You're suggesting the assassin wanted to kill me but protect the city. That doesn't make sense."

"No, it doesn't, you're right." He looked at me for a moment. "Look, Mac. This is delicate."

"Go on."

"Renée is lucky she was behind that outcropping when the blast went. But the fact is, it wasn't a huge explosion anyway. I've seen the video of it."

"Maybe he was hoping the torpedoes would also detonate."

"That's possible, but they weren't armed. They may have known that the weapons wouldn't explode. But there's more, Mac."

"What?"

"The location of the bomb. It actually wasn't close to the launcher. It was twenty meters from it."

"So the person didn't want the torpedoes to explode."

"That's right."

Which gave further credence to the notion that the assassin actually wanted to keep damage restricted to a small area. It was mysterious.

Cliff remained silent, waiting for me, which was a character trait of his that I appreciated. He was staring at me.

"Anything else?" I asked.

"One thing. The mining division has narrowed the explosive type down to either TNT or AN."

"Ammonium nitrate? Really?"

"We use both extensively for undersea blasting. It would have been easy to get the explosive, even from our own activities." Before I could ask for it, he continued, "I'm investigating our mining division procedures for securing their supplies, of course. Someone could have stolen it, or the perpetrator could even work with us here."

"Understood."

"I'll be in touch when I know more."

He signed off and I sat in the chair, in *SC-1*, powering through the Atlantic in a bubble of air at 450 kph, staring outside for long minutes.

Richard was silent too.

—••—

CHURCHILL SANDS WAS LOCATED ON the sandy bottom of the English Channel at a depth of thirty meters, like all other large underwater colonies. Global agreements had mandated all structures underwater to maintain four atmospheric pressures, to make movement between them practical—no need to depressurize, and docking between vessel and module was simple, through the use of umbilical.

There were of course many undersea habitats and modules located at much deeper locations, for mineral extraction, research, military purposes and so on, but even those maintained four atms as well. It made travel through the oceans as simple as on land; the only restriction was that people who lived in the colonies couldn't travel to land without an extensive period of decompression first.

The currents were strong in the Channel, and the water murky as a result. I'd experienced it before at the French undersea colonies as well. The view outside was nowhere near as pristine as ours at Trieste, where the water was clear and warm. This water was dense with churning sediment and visibility out the city viewports was low.

The city consisted of several modules and the population was greater than 100,000 people. Its purpose was mostly fish farming for the United Kingdom, though I noted with interest a large cluster of modules in the southeastern quadrant. It was one of the more famous institutions of study in the undersea world: Churchill University.

We piloted into the Docking Module, secured the seacar, and prepared for our meeting with Sahar Noor, the city's Mayor.

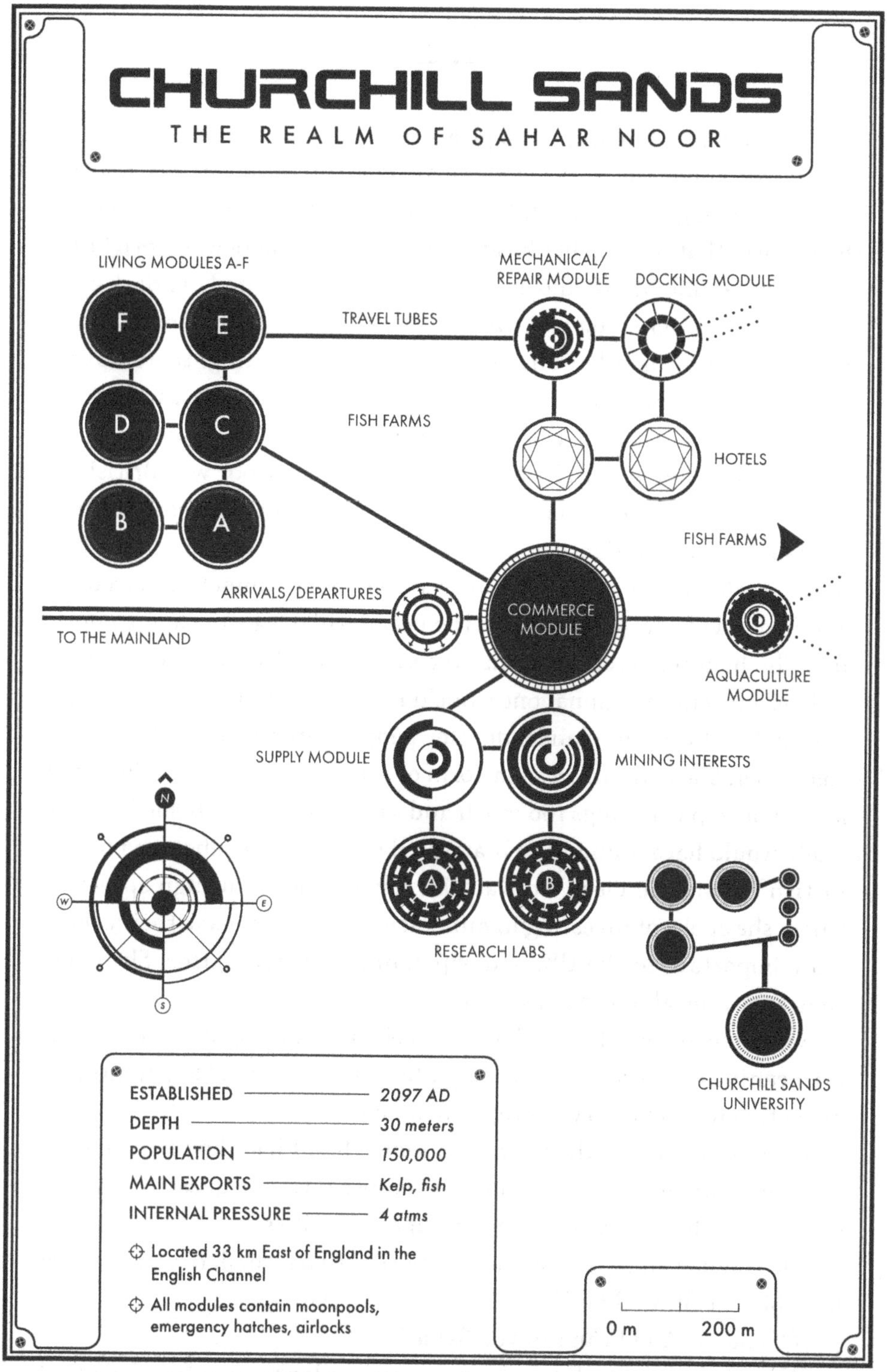
CHURCHILL SANDS
THE REALM OF SAHAR NOOR
LIVING MODULES A-F
F
E
D
C
B
A
TRAVEL TUBES
MECHANICAL/
REPAIR MODULE
DOCKING MODULE
FISH FARMS
HOTELS
FISH FARMS
ARRIVALS/DEPARTURES
TO THE MAINLAND
COMMERCE
MODULE
AQUACULTURE
MODULE
SUPPLY MODULE
MINING INTERESTS
N
W
E
S
A
B
RESEARCH LABS
CHURCHILL SANDS
UNIVERSITY
ESTABLISHED 2097 AD
DEPTH 30 meters
POPULATION 150,000
MAIN EXPORTS Kelp, fish
INTERNAL PRESSURE 4 atms
Located 33 km East of England in the English Channel
All modules contain moonpools, emergency hatches, airlocks
0 m
200 m

— ·· —

"GREETINGS MR. MAYOR, IT'S A pleasure to meet you."

I stared at her, taken aback for just a moment. "And you, Ms. Mayor," I finally managed. She was tall—probably five foot seven—and wore a black hijab that covered her head, ears, and neck. There was a bright topaz scarf around her shoulders, and makeup accentuated her dark eyes. Her eyelashes were long and thick. She was also wearing red lipstick, a nice contrast against her olive skin. She was captivating, there was no doubt about it. There was a magnetic aura to her personality, and I could immediately see why she was so popular in the undersea colony.

I had done my research before the visit. Sahar Noor was British by birth, but her heritage was Saudi, though her parents had emigrated to England in the 21st Century, so there were other nationalities mixed in now as well. She had a reputation as a free diving competitor as a teen, and had obviously grown to love the ocean while training and competing. She held numerous national records in the deep-diving sport, as well as a few international ones. She'd run for election three years earlier, and had won in a landslide. Her people didn't just like her—they *adored* her. She had run on a platform of self-reliance for the colony, but knew not to push things too much and say *independence*. If she had, she likely would have found herself arrested or her career sabotaged by the British Submarine Fleet. I'd watched some of her campaign speeches, where she spoke of investing in mineral extraction to make their colony more important to the UK, and expanding their fish farms. She knew they were crucial to the UK's economy.

Sahar meant "just before dawn" and Noor meant "light" or "divinity." Its meaning was clever, and I thought for a moment that her parents had given this woman a very appropriate name.

Richard had researched her even more than I had, however, and he seemed to know that she would be receptive to our quest to achieve *Oceania*, a collection of independent undersea cities.

She laughed and said, "We don't have to be so formal, now that we've met. May I call you Mac?"

"Of course. And I can call you Sahar?"

"No." She paused and stared at me, a serious look on her face. I glanced at Richard and he seemed concerned. He also looked at me.

Then she laughed again and said, "I'm just joking, Mac. Sahar is great."

I couldn't help but smile. "That's nice, thanks."

"I have followed your career closely over many years."

"Really?" I'd heard such things before, of course, but wanted to be polite about it.

"Yes. Your dad, his quest for independence, his murder, your sister and your current activities in the oceans."

It was a lot all at once, and I swallowed, not knowing exactly what to say. Her mention of Dad's *murder* implied that she felt it had been an unlawful action.

I glanced around at her office, stalling. It was larger than mine, but still sparse. She didn't have many luxuries—even her chair was metal—but there was a single red flower in a vase on her desk—rare, in the underwater world, like her—and some photos of her family on the bulkheads. Most were pictures from topside; the sun and sky visible in them. Only Richard, Meg, and I were with her; her staff had ushered us from the Docking Module, walking us through the central Commerce Module to the upper level and her office. She'd said something to her assistant about a "Clarke," who I guessed would be joining us. I didn't know who that was, but I'd noticed Richard nodding when she mentioned the name.

I finally said, "They killed our dad for his beliefs."

"Independence, yes, I know."

Meg, who had been silent up until then, said, "It's a touchy subject nowadays."

"But a common one." Sahar focused her dark eyes on my twin. "I have heard about your family for many years. I know what you've been through. I know about the drive for independence now."

I shifted on my feet. "It's growing more common, you're right."

She gestured to a seating area in the corner of the cabin, and we lowered ourselves. I noted that she waited for us to sit before she herself took a chair. "I have watched your career closely."

"You said that, yes."

"I know about your SCAV drive. I know about your efforts to increase technological development in the oceans. I have heard rumors about a deep diving technology as well." She frowned, tilted her head, and watched my reaction. "I've heard your subs can dive to over six kilometers. Is that true?"

"Purely rumor."

"But other mayors are mentioning this to me. Six thousand meters! Some are saying even deeper, perhaps *eight kilometers*."

I shot a glance at Richard. He had a smile on his face, but he was quiet as he watched Sahar. She transfixed him too, I felt.

"We've been able to dive that deep for a century or longer."

"Those are exploration vessels. I'm hearing that your common seacars can do it. Not even large warsubs!"

"If that's true," I said, "it would give us an enormous edge in ocean colonization." Inside, I shuddered. Knowledge of our Acoustic Pulse Drive was getting out. I'd expected it, since the USSF had watched our battle against the Russian dreadnought, but it was the last thing I'd expected at this meeting.

"It would give you ocean superiority. You could simply sail under your enemy and shoot up at them. Like air superiority on land, but inverted."

"That would be . . . a magnificent advantage in the oceans," I managed. I was growing uncomfortable, but not in a bad way. I felt that she was not criticizing me . . . that she wanted the tech for her colony as well. And that signified the possibility of a treaty with her.

She watched me for a moment, deciphering my thoughts. "We can wait for the Commodore to arrive to discuss it further."

"The Commodore?" I immediately grew nervous.

Richard turned to me. "I didn't mention this to you."

Meg's face hardened and her eyes flashed. "I didn't agree to this!"

"Now just a—"

"I won't fraternize with some BSF asshole who thinks we're going to join him in partnership!"

Richard glanced at Sahar nervously. "I don't think this is the time for—"

Meg interrupted: "You just listen to me, Richard! I am not going to deal with senior military officials who are only good at inflicting pain and torture!"

She was breathing hard and her face was flushed. I touched her hand. "Meg, just hear him out." I eyed Richard. "I'm sure he has a reason for this."

Sahar Noor had watched the entire exchange with a perplexed expression. Then she leaned forward and put her hands on Meg's shoulders. "I understand where this pain comes from, trust me."

"How could you?" Meg snapped, but she wasn't mad at the woman. Her fury at that moment was directed at Richard, for leading us into meeting someone for whom we were not exactly prepared.

"Easy." Sahar sighed and eyed me for a moment. Then she looked back at Meg. "You and your brother moved to Trieste when you were young. The CIA and USSF—senior military leaders who no doubt pretended to be friends—ended up betraying your dad and killed him in a travel tube in 2099. You fled to Blue Downs when you were eighteen, which a senior military officer—Captain Ventinov of the Russian dreadnought, *Drakon*, later destroyed. Then, back in Trieste, after you'd rejoined your brother and his quest to be Mayor and bring the world's undersea cities into economic and military partnerships, you had dealings with Captain Heller and then Admiral Taurus T. Benning." She frowned. "Heller died later in battle somewhere in the Atlantic; the circumstances are still murky. As for Benning, I'm not precisely sure what happened, but it's common knowledge that he had in fact played a role in your dad's death thirty years earlier. And now, he is either dead or missing, but your anger toward senior military—especially men—is totally understandable."

I didn't want to tell her exactly what had happened to Benning—Meg had murdered him to avenge Dad's death—but Sahar's omniscience surprised me. She had certainly done her research, and her calm, deliberate manner was soothing and reassuring at the same time.

And then the hatch suddenly slid aside, and an older man with white hair, wearing the dark blue uniform of the British Submarine Fleet, entered the office.

Chapter Three

HE WAS EASILY OVER SIX feet tall—six four, I guessed—with broad shoulders, receding hair, a narrow waist, and a sharp nose. His eyes were piercing, and the man radiated pure authority. There was no doubt that when he walked into a cabin, people noticed. He'd probably held that quality all his life. His uniform was the signature dark blue of the BSF, and the rank on his shoulders signified *Commodore*. This meant he outranked Captains and held authority over multiple ships simultaneously. He could command and organize numerous vessels to engage in broader actions.

His name was Commodore Bertram A. Clarke, and in the undersea colonies, he was infamous.

I immediately felt the same bitterness as Meg surge within me. I glared at Richard. "What the hell is going on? I didn't agree to this."

"I know," he said. "I didn't tell you, I'm sorry."

"But why?"

The Commodore stepped toward me. "Because he felt you wouldn't trust me, Mac." He had spoken in a thick Scottish accent.

"I wonder why." My tone was blunt.

"Because I represent the military. Because I represent power of the topside nations over the ocean dwellers, such as yourself. Because I am a tyrant, or I am the tool of one, I suppose. Am I correct?"

Meg snarled, "You could say that."

He turned to her. "I assure you, I'm not all that bad."

Sahar said, "I'm sorry Mac. I apologize, Meg. I was unaware that this was a surprise for you." She turned to Richard. "Why is that?" Her tone was calm and reassuring, but there was a pointed quality to it.

All eyes were now on my most senior advisor, who seemingly had arranged this meeting without our consent.

He nodded. "Yes, I have manipulated this event. But there is good reason."

"We're listening!" Meg snapped again.

Richard paused and looked at all of us. Then he gestured back to the chairs. "Perhaps we could all sit again to talk in a less . . . tense environment?"

Commodore Clarke grimaced and said, "Yes, that's a good idea, Richard. Perhaps a drink would be a good idea as well. Whiskey?"

Sahar said, "You know that won't happen, Clarke. But I can offer you tea." Her voice was now a knife in the silence, and I realized that she would never serve alcohol in her office. There wouldn't even be any nearby, and surely Clarke had known that. His expression showed that he had; he was smirking.

"Now why go and do that?" I asked.

Clarke lowered himself to a chair and looked at me. I stood over him now. "Do what? Request a drink to reduce tension a bit? It's a bit stressful—"

"You deliberately insult—"

"It's okay, Mac," Sahar said, soothing me with her tone. "Clarke and I know each other well. He is taking a jab, yes, but I'd rather it be words than torpedoes." She glanced around at the eyes focused on her. "Less casualties, no?"

"One is still too many," Meg growled.

Besides, I thought, there was absolutely no reason to be so abrasive to Sahar because of her culture.

Another deadly silence descended over us, but we eventually found our seats and stared at Clarke. He still had a slight smile on his face, and he eyed each of us in turn.

He did not apologize for his comment.

Tea arrived, and we waited until the assistant left.

Then, a minute later, Richard finally cleared his throat. "Mac, sorry about this. I have never told you about Commodore Clarke here."

"What about him? He's BSF. He represents one of the most repressive elements over our colonies." I stared at Sahar. "Surely you're aware of that?"

A look of shock appeared. "Of course, Mac. I am the Mayor here. I know how the BSF treats us. I'm sure the USSF treats you the same way."

"Yes."

"In fact, Seascape, the USSF HQ in your region, blew up six months ago in a fiery Isomer explosion. Do you know anything about that?"

I shifted in my chair. "I believe the Germans have a lot to explain about that."

Clarke sighed. "Interesting, Mac. The US blames the Germans as well. But the elimination of the base that was in such proximity to you is beneficial *to you*, not the Germans."

"What does that mean?"

He chuckled. "It's simple logic. Who has the most to gain from the elimination of USSF HQ? Not the Germans."

"There's no evidence for that. And your accusations are making no sense right now."

I kept my voice calm, but he was absolutely correct. Trieste had indeed been responsible for the destruction of the base, but there was no way I was going to admit it. Especially to this man.

He stared at me. "I don't really care who did it. But what you don't realize is that I worked with your dad back in the 2090s." He gestured at Richard. "And with Richard. We worked for Trieste. For independence."

— ·· —

I CHOKED BACK A LAUGH. "Bullshit. You're a British Commodore. You control BSF forces. You repress the colony here. You're an occupying force." It occurred to me again that he could arrest us all in an instant and haul us to prison; we were far from Trieste and the protection our own citizens provided.

He said, "You could ask Ms. Noor about that. I am not a tyrant, as I said earlier. I try to work with her to make sure her colony succeeds."

"There are others far worse than Clarke," Sahar said.

I stared at the pair of them. "You knew our father?"

"Indeed." He sipped his tea and stared at me. I noticed his eyebrows over the teacup; they were white but closely trimmed. "We fought together for independence."

"I don't believe it."

Richard said, "We all worked together before the CIA killed your dad. Before Benning did."

Meg said, "You're saying that you were on Dad's side? Fighting for independence. And now you're . . . " Her eyes showed confusion. "Working for the BSF?"

"Correct," Clarke said in his thick accent.

"But why? Why didn't you stay with the movement?"

"And why didn't you stay in Trieste after they killed him?" I added. He could have fought back, I wanted to say. Sought revenge against those responsible.

"For revenge?" he asked. He shook his head. "I understand what you're saying. I was all-in on independence for the underwater settlements. Then I saw what governments would do to preserve their power over the ocean colonies." He sighed and looked down at the deck. "Look. I'm from a town called Kilmuir on the Isle of Skye in Scotland. Rising waters are killing us. It's devastated the economy there. I'm also Scottish, and I know a thing or two about repression and the fight for independence." His voice was gaining strength now, and I could sense his anger. "I wanted to fight with your dad. I respected him greatly. But then I saw what could happen."

"So you ran?" Meg hissed. "You gave up!"

"You did too," he replied in a calm voice.

It was the wrong thing to say. She bolted to her feet; the chair slid back five feet across the steel deck, screeching the whole way. "I was a child! They killed our dad!"

Sahar said, "She's right, Clarke. And you know better than to be so rude. Especially when you're a guest in my colony."

He turned his gaze on the Mayor. "*Your* colony?"

"Are you about to say it's British?" I asked.

He nodded. "I see where you're going with that. I guess you're right, if I'm supposedly on the side of independence." He paused. "Look. When they killed your dad, I realized that staying in Trieste was not going to help. So I came back here. Joined the BSF. Worked my way upward. Now I'm in charge of a fleet, and in a much better position to help."

A sudden shock descended on the group.

"Wait a minute—" I glanced around. Meg was lowering herself to her chair again, staring at Clarke. I continued, "You're saying you want to help us achieve Oceania?"

"By helping bring Churchill Sands into your fold. Yes."

—••—

IT WAS A STUNNING DEVELOPMENT. Sahar had a smile on her face. Clarke was looking at Meg and me. Richard also was grinning.

I said, "But it doesn't make sense. You come here and insult Sahar. You claim that your BSF has control over this colony." I shook my head. "I'm sorry Richard, but I'm not buying it. It's bullshit. He's here to entrap us, more likely."

Sahar said, "He has a caustic personality sometimes. I admit to that. He is a senior official for a mainland submarine fleet. But I have been working with him now for years. He isn't *too* repressive. He is kind to our people, for the most part. And he seems to want to help us."

I stared at her. "What are *you* asking, Sahar? I still don't know why Richard brought us here."

She paused, and then, "Simple, Mac. I want to join Oceania. I want to help you. And Clarke is here to assist."

—••—

TEN MINUTES LATER, MEG, RICHARD and I had left the office with plans to meet Sahar later to discuss the development in more detail. I stared at Richard as we marched through Churchill's version of City Control—there were consoles and equipment throughout the chamber to monitor environmental conditions in the city and resource extraction activities outside—and his eyes were bright. He glanced back at me and said, "Surprised?"

"You could say that," I muttered.

We continued through the corridors away from Sahar's office and City Control, and wound our way through travel tubes toward the southeastern area of the city. I didn't know where we were going, but Richard had an agenda. I had agreed days ago to let him organize this trip; I was just along for the ride.

So far it had been interesting, I had to admit.

Eventually we stopped in a travel tube and stared at the murky water outside. Meg was still angry; she was silent and her freckled face was still flushed. Soon we were alone, and I said to Richard, "Why didn't you tell us about this?"

"Would you have come?"

"To meet Sahar, of course. But Clarke . . . I'm not sure."

Meg said, "You realize he might have played a role in Dad's death."

Richard said, "No. I know the man. We worked together, with Frank McClusky. He was totally devoted to the movement. He did exactly what I did after the assassination, Meg. He left to prepare for a better opportunity."

I considered that. Richard had indeed done that. He and Jessica Ng, his partner, had gone to Ballard City off the coast of Louisiana. There they waited for nearly thirty years before contacting me and rejoining the movement.

"But you don't have proof," Meg snapped.

"It was a long time ago. I don't think I'll be able to prove it to you with evidence from those times. The USSF destroyed or hid it all anyway." He sighed and stared at the Channel waters. "But I do have a way to prove it to you."

"How?" I asked.

"By his actions now. I have someone you need to meet. And when you hear what she has to say, you're going to flip. And Clarke is going to help us, and prove that he is on-side with us. He and Sahar are going to help get Churchill and her people into Oceania."

"What *who* has to say?"

"The inventor of the weapon, Mac. Did you forget?"

—••—

IT WAS A LOT TO take in. Many developments in a short period of time.

The assassination attempt on me in Trieste.

Meeting the charismatic Sahar Noor, Mayor of Churchill.

Commodore Clarke.

But the fact that yet another city might be interested in joining the independence movement was huge. And not only that, a *Commodore* in the British Submarine Fleet—the purpose of which was to maintain control over the colonies—might be willing to help.

I let Richard lead the way into a small lounge in a module in the southern quadrant. It was a Research Module. I worried that perhaps this was all a setup, and mentioned to the others not to say anything incriminating. We were just going to listen, for now.

Within minutes a black woman in her fifties walked in. She had an intense look on her face, but seemed to recognize Richard immediately. She shook his hand before turning to me and Meg. We exchanged introductions—her name was Alyssna Sonstraal—and sat facing each other.

She smiled at me. "Of course I know who you are. I'm pleased to finally meet you, Mac."

"Thanks." It was a common thing; people everywhere in the underwater colonies knew about my dad and his history with independence. It naturally struck a chord with the other underwater cities, and his death most certainly galvanized their sympathy and mutual desires.

I stared at Alyssna. She was watching me, waiting. I said, "I'm sorry, I don't know what your field is."

She looked to Richard, who said, "I haven't told him anything."

She grunted. "I'm not surprised."

"What do you mean?" I asked.

"Because most people think what I'm doing is a lie. Fake science."

"Why's that?"

She shrugged. "It does seem ridiculous, when you first hear it. I'm sure Richard worried that if he told you, you would refuse to come."

"It's already been an . . . *interesting* trip," I muttered.

"Indeed," Richard interjected.

Meg said, "You could say that again."

Alyssna glanced at us. "I hope in a good way. But I promise, when you hear what I have to say, and you think about it for a bit, you'll understand."

"What are you proposing?" I asked.

"I know all about your quest for new technologies. I know about your SCAV drive and I've heard about your deep-diving system. Some say eight kilometers by any standard seacar, without adding hull plating!

That's incredible."

I remained silent and simply stared.

She continued, "I want what's best for the underwater colonies too. I know that it involves technology. To prosper in the oceans, you have to prove yourself superior. You can't give the mainland superpowers reason to crush you. You have to always stay ahead of them."

"Sounds logical."

"It is." Alyssna was all business. She had an intensity that I'd seen in other scientists before. Most were quirky and their social skills weren't exactly well developed, but *polished* and *rehearsed* were appropriate terms to describe her. She clearly had prepared for this meeting. I still wondered what exactly she was going to tell me.

"You have worked at Churchill for a long time?" I asked.

"I grew up in Africa. Zambia. One of eight children, all girls. My dad said we'd never amount to anything. He wanted boys. So I fought to learn. I found a place in science, and ended up at Cambridge. Then I worked for the British government at a facility researching a new type of weapon."

I perked up and leaned forward.

"But I felt marginalized there. I felt that the administrators did not appreciate me. They took my advances without gratitude. The others on the team took credit for them." She sighed. "It's not that I want total credit . . . I just want acceptance."

"And you think you can find it with us?" Meg asked, curious.

"Maybe. I want to show the BSF what they missed out on. I want them to know they screwed up with me. But most important, I want to help you, Mac and Meg." She smiled. "You two are famous! I know about your struggle."

"It might all be rumor," I whispered. "We are not responsible for—"

"Seascape just blew up! It was an Isomer Bomb, the first of its kind!"

"Germany—"

"Bullshit! People have been searching for a new category of weapon for decades. You *did* it!"

I clamped down on what I was going to say and just stared at her.

"You also developed the SCAV drive."

"Katherine Wells did that," I said. "She was responsible."

"She used a fusion reactor to generate the thrust, yes. But it happened at Trieste. And the purpose was for independence."

"She's dead now," I whispered. "Killed."

Alyssna grew silent. "I know, but the circumstances are unclear."

"We buried her at sea," I continued. Katherine Wells—or Kat—had been my lover. We had started our journey together to recover her stolen invention from the Chinese, and in the process had fallen in love. Then, the French Submarine Fleet had killed her in battle in the Mid-Atlantic Ridge a year earlier. Her invention had changed the world, but she had died in the ensuing fighting.

"How did she die?" Alyssna asked.

"No comment."

Alyssna stared at me and Meg and back again. "I see," she said finally. "I hope I gain your trust, and you can tell me. Eventually."

"Tell me what this weapon is you've invented. The one you want to give us."

"It's not that easy. I don't have it."

"What?" My mouth dropped and I stared at Richard. "What the hell is this?"

Alyssna continued before he could answer, "I created it, but I left my post. Quit."

I shook my head and stared at the deck. "This is not what I was expecting."

Richard said, "Keep listening, Mac."

Alyssna said, "I want to help you. I want independence for the undersea colonies too."

No doubt she wanted to prove herself to the scientific community. Prove herself to her father. A part of me knew this was a powerful motivator, depending on what the technology she claimed was.

"I still don't know what it is."

She paused and eyed me in total silence. Then, "It's an energy weapon, Mac. To use underwater."

I STARED AT HER. NOW my jaw was on the deck and my eyes showed my disbelief. "Is this a joke?"

"Not at all." Her face was accepting, as if she'd heard it all already. Dealt with disbelief before.

"Don't tell me this is a laser to fire underwater." I rose to my feet, prepared to walk out. "This is a joke after all. Richard, how could you—"

"Keep listening, Mac. Alyssna reached out to me a few weeks ago. It's important enough that I brought you here. You have to trust me."

"This is not happening," I muttered. "It is not possible." I repeated, my voice harder than before, "Tell me this is not a laser beam to fire underwater."

"It's not," Alyssna said. "It's far, far better. And it will completely obliterate your enemies. But the big problem is that I don't have it right now. But we can get it." She moved her face forward until it was only inches from mine. Her eyes flashed. "*We just have to steal it from the people who do have it.*"

Interlude: The Mid-Atlantic Ridge

One Year Earlier

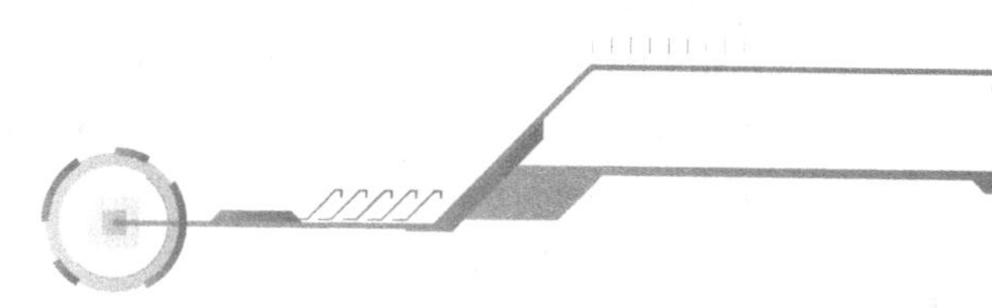

Interlude:	The Mid-Atlantic Ridge
Date:	March 2130 AD
Depth:	2,583 meters
Latitude:	27º 55″ 10′ S
Longitude:	17º 35″ 42′ W
Time:	2015 hours

KATHERINE WELLS SAT AT THE controls of *SC-1* and stared at the readouts before her. The depth was 2,583 meters, speed was low—and quiet—at 8 kph, and the view outside the port was as black as night. But just outside, one of the largest naval battles in history was gathering, and she was a part of it.

Her lover, Truman McClusky, had cleverly manipulated the forces of the USSF and the FSF into engaging in conflict in the Mid-Atlantic Ridge. Both Fleets wanted to capture him, and he had fed Captain Heller incorrect information to lead ninety-eight USSF warsubs to this location. Meanwhile, the FSF had nearly three hundred warsubs approaching from the opposite direction, on a hunt to find Mac and kill him. The two fleets would collide in only minutes, and Kat Wells had a ringside view. She was currently piloting the seacar at the eastern peak of the Mid-Atlantic Ridge at a depth of slightly more than two and a half kilometers, essentially looking down at the battle. When Mac gave the word, she and her small grouping of twenty-two other seacars would crest the peak and fire down at the enemy vessels in The Rift below.

Her heart was in her throat, and her stomach felt hollow.

This battle was largely because of her invention. She'd created the SCAV drive, intending to lead the undersea colonies into war against the world's superpowers.

And now it was happening.

People were about to die.

Mac was currently piloting his own vessel—a *Sword*—with his friend Johnny Chang at his side, and also scientist Manesh Lazlow. They led a contingent of thirty Triestrian vessels which could dive extremely deep. Not even mines and torpedoes could hit them. According to Mac, it would be an advantage impossible to overcome. The USSF and FSF forces would eventually lose this battle, he claimed. Mac and his people would fire from below. Kat and her group would fire from *above*, catching them in crossfire. It was a brilliant strategy, possible because of their technological advances.

Kat had faith in him.

She took a deep breath and waited for his signal.

The two fleets were on her sonar, and they were converging in The Rift, just below her.

Her heart pounded.

"I don't need a friend who changes when I change
and who nods when I nod; my shadow does that
much better."
—Plutarch

Part Two: The Plan

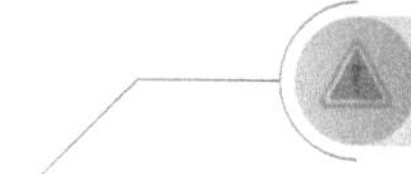

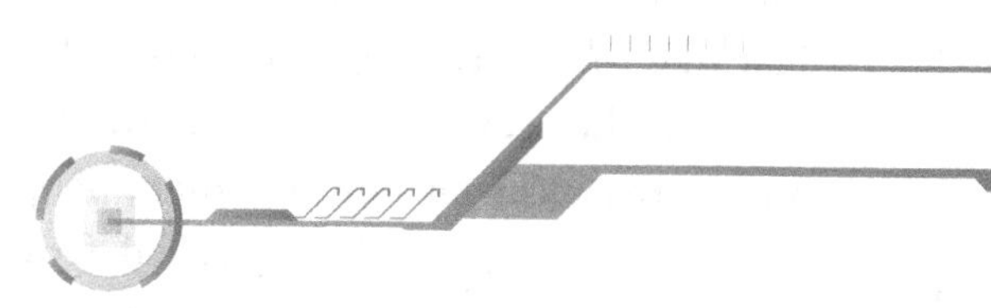

Chapter Four

Part Two: The Plan

ALYSSNA, THE SCIENTIST WHOSE PRESENCE Richard had arranged for us in the Research Lab Module in Churchill Sands, sat silently, watching me process the information she'd provided. She'd just told us that her invention was an energy weapon of some sort.

To use underwater.

Against warsub hulls.

I was pacing in front of her, Richard, and Meg, and I was not happy.

"I can't believe you, Richard," I said. "Can't believe you brought us here for this." I wanted to strangle him.

Richard tilted his head. "We also came to meet Mayor Sahar Noor, and Commodore Clarke. It's all part of what I'm suggesting—"

"This is bullshit!"

"It's not." He rose to his feet and grabbed my arm to keep me from moving. He pulled me down into my chair. "Listen to this. Just—*listen*. And let's try not to be too rude to Doctor Sonstraal here."

Alyssna sighed. "I've heard it all before. Trust me. But then we started testing, and the results proved me right. Senior BSF military fell in line easily." She chuckled. "It was funny, actually. One second they were just like Mac here. Then the next, after the first open-water proof of concept, they gave me whatever I wanted. A facility to broaden the beam and increase the output. A team of people. A massive budget."

"So what happened?" Meg asked, frowning. "How'd you end up here?"

"You mean, trying to convince you people to steal it back for me?"

"Kind of." Meg shrugged. "It's a contradiction, you have to admit."

"I told you. They wouldn't give me credit. They stole my work. They marginalized me and gave my command to other people . . . other Brits."

"But you just said they gave you whatever you—"

"Oh, at first, yes. Definitely. But bit by bit they took pieces of my work. The team that helped solve the blooming problem at short distances, for instance—removed from my control and put under someone else's. The team that solved the power supply issues—taken away. It started small, then escalated. Before I knew it, I had very little control, but the test results were improving. We were hitting targets in the open water at larger distances, and still they kept stripping my responsibilities. I eventually quit out of resentment."

I stared at her. It occurred to me that she was just bitter and wanted her invention back. But if that was the case, what of it? It would still give Trieste a weapon no one else had.

Then I shook my head and forced myself to stop thinking like the Director of TCI. "I still don't believe this."

Richard said, "Look. Mac. What are the limitations of torpedoes as weapons?"

I turned my eyes slowly to his. His eyebrows had lifted and he had a look of genuine inquisitiveness. "What do you mean?"

"We use torpedoes against enemy warsubs. Why? Let's think this through. You'll see what I mean."

I sighed, deciding to play his game. We'd come all the way to Churchill for this, and we might as well hear it all out. "If we're facing an enemy—"

"Or many."

"—we have to launch weapons to take them out. The weapons have to travel toward the warsubs. Conventional devices move at 80 kph, the limit. SCAV weapons move at around 1,000 kph. Pretty damn fast."

"Go on."

I leaned back, thinking. "The weapons have to lock onto target, unless someone on board in Fire Control aims them manually. But even if they detonate nearby, the initial concussion can compromise hull integrity. If not, the aftershocks can do it."

"You mean, when the void in the vaporized water crashes in on itself."

"Of course." I pursed my lips, continuing his game. "Countermeasures can be a problem. They can distract and lure torpedoes away from the target. The pressure is an issue too. Too much pressure can decrease the potential for damage."

"So deeper is more difficult to kill a target."

I nodded. "Storage is a problem too, I guess. A warsub can only carry so many torpedoes." I thought back to our battle with the dreadnought. That Russian vessel had had thousands of torpedoes on board and over sixty torpedo tubes. "A seacar can only hold maybe ten, like *SC-1*."

"Go on."

"Each one costs money. It's an expense that someone has to pay."

"How much?"

I shrugged. "Trieste picks up the bill. Thousands per weapon. But we're making them out at The Ridge now, and—"

"What about the noise?"

I hesitated. "Well, they're loud of course. They show up clearly on sonar screens, as bright as suns. They attract enemies, but most warsubs leave, to avoid torpedoes."

"How long are they in the water?"

"Minutes maybe. Tracking and locking onto targets."

"Creating a lot of noise."

"Sure."

"What else?"

Meg had been listening intently. She said, "They take up a lot of space on board a warsub. And they're dangerous keeping them all together, in the magazine."

"Indeed. Ships have sunk because of a well-placed explosion."

Like Arizona *during Pearl Harbor*, I wanted to say. An enemy armor-piercing bomb had made it to the magazine, detonated, and split the warship in half. The wreck was still in Pearl Harbor, though the memorial structure was now also submerged due to rising waters.

"You also have to lead the target, sometimes," Meg interjected.

Meaning you had to fire where the target might be in a minute's time, instead of where it was when you fired. And you had to hope that the warsub didn't change course or buoyancy during the battle.

"What more?" Richard pressed.

Alyssna was leaning back in the chair, staring at the ceiling, as if she'd heard it all before. "The charge to propel the torpedo," she said in monotone. "It runs out, whether it's fuel or battery."

I said, "And the torpedo can't go too deep. The pressure could damage components."

"What's the threshold?"

"Five kilometers is the usual Crush Depth." I chewed the inside of my cheek for a moment. During the battle in the Mid-Atlantic Ridge, we'd simply stayed below 5,000 meters and fired *up* at the enemy. "It could be a dud, although I'm clutching at straws at this point." Duds were extremely rare, but it did indeed happen. During the Battle of Midway, for instance, when the weapons were still in their relative infancy, many of them did indeed fail upon impact.

"Let's stop there," Alyssna said. "That's a lot of drawbacks you just listed. Now imagine this. A weapon that costs only a dollar a shot. Imagine that! Kill a warsub for only *one dollar*. The noise underwater lasts only a fraction of the time that a lengthy torpedo chase will. A warsub doesn't need to carry dozens of weapons. Just one. There's not a lengthy tracking time, or hoping the torpedo homes correctly on the target, or firing and leading a target, and so on. Imagine a weapon that fires at the speed of light underwater. It just has to track the target, which is slow moving—say 70 kph—and stay locked on for a bit."

I shook my head. "No, no, no. It's still bullshit. I know about lasers on the surface. I know about their drawbacks. Designers make missiles coated with ultra-reflective material, so most of the energy bounces off."

"But Mac—"

"And the sub just has to maneuver to make sure a computer can't lock the beam on. In the air, the missiles rotate—say, once per minute—to keep the laser from doing damage. And blooming is a huge issue." Meaning that the farther the beam traveled, the more particles in the air, dust, pollen, water moisture and more, scattered the energy, making it largely dispersed and ineffective. That would be an immense problem in the water.

"Engineers solved those issues on land, Mac, decades ago. The superpowers have invested a lot of money. Their beams travel hundreds of kilometers *without* blooming. And they are *powerful*—" She cut herself off and grunted.

"What is it?" I asked.

"I forgot. I'm defending lasers on land, in the sky. But as I mentioned . . . this isn't a laser." Then she frowned. "Not really, anyway."

"So what is it?"

She paused. "Look. I know the hesitation. I know the worries. Trust me! I've heard it all before, by people I respected a hell of a lot less than you and Meg. But an energy beam underwater eliminates most of those drawbacks you just listed." She ticked each off on her fingers as she said them. "It's cheap, once engineers build the device. It's fast. It's effective, I promise you this. It's reliable. It saves space on the warsub. It doesn't explode if a weapon hits it. And the best part? *It works*, and damn well."

I stared at her. She seemed sure of herself, I had to give her that. But so did every inventor of every crazy invention ever made, even if they didn't work. "So tell me this."

"Go ahead."

"Tell me the drawbacks now."

She smirked. "Every weapon has drawbacks."

"I'm listening."

"Okay," she said. Then she sighed. "Blooming is an issue underwater. It lowers the range to only a few hundred meters."

I nodded. It was as expected. "So on land they shoot hundreds of kilometers. But down here, only . . . ?"

"Two hundred meters at most. Less than one hundred is best. But on land they deal with a target moving at thousands of kilometers per hour. They deal with the curvature of the Earth, the weather, tracking an object at large distances. We don't have to deal with all that here."

"But you have to get *close* to the enemy. Really close."

"Yes."

Richard said, "But Mac, think about Trieste. Think about what we're looking at right now."

I hesitated. "You mean, if an attack is coming. From Russia."

"Yes. If we had this weapon, we could place it—or a few—at our perimeter. Say five kilometers out. Then when a warsub comes close and passes over . . ."

"We fire upward and puncture the hull."

"Bingo."

"From beneath."

"Yes."

"And the range would be short, because we're so shallow anyway."

"Again, you got it."

I frowned and leaned back. He had a point. A *good* point. I stared at Meg, who was watching me right back.

I turned to Alyssna. "Tell me more about it."

She looked at me, silent, for a long, pregnant pause. "Not yet."

I flinched. "What? But we came here to listen to *you*."

"No, you didn't. You came to steal my device from me, like so many others."

I glanced at Richard. "What is this, Richard? You spoke with her first, I'm assuming."

He opened his mouth to reply, but Alyssna interjected first. "I'll give you everything, I promise. But I want reassurance."

"Of what?"

"That I will play a role in the theft. That I get to work with it afterward. That I get a lab to *keep* working with it. That I am in charge of it. I don't want it taken away from me again."

I paused. Like most scientists, she felt a driving proprietary force over her invention. What she was asking was no surprise, and it was not difficult. It was what I'd willingly given Manesh Lazlow and Max Hyland, our two brightest minds back in Trieste. Lazlow had invented the deep-diving Acoustic Pulse Drive, and Hyland the Isomer Bomb that had destroyed Seascape. Both had extensive labs and free reign for whatever research they wanted. I had no problems offering Alyssna Sonstraal the same privileges.

"You can have a lab and work exclusively with it all you want," I said. "But I have not agreed to any theft yet. I don't have any details." I glared at Richard. "But I'm sure we'll get some soon." I paused and then, "But I need to know more about this weapon too. You keep saying it's not a laser. What is it?"

Alyssna grinned. "Not yet. I need your assurances first."

Meg said, "You want us to make promises before we even know what this is?"

"In short, yes."

"But how can we do that?"

"Trust," she said, staring at me.

I sighed and locked eyes with her. "Tell us this, first then. Where is it?"

"If I tell you, you'll agree to work with me?"

"I'm not saying that," I replied. "But it will give me something to think about."

She stopped and stared at each of us in turn. Then she sat silently for a minute, considering the compromise. I didn't see why there would be an issue. If she didn't tell us any more, we'd just leave and return to Trieste, nothing lost.

But if what Richard was saying was true, it would indeed be a great deterrent. I had to agree with him. Imagine an enemy warsub approaching Trieste and then suddenly getting carved from below like a knife through butter. There would be no warning whatsoever, and the underbelly of the warsub would be only a few meters from the sandy bottom. It would be an easy target. In the back of my mind, in the deep recesses that I didn't like to dwell on because they caused just too much anxiety and fear, I knew that Russia was putting three more dreadnoughts to sea, and very soon. Their first target was obvious, after what we'd done to *Drakon*.

Alyssna finally said, "All right. That sounds fine. The first component is here, in Churchill Sands. In the very module we're sitting in right now."

—••—

"*FIRST* COMPONENT?" I ASKED.

Meg was staring at Alyssna, and Richard also had a curious expression on his face.

"Yes. The device requires four components to make it work. One is here."

"And where are the others?"

She grinned, but not in a malicious manner. "I like compromises, Mac. I just gave you one. Let's come to an agreement first, and I'll tell you where the other parts of the weapon are. Then we'll go steal each."

Chapter Five

"I NEED PROOF, RICHARD," I said minutes later, outside in the corridor. Alyssna Sonstraal had left, but we had agreed to a meeting later, to gather more information.

"That comes next," he replied with a smile.

"What do you mean?"

"There's someone else we have to visit."

I stared at him. "You are leading us on a merry chase here."

"What are we chasing?" He had a playful look on his face.

"It seems we are chasing a mysterious weapon that doesn't seem possible. And for some reason you've included Sahar Noor and Commodore Clarke in this."

He raised a finger. "We need both of them to get this weapon. Part of it is *here*, where we're standing right now!" He looked at the deck. "Just beneath us. But it's heavily guarded. And Clarke has authority over the BSF in this city, and he's willing to join us in the quest for independence! It's not rocket science."

I paused and studied his face for a long moment. He seemed earnest. Meg was concerned though; it blasted through her eyes as clear as day.

She said, "I don't want to work with military officials anymore. They will betray you and turn you in before you know it!"

Meg had borne the brunt of that only six months earlier. USSF Admiral Quintana and CIA Investigator Zyvinski had arrested her for Benning's murder and tortured her for weeks at Seascape until I'd managed to arrange a rescue. I understood her hesitation.

"This weapon does seem to have advantages, Meg," I said.

She stepped toward me. "Now you're arguing *for* it? It sounds insane."

"Yes. But if it does actually work, then we have to go for it."

"Steal someone else's invention."

"Yes."

"That sounds awfully familiar, doesn't it?"

That made me stop short. It did indeed. The Chinese had stolen our SCAV drive and forced me on a global chase to get it back. Many people had died, and a battle had ensued in 2129 as a result: The Second Battle of Trieste. "It does," I finally managed. "But that's the world we live in, Meg. That's the point of TCI. And the best part . . . we don't have to design and build the thing. Someone already has. We just have to take it and use it to defend Trieste."

She sighed and processed that, but she remained silent.

I turned to Richard. "Where next, Richard?"

—••—

HE HAD PLANNED YET ANOTHER meeting for us, with another Churchill citizen, though I was unsure why, exactly. I'd allowed him the latitude to plan this trip for us, and I was just along for the ride.

For now.

So far, it was at times frustrating, but also interesting. Sahar Noor, for example, had captivated me. I could see why so many in the British undersea city had voted for her. She had an uncommon quality that few others held: magnetism. You couldn't help but watch her, listen to her, agree with her. She had already proven her stoicism, humor, and compassion in just our first short meeting. Especially when we'd dealt with Commodore Clarke's surprise appearance. We would be seeing her again, for dinner, and I was already looking forward to it.

Before we entered the next recreation lounge, also located in the Research Module, I drifted away from Richard and Meg and contacted Trieste City using my PCD. I wanted to check in on Renée, to make sure she was recovering, and also get an update from Cliff on his investigation. I was anxious about it and wanted to know who exactly wanted me dead.

Within seconds I had Trieste City on the line and Zira Miller transferred my call to Renée. She was in her living cubicle, resting.

"Hiya, Mr. Mayor," she said with a half smile on her face. Her French accent was thicker than usual, though her words were slurred and lazy. Her short, dark hair was pressed sideways, and the wrinkles at the corners of her eyes were deep. I found them so attractive. *Maturity is enticing*, I thought to myself.

I grinned in return, though I felt guilt over her injury. "How are you?"

"The drugs are keeping the headache away, though I feel a tad loopy. High."

"No pain?"

"None. Thankfully. I'm a bit dizzy and lightheaded though. And the light bothers me."

Which I assumed was why it was dark in her cabin. "Right. The concussion."

She tilted her head as she watched me. "What's wrong, Truman?"

"I just feel responsible."

"Don't. It's not your fault at all."

"Of course it is."

"You're not to blame for people who want to be violent."

"Someone wanted to kill me."

She smiled again. "Isn't that always the case? Shouldn't I be used to it now?"

"You mean because you once wanted to kill me?"

It was a fact. Renée had spent months trying to track me down and sink me because I'd damaged her warsub in battle while chasing the Chinese theft of the SCAV drive. The FSF had demoted her and she'd translated that into rage directed at me.

"Maybe," she murmured. "But I still love you. Doesn't matter that someone wants you dead. They won't succeed."

"If they do, would you miss me?"

"Of course, and don't say such things."

Her eyelids were flickering, and I got the point quickly. "You need rest, Renée. I have another meeting. We're staying here the night, then we'll come straight back."

"Gotcha," she muttered.

We signed off and I stared at the screen, morose. People around me kept getting hit. Kat had died in battle in the Mid-Atlantic Ridge because of me.

I thrust that thought away as soon as it brushed my consciousness. Kat had wanted to fight for independence more than anyone, even more than I did. She'd died in the fighting. Her SCAV drive had been down, and a couple of torpedoes had detonated too close. Her control console had exploded, impaling her with debris.

A shiver coursed along my spine.

I'd buried her at the bottom of The Rift there, six kilometers down. Her body was long gone . . . sea creatures had devoured it.

There was no trace of her.

Kat was now part of that which she'd loved all her life.

I had to keep Renée alive now, at all costs. I couldn't let someone hurt her; I had to find out who was now trying to kill me.

An instant later I had Cliff on the device; he was in his office. Despite the small size of the holo image, his musculature was clear. His head was bald and his shoulders broad. He was sitting down, but even so, he seemed towering. His eyes remained hard at all times; he rarely showed emotion.

"Boss," he said with a nod.

"It's been two days, Cliff. What have you found?"

"I've been investigating the mining division. They use both types of explosive. There's a rigorous process to access the stores."

"Any names pop out to you?"

"Nothing unusual."

I paused, thinking. "Let's think, who might want to kill me? The French for sure."

"You're right; they've tried before. They depressurized a module here to do it. You damaged their fleet too. They have reason to be mad." He stopped and thought about that. "You're suggesting a French worker here in the Mining Division might be the culprit?"

"It's possible."

"Anyone else?"

I thought over recent events. "A German?"

"Go on."

"A Chinese national?"

"Keep going."

"Perhaps a visitor from the United States?"

"And?"

"Let's not ignore the Russians."

Cliff looked down at his notes, then back up to me. "So let me get this straight. Any Russian, German, Chinese, French, or American could be the possible assassin?"

I couldn't help but grin. "That's right."

"Come on, Boss. We're American too."

"I said a *visitor* from the mainland."

"But on that list we have *thousands* here in Trieste. We're a magnet for immigrants, you know that."

And we appreciated it. We were the New, New World, in a way. We were the future of the human race, and for the oppressed and suffering on land, if they didn't already know it, they were learning it, *fast*. We didn't have a lot of space, didn't live in open air, we worked hard, eighteen hours each and every day, and were under a constant threat from implosion or drowning . . . but we were *happy*. Damn happy. Our citizens rarely complained about too much work. They also saw us as the future of humanity, and they were doing everything they could to prove it to the United States. It's why they had followed my dad so fervently, and why they had translated that devotion into a love for Meg and myself. Triestrians were resilient and loyal. Last summer, when the USSF had arrested Meg and taken her away for interrogation—torture, really—only I had kept them from escalating their anger into outright war. I'd had a plan, had asked them for calm, and I'd carried the plan out and rescued Meg.

I couldn't help but grin at Cliff. He stared at me, barely moving, but I noticed his jaw clench. He was enjoying this.

"It could be one of my ex-girlfriends too," I added.

He blinked. "You have some?"

"A few. From before I was Mayor." I'd had a few relationships, though they had been purely physical. I hadn't been able to have an emotional bond until I'd resolved the issues with my dad's murder and my anger at his obsession with independence, but I'd eventually managed it.

He made a show of writing a single name on his notepad. "I've added that. I'll investigate."

I smiled and then let the silence linger for a moment longer than necessary.

He said, "What's happening there?"

"I'll fill you in when I'm back. It's . . . interesting."

"I'm intrigued."

"Keep digging at the mining division. Don't mind the pun." The solution could lie with the explosive.

"You know, the culprit could just have come in on a scooter from a nearby warsub."

"It's possible."

"But we have to check all options here, I know."

"Any French, German, Russian, American, or Chinese warsubs come by lately?"

"USSF, yes. None of the others, thankfully."

"Keep at it, Cliff. Keep me updated." I signed off and stared at Richard and Meg. They were ten meters down the corridor, standing in front of a hatch, looking at me. I waved and started walking toward them. Time for the next step in Richard's agenda.

At that moment, a pair of BSF troops appeared in the corridor. They were marching in tandem, with hard looks on their faces and their eyes blazing. They were on patrol and passed by without incident, but there was something off about them. There was a unique patch on their shoulders that I'd never noticed before. It was a red and black logo.

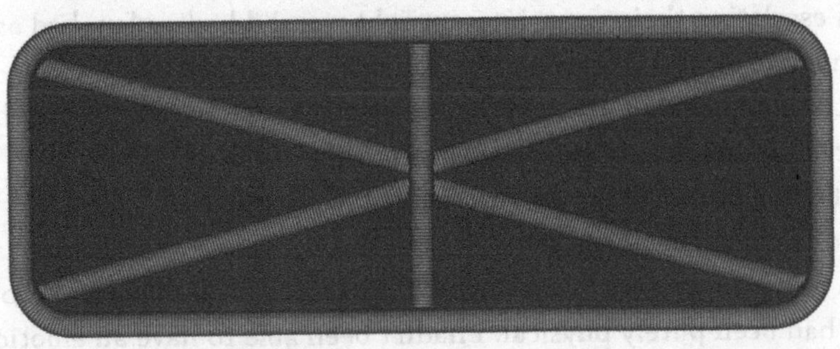

They glared at me as they passed.

—••—

Richard said, "Listen, Mac, before we go in there—" he gestured at the hatch to the private lounge "—I have to tell you something." He paused and took a deep breath. "I know you think Alyssna's idea is a bit wild."

"To say the least."

"Energy beams underwater don't really sound like they would work."

I snorted. "Yeah, I got that." Then again, Alyssna had some strong points.

"But there is a benefit to newer weapons."

It was just like the Hafnium Isomer Bomb. We had to always stay ahead of the competition. And even if the concept didn't work, we still had to keep our irons in the fire, so to speak, in case someone *else* came up with a working device before we did. That would be a disaster.

"I know that," I said. "Torpedoes have been in use for over two hundred years now." I shrugged. "Hell, maybe it's time to start looking for a substitute."

He raised a finger. "Not a substitute. But perhaps something to complement them. Both used in concert could be highly effective."

I considered that. It made sense. I didn't want to ignore something important and then later face great regret.

He said, "Let me tell you something. The US Navy started experimenting with a working device on board USS *Ponce* in 2014. They called it XN-1 LaWS. It stood for *Laser Weapon System*."

"Go on."

"It was effective. It worked. It was only thirty kilowatts of power, and it cost less than a dollar a shot! They were shooting down drones and other flying craft as a proof of concept."

"But it's still underwater here, Richard. The water has to vaporize, the beam would scatter, the range would be—"

"They hit 150 kilowatts by 2020. Only six years later."

I processed that.

He continued, "That was a solid-state laser mounted on USS *Portland*."

"Solid-state?"

"Not a chemical gas laser. No harmful gases stored somewhere. But think about that. They called that laser the MK 2 MOD 0, also known as 'Laws-D.'"

"What does the D stand for?"

"Demonstrator. Laser Weapon System Demonstrator. Their R&D department had increased the beam output by *five times in only six years.* When it comes to weapon development, that's huge."

"Your point?"

"That was over a century ago, Mac! They've had a hundred years to continue development since then. We haven't heard much about it, but back then they were shooting down aircraft, missiles, even artillery shells with ease. A century!"

"So?"

"Engineers measure those lasers in the *terawatts* now, Mac. Imagine that, underwater. The range would be lower, for sure, but other nations will be doing it soon. They weld underwater without issues. Been doing it forever. They've used small lasers for measurement in underwater construction, for just as long."

I exhaled. There was no doubt that he was correct. And if other nations were doing it . . .

"And if they're doing it, we need to do it first." He swore. "Hell, Alyssna Sonstraal was the lead on that team! We're lucky she came to us for this."

Meg, who had been watching the exchange quietly, said, "Tell me something, Richard. How do you know so much about lasers?"

"Researching them, of course. Alyssna reached out because of your reputation. I needed to know more about what she was talking about. But word is getting out about us."

"Word?" She frowned.

"About the fight for independence."

"That's not good," I muttered. I wanted to fly under the radar until it was too late. Until the final battle.

"After the Hafnium Bomb, it's going to be difficult. They're going to figure out it wasn't Germany that destroyed Seascape. Eventually."

Meg said, "But why are you talking about lasers? Alyssna kept saying that's not what it is."

He shrugged. "I don't know everything yet either. But I think there's a comparison we can make. I hope to learn soon, too."

I considered what he was saying for several heartbeats. "And who exactly is meeting us in there?" I asked, pointing at the hatch.

He grinned. "The next part of my plan to convince you. Come on, let's go in."

Chapter Six

THE CABIN WAS SMALL WITH comfortable benches around the perimeter, low tables for drinks, and an entertainment unit built into one bulkhead. It was available to rent for small parties. One bulkhead was a deck-to-ceiling viewport, and the view outside was to the south. It was difficult to make out large distances because of the swirling sediment, but I could see multiple seacar navigation lights as they threaded between the underwater city's modules. There were scuba workers nearby welding an antenna of some sort on a nearby module—bubbles churned out as they melted metal underwater—and a wall of shimmering bubbles rose to the surface at a fish farm located to the east. I knew they had large farms there, to keep the British mainland population fed. Fish and Chips was no longer the national dish of England—Chicken Tikka Masala took that role in the early 2000s—but Fish and Chips still held an important place in the English diet and culture. Churchill Sands supplied much of the cod now for the Southern United Kingdom. Bubble walls contained the fish while they grew, and workers used nets to harvest the schools once they were adult. Fish was the main export of the city, and kelp a close second.

There was a man in the lounge, and he rose as we entered. He was East Indian, young and well-groomed, and wearing a stylish white shirt with collar. The clothes were tight and the hair short, as was common in the underwater world where people were always getting wet. Long hair was a drag; shorter was just more convenient.

I remembered that Kat, my former lover, had kept her hair long despite the drawbacks. It was one of her unique characteristics that I missed so much. She had been a brilliant scientist. In fact—

I shook myself out of it. Why was I thinking about her? And now, of all times? Twice in just a few minutes!

Perhaps because Alyssna was also a scientist fighting for her invention, the same as Kat had done.

The man grinned as he stared at me and Meg. He recognized us instantly; the expression on his face was obvious.

"I'm Truman," I said. "This is Meagan."

"I know you! Of course I do!" he said. His voice was energetic and young. He looked to be in his late twenties.

"And this is Richard." I nodded at the older man with us.

"We've communicated already," Richard said.

We shook hands and sat. There was a pitcher of cool water there, so I poured glasses and we stared at each other for a moment. I realized dimly that I was rapidly growing hungry.

"My name is Chalam Kaashif. I'm a geologist here."

"Nice to meet you," I said. "You work for Churchill?"

He shook his head. "Oh no. Not yet, anyway. That's my goal, but I'm a PhD student at the university. My brother and I both were. We picked geology because we wanted the best opportunity to live and work underwater."

I nodded. "Makes sense. Farming would be the other natural choice."

"Yes. But mineral ore prospecting really appealed to us because it offered a choice for travel and exploration as well." He stopped and a look passed over his face. He suddenly seemed sad.

Meg said into the silence, "I did the same thing, but I chose aquanautic engineering. Sub repair, design, construction, and so on."

"Not many jobs like that topside, I'm guessing," he replied after a moment.

Meg laughed. "There are companies topside, but I wanted to work underwater, in a city."

"Trieste?"

She blinked. "Well, you know about me, I guess."

"Of course I recognize the McClusky twins. Everyone does, in every underwater colony. I know the history."

"Well, I actually chose Blue Downs. I worked there."

He suddenly looked shocked. "Oh my god. Were you there when—"

"When the Russian dreadnought destroyed it? No, but my friends were."

I remember watching her friend in the Repair Module when *Drakon* attacked. He'd died before our eyes, crushed and drowned by the Tsunami Plow, its deadly weapon.

"Terrible," he sighed. "There's so much death underwater."

"There is," I replied. "Lots of people die extracting resources too. It's the new frontier, Chalam. Which is why you picked it, I'm guessing. The hazards are everywhere. Natural and manmade."

"Yes, of course. Mahiransh and I wanted this life. The danger didn't matter." He looked up. "The roof could collapse at any second."

I frowned. "We're at four atms in here. It's four atms outside right now. There's the same amount of pressure as on a house at the surface." But I knew at great depths, where the pressure increased dramatically, the roof *could* easily cave in. He was right. And in the Channel, where the currents were strong, it was like facing a hurricane on some days. The modules did need great structure and stability.

He shrugged. "Maybe I'm just speaking in remote possibilities. I agree with you. The danger never bothered us. Until the worst thing hit, actually."

I watched him. That look was on his face again. "Where's your brother now?"

He raised his eyes to mine. "Dead. He's gone."

Meg said, "That's terrible. We're so sorry."

Chalam sighed and leaned back. "It's not your fault. It's a bizarre and tragic story. I'm lucky to still be alive, I guess."

I shot a look at Richard. I had a sudden revelation as to why we were here to meet this man. "Do you lecture at the university?"

"Yes."

"In geology?"

"My specialty is locating iron ore deposits. I use a magnetometer to help." He shrugged. "It's the focus of my thesis. I also enjoy tectonics. I research trenches and tectonic boundaries. I was just, a few weeks ago, researching one that has all three boundary types in a very small area! It's astonishing, really."

"Where is it?" Meg asked.

"The Chagos Trench."

I searched my memory. It was in the Indian Ocean, south of India and Northeast of Madagascar.

He continued: "After the . . . *trip*, I guess you could call it, I spoke to Richard Lancombe at Trieste."

"Why?" Meg asked.

He shrugged. "Because of what happened. I know Trieste's history." He snorted. "I actually tried to contact you, Truman, but the call was somehow redirected."

My assistant, Kristen Canvel, had likely screened the call and decided that Richard was the person who could best deal with it. My inbox and incoming calls overwhelmed me each day, and Kristen helped me deal with it all. TCI business was left for me, Cliff, Richard, or Johnny Chang.

"And you told Richard the story," I prompted.

"And I thought it was important enough to meet Chalam to talk about it in more detail," Richard supplied.

"Fair enough."

Chalam sighed and leaned back. He looked down. Waves of emotion crashed over his face; he was having difficulty speaking.

"What is it?" Meg asked in a soft tone.

"It's so hard to talk about. I don't even know where to begin. I tried telling the authorities after, but no one believed me. They just chalked it up to *accident* and left it at that."

I mulled it all over. It was clear where he was going with this. "Your brother died on the trip to the Chagos Trench. Is that right?"

He blinked. "Yes." He cleared his throat. "That's where it happened."

"Where what happened?"

"The BSF ship that rescued me investigated. The Captain did, anyway. Or that's what he claimed. He decided that our seacar's hull just failed and I was lucky to have survived." He paused and stared at something over my shoulder. "But that's not what happened, Truman."

"Mac, please."

He offered a small smile. "Mac. Thanks. It's not what happened. I was *there* dammit. I experienced it too. It wasn't a simple hull failure, or a microscopic flaw, or a design flaw, or whatever else they tried to say."

This intrigued Meg now. "You think they were lying? Those things *do* happen, you know."

He snarled. "Not only were they lying, they were covering it up. They knew exactly what had happened to my seacar."

I said, "You think they were in on it?"

He pounded his fist on his knee. "Yes! Those bastards were just trying to hide the truth!"

"And what is that?" Meg asked.

"I actually have no idea. It's why I'm so frustrated. But the story might shed some light." He sighed and stared at her. "It might take a few minutes."

"That's why we're here," I said. "Tell us."

"We were in the Indian Ocean. The seacar was a rental but there were no major issues with it. We'd loaded our equipment and were planning on a four-week journey. We were investigating the Chagos Trench and I was also searching for iron ore deposits."

"I assume your brother was with you?"

"Yes. He was a geologist too. We were both PhD students at Churchill University. We both love living underwater. We were so close." He stared at me and Meg. "People thought we were twins, like you two." He paused and wiped his eyes. "We both had women with us too. His girlfriend was piloting on that final day. Mine was—I mean, the person I was with— was still asleep in the bunk. Her name was Preet." He sighed. "I still don't know what happened to her. If she was still asleep when . . . " His words died in a strangled choke and he fought to maintain control.

"Take your time," Richard said. "There's no rush."

Chalam continued after a moment, "I didn't see her again. She must have died. I just hope it was quick for her."

"What the hell happened?" I asked. I was curious now, but it was not the most sensitive way to ask. Meg shot me a sharp look.

"Our sonar alarm started. It was detecting something nearby. Everyone was wondering if it was a malfunction or a failing weld on the seacar."

I frowned. "What kind of alarm?"

"It had detected a noise. It was saying *fish farms*."

I knew that most seacar sonar computers had a comprehensive list of many sounds in the oceans, from sea life to vessels. The best ones could even tell you what vessels you were near, based on the frequency, pitch, noise oscillations and other associated sounds from the ship. They were heuristic systems as well, meaning they learned for themselves as they detected new subs and sounds. Users could also add programmed explanations and ship names for underwater sounds and vehicles, and a global network connected the systems to share knowledge and increase their database for underwater noises.

"Let me guess, there were no fish farms nearby?" I asked.

"No."

"And the depth—"

"Was 500 meters. Too deep. I thought maybe the seacar was leaking, and bubbles were streaming to the surface."

"And?"

"The seacar was fine."

"Marine life?"

He glanced at me. "Because whales use bubbles to trap schools of fish?"

I shrugged. "Killer whales do."

"Yeah, they're really smart. Good hunters and killers." A sigh. "It wasn't a whale. The sound was long and sustained. It went on for minutes."

"Did you stop?"

"Yes. Turned around. Changed buoyancy to positive. We knew there was a nearby BSF and USSF base. If we got into trouble, we could call for help."

This was news. "What base?"

"Diego Garcia. It's a warsub base now."

I knew that island; it had flooded years ago. The majority of the land had only been two meters above sea level, though there were places nine meters ASL. But water had now inundated the entire place. The British and Americans still used it as a warsub base. "You were close to it?"

He grunted. "Not too close. We hadn't passed into their territory. But I did see something interesting . . ." He trailed off.

"What?"

"A facility on the seafloor. Modules. It wasn't on the charts."

"What was it?"

A shrug. "Who knows?"

I shot a look at Meg and Richard. Then, "Go on."

"The sonar alarms continued. Fish farms. Then Manse noticed an issue with the hull."

Manse must have been short for Mahiransh, I figured. "A flaw after all?"

"No." His eyes widened and began to look wild. "No! There was no leak. No sweat. No bulging. But it was . . ."

"What?" I prodded. He replied, but I couldn't hear. "Say again?"

"Shimmering. Glowing. I don't know."

I shot another look at Richard.

Chalam continued. "Pulsating. Manse got up to go look at it. I warned him to be careful."

I was completely still by this point. Couldn't have torn myself away from the story if I'd tried. It had transfixed me. "Was it hot?"

"No! That's another weird thing. It was cold. Manse mentioned it. I even saw mist coming from his breath. Then . . . then . . ."

He stopped and gasped. He took several deep breaths and Meg put her hand on his shoulder. He said, "He touched it. The result was instant."

He explained how Manse's hand had dissolved before their eyes. Had turned to jelly then liquid and dripped to the deck. His brother had screamed in pain and fear, stared at the dissolving stump, and then passed out. "The hull was bubbling by then."

"And it wasn't hot?"

"No. It was still cold. There was even frost on the bulkhead! Then it started to creak."

Oh, shit. I knew what that meant.

"The integrity was failing. It was about to split wide open. I knew I only had seconds left. I screamed at Preet, who was asleep, and Kalinda—Manse's girlfriend—to get in their scuba gear. I hoped I did anyway." He choked back tears. "I can't remember exactly. I *wanted* to, but I'm not sure if I did. I didn't have more than a few seconds. I grabbed my own gear, and then—"

He stopped then. "It's the last thing I remember before waking up in a BSF airlock. A warsub had come out from the base. It had rescued me." He shook his head. "I'm not sure what happened. I was scrabbling at the gear, and then there was a huge *crack*. I mean, it was *loud*. Then a sensation of cold." He paused, crinkled his head as he fought to remember the details.

"Were you in the airlock?"

"I was near to it. I may have opened the inner hatch." He shook his head violently. "I'm sorry! I can't remember."

I rose to my feet and walked to the expansive viewport and stared outside. Behind me, I could hear Chalam wiping his tears and blowing his nose. I gave him a minute to compose himself.

"What do you think it was?" he asked finally.

I turned back to him. "You don't have any idea?"

"No."

"When did it happen?"

"A few days after New Year's."

"And no one else lived?"

"No. Kalinda, Preet, Manse. Gone."

I thought it over. "And you watched Manse's hand . . . melt? Evaporate?" It sounded so odd, but Chalam himself had described the events as *bizarre and tragic.*

"Yes, I did," he said in a soft voice, staring at the deck.

"Do you have a theory?"

He sighed. "I'm a geologist. A scientist. I've gone over it a thousand times. It might have been tectonic. Bubbles from an outgoing magmatic extrusion? Like in the Pacific along Ridge-Axis Boundaries? At thermal vents? Or even an intrusion?"

Meg said, "You did mention there were many types of boundaries at the Chagos Trench."

"But that was hundreds of kilometers to the East!" he cried. "We were away from the boundaries!"

"A seacar flaw? A tear in the ballast system?"

"The ballast was functioning perfectly."

I said, "That wouldn't explain the sensation of cold, or the injury to Manse's hand though."

"No," Meg answered. "It wouldn't."

Chalam said, "Richard was interested in my story. In fact, he contacted me quickly to ask for more information." He pierced the older man with a glare. "It's time for you to tell me what you know."

Richard blinked. "Pardon?"

"You know something! Just by the way you responded to me! Now, what is it?"

"Why do you need to know?"

Chalam had switched from grief to full-blown anger and rage. "Because

I want revenge, dammit! I want to know what—and *who*—did this!"

I turned again and looked out at the work being done outside the Research Module. The welders were still at work on the antenna. I muttered, "It seems clear, doesn't it, Richard?"

"Indeed."

Chalam didn't reply. I could hear his confusion from the silence now. Eventually he managed, "You know what it was, Mac?"

"I think so," I muttered.

"But how?"

I exhaled. "Just putting a few facts together. A few things I know that you don't." I glanced back over my shoulder. "And I know what Richard's mission is right now."

Chalam said, "I don't understand."

I exhaled. "Richard is trying to manipulate me into going after something that doesn't seem logical or likely. And yet the facts are coalescing before our very eyes here."

"Meaning?" Chalam was still confused.

I shrugged. "Just based on the people he's introduced me to today. You being the final piece in the puzzle. It's all just come together."

"I still don't—"

I whirled on him. "How long was your sonar going off before the hull split?"

"Ten minutes I think."

I frowned. "Seems like a long time."

"They turned the ship," Richard interjected. "It might have played a role in delaying things."

"Possibly," I said. "But it's not as fast as Alyssna led us to believe."

"It's still in testing phase, Mac."

"Again, it's possible." I shrugged.

"They may have changed targets. From the port to the starboard when they reversed direction. The range may have been large."

Chalam was staring at me, to Richard, and then back to me. "Listen, Mac. I'm trying to be polite here. Three people died under mysterious circumstances. The BSF sailors didn't believe what I was saying. I've been living with the death of my brother for a few weeks now with no explanation. Preet was still asleep! Kalinda was piloting—"

He was starting to panic again, getting frustrated and angry. I said, "Chalam, tell me what the BSF sailors said to you."

He stopped and his eyes fixed to mine. "I woke up in the airlock. Cold and tired. Had a headache. They were pulling the facemask off. I was gasping for air." He looked away, and his eyes darted back and forth as he remembered. It seemed totally, completely authentic.

The man was not lying.

I had no doubt at all—he'd lived through a traumatic experience.

"You told them about the alarm? About the hull?"

"They didn't believe me."

"Did they ask you for the entire story?"

"They didn't really pay any attention to it."

I frowned at that. "They were from Diego Garcia? What ship?"

"I think it was *Trafalgar*. Their divers pulled me into an airlock. The doctor fixed me up and they transferred me to another warsub that was coming back here. I only arrived a few days ago."

"You say they didn't pay any attention to your story? Did they ask questions?"

He snorted. "Not as many as you have, and I was on that ship for a couple of days. They just kept repeating that the hull must have failed because it was a rental."

I muttered, "Clearly they were hiding something."

"But what?"

I pointed outside at the maintenance work. "What do you see there, Chalam?"

He rose to his feet and peered past my finger. "Workers." He grunted. "Working."

"And what's that?"

He followed my gaze. "A stream of bubbles."

"From?"

"They're—" He choked off his thought. "They're welding." He turned to me. "You think there were people outside our seacar? But we were moving—"

"Not people. But it was something like that. Hitting your hull."

He paused and I could see the thoughts churning through his head. "That is . . . that is . . . " he trailed off. Then he shook himself. "But if that's true, *why*? And why us?"

I shrugged. "A test maybe? Were there any other vessels near you?"

"Nope."

"You searched?"

"Yes."

"With passive sonar?" Meaning listening sensors on board the seacar capable of detecting distant noises.

"Yes."

"What about active sonar?" Seacars could send out loud noises—or *pings*—that would rebound and inform a sonar system what exactly was close.

"We didn't send any."

"Then there could have been someone near."

"I guess."

"*Trafalgar* was obviously near."

He sighed. "They might have been responsible, even if they did save me."

"There was also something you said, about modules on the seafloor."

"Yes. We passed over them. My magnetometer detected them."

"Could you tell me where that was on a map?"

He stared at me in total silence. He looked at Richard and Meg, then back to me. "I could. But I won't."

I blinked. "But why not?"

He snorted. "Because I don't trust people as much as I used to."

"You came to *us*, remember?"

"Yes. But I want revenge for Manse. His goddamn hand dissolved before my eyes! Then our hull mysteriously caved in and killed three of us! I want to kill the people responsible! Now tell me what it is!"

"It caused bubbles, right?"

He stopped to catch his breath and his brow furrowed. "So, you think this is some kind of . . . *welding* weapon?"

I didn't want to tell him the truth just yet so I settled on, "It's very possible," I said.

He leaned toward me; his mouth was inches from my face. I didn't back off because I knew he was not a threat. He hissed, "Then I want in, Mac. I want to be a part of this. Whatever you're planning. Killing them, stealing it, *whatever*. I'm a part of this now, and I won't tell you where it is unless you include me."

Chapter Seven

We were back in *SC-1*, cleaning ourselves up before dinner. We were to meet Sahar Noor at the most exclusive restaurant at Churchill Sands, and we had to dress nicely for the occasion. She and Richard had arranged it before our visit, and he had warned me to bring something nice. Meg was already in a black form-fitting dress. As her brother, I had long been aware of the attraction she held over other men.

She noticed me staring at her and she flashed me a grin. "Worried?"

We were in the living compartment of the seacar, a small carpeted area with two couches facing each other across a tight space. The steel bulkheads, which curved upward into a low ceiling, were featureless, unless you considered welded pipes and wiring fixed to the space "decoration." "About?" I asked.

"Other men trying to take advantage of me?"

I snorted. I knew she could handle herself. She worked as an aquanautic engineer and mechanic, a field usually male-dominated, and she held her own just fine. She was in charge of a large crew and was an exceptional mechanic. Engine grease usually covered her arms up to the elbows and she was often in coveralls. This look was a bit different for her, but she certainly appeared glamorous. "Not at all."

"Just don't look at my scars."

Her legs were still healing from the torture she'd received at CIA Investigator Zyvinski's hands six months earlier. "They're getting a lot better. You look amazing."

She grinned again. "You don't look so bad yourself. Those broad shoulders will attract every Brit from here to Dover."

I frowned. "But Dover is only a few kilometers—"

"Whatever." She rolled her eyes and it made me laugh. She continued, "Excited about dinner?"

"I'm not sure." I thought about what we'd been through that day. "The developments are . . . incredible. I don't know if I believe it all, really."

Richard stepped out of the lavatory. He was in slacks and a pressed shirt with a collar. He looked distinguished and respectable. "How could you not? You heard everything, Mac. I didn't plant or insert anything. I let those people tell you themselves. You questioned them. They answered."

"Still."

"Doesn't it all add up?"

"It adds up to a bigger mystery than when it started." I frowned and lowered myself to a couch. If the weapon was real, and a superpower was already testing it underwater, then it was something TCI had to pursue. Our lives in the oceans depended on advancing technology, locating new resources, developing our militaries, and always being one or two steps ahead of our competitors, like the United States, China, or Russia. We couldn't let them get the advantage. The future of the human race was at stake.

Our cities supplied a growing amount of resources for the land nations. Countries around the world used kelp in their diets. We had been managing and growing kelp forests now for decades, and when it grew a meter a day in some locations, it was a natural choice for economies. Researchers had discovered forests in the Arctic Ocean in the early 21st Century that were exploding in size due to warming waters.

And so the flood was coming . . . but the other way, this time. Humans into the water. Cities on the seafloors. Transportation between settlements across the oceans.

And technology was the key. We needed to farm more efficiently to prove our existence to the superpowers. We needed to mine richer deposits, which meant locating them in areas easy to access. We needed to stake these claims first.

And this included needing better militaries and better transportation.

And this energy weapon was yet another advance, whether I believed in its logic or not. If a nation was developing it, Trieste needed it too.

It was one of the reasons why we were fighting to create Oceania, the military and economic partnership among the undersea colonies. We were doing it as secretly as possible, for the superpowers were fighting it, but knowledge was getting out, as Richard had mentioned. We had fourteen cities in our sphere so far, and there were twenty-nine major settlements in the oceans. At some point, when we felt confident enough, we would make the announcement and brace for the fallout. Our colonizing nations would not sit back while we claimed independence; they would occupy and fight us.

And war would result, in the oceans.

It was coming, and soon.

Meg and Richard were both standing at the ladder's base, staring at me. "Ready?" Meg asked.

I shook myself out of my reverie.

—••—

THE WALK THROUGH THE CITY was fascinating. Whenever I went to an undersea colony, I marvelled at the differences. Seascape, for example, had been for tourists. Most of the bulkheads and decks had been transparent, allowing incredible views of the marine life and clear, bright waters in the Gulf. Blue Downs, in the Tasman Sea, had been light, bright, and airy. It was clean and more spacious than other cities. Trieste was more industrial—the decks were steel grates with exposed wires and conduits—but the central Commerce Module was spacious, nine entire stories—four stories up and five down into bedrock—with a skylight at the top, vines and plants ringing the balconies around a large atrium, with restaurants and bars and retail in the sunlit space. But no matter the colony, the people remained the same. We were workers, dedicated to a common goal. We weren't weak, fragile, or lazy. We didn't take days off. We worked two out of three shifts every single day. We wanted our freedom and we worked hard for it. And no matter where you went in the oceans, each underwater colony seemed the same in this regard.

Churchill's citizens stared at us as we marched toward the Commerce Module. They recognized us. There were smiles, waves, greetings, and high fives from children. They knew about our father and his quest and how we now represented his ideal for the world's ocean dwellers. They loved us.

At times I understood—and appreciated—it. At others, I found it tiresome. There was too much pressure some days.

I saw more BSF troops in the city. Some were smiling and friendly, chatting with the citizens and exuding an aura of friendliness. Others were in pairs, marching robotically, with eyes like embers and dark, stony faces. Those troops had the same black and red logo on their shoulders, and I noted that the citizens stayed away from them. They parted as those patrols approached, avoided eye contact, and hugged the bulkheads as they passed. It was obvious what had been going on; only violence and power could cause such a reaction.

I thought about Chalam and how he had spoken about the water all around. It was a reality of life where we lived, but I also felt the emotional weight for what we were doing. People depended on us for our continued existence. I couldn't let them down, but I also couldn't expose them to danger. I especially felt that when I saw the children running through the travel tubes and corridors of Churchill. They were innocent and didn't deserve war. The path I was on—which Dad had started and which I had reluctantly joined after learning about the SCAV drive— had forced me to recognize the dangers all around. People's lives were on the line, and the weight of this was squarely on my shoulders.

I glanced up at the travel tube we were in. The ceiling was transparent, and thirty meters of water was immediately over our heads.

At times it made my heart pound. Anxiety . . . but not from the water.

—••—

THE RESTAURANT WAS AT THE Commerce Module's apex. There was a skylight but it was dark topside now, and moonlight shone downward. There were lights on wires crisscrossing the room, hanging above the tables, and in the dark chamber it was like a starlit sky at the surface. There were vines on trellises along the bulkheads, and everything combined gave the impression of an outdoor café topside at nighttime. It was beautiful. There was even a breeze through the restaurant, shifting in direction and speed, which simulated the outdoors. The lights were low and the moonlight flickered over everyone. I smiled as I walked in and looked around. People eating glanced at us, looked back to their meals, then shot us a second look as they realized who we were. I smiled at a few tables and waved, then wound my way among the patrons to the table where Sahar Noor was waiting.

She was by herself, which made me happy. I didn't feel like eating with the BSF officer, Commodore Clarke. I needed more information about him, but didn't want to discuss anything sensitive in his presence just yet. The fact that he had known Dad when the CIA assassinated him didn't sit well with me.

"Hello Meg," Sahar said, rising as we approached. "Mac, Richard," she said to each of us in turn with a slight bow of her head.

She was wearing a dark hijab and matching long dress. She had draped a long yellow scarf around her neck that flowed down her back. From what I had heard, the bright scarves were her trademark. This one had intricate turquoise weaving throughout, mimicking the ocean currents outside, I assumed. Her eye makeup was dark, lashes long, and lips red. Her smile was demure and welcoming at first, then grew broader as we sat.

"Thank you for this invitation," I said. People at the nearby tables had noticed who was next to them, and they kept their eyes down, but they could not contain their excitement; it showed on their faces. At first I thought it might be for Meg and me, until I saw eyes shooting toward Sahar.

She was the celebrity here, I realized. Not us.

It made me laugh inwardly, and squashed my ego just a bit, which was a good thing.

"I hope you've had a nice day at our city," she said.

"It's been interesting, Sahar."

"I'm sorry I hit you this morning with the Commodore. He can be abrasive."

Meg's eyes grew slightly hard, which someone else may not have noticed through her makeup. I did.

"We just have . . . reservations about colonizers and their military," Richard supplied.

Sahar had already proven her knowledge about our history, and she remained silent at that.

Drinks arrived, without us ordering, and I stared at mine, surprised. It was a fruit juice of some sort, sparkling, with slices of peach on the rim.

"I took the liberty," Sahar said. "I hope you don't mind."

I continued staring at the glass.

She added, "Is it okay?"

"It's the fruit. We don't see a lot in Trieste." We had to take vitamin supplements to make up for it. "What we do see comes in cans."

"It's a special occasion, Mac. Non-alcoholic though. I hope you don't mind."

I knew that her religion would have prohibited it at the same table. "Not at all. This is even better," I murmured. I touched one of the peach slices and felt the texture. The smell was intoxicating. "It's amazing how something can be so . . ." I trailed off.

Sahar laughed. "You already said it."

I stared at her for a moment. "Do you get this each day?" A part of me rebelled against the notion; my quarters at Trieste were the same size as an average citizen's. No extra luxuries for me. I felt that I didn't deserve special treatment in any way. The people had elected me, and they could just as easily vote me out. I was no different from them.

A puzzled look appeared on her face as she thought about the question. Then she realized. "Oh no! This is a special occasion. I usually drink water. This is for you three, not me."

Meg said, "It's wonderful." She took a sip and closed her eyes. "Oh, my . . ."

Sahar laughed again. "Thanks for letting me see this."

"What?" I asked as I also took a sip.

"The two McCluskys, together at a table in a restaurant underwater."

I glanced around. "Designed to simulate a topside café. It's incredible, really. If my hair were longer, I might feel it blowing in the warm breeze."

"The moon is an added bonus. I added it just for you three." She shrugged into the silence. "Morning prayers."

We laughed and looked upward. It did seem perfectly placed at the zenith, shining right down on us. The meaning behind her name seemed even more perfect. "You've done a fabulous job here, Sahar. The people seem so happy. The city is producing large amounts of produce to ship topside. The UK seems content too."

"We all work hard, same as at Trieste."

"Why do you want to risk it?" Meg asked.

Sahar paused, then, "Let's eat first. Then business."

—••—

THE DINNER WAS FABULOUS. IT was mostly produce from their own farms—with the exception of the fruit in our drink—and conversation ranged from life in Churchill to her own background in England and decision to move to the colony and enter politics.

"I've always felt a need to help people," she said as we nibbled at platters of fried cod pieces, kelp puree, and pita with a variety of dips. "I volunteered at places as a child. Mostly helping refugees from the coasts relocate. Then I studied social work and politics in London." She shrugged. "Then I came here."

Meg said, "Are there many Muslims living here?"

"Yes. It's a growing community. There are challenges, but those exist on the surface as well. But I am a practicing Muslim and I do just fine here."

"You swim outside?"

The question made me frown. It was something I hadn't actually considered, but I knew of Sahar's free diving records from her life before politics.

She laughed. "Yes. All the time. I couldn't live underwater without scuba. And the people would never have elected me! Imagine an underwater mayor who never went out!"

"I'm sorry," Meg quickly said. "I didn't mean—"

"No, no! Not at all. I know I'm . . . unique I guess. But it's part of how I got elected I think."

I said, "Because you are rare, living underwater?"

"No. There are other Muslims too, which I mentioned. But people always underestimate me. Then I surprise them."

"But does it cause friction?"

She paused. "You mean, do they get angry?" She considered it. "Not at all. I surprise them at first, then they embrace me. I work hard for them."

Meg said, "And you swim . . . " she trailed off, but her eyes lingered on Sahar's hijab.

Sahar's eyes flashed comprehension. "Oh, we wear wetsuits with hoods. The wetsuits are more like burkinis." Meaning they covered the swimmer from head to toe, with looser material stretching down to the knees.

"And the refugees topside?"

A shadow passed across her face. "It's growing terrible on land. Refugees arrive daily. The economy is suffering. There's not enough work for them, but they're surging across Europe from the coasts, especially Bangladesh. Citizens are not happy, to say the least. It's fueling right-wing groups everywhere, not just the United Kingdom."

I'd seen stories about it on the news constantly. It was a global crisis, but the oceans—which had caused the issue—actually sheltered us from it! When we did see immigrants arrive at Trieste, homeless due to rising waters, we were happy to see them. They were especially hard workers.

More food arrived, and it was wonderful. There were English touches to it, like fish pastries, and even East Indian touches like a coconut chutney to dip our pita in. More fruit drinks appeared. The music was soft and quiet, the flickering light from above, the simulated starlight, the water sighing against the skylight . . . it was magical.

The thought of Chalam and the tragedy he'd suffered only three weeks earlier flashed into my mind, and I wondered about him.

"What's wrong, Mac?" Sahar asked.

"Pardon?"

"Your face suddenly got dark. What is it?"

I sighed and leaned back, away from the food. "This has been fantastic; thank you so much. I'm bursting."

"It's more than that."

"I don't want to put you in danger. We've added many cities to our quest. But I'm not sure you are aware of what will happen."

"I've been watching current events. Things are worse on the surface. We're their only hope, maybe."

"But you can help them without exposing yourself to war."

"I don't intend to cause death. I think we can do it peacefully."

I frowned. "What's your motivation? Why do you want to join Oceania?"

"I said I wanted to help my people. I wouldn't do something without their support."

Meg frowned. "You're saying that it's what they've asked for?"

"Exactly. They are growing vocal about it with me. It's what they want."

"And you're willing to risk war? Risk their lives?"

Now her eyes flashed. "Quite the opposite, Mac. If I wasn't Mayor, and it was someone else who wasn't as . . . *thoughtful*, I'll say . . . then he or she might jump into it without fear. Fear is a good thing. It makes us question our actions. I can do this without causing trouble. Without violence. I think we can achieve Oceania through negotiation."

It was what I had said before as well, on occasion. If we forged economic partnerships which benefited people, instead of military action which cost money and lives, then the superpowers might just listen. If we could make it profitable for them. Make ourselves useful as an independent nation instead of an angry colony of repressed people.

I said, "You think you can do this peacefully." I was repeating what she'd said, but it was more so I could process it and figure out how to respond. I didn't know at that point if she was brilliant or oblivious.

She lowered her head. "I'm going to try. It's what *they* want." She shot a look at the citizens around us. "I can't ignore them, or I wouldn't be in this position."

I sighed. "But Sahar. War sometimes happens. Fighting breaks out. It's a cold war, but it flares bright at times."

"Like in the Mid-Atlantic Ridge? Or the fight against the dreadnought?"

I blinked. "Yes. You could say that. People die."

"I won't kill anyone, Mac."

"I'm not asking you to. But that dilemma will hit you, eventually, if you join us."

"I can avoid it. I'm sure I can."

I pondered that. "And if you can't?"

"You're not understanding, Mac. I will find a way around it. I always will. And if I can't, then I won't be in this position."

"You'll quit?"

"I'll find a solution." She said it adamantly and with a smile on her face. I couldn't help but grin back.

But a part of me wondered if she was being realistic.

—••—

SHE LEANED BACK AND LOCKED eyes with me. Then she studied Richard and Meg, then back to me. "Why don't you fill me in on your meetings this afternoon?"

That startled me. "I beg your—"

"You met Alyssna Sonstraal. I know all about her."

I choked back a startled gasp. "You've been watching us?"

"We have a network of . . . *agents* too, Mac. We're just curious about what you're doing."

"By spying on us?"

"You're in the thick of a cold war. You said so yourself." She paused. "I meant nothing by it. It was more to keep you safe. But I know who Alyssna is. I also know Chalam Kaashif's story. What are you working on now?"

I remained silent.

"Mac," she said, leaning forward. "I want *in*. I want to help. So does Commodore Clarke. We're here for you. Tell us how to help."

I stayed silent as the worries churned through my mind. I didn't know what exactly to say.

Richard interjected, "It's why we came here, Mac."

"We came to discuss a partnership with Churchill. Now it's turned into something I wasn't expecting."

Sahar said, "I know Doctor Sonstraal worked on some sort of secret project in the Indian Ocean. Then she came here and has been upset at the BSF since. She's been quite vocal. As for Chalam, a BSF warsub dropped him off three days ago. I spoke with him to find out what was going on. He told me a strange story. The interesting thing is, it *also* happened in the Indian Ocean."

"Yes," I muttered. "He told us too. They all seem to add up to one thing."

"A new and peculiar weapon, which you want to steal."

"Perhaps," I murmured. "We haven't decided yet."

"Well, I can help you. Commodore Clarke can help you." She looked at us in turn. Then, "Listen Mac, the labs are here, in *my* city. Clarke is a BSF officer. Let us help you steal it. If you're going to try anyway, then I at least want in, to keep people from getting hurt. Now . . . *what's the plan?*"

Chapter Eight

"But it doesn't make sense," I said. "You want to avoid violence. Why help us steal Doctor Sonstraal's weapon?"

She smiled. "Mac, haven't you been listening? I want to do things peacefully. Without death. If someone else was in charge, they'd just barge in, guns blazing. People in Churchill would be hurt. But I can help you do it silently. Without killing."

"But the weapon, by nature, is meant to kill! It's still doesn't—"

"It's about maintaining the balance of power," she said. "I'm a student of history too. I know about the first Cold War. Mutually Assured Destruction. The constant struggle to maintain equality. The Atom Bomb. The Hydrogen Bomb. If both sides are equally strong, it'll *prevent* war, not cause it."

I hesitated at that. She was correct, I had to hand it to her. But I didn't want to tell her that we had the Hafnium Bomb, or maybe she'd suggest handing it over the CSF, RSF, and the USSF. That thought made me shudder. The Bomb would actually stop fleets from attacking us, I hoped, and prevent death that way. I also didn't want to stress the flare-ups that had happened during the Cold War—the Korean War, Vietnam—not to mention the perpetual, ongoing issues in the Middle East, or the ones that had happened during our own struggle, and how many had died because of them.

I realized in a flash that Sahar was vocalizing the exact thoughts I'd had only an hour earlier. I hadn't wanted the people of Churchill Sands—or *any* city—to suffer because of my quest for independence. Already so many had died, and I felt tremendous guilt about it. But Sahar was very self aware. She wanted to succeed without causing death right from the beginning. She understood what the results could be, and she wanted to avoid them rather than deal with the fallout, as I'd had to do. It was a clever and mature way to move forward.

"How do you know that Sonstraal's weapon is here?"

"I beg your pardon?" Sahar asked.

"You said you want to help because the labs are in Churchill."

"Alyssna has been vocal, as I said. We have agents watching her of course. I need to know what's going on to be an effective leader."

But there were four components to the weapon, I knew. I didn't say anything about that.

Yet.

I pondered the dilemma confronting me. There was a whole other line of thought that suggested that if one side held *more* power over the other, then that would also keep conflict from occurring. It was the opposite of what Sahar was suggesting. At times during my leadership—as Mayor of Trieste and as Director of TCI—I'd subscribed to that philosophy. Moreover, I'd actively used the advances in technology to encourage the other colonies to join with us by giving it to them. The SCAV drive, for instance.

Regardless of the debate, I knew that if Sahar wanted to help us steal the weapon, I would of course have to let her.

Meg said, "You could just let the BSF develop the weapon on their own. I still don't understand why you want to help us."

Sahar offered her a smile. "I know your history. I know what the future holds. I also know what my people want. I have to join your efforts to form Oceania. And that means helping to steal the weapon."

"Without causing death."

"That's right."

"And Clarke is actually willing to help?" Meg snarled. "It just doesn't make sense. He's a Commodore in the BSF. I can't see him turning his back on that."

Sahar looked away. She appeared to be collecting her thoughts, or deciding what exactly she was going to say. "Meg, he is not the nicest person. I'm sure you could tell when he was with us in my office earlier. He was cold and callous."

"He insulted you by demanding whiskey. Why, exactly?"

She shrugged. "It's his way of joking. It was offensive; you're right. To me. To Muslim women. But I also know that he is with us on this."

"How?" I asked.

She leaned forward. "He has told me about his past. And yes, even about your dad. He has a great deal of guilt over that, trust me. He knows that independence is inevitable, and the longer it takes, the more people will die to achieve it." She paused. "Alyssna's weapon is in the Research Module. Clarke has seen to it that people under his command are guarding it. *Some* of them, anyway. He can make sure they're . . . not alerted when we make our move."

"What do you mean, *some of them*?"

"From what I understand, the BSF has guards at the labs. They watch the hatches, monitor the alarms, and so on. Since this area falls under Clarke's command, he can help with them. But the organization currently developing the weapon *also* guards it. They also operate a covert lab, located somewhere in the Indian Ocean. We don't know exactly where the facility is. But that's a division of the BSF much like your DARPA in the United States. The Commodore has little authority over those sailors."

"So he can't order them to . . . take a break or something?"

"Precisely. If he tried, they might think there was something up. They only take orders from their superiors."

I pondered that. "What if Clarke tried?"

"They would think it odd."

"You've asked him?"

She nodded. "We've spoken at length about it. We know Alyssna. She's a brilliant scientist, Mac. If she claims to have created a new weapon, we have to listen to her. I've researched her history."

"Has she approached you about it?"

"No. She has an extreme dislike for the BSF at the moment. And for me."

"How do you know?"

A shrug. "You know the game."

I pursed my lips. It made sense. Alyssna Sonstraal wanted to help Trieste, not Churchill. But Sahar Noor was going to assist anyway, just to help Oceania. "How many troops are guarding it?"

"Close to a dozen at any moment."

My eyes widened. "Is that all?" I muttered. It was meant to be sarcastic, but Sahar ignored it. She was all business now.

"But those are just the guards. I'm not including the scientists and assistants who work here."

"And you don't want anyone killed," I said. It wasn't a question. I was just thinking out loud.

"Exactly. We have to get in and out silently, so no one knows we were there."

I frowned at that. Surely they'd know we'd taken it. "How large is the lab here?"

"A couple of decks in Research Module A. It's big."

"Is there a moonpool?" It was the usual way to infiltrate a city.

"Yes, under the lower deck, but it's always under guard and closed tight."

"Opening it triggers alarms?"

"Yes."

I thought about the situation. Guards to distract. A moonpool hatch that was always sealed. A weapon of some sort to carry out. Other workers to sneak past. There was still so much to learn. We didn't even know how large the weapon was.

Richard spoke after remaining silent for so long. "You work on three shifts here?"

"Yes."

"The scientists too?"

"From what I gather, yes."

"Is there a holiday or event coming up that will take care of some of the workers for us?"

Sahar considered that. It was currently January 30. "I'm not sure how much preparation you'll need. Chinese New Year, Valentine's Day, Shrove Tuesday and Ash Wednesday are in February. Also a Jewish holiday called Purim."

"Are any of those national holidays in the UK?"

"No. In March there's St. David's Day and Maha Shivaratri."

"What are—"

"Neither of them are national holidays either. The latter is Hindu."

She looked upward at the surface thirty meters above the skylight.

Moonlight bathed her face in its glow. Then her eyes opened and she stared at me. "We're very multicultural here. We love it. Embrace it. But there is one coming up that is a major celebration across cultures. It might work." She offered a slight chuckle. "It's not one I'm fond of, but I can't fight the culture. And it's one that the majority of the city basically stops to celebrate."

—••—

"St. Patrick's Day?" I said.

She nodded. "Most of the city stops. There are many parties. Even the children participate. Other cultures engage in the festivities, including Muslims, though they celebrate in a more subdued fashion."

I stared at the fruit drink before me. "No doubt," I said. "But your idea has merit."

"It's also slightly ironic," Meg said.

Sahar nodded. "Alcohol is *haraam*." She shrugged. "I do see the irony though, Meg, you're right."

"St. Patrick's Day is 17 March, correct?" I did a quick calculation in my head. "That's about forty-five days."

"Is it enough time?"

I sighed. "Thankfully we have a SCAV drive to move quickly back to Trieste and plan. We'll have to leave tonight. Are we able to communicate through a secure line? From Trieste?"

"I can arrange it."

"And Clarke will be available to participate?"

"Of course."

"Then I think it's time we depart Churchill and get started on the plan. Thank you for your hospitality, Sahar. We really appreciate it."

She smiled at us. "Richard, Meg, Mac. *Ma'a salama.* Go with peace."

—••—

"So you're going to do it?" Meg asked.

We were marching away from the Commerce Module, our feet ringing on the steel deck. There were few others around and the sea outside was dark. I was leading them on a westerly direction, even though the Docking Module was to the north.

"I don't think we have a choice." I gestured at Richard. "What do you think?"

"I wouldn't have brought you otherwise. We need it."

"The British have it now," I whispered. "They're already testing it. The geologist Chalam Kaashif is proof. And soon others will find out too."

"Can you imagine if the Russians get it before we do? They could carve into Trieste if they got close enough, and it would happen without warning."

That thought made me shudder. They wouldn't even have to be in an RSF warsub. It could just be a cargo ship or a privately owned seacar with the weapon installed within, and the energy *emitter*—if that's what an engineer would call it—at the bow. Pull up to within a hundred meters, and fire. Collapse the modules one after another. It would be a disaster.

Or even a scooter might be enough. We paid little attention to smaller craft around the city. People came and went as they liked, as in most other undersea colonies.

Meg glanced at a sign as we passed under it. "Tru, where exactly are we going?"

———••———

FIVE MINUTES LATER WE WERE knocking at a partition hatch in one of the Living Modules. A muffled voice swore from the other side and the hatch slid aside. Alyssna Sonstraal glared out at us, rubbing her eyes. "Don't you have a PCD? You could have called."

"This is the best we could do," I answered. "Can we come in?"

She grunted. "There's not much space, but come on."

We pushed our way in and found ourselves shoulder-to-shoulder in the small compartment. It was the same as at Trieste, where space was at a premium. Alyssna sat on her bunk—where she'd been sleeping only seconds before—and the rest of us remained standing.

"Tell me about the four components of the weapon," I said.

She shook her head savagely. "No way, Mac. I want to work with you.

And you have to host me at Trieste before and after. With a lab to continue my work."

"That doesn't mean you can keep everything to yourself. What are the different components?"

"Not yet."

I exhaled. "What about the one that's here? Is that enough to work on its own?"

"Not effectively. You need all four."

"Do you know where they all are?"

"One is here. One is on a BSF warsub, moving around in the South Pacific. I know the name of the vessel, so we can find it. And two are at the facility in the Indian Ocean, where I once worked."

"What are the coordinates?"

She sighed. "I can't lie. I don't know the precise coordinates. Just the general region."

I glanced knowingly at Meg. "And how big is the completed weapon, once you connect all components?"

"The four together are the size of a small seacar. Six meters or so in length; two across."

"And the one here?"

"Larger than, say, several connected couches."

"Weight?"

Her features screwed up as she thought. "The one here is five hundred pounds. It's the largest."

I swore. I had hoped that one person could sling it across his back and just walk out with it. I wondered exactly what the hell this weapon was. But this first component was huge. We'd need a large trolley to cart it out. Or a crane.

"Can it get wet?"

She looked horrified. "No way. It's delicate electronics!"

"And the other three parts?"

"They vary in size. One is small."

I swore again. She wasn't making it easy. I stared at the ceiling and tried to work out the puzzle. The timing was an issue too. The one great thing we had going for us was that we had a lot of help, and a specific day to make it happen.

At least for the mysterious first component.

"Grab a bag, Alyssna, if you want to work with us."

She stared at me, her eyes wide. She wasn't blinking. "You accept my terms?"

"Of course. I keep hearing that you are a brilliant scientist. That alone is enough for me to want you to live with us at Trieste. This weapon of yours, which I'm still skeptical about, is an added bonus. We're going to steal it, if you'll help."

"And I'll get to work with it, once it's back at Trieste?"

"To connect the components and make it operational, yes. And make more, I hope." *If it works*, I wanted to add. It was a dark thought. We were going to steal four components to create a working weapon. But I realized that there were already working models out there . . . one of which was in the Indian Ocean.

"Then I accept," she said with a grin. She thrust her hand out. "It's a deal!"

Meg and Richard also shook hands, with smiles all around.

"And we're going *now*?" she asked, surprised.

"We're in a hurry. Time is an issue."

"Are we bringing Chalam back too?" Meg hissed at me from the corner of her mouth as Alyssna grabbed her belongings.

I shook my head. That would not be a good idea, just yet, but eventually they would have to meet, because only he knew the exact coordinates of the facility in the Indian Ocean.

The facility where two of the weapon components were locked securely away.

Chapter Nine

Within an hour we were on our way back to Trieste. We'd originally planned on staying overnight, but now there was an urgency to our decisions and an impetus to our movements. I needed to brief the entire team about the happenings at Churchill Sands, about Alyssna and the weapon and the proof that it did indeed seem to work. I would involve Chalam at a later date, if we were successful with the first component on 17 March.

Alyssna's bag was small—she didn't have a lot of possessions, and didn't feel tied down to Churchill at all—and there was a grin on her face as we boarded *SC-1*. Despite the bitterness she felt about the weapon and how others had taken it from her, she was thrilled that there was a plan brewing that involved not only her getting possession of it again, but also working with it, improving it, and even putting more of them to use at some point in the future. I wondered to whom she was allegiant, but I was sure I'd find out at some point. She'd mentioned Africa and tensions with her dad, and also England and tensions there with her superiors. If I could show her anything at Trieste, it would be a place that would support and honor her, embrace her, and offer her a home that she could work and fight for. I knew it would thrill her, as it had our other science staff in our research labs.

As we pulled away from the colony, I brought us close to the Living Modules. We soared past, banking to port and toward the south. The lights on each were bright, but the dark and thick water scattered and dispersed each greatly. The blue light at the top of the Commerce Module was especially bright, however. Alyssna, standing behind me and watching over my shoulder, said, "That's close to the wavelength that best penetrates water."

"I beg your pardon?" I adjusted the ballast to keep us close to the seafloor as I increased speed. The floor dropped away below us, but I maintained the thirty-meter depth.

"Light blue. Well," she said, "cyan or green, really. A wavelength of about 520 nanometers penetrates best, though it depends on the salinity, dissolved gas content, and temperature."

"Better than white?"

She snorted. "White is every color combined. It doesn't really have a wavelength."

"I guess you'd know." I looked back at her. "You said you studied at Cambridge?"

"Particle beam physics."

I pursed my lips.

"It's not a laser," she said again, anticipating my comment. "Well, not really."

"When will you tell me?"

"Soon. When I know you're serious."

So, she wanted to ensure that I was actually going to go through with this. She was keeping her cards close to her chest, but I thought I had a way to start getting her to trust me.

"You know, revenge isn't a great driving force," I said. "It is powerful, but it causes . . . problems."

She hesitated for a long moment. "Why the hell would you say that to me?"

I shrugged, though I was sitting in the pilot's chair and she may not have noticed. "I've had a great deal of experience with it. My entire family has. Revenge is sweet, but it also has a price." I thought about Rico Ruiz and his obsession with finding and killing the German. Or Meg and what she'd been through after murdering Admiral Benning. The torture . . . prison . . .

I shuddered.

"You don't know what I've been through."

"I can tell," I said. "I want to welcome you to Trieste. You're free to work there. We'll fully fund your lab. But sometimes it's better to forgive and move on. Just start a new life."

"Forgive who, exactly?" she snapped.

"The BSF in charge of your project," I replied. *Your dad*, I wanted to add, but didn't. I felt that it would trigger a massive emotional response, which I wanted to avoid.

"How much do you know about Trieste?" I asked.

"I've been isolated a bit for the past few years. We didn't get a lot of news at The Vault."

I blinked at that but didn't say anything. I filed it away for future use. "I think you will be happy with us."

"I guess we'll see," she murmured.

I opened the panel using my thumb print and triggered the reactor. A rumble reverberated through the seacar.

She glanced around. "Is everything okay?"

"Perfectly." I pushed the throttle forward and the noise grew to a dull roar. I felt myself pressed backward, and vibrations moved up my legs. "I'd sit down if I were you." I gestured at the chair next to me, which was empty. Richard and Meg were both in the back, getting ready to sleep, I assumed.

Alyssna pushed between the chairs and sat down, staring out the canopy. Bubbles were churning from the bow and flowing backward; a film was growing and moving slowly past the transparent material.

"Holy shit," she gasped. "Is everything working okay? That's a lot of cavitation. The bow of your seacar—"

"Is designed to do this," I finished for her. "And the rumble you hear is a fusion reactor in our engine room."

She shot a look at me. "What the hell are you saying?"

"You've been away for several years?"

"Two. A bit more."

I grinned. "Alyssna, you're about to experience something few others have, but more and more nations are building them right now as we're speaking."

She continued to stare out the canopy, leaning forward to watch the distorted view. She was fighting acceleration though, and I pointed at the readout. Her jaw dropped. "That can't be right."

We were pushing past 300 kph and steadily climbing toward 400. The bottom had dropped away from us, and I lowered our depth to 1,000 meters, to take advantage of the cold-water Atlantic gyre that flowed southward from the North Sea. It was essentially an underwater river. At surface, the water moved northward. If we'd stayed there, it'd be like fighting a headwind. "Trieste has numerous advances in technology, Alyssna. This is just one. I hope we can add your discovery to the list."

"On your quest for independence?"

"You got it."

She remained silent and simply stared in amazement.

—••—

"I GUESS I'VE BEEN AWAY for too long," she muttered after a while. The sound of the fusion drive had faded into the background, along with the ballast and life support systems meant to maintain course and keep us alive—it was all white noise. She'd been staring at the blurry image before us, the twisting and swirling and ephemeral nature of the SCAV bubble that lowered friction with water to nearly nothing, and sighed. "I wonder what other revelations I'll realize I've missed."

I grinned. "There are a few."

"I'm sure I'll learn."

"I hope." I filled her in about our research labs and the other scientists who worked there. I didn't provide detail about the other inventions we'd been using, like the Isomer Bomb. Eventually I found myself talking about the past, while Meg and Richard slept in the recessed bunks behind the pilot's cabin and before I knew it, I was telling her about Dad and his struggles and how the authorities had murdered him to prevent further violence in the underwater colony. I told her about my own pain trying to deal with the heartache of a shattered family and lives torn to pieces.

She listened in silence as the ocean whirled past us and the rumble of the SCAV drive comforted us with its powerful presence. Then, after thirty minutes of me talking nonstop, and a few more of silence, she said, "And you wanted to follow your dad's path, like so many sons." She nodded to herself. "It makes sense."

"Actually, no. I didn't want anything to do with his plans or goals."

"What do you mean? I thought you embraced it. You're fighting for independence now, aren't you?"

"Yes, but it took me a long, long time. I hated him for bringing pain on us. My mom never recovered. Meg ran away to Blue Downs when we turned eighteen. The assassination destroyed the family. I resented him for years."

I could tell from the corner of my eyes that she was staring at me. I knew that her own tensions with her dad had led her on the path she was on now, the same as me. She had done it to prove him wrong though . . . to prove that women were just as smart and as powerful as men. I wanted to know where her dad was now, but decided not to ask.

She said, "So you didn't want anything to do with independence?"

"Nothing. I knew it would cause more pain and hardship. Cause death. Not just for me and Meg, but for all of Trieste. We're so vulnerable, living where we do. A small explosion or torpedo could end it all for so many people in a split second."

"And what were you doing?"

"I was working for the city," I said. "In intelligence. I ended up captured by the Chinese and tortured for months. Then after, I worked the kelp farms just to contribute. Eventually I did find myself back in TCI and espionage, after seven years of farming, and then it all changed for me."

"You mean about your dad?"

"When I learned the truth about the SCAV drive. I *knew* it would be the trigger point. With it we could drive the colonies to the future. It was a watershed moment. It would give us the edge, *and* give me a massive advantage over our enemies." I snorted. "And that's where we are now."

"Fighting for independence."

I'd come to terms with my father now and how he had lived his life. And then when I'd come across his killer—Admiral Benning—I had even spared his life.

Though Meg hadn't had the same ideas. She murdered him in her cabin, and we'd all had to deal with the violent aftermath.

It had angered me at the time, though I understood Meg's rage. Our entire lives had shifted in 2099, the year Dad had died. It had been a monumental event in our journeys, but since reconnecting in Trieste, and starting on the path he'd started, Meg and I had found peace with the events, finally.

Doctor Alyssna Sonstraal would have to somehow find the same

peace with her dad and their history, if she was ever going to find happiness in life.

—••—

EIGHTEEN HOURS AFTER DEPARTING CHURCHILL, we pulled into Trieste.
The SCAV was off and we were under conventional thrusters only. The
waters were light and clear, and myriad fish swirled about the many modules. Seacars approached or departed, their navigation lights blinking,
and scuba divers swam close to the seafloor. Some of them disappeared
under the city modules and swam up into moonpools, and others appeared as they dove into the water and emerged from under them. The
modules were all maintaining four atms of pressure, matching the surroundings, so the water didn't flow up into the module and the air didn't
rush out. It was a perfect balance, at all times. Moonpools were open areas
of water at the seafloor level of each module. Alyssna watched the scene
with wide eyes.

"I've seen images like this on the news or in movies. But this is beautiful."

"Churchill is darker. The water isn't as clear, and the currents in the
Channel are stronger."

She continued to stare in fascination as we powered into the Docking
Module, rose into the moonpool, and moored in the large open area. I'd
been communicating with Grant Bell in Sea Traffic Control the entire
time to ensure there were no collisions.

"It's like a postcard. Or a travel poster. It seems like paradise."

I turned to her. "Welcome home."

—••—

A FEW HOURS LATER, AFTER getting Alyssna settled in a living cubicle
and asking my assistant, Kristen Canvel, to arrange a research lab space,
I was at Renée's cubicle to see how she was doing. She was awake and
bright-eyed, thrilled to see me, and seemed nearly recovered. We kissed
like we'd been apart for weeks, although it had only been four days.

"Later," she whispered, her breath hot on my neck. "I have missed you
so much."

I held her face between my hands and stared into her eyes. I was so happy to see her again. "You won't believe what's happened," I said, as I continued to kiss her.

"Tell me."

I told her about Sahar Noor, Alyssna Sonstraal, Commodore Clarke, and what Churchill had been like. Then I mentioned the weapon.

She pulled back and eyed me, shocked. "You're serious."

"Absolutely."

"And you want to steal it."

"We *have* to steal it. We don't have a choice."

She glanced away as she processed it. "Do you believe it?"

I shrugged. "Doctor Sonstraal is here. She claims it works. I've spoken to someone who experienced it firsthand. It didn't end well for him."

A frown. "What do you mean?"

"His brother died. And two other women."

"So it works. Amazing." She shook her head. "I never would have imagined it." She turned to me and said, "Do you know what I'd love to do right now?"

I tilted my head and gave her a lopsided smile. "I thought you said—"

She laughed. "Not that, Mac. I want to swim. I haven't been outside in days." She gestured to her bunk angrily. "I've been here recovering. I feel better, but I also feel locked up in here. I'm frustrated. I need to get outside."

"Are you okay to swim?"

"Of course. No dizziness. No headache. No pain. I feel nearly back to normal." She stood and reached out to me. "Care to go for a walk outside, lover?"

—••—

I HAD ONE ITEM ON my agenda before I could go out with her, so I quickly took care of it. Laura Sukovski led the Mining Division, located in the Mining Interests Module. Her face soured when she noticed me approach, and inwardly, it made me smile. I knew what it was like to be in her position, with a team of people depending on her and a quota to hit every week. Malfunctioning equipment or a lack of labor affected their output, and it was a constant stress.

And it didn't help that I was always asking for new minerals.

"Mac," she said with a scowl. "You're back."

I chuckled. "Hello, Laura. How are things in the mines?" We had claimed mineral deposits scattered all over the gulf and the Atlantic, and workers were currently at the sites, living and working the claims.

"Fine." Her response was curt, to the point.

"Anything interesting happen?"

"You mean, injuries?"

I saw the injury reports each week, so I already knew the answer. "No. I mean in terms of ore prospecting. Have you found anything . . . *big*?"

Her face brightened as she realized I might not be there to demand something. "We did find a large aluminum deposit. We'd already been mining it, but it's much larger than we'd expected."

"Excellent." She continued to stare at me, not volunteering any other information. I continued, "Uh, Laura, I'm wondering about the explosives you use here."

Realization spread across her features. "Chief Sim was already here, investigating. Only approved people get their hands on ammonium nitrate, Mac. The construction contractors were here too, because they're still finishing up the underwater shelters that they've been building now for a while. Richard was asking about this too, you know."

I nodded. The shelters were crucial. If an attack came, people had to be able to escape to safety in a pressure-controlled environment *within* the bedrock, able to sustain them with air and supplies until rescue could come. We used explosives to carve out the rock.

"So no one else has been here?"

Her face screwed up. "Well, the mines are asking for explosives, all the time. We're always shipping them out. I told Chief Sim this—"

"And have any shipments gone missing?"

"No. They've all arrived safely at their destinations."

"And the supervisors at the mines can account for it all?"

"Yes, Mac." Her tone was growing exasperated.

I waved at her as I marched away. "Thanks, Laura. Keep up the great work."

—••——

MEG AFFECTIONATELY CALLED RENÉE *FRENCHIE*. She'd been a French national when we'd first met, though calling it a conventional meeting was putting it kindly. It had been violent. As had our next. I'd fired on her warsub to damage it so I could continue on the chase to recover the SCAV drive from the Chinese spies who'd stolen it. Renée's career had never recovered. She'd been a warsub Captain in the FSF. Her superiors had demoted her to a much smaller ship and punished her for the death of her crewman. She'd translated her anger into rage toward me, and had embarked on a mission to kill me. She'd nearly succeeded, but I had captured her, and she had eventually seen the logic behind our push for independence. Now she lived in Trieste, with me, and was in charge of our city defence network.

Outside, in the warm waters, she grinned behind her full facemask as we swam, holding hands, away from the city, then turned back to see it in the daylight. The light from above shimmered down. It was warm enough that our wetsuits didn't cover our entire bodies; they ended at our knees and also left our arms exposed. Our bubbles soared up as we exhaled, and we stopped and lowered ourselves to the sandy bottom. We sat together like that, cross-legged, staring at the city.

"What are you planning?" she asked after a minute.

"With the weapon?"

"How are you going to steal it?"

"Sahar Noor will help. And Commodore Clarke."

"If the BSF catches you, it'll be prison. Or worse." She sighed. "After what we just went though with Meg, are you sure you want to?"

"It's what TCI does, Renée. I can't stop. If I did, I'd have to leave TCI and abandon the city."

"I guess that's a fact. Do you really think an energy beam will work underwater?"

"It has advantages over torpedoes, though its range is likely short."

We sat like that for several more minutes, just staring at each other and watching the city. Fish swam near us, investigating, wondering what we were doing. A few shellfish crawled by, also curious. We were sitting on a bare patch of sand; there were grasses nearby, and there were far more species living in them than were near us on the sand. There were dangers, I had no doubt, but as Triestrians we had come to just accept them, and not worry. She glanced at her PCD once, and her brow furrowed. Then she put it away.

My comm beeped. Renée stared at me for a moment, giving me a look I recognized instantly. She sometimes complained that I was always working, that I never took a break. I shrugged and offered her a smile.

"Go ahead," I said.

"Mac, it's Sahar Noor."

I blinked. "Hi, I'm just outside right now. Sorry, there's no video."

"It's quite all right. I'm sending you an information packet right now. It's in your inbox. A schematic of the labs. It'll help with your plans."

"That's great, thanks." I glanced at Renée. Her eyes were closed as she waited for me.

"The Commodore will try to get us the guard stations. He's working on it. I'll send it when I have it."

"Sounds great." I stared at Renée. I nudged her, and her eyes opened. She smiled back. I mouthed to her, *Are you okay?* She didn't acknowledge it. Her eyes closed again. "Thanks again, Sahar. I'll be in touch."

"I wanted to also say—" The comm cut out with a squawk, and I frowned. Renée's eyes were still closed.

"Hey," I said. "Sorry about that."

She opened her eyes. "No problem. Work never stops. I know."

Renée's eyes closed and then snapped open a moment later. It was like a long, sustained blink in slow motion.

I frowned.

Then they closed again, but took longer to open this time.

"Are you okay?" I asked.

"Fine. I'm fine. Just tired." Her words were slurred though, it didn't seem like simple exhaustion.

"You said you felt okay to swim."

Several heartbeats passed. I was about to ask again, then, "I did. Something's . . . wrong, Mac." Her voice was quiet. "My headache is back. It's like a . . . like a knife. I don't think . . ." She gasped and then her words trailed off.

Then she passed out.

———••———

I keyed City Control in an instant and roared, "I need help out here! It's Renée!"

There was no reply.

"Grant! It's Mac!"

Still nothing. Then there was a burst of static and a garbled voice, but then nothing.

I swore.

I scrabbled at my emergency regulator; it was easy to find. Divers used their right arm to reach back, next to their ribs, and then sweep their hand forward. The reserve would be there. I grabbed it and tore the tube from Renée's mask. I thrust my reserve into it and hoped to hell it would work.

"Renée!" I yelled. I wondered if it was the concussion, but there was another possibility here . . .

I pressed the button on the side and watched as bubbles churned out from the mask edges. I'd exchanged the air in her mask with air from my tank. "Renée," I said. "Come on. Wake up. Are you there?" I grabbed her shoulders and squeezed. I was on my knees, in front of her. Her head had fallen forward, completely limp. I pinched the skin at her hip. "Hey, wake up."

I heard a cough. "Mac?"

"Are you okay?"

"Headache . . ." She looked up and blinked her eyes. "Everything's blurry." Then her eyes closed again. They didn't reopen.

"Shit," I snapped. I stared at Trieste. There was no more time to waste. I grabbed her around the waist and pulled her up. I started to pump my legs, swimming with everything I had, dragging her back to the city. I had to make sure my backup didn't get yanked from her mask, though I still wasn't sure that was the problem.

I tried to contact STC again. "Grant! Where are you!"

Still no answer.

Chapter Ten

IT WAS DIFFICULT PULLING RENÉE while swimming, but luckily I was fit and the flippers were an enormous help. We were also relatively close to the Docking Module and Living Module B, and both had moonpools. Within ten minutes I was at the Living Module and frantically gesturing for help from other swimmers. We hauled her up to the deck around the pool, and I tore the equipment from her back and the mask from her face. I kept calling to her the whole time. She seemed to be breathing, but I turned her face to the side in case she threw up.

"What happened, Mac?" one of the swimmers asked.

"She passed out during the swim. Not sure." I looked up at him. "Call for medical—*now!*"

—•••—

"WHERE'S HER TANK, MAC?" STACY Reynolds asked, only minutes later. We were in the clinic, and Renée was back on a procedures table. It seemed that we'd only just been there, following the explosion outside.

"Back by the moonpool."

Stacy was studying the readout on the bulkhead next to the table. "Her CO level is extremely high. How long has she been on your emergency regulator?"

"Twelve minutes now maybe."

She blew her breath out. "Wow. Her CO level must have been extreme." She leveled her eyes on me. "We need her tank. I think someone has tampered with it."

Cliff was there an instant later, with the tank in his hands. "Boss, I just ran a check on it."

"And what—"

"The mix is off. *Way* off."

I stared at him. "You mean, deliberately."

He nodded.

I stared at the readout. I hadn't given much thought to the first attempt on my life earlier, when the bomb had hurt Renée. I'd returned to Trieste from the trip and had simply gone about my business. Damn. Stupid of me.

"Where'd you get the tank?" he asked.

"From the moonpool in our Living Module. Same place they always are."

"From your locker?"

I thought back. "One was from mine, yes."

"And the other from Renée's."

"Yes."

"Did you get them mixed up?"

I sighed. "I wasn't paying attention. We put the gear next to the pool and got ready. Put the tanks on our backs." I shrugged. It was just a normal part of life in Trieste, like putting shoes on in the morning. You didn't really pay attention to it. And air tanks weren't like wetsuits. They weren't personalized. You could use any tank, and often they were just lying around, against the bulkheads, for anyone to grab and recharge. The regulators were personal, but they were easy to attach to different tanks.

"It's another attempt on your life, Mac. You have to be more careful." His face was hard; he clearly felt guilt at this happening again. "I'll have my people pay more attention to you. We'll check over your equipment more closely." There was something in his expression, but I didn't think more about it at that point. I was too concerned with Renée.

Her eyes opened a minute later. "Mac," she whispered. "You got me back home."

I clutched her hand. "I'm so, so sorry." Tears welled up behind my eyes.

"You saved my life."

"I *risked* your life," I hissed.

"No." She took a breath. "If it wasn't for you, I'd have drowned out there."

I didn't want to argue with her right then and there, so I left it.

I put my head on her chest and listened to her breathing.
And cried, silently.

———••———

AN HOUR LATER WE WERE in my office in City Control. Richard, Alyssna Sonstraal, Meg, and Cliff Sim, my CSO. His people were investigating the second attack and reviewing video, but I'd wanted him at this meeting. He'd agreed, though I could tell it had bothered him. He wanted to solve this mystery because it kept growing.

Meg was as concerned about Renée, but the doctor assured us she was fine. Her blood was fully oxygenated, the excess carbon monoxide flushed from her system, and she was resting peacefully. I felt massive guilt for it, and knew I'd have to be careful. Cliff wanted to put a guard on me at all times, but I was against that notion. However, I couldn't allow those around me to face the same risk I did.

Johnny Chang, my Deputy Mayor, was also there. We'd filled him in on the trip to Churchill, and he had an idea of what was going on.

After the introductions were done, I said, "So. We know the dangers facing us. This new weapon is something Trieste needs. We can't let other nations get their hands on it."

"The BSF *already* has it," Meg said.

"Doctor Sonstraal invented it." I gestured at Alyssna. "She knows where it is, for the most part. We have to plan. We have just over six weeks."

"Why the hurry?" Cliff asked.

I filled him in on plan to infiltrate the Churchill labs and steal the first component on 17 March.

He nodded. "Most people will be busy celebrating. And what of the guards?"

"Commodore Clarke can distract his people. For the others, we have to come up with something. We also have Sahar Noor to help."

"What was she like?" Johnny asked me.

I couldn't help but smile. "Incredible. More than I could have hoped for."

"Do you trust her?"

I thought about that, but only for a second. "Implicitly. She's honorable. She's with us."

Meg interjected, "But she doesn't want people to die. She'll object to that and likely won't help if it involves war."

"Seems slightly ironic," he muttered.

I shrugged. "She has her reasons, and they make sense. But it doesn't matter. We need her and Churchill. They'll join with Oceania. They'll be the fifteenth city."

There were smiles all around. "That's incredible," Johnny said.

We had started with just Trieste, only two years earlier. Against all odds, we had defeated the superpowers and had grown steadily.

"How are we going to steal this?" Richard asked. He had lowered himself to a metal chair and had his elbows on his knees.

"I think we need to know more about it first." I looked at Alyssna. "It's time to fill us in." We had given her a lab, a place to live, and a new home. I'd hoped my intentions were clear, and she could finally end the evasiveness.

Her smile was genuine. "Absolutely." She took a breath and gathered her thoughts. "I first had the idea while at Cambridge. I was doing a research study on a US program called an electrolaser."

I practically growled. "You told me this was not a laser."

There were a few hooded looks in the office; they were impossible to miss. The concept of an underwater laser—even though underwater engineers had used them for over a century—as a weapon seemed unlikely.

"It's not." A shrug. "Well, not *really*."

I frowned. There was that statement again. I wanted her to finally explain.

She continued: "The electrolaser is fascinating. It uses a powerful laser to deliver an eventual electric pulse or shock. It's a two-stage weapon. First, a laser would fire at the target and create a type of *channel* leading right to the target."

"Channel?" Johnny asked. "Like, a pathway?"

"Exactly, Mr. Chang. It heats the path and vaporizes the air, rapidly heating it to a plasma, or a gas. The part that matters is that it's electrically conductive! And it's basically straight as an arrow, leading directly to your target."

I raised an eyebrow at that. Her weapon had four components, and only the first was at Churchill Sands. I wondered if her weapon was in fact this electrolaser device with multiple parts.

"Then what happens?" I asked.

"The electric charge is massive. It's like a non-lethal taser weapon. It's used on the surface though, mostly against human targets. There are rumors that it's been tested against aircraft and missiles—the *Phoenix Project*."

"But you said *non-lethal*," Johnny said.

"Yes, for crowd control at large distances. But it can be fatal at higher energy levels against vehicles and planes and so on." She raised a finger. "But this is just where my idea came from, remember. My weapon is *not* an electrolaser."

Complete silence met her comment. Some of us were on the edges of our seats. She glanced around, a smile in her eyes. "I'll continue." She took a breath. "The notion of creating a conduit or path to the target triggered something in me. I realized that it might be a useful way of first marking a target—to make sure it's correctly aimed—and then secondly, delivering a massive blast of some sort. But still, a major issue blocked this notion."

"The water," I said.

"Exactly. Water is *the* major problem! It's very dense. It's full of material. It causes massive blooming issues with any light beam."

"Light only travels two hundred meters or so underwater," Johnny said.

"From the surface, yes. The brightness of the sun can only penetrate that far. But we can create something far brighter, Mr. Chang."

"So, it's a laser?"

"In a way," she said with a smile.

"Wait a minute," I snapped. "Just—"

"Let me continue, Mac," she said. "I do use lasers to mark the target. But it's not the real weapon."

My heart dropped. Damn. I hoped that she hadn't hoodwinked us.

"I use an insulating beam of ten extremely powerful lasers to fire at the target. The beams enclose the eventual channel. They vaporize the water in a path, and it's down that channel that I fire the *real* weapon."

—••—

I exhaled. Then I swore. "So, it's a laser."

She shook her head vigorously. "No, Mac."

"How powerful are your lasers?" Richard asked. I recalled what he'd said earlier, about the LaWS system being thirty kilowatts over a century earlier.

"Each is a terawatt, firing at the wavelength that best penetrates water, but it's an adaptive weapon. It samples the salinity, temperature, and suspended sediment first. It decides the best wavelength before it fires."

"*Ten* terawatts?" Richard gasped.

"It's a massive cluster of lasers, yes."

"My god."

Fish farms, I thought.

The alarm that Chalam's sonar system had been screaming.

It was bubbles, created by that laser cluster.

It was definitely not a quiet weapon, but the sonar system had signaled the only thing it could interpret from the noise: a bubble fence meant to contain fish.

"What is the size of the channel you create?" I asked.

"It's about twelve inches across."

"And it's full of . . . what?"

She frowned. "It's hard to answer. At first it's a plasma. Superheated gas from vaporized water. But after a prolonged period of firing, it actually turns to vacuum."

This made me perk up. A *vacuum* channel, underwater? And they could control and sustain it for minutes, and aim it directly toward a warsub target?

"And what happens next?" Meg prodded.

Alyssna Sonstraal nodded. "Right. There's a period of adjustment. The wavelength cycles to maximize the range and the power. The ten terawatts are vaporizing a long channel of water, and within that insulated void, the real beam fires. But to do that, you need the Staging System. It regulates the power from the supply, feeding it to the lasers."

"The second component?" I asked.

"Yes," she replied. "It's located in a BSF warsub."

"Currently in the South Pacific."

She stared at me, then seemed to make a decision. "It's on *Aurora Rex*. The Staging System is there."

"Why is it currently broken into four pieces and scattered around the world?" Johnny asked.

"To prevent its theft. Trust me on this one, I know what the project senior administrators are thinking. They know others will try to get this when word gets out. They're trying to keep that from happening."

"But Mac," Johnny said, turning to me. "There's a functioning version in the Indian Ocean right now. You said that. Why don't we just steal that one?"

"I have a plan," I muttered. "If things work out, then after the heist, no one will know we have it for some time. It'll keep it covert. We'll leave them with their working model, and no one will be the wiser."

Until we use it in battle, I wanted to say.

Eyebrows raised at that, but I said no more.

———•———

"So that's two components," Richard said. "What are the other two?"

Alyssna replied, "The third is the Aiming Module. It takes data from the sonar system. The location of the target, including velocity, depth, any course changes and so on. It keeps the laser cluster firing on the correct location, and the sonar constantly feeds data to it. It's crucial . . . otherwise, you're just firing blind and turning water to steam. The weapon is useless, unless you have the enemy directly in front of you, that is."

"And what's the final component?"

She turned to me with a sly smile. "That's the real weapon. The most important component. Both it and the Aiming Module are in the same guarded facility. You'll need to infiltrate it and steal both simultaneously." She glanced at me and frowned. "And somehow keep people from realizing that we've taken them." She shrugged. "I'm not sure how you'll do that though . . ."

"Where are they?" I asked, exasperated.

"They're at The Vault."

—••—

"The Vault?" That was the second time I'd heard her mention it.

She nodded. "The facility in the Indian Ocean. It's where we developed the weapon. The BSF is testing it in the area now, but there's a newer version of the final component in The Vault. More powerful."

I sighed. "Alyssna. You have led us on a merry chase here. Four components. First, the insulating lasers and the power system, located in the labs at Churchill Sands. We have to be prepared to steal it in six weeks. Second, the Staging System, in the BSF warsub *Aurora Rex*. It's *somewhere* in the Pacific." I snorted. "We'll have to find it and steal it without anyone discovering it." I looked up at the eyes staring at me. "Then the final two components are in The Vault, a location that only one person knows of. Those two are the Aiming Module and the actual weapon. We're going to steal all four components and assemble the weapon here." I turned to Alyssna. "Now, Doctor Sonstraal, it's time for you to tell us the truth. You've held it back from us for days now." I exhaled. "*What is the weapon?*"

She smiled. "The lasers create the conduit, which is plasma initially, then becomes vacuum. The final component is The Accelerator. It generates the real beam, which fires down the channel and hits the hull of an enemy warsub, and simply put, kicks the protons out of the nuclei from atoms in the titanium or steel. It literally rips apart the vessel's pressure hull. Weakens it. It would eventually dissolve it, but water pressure acts first and breaks through, sinking the sub. It's highly effective."

My stomach lurched at her mention of *dissolving* material.

I thought of Chalam's brother's hand . . .

She continued, "The beam penetrates several inches into the hull. The thickness doesn't really matter, because ocean pressure takes over. In this respect, it's way more effective than a laser."

"Alyssna, *what is it?*"

"Oh." She grinned. "It's a neutron beam."

Interlude: The Mid-Atlantic Ridge
One Year Earlier

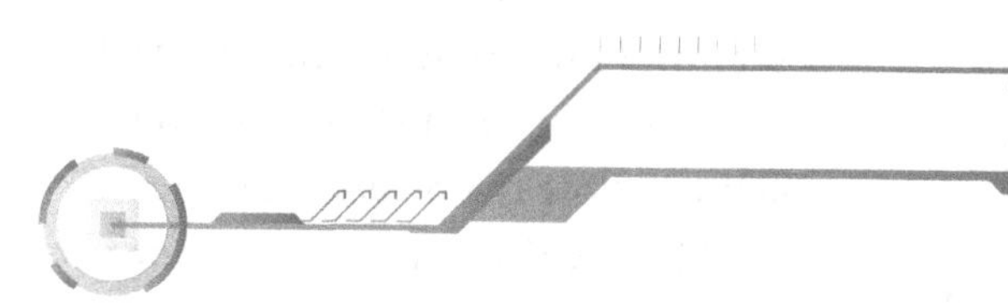

<table>
<tr><td>Interlude:</td><td>The Mid-Atlantic Ridge</td></tr>
<tr><td>Date:</td><td>March 2130 AD</td></tr>
<tr><td>Depth:</td><td>2,577 meters</td></tr>
<tr><td>Latitude:</td><td>27° 55" 10' S</td></tr>
<tr><td>Longitude:</td><td>17° 35" 42' W</td></tr>
<tr><td>Time:</td><td>2033 hours</td></tr>
</table>

KATHERINE WELLS HAULED THE YOKE of *SC-1* to the port and the vessel heeled to the side, avoiding the torpedo on her tail. She swore. Far below her, torpedoes and mines crisscrossed the theater of war, clogging the sonar screen with trails and echoes and pulses of sound. Explosions lit The Rift, their reverberations rebounding off the cliffs on either side, and vibrations in the deck—companion to each detonation—coursed up her legs in a sick and violent rhythm. It was orchestral, in a way, and Mac, far below, was conducting the events. The battle had raged for thirty minutes now, and compounding the clutter on the sonar were his *Swords*—seacars equipped with the SCAV drive, flitting about the battle and difficult for the enemy to kill. The bubbles churning from the aft vents erupted fifty meters or more behind each vessel, before soaring to the surface and leaving a long churning curtain behind each seacar. On the screen, each SCAV drive shone like a star and obscured anything nearby. On top of this, the deep-diving pulse drive—the APD—using sound waves to shove the ocean back on itself to allow the *Swords* easy access to depths of over six kilometers, flared like white suns on the sonar screens. The computer was having difficulty deciphering the events in the battle. The algorithms could not identify every warsub in range, the screen flickered at times, there were question marks on the popup callout labels where normally there would be information about depth, speed, vectors, and so on, and whole quadrants sometimes flared completely white for long moments as huge detonations ripped out through the underwater canyon.

The battle was enormous; Kat had never experienced anything like it, and sailors were dying by the dozens, and she knew that by the end of the day, the number would be in the hundreds. It was due to her, her invention, her quest for independence for Trieste, and because of Mac's decision to not only include her city, but to attract *every* underwater city to the movement. He wanted all the colonies to join Oceania and declare independence from the superpowers. The current enemies were the USSF and the FSF, but she had no doubt other countries would be involved soon as well.

SC-1 had performed admirably in the battle, despite its SCAV being down. She was with a smaller group of subs, hiding on the other side of the peak of the Mid-Atlantic Ridge, peering down at the action below. An errant torpedo had made its way over the peaks and had momentarily acquired the seacar, but a countermeasure had distracted it.

Below, the battle raged. She could hear the communications between Mac and his people. They were shooting from below the USSF and FSF fleets, and the enemy returning fire with torpedoes that could not descend far enough to have an impact. At 5,000 meters, the weapons imploded. Mines went inactive and fell as expensive ball bearings into the depths.

Mac's strategy was effective, and Kat felt a thrill of joy and love surge through her.

"It's working!" she cried to the two people on board with her. On the flickering sonar screen, FSF and USSF warsubs foundered. Bubbles streamed from gaping holes in the hulls, the boats listed and tilted at unreal angles as they fell to Crush Depth. Bodies and debris littered the area, oil rose serenely through the battlefield on its journey to the surface, flashes lit the area, and the hulks of dead warsubs plunged downward before imploding violently, the twisted debris settling to the magmatically active ocean floor so far below.

One of her companions was at her side in an instant. "So, Mac was correct."

"Yes," she said, smiling. "His strategy . . . it's brilliant."

"It's finally going to work." Her companion grinned. "I can't believe we're watching the destruction of two enemy fleets right now."

Kat felt a thrill of excitement surge through her again. The adrenaline was coursing through her veins. Her face felt flushed and her hands tingled. The superpowers had repressed the ocean colonists for too long. They treated the city dwellers as slaves. As the surface descended into chaos because of the climate crises, as economies fell and rebellion and wars raged on the surface, they had demanded more and more from Triestrians as well as the other undersea colonies. There was little thought given to them except a need for more resources, more work, more sweat, more blood. Meanwhile their fleets invaded the colonies and their sailors abused the citizens.

Kat was through with it all, and her SCAV drive had been the trigger.

A flurry of voices crackled from her comm. The sounds of battle.

"—that *Matrix* is almost out! Take another shot at her!"

"Got it!"

"That rock outcropping over the *Typhoon*! It's ready to go. Can someone fire on it?"

"Just did."

"It's crumbling onto the ship! The damage is—Whoa! The *Typhoon* just imploded, everyone! The rock must have ruptured the hull!"

"Watch out for that homer! It's a SCAV!"

"Get out of there!"

"That *Trident* is trying to use his grapples for fuck's sake! Does he think we're slow-moving or something? I'm taking him—"

"Another USSF warsub just left the battle!"

"Another just imploded!"

Kat shook her head. By all signs, they were doing extremely well. The battle continued for close to thirty more minutes, with few casualties at Kat's end. She was starting to get antsy, just sitting up there, waiting for orders. She wanted to be involved, to *fight*.

Then Mac's voice echoed over the comm. "Kat, are you there?"

She pressed the transmit button on the yoke. She could barely keep the smile from her face. "Right here."

"It's time."

Kat signaled her team of *Swords* that had been hiding behind the Ridge peaks, and they turned toward the fighting.

Finally.

They angled down, made ballast negative, targeted the enemy vessels, and, en masse, fired their torpedoes.

A wall of steel churned down toward the warsubs.

"There is no light without shadow, just as there is no
happiness without pain."
—Isabel Allende

Part Three: First Component

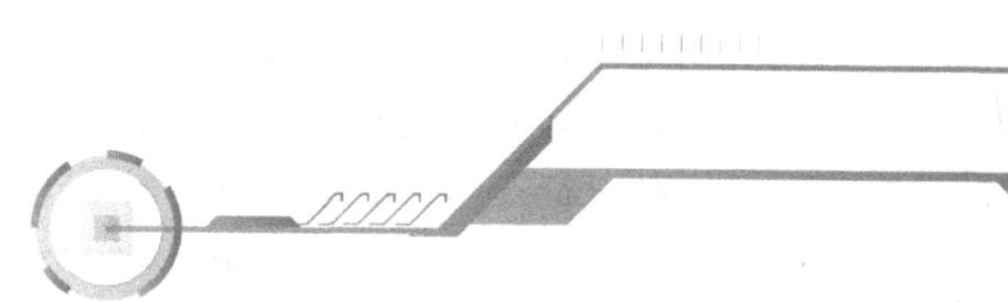

Chapter Eleven

WE WERE STILL IN MY office, where we had held so many strategy meetings over the years. Doctor Alyssna Sonstraal held us in her grip; we stared at her, amazed at the revelation.

The sighs of the ventilation fans, the whisper of a breeze in the ducts over our heads, the *clicks* of the pressure monitors always maintaining four atms, and the murmur of water as it churned past the bulkheads were the constants, but there was complete silence otherwise.

We studied the doctor in amazement.

Then, "A neutron beam?" Johnny whispered.

"Or 'neutral' beam, to be more precise. Neutral Particle Beam. NPB."

"What is it?"

She shrugged. "It's a stream of deuterium, generated by the fourth component—The Accelerator. It creates particles without an electric charge and fires them at nearly the speed of light."

"How does it do that?" I asked.

"It first adds electrons to deuterium—a form of hydrogen. This *gives* the particles a negative charge and magnets can manipulate, or aim, them. The Accelerator increases their speed and then the beam passes through a thin gas, which neutralizes them by taking the electrons back. The beam of deuterium blasts down the vacuum channel. Blooming isn't an issue because it's held *within* the path that the lasers have created! It's a straight shot at nearly the speed of light. Right at a hull."

Jaws were on the deck.

She continued, "It has to be a neutral charge because blooming would be a huge problem. If each atom had a charge, the particles would repel each other. So we neutralize the atoms before firing. Since deuterium's nucleus is made up of a neutron and a proton—a *deuteron*—the beam is essentially a stream of these particles moving at nearly the speed of light. It slams into the hull and destroys it at a molecular or atomic level."

Complete silence. Then, "Oh my god," Richard muttered. "You came up with this notion?"

"Not for the neutral beam. But for the entire four-stage weapon, yes."

"What's it called?"

She grinned. "Technically it's a LaWS Encased UNPB."

"What does that—"

"The Laser Weapon System Encased Underwater Neutral Particle Beam."

Meg snorted. "I think we need a better—"

"But at The Vault we just called it *The Water Pick*."

A deadly silence fell across the group. A few of us smiled at that.

I shook my head. "Crazy." I glanced at her with new respect . . . but also perhaps with a bit of fear. "But a different weapon gave you the idea."

"The electrolaser. It was the impetus."

"And the BSF let you develop it, then stole your idea."

She shrugged. "They marginalized me. They let me keep working on it, but others took over. I didn't like that."

I studied her. It was why she had left The Vault and was now at Trieste. They had done to her the same thing that her father had. I made a mental note to never do the same, and to respect her at all times.

At all costs.

"Why is this neutral beam better than a laser?" Johnny asked.

"The lasers only create and confine the vacuum channel. The beam nullifies any reflective surfaces on the hull, because that doesn't have any effect on the high energy particles. They penetrate inches into solid steel easily, and tear the material apart."

"Then ocean pressure takes over . . ."

"That's the thing!" she blurted. "The beam doesn't even have to fully penetrate or open the hull. It only has to *weaken* it. Then the surrounding water takes over. It's actually easier to destroy warsubs than aircraft."

Water is relentless, I thought.

That's what Chalam had noticed on board his seacar. The neutral beam had obliterated the structure of the hull. Then his brother had done something that made me shudder: he'd *touched* the beam.

And it had destroyed his hand.

Then the hull's integrity had failed. The titanium alloy itself had started to bubble as the beam knocked protons and electrons away, and the water pressure outside had worked its inexorable force.

"Did you invent the neutral beam?" Johnny asked.

"Oh no," Alyssna said. "They've been around for more than a hundred years. They were first tested at Los Alamos National Laboratory in the United States. Then they tested it in space, for use in a space-based anti-missile defense network. In July 1989 the US conducted the BEAR Project, which fired a neutral beam from space. It fired successfully for four minutes."

I thought about the size of her weapon—six meters long and two wide—and the weight of just one component. "How big was that prototype?"

"The accelerator then was just over a meter long. It wasn't large. But it *worked!* It was part of their Strategic Defense Initiative, or *Star Wars.* President Reagan's program."

"And now the BSF is doing it, *under water.*" I shook my head. It was insane. But a part of me was thrilled that it wasn't actually a laser weapon, which had so many drawbacks in this environment. The weapon still had a limited range, likely of only a few hundred meters, but it was a brilliant concept.

"And now you want to steal this?" Johnny looked at me, shock in his eyes. "Damn Mac, you went to Churchill Sands to meet Mayor Noor. And you came back with this idea?" He shook his head.

I started to tell him of the importance of not just balancing power in this Cold War, but achieving dominance over our enemies so they wouldn't attack us. How we had to always be a step or two ahead of the other underwater powers.

He held his hand out and waved me off. "Hell, you don't have to convince me. I agree with you. I know we have to get it. But I still think you're crazy. This isn't a simple infiltrate and grab. This is far, far more difficult." He took a breath. "You need to infiltrate the Churchill Sands lab, a BSF warsub at sea, and some super secret facility called *The Vault*— The Vault, for fuck's sake—and steal four parts of a super weapon, and somehow make the BSF think that no one has been in those places, and the weapon isn't gone!" He tilted his head. "How the hell are you going to do that, exactly?"

"*We*, you mean." I sighed. Then, "I'm not saying that they'll never realize. I just mean to give us time to assemble it and perhaps use it to defend ourselves before they're aware."

Alyssna said, "They'll know as soon as we steal the laser component from Churchill, Mac."

I turned to her. "No, they won't Alyssna."

"But—"

"Because you're going to build a duplicate here. One that doesn't work."

—··—

COMPLETE SILENCE MET MY STATEMENT. Then there was a babble of voices.

I said into the chaos, "You see, the components don't work apart, anyway. To work, someone has to assemble it. At this point, they're just storing it." I looked at Alyssna. "You know what it looks like. You can make a replica. A façade. Then we'll just substitute it."

She frowned. "Hell Mac, I could just remake the entire weapon for you. It'll take time though—"

"How much?"

"Oh, two years maybe. I might be able to get it down to eighteen—"

"You see?" I said. "You'll need an entire team and months. This way we'll have it in one." *I hoped*, I wanted to say. "The Russians are coming, and soon. There's no time to waste here."

That stopped them. They immediately saw the logic behind my statement.

Alyssna said, "But Mac, I can't make the laser component in only six weeks! March 17 is coming—"

"No, no," I replied. "It just has to *look* realistic. They can't use it anyway. So fashion a duplicate. Make it the same size. The same shape. The same *exterior* appearance." I shrugged. "We'll swap them out. It'll take them months to realize, maybe."

Johnny was eyeing me. "So that's how we'll take the first component without them knowing. What about the other three?" He swore. "Hell, you're talking about a BSF warsub and a facility called The Vault. Surely they'll know."

"One thing at a time, Johnny. First thing, we plan for Churchill Sands."

Alyssna was staring at the deck. "Wait a minute. This is what you want me to do?"

I sat next to her. "Alyssna, you're going to get the complete weapon, with the new accelerator that you say is better than the version they're currently using in the Indian Ocean. You'll have to assemble it and get it working as soon as possible. Then you can test it and build new versions. But first, we have to get your invention back. That's what you signed up for."

"But make a fake—"

"It's how we're going to steal the real one. It *has* to be."

Her eyes showed confusion. "But why?"

"Think about it." I looked at everyone in the cabin. "If we steal it from Churchill, and they find out, then what will the BSF do?"

"They'll immediately put the other three components into lockdown," Richard said. "High alert."

"Exactly! Then we'll never get the other pieces. We can't give them advance notice that we're coming! We have to keep their guard down."

"But how are you going to get it from The Vault?" Alyssna asked.

"Like I said, one thing at a time. But we have other people who can help. I think Max Hyland is going to be useful here, as well as Chalam Kaashif."

Meg's eyes showed horror. "You want to destroy it with a bomb?"

"No. I have another idea. But first we have to infiltrate Churchill, Component One, Meg. That's what we have to focus on now. We have six weeks."

Johnny was nodding. "So we need a plan. How are we going to do it?"

I exhaled. "We'll need precise info from Sahar Noor. But I do have an idea."

"What do you know about it?"

I brought up the schematics Sahar had sent me. The holo projector displayed it in the center of the cabin, in 3D. I rotated the display until the lab centered in the frame. I hadn't had a chance to view it yet, so I was seeing it for the first time too. "This is it."

"Where?" Johnny asked.

"Those are the labs."

He blinked. "It's two full decks. Huge." He peered at the bulkheads and partitions. "Where is the . . . *The Water Pick?*"

Alyssna said, "It's just the power system and the laser pack here, remember. It won't work on its own."

"Not even just the lasers?" Richard coughed. "That's ten terawatts of power."

"It needs the Aiming Module and the Staging System too."

I peered at the map. Sahar didn't know where the component was. Alyssna had told us how large it was, but we had no other information. "Do you know where it is, Alyssna?"

She was studying the schematic. "No. We can likely eliminate these smaller rooms. They're likely just offices." She pointed at them, and I changed their color to gray. "Which leaves all these larger ones."

"Would this fit through an airlock?" Johnny asked.

"Depends on the size of the airlock."

I identified the larger airlocks on the map and changed their colour to green.

"There's also the moonpool," Meg said. "They could have brought it up through that."

I changed that to green.

"What about the corridors?" Johnny said.

Richard frowned. "What about them?"

"Well," he replied, "you told us how large Component One is. It's five hundred pounds too." He pointed at a few corridors. "Look at these. They aren't main passages. You couldn't get this device down there, or even around one of those corners."

It was an interesting idea. I made those areas red, and that also blocked off other areas that didn't have access to the wider corridors or the airlock and moonpool. They couldn't have carted the weapon there, so it eliminated them as options.

But it still left several large cabins on both decks.

"Anything else?" I asked.

"Could we just search the entire area?"

I said, "You mean, infiltrate and pretend to be there for something else."

"Sure," Johnny replied. "An engineering team. Senior administrators. I don't know . . . even cleaners. Then spend time searching."

"They'll catch on pretty fast." I made a decision. "We can't do this unless we know *exactly* where it is. We have to be calculating. In and out, fast. Deliver the decoy and grab the real thing. That alone is not going to be easy. We can't waste time searching."

"What about an advance team, a few days before?" Meg asked.

I turned to her. That was interesting.

I checked the time on my PCD. We had already been there for two hours. I sighed. "Let's meet again in a few hours. Everyone go and think the dilemma over. Come up with some ideas. The best one wins." I turned to Alyssna. "Except you."

She frowned. "What am I supposed to do?"

"You have to start on the decoy, and there's no time to waste."

—••——

A FEW MINUTES LATER, ALONE in my office, I keyed the comm. I was in my chair behind the small desk, and as was usual, there was a pile of paper on the corner. Things to do. There were also hundreds of messages in my inbox, also things to do, but digitally. Both were added pressures—city business—but some of them I could hand over to Johnny or Kristen. They were both highly effective at helping run and lead Trieste.

An instant later, the comm beeped and Max Hyland's smiling face appeared on the screen. "Hiya, Mac," he said.

"Hi Max. How are things in your lab?" Doctor Max Hyland was the man who had invented the Isomer Bomb. It used a nearly stable element—hafnium. The isomeric version of the atom decayed steadily and had a half life of thirty-one years. But Max had figured out how to bring the nucleons of the excited element down to ground state instantly, releasing all its energy at once in the form of Gamma Rays. It was a nuclear-sized detonation, but not a fission or a fusion explosion. It was a new form of weapon in a very small package.

The detonation and subsequent implosion of Seascape had sent shudders around the world as it ushered in the Isomer Age. Nations were still trying to figure out who had been responsible.

He grinned back at me, showing his dimples. He was exceptionally sociable and likeable and had fit in at Trieste instantly. He'd arrived roughly half a year earlier. "Fantastic, thanks."

"Do you have more hafnium?"

"Yes, the synchrotron you contacted has manufactured more for me." He tilted his head. "I told them it was for medical uses—to burn tumors—which I am working on. But eventually someone's going to put two and two together."

The element he used was Hf-178m2. Exceedingly rare, and very expensive, but hafnium occurred naturally within zircon deposits. The trick was converting it to the isomeric version. The US and Germany would soon figure out who had used the Isomer Bomb on Seascape, and mentions of or interactions with Hf-178m2 were like breadcrumbs leading directly to Trieste, but we had no choice.

"And it's ready to use?" My implication was clear. *Do you have any more bombs?*

His smile immediately disappeared. He took a massive breath and exhaled slowly. "Mac, what do you have planned now?"

—••—

A MINUTE LATER THERE WAS another face on my comm. It was Chalam Kaashif, the geologist at Churchill Sands. His lips were turned down and his eyes dark. He was in his small cubicle; there was bare bulkhead behind him. I could see his bunk with a crumpled bedsheet and a small, wrinkled pillow. He nodded, waiting to hear me speak.

"Are you okay, Chalam?" I asked.

He sighed. "I'm tired. I'm having difficulty sleeping."

"Once again, I'm sorry about your brother."

There was a silence as he stared down at the deck. "It's still so recent. When I get distracted, I sometimes forget that it happened at all. Then it all comes rushing back." He sighed and ran his fingers through his dark hair. "I just wish I had more answers."

"I understand."

He raised his eyes; they were piercing. "You don't know anything more, do you?"

I shifted in my chair. I didn't want to be too open over the comm. "I'm still researching the problem. I'm hoping to meet with you at some point soon. But for now, there's someone I need you to speak with. I'm hoping you can help him."

He tilted his head and his expression changed. "Who is it?"

"It's a scientist who works here. His name is Max Hyland."

"A geologist?"

"No, not at all. But he needs geologic advice, you could say."

He stared at me. "I guess, if it'll help figure this all out."

He'd been though a highly traumatic event. He'd watched his brother mutilated before his eyes. Then he'd experienced the death of three people while he'd been the lone survivor. And on top of it, he was also dealing with a mystery that the authorities denied ever happening.

He knew better.

As did I.

I made the arrangements with him, and signed off.

—••—

MY NEXT CALL WAS TO Cliff Sim. He had only just left my office, but his people were looking into the latest attempt on my life. Someone had tried to hit me yet again and had hurt Renée, which made me feel miserable. There was a weight on my chest now and a dark cloud around me. I needed more information.

He was on my screen quickly. He said, "Mac. I have some information for you. Come to my office. Now."

Chapter Twelve

Cliff was sitting at his steel desk when I stalked in. His office was just down the corridor from City Control; he was always close. He was in charge of all security at the city, and he took his responsibilities seriously. Anytime someone got hurt, the investigation would inevitably involve his division. Injuries on the farms were common, but the ones he was more concerned with were crimes and assaults, often caused by USSF sailors while on leave.

"Mac," he said as the hatch ground shut behind me. "My people have news."

I'd checked in with Renée during the short walk; she was sleeping in the clinic, under guard, but all signs were that she was fine.

"Go ahead," I said, instantly worried.

He frowned. "Someone sabotaged your comm."

I exhaled. "I figured something like that. I'd been talking to Sahar Noor when it suddenly cut off. Then Renée passed out, and I couldn't call for help."

"Apparently the transmitter broke at the worst possible time." His tone was dry, and it held a deeper meaning.

I stared at him. "How?"

He pushed something across the desk. It was the size of a grain of rice, but black.

I stared at it. "What is it?"

He gestured to it. "Pick it up. Smell it."

I did as he asked. "It's charred. Burned."

"It's an explosive. Just big enough to cut a few connections."

I swore. "In my comm?"

"It was in your facemask transmitter/receiver. None of your transmissions got out because of it. There was one in Renée's mask as well."

"Shit."

"The carbon monoxide meant to knock you out, then kill. The comms were cut to prevent either you or Renée from asking for help. Simple but effective." There was that look in his eyes again. I assumed it was because it had occurred on his watch.

"And the tanks got mixed up, and I was able to drag her back for help."

"You didn't go out too far. If it had happened while you were out a kilometer or more, it would have been tragic, Mac. No returning fast enough."

I shook my head as I stared at the grain. It had left a charred residue on my thumb and finger. "How did it work?"

"Timed to go off in salt water. The outer skin dissolves, then there's a reaction when the salt hits it. Simple, effective, but hard to be precise." He leaned back. "Look, Mac. This isn't going to stop. I want you to consider a guard."

I snorted. "I'm a trained operative, Cliff. I can take—"

"You're the Mayor and the Director. Trieste can't lose you. It doesn't matter if you're good in a fight. I've seen you, I know. But an explosion or a torpedo or a sabotaged bulkhead is all it takes. Let me put someone with you."

"I'll think it over."

"Dammit, Mac. You have to—"

I stood up. "I said I'd think about it."

—••—

I REALLY HAD NO INTENTION of having a guard follow me everywhere I went. Cliff might even suggest calling it an 'honor guard' or something, just to distract from the true purpose of the squad, but there was no way I'd allow it.

Still, the attempts on my life kept putting Renée at risk. I really couldn't keep letting collateral damage like that happen. I'd already lost Kat. I couldn't handle that again.

Renée filled my thoughts for a few moments as I wandered Trieste's corridors and travel tubes. Before I knew it, and without thinking, I was back at the clinic, staring at her as she slept. A deep feeling of remorse churned through me. She looked so peaceful, her head cradled in the white pillow, as the IV dripped fluid into her arm and a diagnostic machine beeped softly somewhere nearby.

I exhaled softly.

—••—

JOHNNY WAS IN HIS OFFICE, staring at a computer monitor and leaning back in his chair. He stood when I entered and a broad smile split his face.

He was my best friend. We'd been partners in TCI years before, had been on many covert missions around the world, and then, on one mission to a Chinese city, he'd betrayed me. He'd turned to the other side. I'd endured four months of torture before a prisoner exchange. Following that, I'd abandoned TCI and worked the kelp farms for seven years. Then I'd rejoined TCI on a mission to recover the SCAV drive, and Johnny had re-entered my life. We'd reconciled and now he was invaluable to my efforts in the city and in TCI fighting for independence.

"Sounds like quite an adventure at Churchill," he said.

We hadn't had a chance to really talk about my visit to the city, although he knew about the weapon.

He continued, "This is quite a mission you've got planned."

"That's what I'm here to talk about." I lowered myself to the chair before the desk. I looked around. There was a large viewport showing the exterior. Seacars were soaring past the city and people in scuba gear swam peacefully about.

It made my heart pound. It was so beautiful.

Worth fighting for, without question.

Then I remembered what had happened to Dad, and my heart skipped a beat. I couldn't forget that.

Ever.

He said, "You mentioned Commodore Clarke in your office. What were you talking about?"

I sighed. "Clarke was at the meeting with Sahar. Apparently he wants independence for Churchill."

He shook his head. "Do you believe him?"

"I'm not sure."

"But Sahar does?"

"Implicitly, although there was some tension."

"How do you think we should steal the weapon from Churchill?"

I paused. Then, "Something in that meeting struck a chord with me." I brought up the map of the labs. Some areas were red, some green. "We've narrowed the lab down to these areas, but it still hasn't really identified where it could be." I pointed. "It's still somewhere on these two decks, which is a large area. But what if we did send someone to reconnoiter first? The day before maybe. Just to take a look around?"

"And find where it is, so when we really conduct the operation, we know where we're going. Makes sense. But it'll be dangerous."

"I can get help from Sahar, don't forget. Maybe a uniform and ID. Clarke can help."

"*If* he's telling the truth." He swore. "We can't go through what happened with Meg at Seascape, Mac."

"Tell me about it." I considered it for a moment. "Let's contact Sahar at Churchill. We'll get her thoughts now."

—••—

BACK IN MY OFFICE AN hour later, the entire team met again, with the exception of Doctor Sonstraal, who had begun preparations to build the decoy weapon.

I noted the looks of determination on their features. Despite the difficulty, they knew this mattered. They knew other superpowers couldn't get their hands on the neutral beam. We needed it, and we were going to make it happen.

"Any ideas?" I asked.

Richard said, "We need to discover the location within the labs. Once that's done, it's clear what happens next. We move the decoy in and take the real weapon component out."

I nodded. "The big problem is, *how?*" I waited for them to speak.

No one did.

"Shit," I muttered. "It's that dire?"

"No," Meg answered. "There just don't seem to be many ideas other than a smash and grab."

"That's too dangerous," Richard said.

"Well, I know that, but still. I couldn't think of anything else."

Cliff said, "What about a distraction? A diversion?"

"You mean like a celebration going on somewhere to divert attention? I think we've got that covered."

He frowned. "I was thinking of something else. An emergency perhaps."

Meg said, "That might not go over well with Sahar. She doesn't want anyone endangered."

A silence settled over the group. Then I cleared my throat. "Something came up earlier that might work. Johnny and I have spoken about it." I turned to him.

"We just talked with Mayor Noor," he said. "Clarke can get one or two of us inside the labs the day before. Once there, we'll find the weapon and place a transmitter near it. Then we leave. The next day, the real mission happens."

"*We?*" Meg said.

Johnny said, "I'd like to do it. I'm used to this sort of thing."

"How are you going to get in?" Richard asked.

"They're going to get me a BSF uniform. I'm going to march right in, with the Commodore at my side."

Meg swore. "Dammit, Mac. I don't want to involve this guy. I don't trust him."

I said, "I know. But does anyone else have a better idea? We need to know where the weapon is."

"What if we scan for a fusion reactor? Locate the emissions?"

I knew the lasers used a small fusion cell for power. "Useless. It's not functioning. It's only one piece of the entire weapon. It could be in a crate for all we know."

"Well, how are we going to find out? That would be a disaster. The fake component has to be put exactly where—"

"That's why it makes sense to send someone first," Johnny said. "I can do it."

Meg said, "But the Commodore is a question mark, Johnny."

"Sahar vouched for him," I said. "And we are pressed for time here, Meg."

Her eyes flashed. "It's a danger we shouldn't expose ourselves to."

I sighed. "I agree, actually. His involvement doesn't exactly make me enthusiastic. If anyone has a better idea, please speak up." I turned to Richard. "What about Jessica? Is she available for this?" Jessica Ng was his partner; she'd been involved in the independence movement for just as long, and had also worked with my father in the early days. I hadn't seen her in quite a while, but hadn't thought much about it, because we were all so busy, all the time.

A look passed across his face. It was hard to interpret. "I'll fill her in when I see her. I'm sure she'd agree with you."

I stared at each of them in turn. Then, "Okay, it's time to start working on the details."

—•• —

SAHAR HAD SENT US MORE information than we could have hoped for. The locations of the guard stations. The entry points for each deck. She'd also arranged to prepare a BSF uniform for Johnny.

We worked long into the night. Then we met again the next day, then the next as well. Soon Renée was up and feeling far better, and she began working with us on the plans. Weeks passed like that. She was all smiles at first, excited to be involved and working on efforts to steal the weapon, but I realized that she was likely trying to protect me from guilt at what had happened. She had said that it was a good idea for me to accept the guard detail, but I'd deflected and suggested we get one for her instead.

I was also anxious about spending too much time with her. Although I loved her deeply, I didn't want another attempt on my life to involve her.

Again.

But my idea of a guard for her didn't go over well.

The suggestion infuriated her.

We'd argued after, but not for long. In fact, within minutes we'd already made up.

And that had been *enjoyable*, to say the least.

Now we were back in my office, reviewing the plan details for the tenth time. But, I had to admit, we didn't have much. Richard said, "We still don't know how to get the weapon out. It's damn large."

"They got it in, so we'll get it out." I shrugged. "It'll be a skeleton crew. We'll have to avoid them." *I hoped*, I thought. It seemed that we would be relying on Clarke for more and more. We'd need a way to avoid the guards watching the laboratories, and he was going to have to help us with that as well.

Meg was glaring at me, and it made my stomach churn.

If we'd had more time, we might have come up with something better. We had no choice.

—••—

WE NEEDED TO FIGURE OUT a way to take the device out. An airlock made sense, but we quickly realized that there was no way the device would fit through the umbilical or airlock in *SC-1*. There was an elevator—or hydraulic lift—in the schematic, however, and it led downward to the first deck. I said, "What about the moonpool? If we have to get out, and that's the only way, we need a way to open it."

Sahar had mentioned that it was always sealed shut, to maintain security at the labs. I said, "I can likely get past that."

Meg said, "This isn't a common hatch. It's controlled by security."

"I know." And we can't let anyone know we were there, so we had to be careful not to leave evidence behind. Still, I had an idea on how we could get past the moonpool. "Once we get it open though, we need to get the weapon out. It's large. It can't get wet. Any ideas?" I glanced up from the map at them.

Johnny said, "Why don't we use a large tarp? We cover the weapon with it, seal it shut with a watertight zipper. Then we push it into the pool."

"And it sinks to the seafloor . . . " I prodded.

"And we have a seacar there with a grapple or a harness. Divers connect the weapon and we sail away, dragging it behind."

The thought of dragging a delicate piece of weaponry behind the seacar, watching it tumble over the seafloor, made me shudder. "It would be better to load it into *SC-1*." Still, I considered the Johnny's idea to push it into the moonpool. "So the biggest issue is finding the weapon——"

"Which I'll do, the day before."

"——and then avoiding the guards and getting it to the moonpool."

There was silence at my statement. All looked satisfied, except for Meg.

———••———

TWO MINUTES LATER, I WAS dealing with the full brunt of her wrath.

"Dammit Tru!" she snapped, leaning over my desk with her face only inches from mine. "This is bullshit! We can't trust Clarke. And you can't even call this a 'plan'! There are too many variables!"

I took a deep breath and tried to maintain my cool. Siblings sometimes have tumultuous relationships, and ours was no different from others. I knew that she respected logic, though, so I tried to placate her using reason. She still wasn't having it, however.

"Clarke is the enemy. He's a senior officer in the military!"

"Cliff was in the USSF too. He's trustworthy."

"That's your Chief Security Officer! He's paid his dues and he's proven himself to us a thousand times over. He's dedicated to your survival." She began pacing. "Clarke is unproven."

"Sahar says——"

"We don't know! Sahar might betray us too."

That startled me. "You don't trust her? After meeting her?"

She hesitated. "She seemed totally with us. You're right. And her culture and religion is a powerful force. I don't think she'd betray anyone. But still."

"Yes?" I raised an eyebrow.

"Maybe Clarke has tricked her."

Now it was my turn to pause. "It's possible. You're right. But we're pressed for time on this."

She grabbed me and pulled me to face her. "Tru. If we get caught, it means prison. It means cells. It means no more independence, no more Oceania."

The panic was clear in her face, and her eyes were wide. Scared.

She continued, "It means *torture*, dammit!"

So, this is where it was coming from. The trauma from what she'd endured at Zyvinski's hands after murdering Admiral Benning. I stared at her for a long moment. She was breathing heavily and her chest was heaving. Her face was red.

"Meg," I said in a soft tone. I pulled her to the chairs in the corner and we sat. "You don't have to do this. You can stay here and keep working. We'll do the job and return. You'll see."

Her expression grew angry. "You want me to stay here and repair seacars while you're in danger? While Clarke might arrest you? Haul you away to—"

"If you're scared, then you can—"

It was the wrong thing to say.

"I'm not scared! I'm just being safe!"

I stared at her, silent. I recalled that she hadn't wanted to join with me until we'd learned about the SCAV drive and how we could use it as leverage to convince colonies to join us peacefully. Since then, there had been a lot of pain and suffering and death and fighting, but she had stood by my side the entire time, mostly because we'd thought things through first. She relied on logic and reason, I reminded myself. "Look," I said. "We'll review the plan first. I know you're not scared. But if you're not convinced, then we'll consider changing whatever you're concerned with. But if you think it sounds good . . ."

"Then what?" she snapped.

"Then we go. We do it."

She frowned. "You're giving me the final say?"

"You can lead the heist. It's your mission. You coordinate. If you're worried, then you can abort it. We'll follow your orders." It was a massive gamble, because we didn't have an alternative. I just had to make sure that the plan was solid before we started. "Agreed?"

She stared at me, her eyes lasers.

Chapter Thirteen

RENÉE WAS BY MY SIDE as we marched through the travel tube toward the Research Module. She had fully recovered now, and our relationship had also improved. The evenings had been romantic once again—with meals followed by lovemaking, as was our routine—and there had been no further problems, though Cliff kept warning me to keep an eye out. Just being with Renée in public put her in danger, I knew. When the assassin made another attempt on me, which I assumed would happen, I didn't want her in the line of fire again. Once was too much, and now there had already been two attempts.

My hands were at my sides and I reached out and grabbed Renée's. Her fingers intertwined with mine instantly and she squeezed. I could feel the love and the pressure and it felt like a warm, comforting blanket. I smiled to myself as we walked. People passing us nodded and said hi, and many grinned when they noticed my smile. I barely registered what they were saying because I was so happy.

The danger was so very real, though, and I had to make sure nothing happened to her. A part of me felt that she was actually safer with me, where I could protect her, until I realized that being near me had put her in danger.

I growled inwardly at that.

We were approaching Doctor Sonstraal's lab, where she had been hard at work for weeks. I had assigned a team of people from Meg's division to help her, and they were fabricating the outer components of the laser weapon and the fusion containment structure. All fake, of course, but it had to appear real. Panels and readouts even had to light up if touched. Otherwise, the BSF would figure out what we were doing, and the other three components would immediately go into lockdown and our chances at getting *The Water Pick* would be close to zero.

The guards admitted us to the lab, and soon we were standing in a chamber looking at a device taking shape in the center of the deck.

I swore.

It looked like an artist's sculpture fused with a brutalist's twisted view of pain and death. Curled glass tubing circled a large cylinder, aiming to a common point along the weapon's shaft. Ten large steel barrels, each lined by glass tubing, connected to the barrel. A fusion sphere with injection ports and heavy black cabling led to and from it. There was a large metal Y-shaped cradle, supporting the barrel at three points, which rested on the deck at three equidistant points along the . . . *cannon?* . . . and a console with digital and holo readouts. There were currently blinking lights on the console, and the glass tubes were pulsing with power.

I swore again.

Beside me, Renée said, "*Putain de merde!*"

"It looks deadly," I said. Indeed, it seemed as though she could activate it right there and obliterate the entire facing bulkhead.

"It's still not done," a voice said from my side.

I turned slowly, almost unable to tear my eyes from the lasers. Doctor Alyssna Sonstraal was approaching from a bank of computer consoles.

"It looks damn realistic," I said.

She shrugged. "Still. They'd realize it's fake."

"What more is there to do?" Renée asked.

She pointed at the fusion reactor. "That's not done. It's missing deuterium injection ports. The radio wave plasma generator. We're working on it." She pointed at the barrel. "There, the internal components are not in."

"But we're not doing the internals."

She snapped a look at me, as if to say, *Don't tell me how to do my job.* "The glass tubes . . . you can see inside them. There should be sensors and frequency modulators in there. We have to insert them still." She exhaled, exasperated. "Then there's the fusion control panel, the inputs for the other three components, and the injection point for the neutral beam!" She exhaled again. "And there's more."

I nodded. "Okay, okay. I got it. There's more to do. But good job, so far. It's looking great." I stared at her. "How's the team? Are they working well with you?"

She smiled through her frustration, which seemed to melt away instantly. A warm personality shone through immediately. "They have been wonderful, and highly effective. They can manufacture whatever I want, and *fast* too. They know what they're doing."

Some of them had worked on our fusion seacars—*Swords*—at our secret base, The Ridge. They had extensive real-world manufacturing experience. I knew they'd work hard for a mission that involved Trieste and TCI. "Great," I muttered, staring at the weapon. It seemed to pulse with power and glow with deadly danger.

I peered down the void between the ten "lasers." The channel was twelve inches across. It was difficult to comprehend. An artificially generated vacuum channel two hundred meters long, through which a stream of neutral particles would blast. It would hit a warsub's hull, knock protons from atoms, tearing the structure of the sub apart and weakening its integrity. It would dissolve solid titanium in only seconds and trigger enormous death.

A prickle worked its way up my scalp. I thought about someone using it against Trieste. Ripping into a Living Module. People within would drown, or the water would crush citizens as it churned through the corridors like poisoned blood through veins and arteries.

"How much longer?" I murmured, picturing the calendar in my head. It was now the eighth of March. Travel time was about two days, and we needed to insert Johnny and Clarke on the sixteenth.

Which gave us six more days.

She tilted her head. "Eight days."

"Alyssna, we need—"

"But I'll do it in five." She grinned.

"Shit, Doctor."

She chuckled. "Just teasing you." She turned to Renée. "He is wound a bit tight, wouldn't you say?"

Renée hadn't actually had a chance to spend time with Alyssna yet, but I could tell that she enjoyed the jab at my expense. "He is indeed," Renée said with a matching smile. "But he has good reason." She punched me playfully in the shoulder. "There's a lot riding on decisions that we make. And he takes it all personally."

"I *am* in charge, don't forget," I said.

"You think you are."

"I *am*." But I smiled at her and grabbed her hand again. Then I recalled that I had actually put Meg in charge of the first operation . . . she could abort it whenever she wanted.

I swallowed.

Alyssna studied Renée. "I heard there was an accident recently. A couple of them, in fact. I hope you're doing okay now."

A shrug. "I'm still breathing. I'll be fine." Renée pointed at the object in the center of the chamber. "As long as that's ready, at least."

I smiled at that. Renée always seemed to know what was on my mind, and the things that concerned me most. She also knew my inner demons.

Alyssna said, "I'll have it done in time. I promise."

—••—

MORE DAYS PASSED AND BEFORE we knew it, it was time to depart. We'd been in frequent contact with Sahar Noor, and she with Commodore Clarke. He was going to escort Johnny into the labs the day before the theft. They had to locate the weapon or our plan would not happen. That would be a major setback, for the window was closing. Earlier in the week, Cliff had pointed out an ominous news story.

It was the usual collection of reports of bloody battles on the surface, populations starving, cities flooding, and so on. Ice sheets sheering from massive land glaciers and crashing into the warming oceans. Swarms of locusts, dying cropland, and economies crashing. It was depressing and I'd been trying to avoid it, frankly. I knew what was happening. Dad had predicted it all years before. He had known that Trieste would have great value to the US, and that other colonies would also provide the lifeblood of resources to the topside superpowers.

But these were not the stories that Cliff was trying to bring to my attention. We were in the Commerce Module, having a coffee early in the morning before the shift began. He brought up a news story, and the title immediately froze my heart. My breath caught in my throat.

RUSSIA TO LAUNCH THREE NEW WARSUBS

"Oh my god," I whispered. Then I swore. "It's happening."

"It is," Cliff replied in a hard voice. "They tried to keep this news story from breaking, but it was too difficult due to the size of the subs. Government and corporate satellites can see the construction facilities easily. Look at this." He brought up a section of the text and zoomed in.

The large boat ramps needed for the launch of the new warsubs means that the RSF can only launch one vessel at a time. The ramp at Petropavlovsk is one hundred meters wide, where according to sources on the ground, others are generally only fifty or less. This signifies a substantially larger hull than other fleet vessels. This has worried US officials, concerned about the RSF escalating activities in the oceans. The previous attacks against Norfolk and San Diego, presumably by rogue Russian actors, has resulted in a USSF on edge, particularly after the German destruction of Seascape last Summer. The first of the three vessels is due to hit water in only two months.

I groaned. "When they float the three boats, they'll head straight to Trieste."

"And that means we have until May, *maybe* June if we're lucky."

"Damn."

———•••———

THE RUSSIANS HAD ALREADY TESTED Trieste to determine the strength of our defences. RSF warsubs had arrived following the destruction of their dreadnought, had feinted, and we had flinched and shown our cards. They'd noticed our defensive strategy and now knew how to attack. Three dreadnoughts were more than enough to destroy our fragile underwater colony, but we still had some time to prepare.

The Water Pick would be one way to keep them at arm's length.

There was no time to waste. We needed every weapon we could get our hands on.

We loaded the decoy laser component into *SC-1* through the

moonpool hatch. We brought the seacar into the Repair Module, where Meg hoisted it from the water using a harness system. We brought the tarped device onto the docks on a large wheeled and powered trolley, maneuvered it under the seacar, opened the moonpool and then lowered the vessel to the deck, enclosing the "weapon." It was a large piece of equipment, but it loaded easily and no one looked twice at it. Nations and colonies hauled cargo around the underwater world as frequently as on the surface.

Within hours, we were ready to go. I looked at the team with me in *SC-1*: Johnny, Meg, Richard, Cliff, Alyssna, and Renée. Behind the living area, resting on the moonpool hatch, was the covered façade—the shell of a device that seemed to be a working model, but really was an empty structure. As a result it was lighter than the real thing, and would be easier to move into the labs.

I smiled. "Ready to go?"

—••—

We navigated from the Repair Module, pushed into the ocean, and I opened up the throttle, SCAV drive on full. The roar surrounded us and acceleration pressed us to our chairs. The others sat on the couches, making small talk and preparing for the mission. There would be no killing—I had already stressed this with them; it was a tenet of this operation, not just out of respect for Sahar Noor, but because we had to do this quietly and leave no trace of the operation.

Then a silence fell as we rocketed through the Atlantic toward England. My heart was in my throat.

When this all started, I'd thought the weapon to be a fantasy, a ridiculous dream by a deluded scientist or engineer. Then I'd learned about the mechanics and theory of the thing. But most important, Chalam Kaashif's eyewitness report of what the neutral beam had done to his seacar. It would be a devastating addition to any nation's underwater armory. Hell, on the surface people would consider the thing a superweapon. A ten-terawatt laser alone would be a devastating strike on any vessel or aircraft! Then the neutral beam, which penetrated inches into solid steel, would nearly be overkill.

Overkill.

An appropriate term for this weapon if ever there was one.

—••—

RICHARD WAS SITTING ON A couch in the living area, staring at the tarped, false weapon. His features were difficult to decipher, and I sat next to him. He barely registered my presence.

"Are you okay?" I asked.

He turned to me sharply, as if he hadn't even realized I'd been there. Then he relaxed slightly. "Oh, sorry, Mac."

"No worries."

"I just have my mind on other things I guess."

"Are you worried about the mission?"

He shifted on the couch. "No, not at all. Missions are good. It keeps us focused on the eventual goal."

"The weapon?"

"No." He appeared surprised. "Independence."

"Ah." A moment of silence passed. He kept staring at the tarp. "I haven't seen Jessica lately," I mentioned.

That look crossed his face again. "She's been distant with me, to tell you the truth, Mac. She's back in Ballard right now."

I frowned. "Not in Trieste with you anymore?"

He sighed. "We've been together for so long. She was with us when we fought alongside your dad. She's always been on our side. But lately we've been . . . arguing I guess. There's been tension."

"What happened?"

Something crossed his face that was difficult to interpret. Guilt . . . fear . . . pain? I couldn't tell. He glanced at me and looked momentarily nervous. Then he looked away again. "Marital issues, I guess. Things that have nothing to do with this." He gestured at the tarp.

"I understand." He was basically saying, *It's not your business.* Married couples had lives that no one else truly understood. At least, that's what others had told me. I'd only had two serious relationships. Kat had been the first. Renée was the second.

"Is she still interested in our struggle?" I managed finally.

"Of course. She's always been loyal to us. About achieving freedom for the people who live in the colonies." He looked angry for a heartbeat, as if my question insulted him in some way.

—••—

THE NEXT DAY, WE WERE at Churchill. Renée and I had slept together in one of the recessed bunks, where we had made love slowly and tenderly. Being in the cramped bunk, with the vibrations of the SCAV drive rumbling through our bodies, was comforting and welcoming. We'd done it in the same place many times before, and it was nice to be back together, on a mission, relieving stress, anxiety, and pressure while expressing our love for each other. Renée buried her face in my neck as she moaned, and I groaned into the pillow. I fell to the side, gasping, and she laughed softly beside me as the tremors of orgasm echoed through our bodies.

Then we did it again.

This person meant so much to me. She was beyond important. She was crucial to the independence movement, and I needed her with me forever.

Strange, that someone who had once tried to kill me now meant everything.

I thought for a moment about Richard and Jessica, two people who had been together for so long, but were now experiencing marital issues. I hoped nothing of the sort would ever come between me and Renée.

—••—

WE ARRIVED AT CHURCHILL, WHERE Sahar had arranged for us to moor at the docks.

It was the morning of 16 March.

Sahar met us, and I greeted her as I emerged from *SC-1*. The others collected at my side and I made introductions.

I could sense their excitement, for her reputation had spread throughout the underwater world. She had the personality and power to galvanize entire populations. We marched through the city to her office, where we sat in the corner lounge where earlier we'd had the tense first meeting with Commodore Clarke.

Doctor Sonstraal was on edge, however. She didn't trust the BSF, and Mayor Noor represented authority, which rubbed her the wrong way. Alyssna understood what was happening here, though. I'd wondered if she really even needed to be on the team at Churchill during the operation, until we realized that if something failed on the decoy, we'd need her there for repairs.

"Meg is running this operation," I said to Sahar. "She's going to give the final go ahead."

Sahar nodded. "I understand." She looked at my sister. "The Commodore should be here shortly."

"Great," she drawled.

"Meg," I muttered.

She stared at me for a moment. Then she nodded. "I'll try to behave."

Sahar watched the entire exchange, confused. Then her face flattened. "Ah. Understandable. I do promise that he is going to assist with this." She paused. "He's going in today with your teammate to . . . what's the word?"

"Reconnoiter," Johnny provided.

"Reconnoiter, yes."

"Do you have my uniform?"

"Right here." She pointed to a garment bag against the bulkhead. Johnny stood and investigated it. He checked the time and said, "We go in an hour. Where's my ID?"

"The Commodore is bringing it."

And as if on cue, the hatch slid aside, and the tall, white-haired BSF officer entered the office.

—••—

I ROSE TO GREET COMMODORE Clarke. He offered a genuine smile and shook my hand. Sahar introduced him to the others and he nodded at each in turn. Cliff's face was hard; he wasn't yet sure what to think of the senior BSF officer. Cliff himself had been in the USSF at one point, and involved in the operation that involved Dad's death, meaning he may have once crossed paths with the Commodore. Neither man recognized the other, however, and the moment passed silently.

Clarke either didn't notice Meg's hostility, or, more likely, he decided to ignore it.

He handed a computer chip to Johnny. Johnny put it in his PCD and a holo image appeared in the air before him. It was his face, rotating slowly, and slightly transparent. It was a picture from the previous year, when his hair had been different, but it was clearly Johnny Chang. He was in a simple black t-shirt. A list of details appeared across the frame, including his birth date, title, rank, position, current posting, and more. It included official logos and documentation, with scannable barcodes to check veracity.

"It says you're with BSF command in the North Atlantic," Clarke said in his deliberate, clipped Scottish accent. "Posted to my duty. No one will question you. The hyperlink codes all function." He glanced at the garment bag. "Your uniform. You can dress any time. From this point on you'll be with me. We can go to BSF Command first." Then he hesitated. "Just don't speak, unless you have the accent down."

Meg said, "Why go there? That wasn't the plan."

Clarke shrugged. "Just to get him feeling comfortable. He's got to feel normal in the skin, if you will. To acclimatize him." He stared at Meg, understanding the tension. "I worked with your father, Meagan. I was his friend. I wouldn't jeopardize you or yours. I want to help."

"And yet you left Trieste after they killed him."

He blinked. He paused for a long moment, and then, "I didn't have much choice. They stamped down on the movement. They killed City Councillors too, you know." He was staring down at her, and his eyes had grown hard. "You left too." His tone was sandpaper.

I groaned inwardly. He'd said the same thing during the previous meeting. Perhaps just to cause an argument.

Meg stepped forward, her eyes matching her fury. "I left four years later. You disappeared *that day*."

"I told you, I left to prepare for *another* day." He glanced around. "For *this* day." A silence descended over us. "I want to continue with you on the next stage of the heist as well. I can help with *Aurora Rex*." He sighed. "If I meant to betray you, there would be a team of sailors outside the hatch, right now. I'd just arrest you. But that won't happen."

Meg stared at him for a long moment. Then she shot a look at me.

I said, "What do you say, Meg? Are we doing this?"

Chapter Fourteen

THERE WAS A DEADLY SILENCE. We all stared at Commodore Clarke. He was eyeing Meg, though his face did not show hostility. The quiet was like a cold blanket over a hot ember; Meg was visibly angry, her eyes burning. Clarke had locked his gaze on her, and he just stood still, waiting.

Sahar cleared her throat into the tension. "Meg."

Meg hesitated, then turned slowly to the woman. "Yes, Sahar?" She'd practically growled. But she added quickly, "Sorry. I don't mean to offend you. I'm just concerned about that man, the Commodore." The disdain dripped from her.

Sahar turned to her desk and said, "Look at this." She gestured to the corner of the room. There was a rolled carpet in a steel bin leaning against the bulkhead. It was made of woven fabric. The corners were frayed and there were loose threads. It had an intricate and colorful pattern throughout.

"What is it?" Meg asked, her tone deliberately soft.

"This is my prayer rug. My *Musaleyah*. It belonged to my great-great-great-grandmother. She passed it down to her daughter, and so on through the generations. It came from Saudi Arabia, over a century ago."

Meg stared at it for a few moments, then she looked at Sahar. "I don't understand."

"I face the same direction each prayer. The *qibla*. Toward the sacred shrine of the Kaaba in Mecca. Here it's to the southeast. Five times a day, Meg. It teaches spirituality, discipline, patience, and resilience. It's a tenet of Islam."

"I—I don't—"

"I pray outside too. Underwater, if you can believe it."

The silence was complete now. It seemed as though the ventilation systems had stopped, the vibrations of environmental systems, the pressure monitors. Everything.

Sahar continued, "You have no idea how peaceful that can be. And the solitude is absolute. The water currents are brushing against me, there are some fish about, I can hear my bubbles rising toward the surface. There's *no one* else. And I lower myself to the sand and conduct my prayer."

"You've done this *outside?*"

"Absolutely. We try not to miss a prayer. It's almost like speaking to Allah." She shrugged. "God. Different name, same spirit. I face Mecca and say my prayers. Each one is a different number of units . . . I like fifth prayer outdoors. It's the longest . . . four units in length. It's dark down here. Dusk. The peace is complete." She sighed. "There is nothing like it, and we generally don't speak to others about it."

"Then why are you?" Meg's voice was now soft. "I don't understand what this has to do with the mission. Don't get me wrong, I appreciate you opening up to me—I hope to do the same for you—but we're in the middle of—"

"Meg." She exhaled. "Do you think I, someone devoted to love and peace and hospitality, would bring you here to entrap you? To trick you? There is no way. You are my guests here, do you understand? It's in my nature to now protect you with my very life." She glanced at Clarke. "I'm not his biggest fan, but we are together in this. We want you to steal the weapon. We're here to do whatever it takes, except kill. To lie to you, to trap you, to do anything of that sort, which you are worried about, is a serious insult to my very being." And then she stopped and stood there, in her bright blue hijab and an ornate green scarf, and waited patiently. She was a tall, statuesque figure, radiating power despite her calm demeanor. She was strong and captivating, even though her aura was one of peace. It was a strange counterpoint, but it occurred to me that it was likely how she'd won the mayoral race.

Meg processed that for several heartbeats. She glanced back at me, then to Sahar. "I appreciate you telling me this. I am honored that you showed me your prayer rug." She took a deep breath, then, "I trust you. We will begin the operation immediately." She turned to Johnny. "Get in your new uniform. Get the tracking beacon ready and go do your job. And good luck."

—••—

IN FIVE MINUTES, JOHNNY WAS ready. He looked smart in his dark blue uniform. The rank on his shoulders signified Lieutenant—or *Leftenant*, as the Brits pronounced it, he reminded us—and he attached a micro-mic under the lapel, close to his throat, so he could keep us informed as he explored the labs with the Commodore.

"How do I look, old chap?" he said in a clipped British accent.

Meg's eyes widened. Then she shook her head. "I should know by now not to underestimate you operatives."

Johnny and I had both been involved in many missions across the oceans. Sometimes on our own, sometimes together. Our instructors had trained us intensely, so we could defend ourselves in a variety of situations against a number of opponents. We could speak multiple languages, hotwire simple electronics, and navigate numerous cultures. We had practical, real-world knowledge with weapons in or out of water. I actually spoke Mandarin, though I hadn't had to use it much, but it had come in handy while prisoner in the Chinese underwater colonies. They'd had no idea that I could understand them, which helped me navigate the experience a bit better. Still, torture is torture, and being able to understand the person wielding the instruments of pain sometimes doesn't much matter.

Pain is pain.

They don't care what you have to say.

They just want to hear you scream.

Johnny spent a few minutes reading over the dossier Clarke had provided. The rest of us spoke quietly about the upcoming mission, preparing for the next day, when we'd actually steal the component . . .

If Johnny could find it today.

A few minutes later he closed his display and pocketed the PCD. He turned to Clarke and said in an impeccable British accent, "I'm ready, Commodore. Let's go."

—••—

WE WERE IN THE SEATING area in the corner of the office. We could hear muffled noises from the speaker on the table between us. Then some voices. Then a hatch might slide open, then a few more voices. Commodore Clarke made a few innocuous comments about upcoming assignments, duty rosters, and so on, and Johnny responded with "Aye, sir" or "Acknowledged." He kept his responses brief and to the point, and it made me smile. He was an excellent operative, and he was proving it to us now, even though I'd known for years already. I was proud of the fact that he had volunteered for this. He was putting himself at enormous risk.

But, I reminded myself, all he had to do was get in with Clarke, march around the labs, and note where the weapon was.

Then leave.

Still, a part of me trembled at the danger. We were putting our eggs in one basket here. If an alert sounded, we might as well kiss The Water Pick goodbye. Or, if Clarke was actually setting us up, then Johnny was in serious trouble.

And this was only the prelude . . . the other elements of our extended heist were going to get more and more challenging.

There was a sound of booted feet on the steel deck. Clarke was addressing people in his loud, Scottish drawl. He was asking for information, demanding reports, and so on. His tone was powerful and commanding. Occasionally he said, "Do that for me," or "Have that done for me," and I realized he was giving fake orders to Johnny. With each minute that passed I relaxed a bit more. Meg as well. She was breathing calmly, her eyes closed, but she was concentrating on what was happening.

Then a murmur: "*It's time.*" He was speaking in his British accent, to keep others from wondering why a BSF officer was speaking with an American twang. "We're at the labs. The hatch is right before us. There's a logo. It says BSFRL on it."

Sahar said, "That's the British Submarine Fleet Research Labs. They run the R&D here at Churchill. HQ on the coast is their main base, but they have labs everywhere. At DG too."

"DG?" Meg whispered.

"Diego Garcia."

"Ah."

The hatch opened and there were more footsteps. Then they stopped suddenly.

"Good afternoon, sir. Can I help you?"

"I'm here for inspection. I want to check in on my sailors."

"There's nothing on file about that."

"There doesn't have to be," Clarke snapped. "I'm the Officer in Charge here. My men and women are in this facility. I routinely run inspections."

"Not here you don't."

"I haven't so far, you're right, but that fact has irritated BSFCO. They want me to check up on our people."

There was a pause.

A sound of a keyboard.

"What's going on?" Clarke demanded. "Make a note of this man's name," he snapped, presumably to Johnny.

Johnny said, "Hopkins is it? What's the 'J' for?"

"Jack, sir. Jonathan, I mean. Officially." The guard's voice was full of nerves.

"Noted," Johnny replied.

"Now," Clarke growled. "I have Eyes Only clearance. We're coming in. We'll only be a few minutes."

"There's no problem coming in, sir. It's just that there's no mention of it in the daily report. I'll have to note it in the log."

"That's fine." Then he said to Johnny, "Come on, *Lieutenant*. We have eight people on duty today."

"Williams, Martin, Smith, Kitchener—"

I turned to Sahar. "They're in." I was whispering, though unsure why. Johnny was continuing to recite the names. This was not a two-way comm system, so they couldn't hear me. "It shouldn't take long."

She nodded but didn't respond.

———••———

SOON IT WAS SILENT, EXCEPT for the sounds of their bootsteps. Then Johnny muttered, "We're on the first deck. People moving about; scientists and tech staff mostly. They seem pretty nerdy. Signs on the bulkheads. Seems to be an electronic and mechanical lab mostly. Haven't seen any biohazard signs, so it's not for chemical or viral warfare. Not like the mission we did to that Indonesian lab in Twenty-One, Mac. That was hairy."

There was a long pause. I felt the others staring at me, but I didn't say anything.

He continued, quietly: "There's an odd patch on some shoulders here. Red and black. There's no lettering . . ."

Another moment passed. Then Clarke said, "At ease, Sailor. No worries. Just checking in on you."

A different voice replied, "This is a surprise, sir." It was a woman.

"Just routine."

"Really?"

"It is, though I haven't been so good at it. I heard about it from BSFCO, let me tell you."

A laugh. "Very well."

"How are you doing here?"

"It's fine. Typical of the type of work, sir."

"Meaning?"

"It's a tad boring." Then she added, "Sir. Sorry, sir. Just being honest."

He chuckled. "No worries at all."

Johnny said, "What's your division?"

"I guard this hatch here. Every shift. It's a virus lab." Her tone was unmistakable.

"But there are no biohazard signs here."

"Computer viruses, Lieutenant. Sorry to be vague. The scientists here are doing something with computer software. I hear things about worms, and so on. Coding worms, to be precise. Digital parasites or some such talk. I don't really know much."

"Very well."

"Keep up the good work," Clarke said. "You're doing the King's service, and we're all proud."

She lowered her voice. "I hate working for this group of people though.

The BSFRL people. They don't recognize us as part of their military. Almost as if they're a different group entirely. They treat us so poorly." Pause. "If I could get out into the oceans, it would be a relief, sir. I'm in the BSF . . ."

"Go on."

"I don't want to guard a lab for the rest of my career."

"How old are you?"

"Twenty-three."

"I won't tell you about some of the loos I had to clean in my twenties. It's all part of the service, Sailor."

"I understand." The sound of defeat was clear.

"We *are* out in the oceans, by the by. Every post has these types of duties. Buck up and do your job." Pause. "But . . . I'll keep you in mind if something comes up," he said.

"Oh, that would be wonderful!"

"Carry on."

Their footsteps continued. I took a breath.

—••—

SEVERAL MORE EXCHANGES OF THE same sort took place. Not many of the guards really seemed too enthused with their postings. Then Johnny whispered, "We're on the upper deck. There's a central lift that leads down to the moonpool There's a lot of equipment in the corridors. Electronics, wires, motherboards, quantum computers. I saw a hatch marked 'Energy Beam Research.'"

"Can you go in?" I muttered to myself.

As if he could hear me, he said, "We're going in."

—••—

"THIS IS IT," JOHNNY HISSED. In the background, I could hear Clarke speaking with other sailors, probably BSF guards, or maybe even engineers who worked there. "There are laser components lying around. They look like the ones on Doctor Sonstraal's duplicate. At least, the transparent tubes do. I'm searching for the complete device."

More overlapping voices. Then the rattle of equipment, and a couple of hatches grinding open and shut. Then, "This is it. I see Component One. It looks like Doctor Sonstraal's device. The ten lasers, the fusion core, the barrel, and the empty channel."

I clenched my fist in triumph. The others were grinning.

Johnny continued, "There's a clear route to the hydraulic lift. The device is already on a large, wheeled trolley. But Mac . . . " He paused, and my heart pounded, expecting something bad. He continued, "It's not exactly the same. There's something off about it . . . "

I frowned. "What is he talking about?"

Alyssna said, "I don't know. I made it exactly as it was. Same displays, struts, controls, *everything* as I remembered it."

"Mac. There are *two* fusion reactors attached to it. At the back. There's a new bracket and an identical reactor beside the first one."

I stared at Alyssna. Her face was slack. "Oh no," she whispered. "We'd discussed adding another, for more power. These reactors are small and produce a lot of energy, but we were approaching the threshold. Ten terawatts simultaneous to the neutral beam had pushed the reactor close to its limit. We'd considered—"

"What are you doing here?" a voice rasped from the speaker.

"We're on an inspection tour—" Johnny started.

"You're with the Commodore?"

"Checking in on our people." Then Johnny's tone hardened. "And you better address me appropriately, Sailor."

There was a pause. "What are you doing here? I'll not ask again."

"How dare you repeat yourself. I told you I'm with Commodore Clarke."

"He's not in here. This is strictly off limits."

"I just walked through a hatch. There was no alarm or sign saying it's off limits. Besides, what is off limits to the Commodore? He's from BSFCO. And so am I! He's the CO of this entire region."

A light on my PCD began to flash. I held it up. "He just triggered the beacon." But I listened to the voices with intent concentration. I was clenching my teeth. I hoped he hadn't been found out. I also hoped he could place the tracker before the intruder noticed.

"What's your name?" the other said.

Johnny gave him an indignant reply. "Get Commodore Clarke. I'm on his staff. I won't answer to you. I'm a Lieutenant, in case you can't read rank insignia!"

"You're coming with me. No one's allowed here."

There was a scuffle and the sound of boots ringing on the steel deck. I noted that the tracker was not moving. He'd planted it.

Soon Clarke's voice echoed from the speaker, demanding answers. "How dare you!" he barked.

"Sir, he was standing near the laser pack. He was staring at it."

"So? He's on my staff, dammit. Let go of him."

"I'm sorry, sir. I'm going to have to hold him here."

There was a moment of stunned silence. "What? I outrank you. Leave him with me and I'll deal with it."

"Sorry, sir. You don't outrank me."

"I'm a Commodore—"

"You're with BSF."

"So are you!"

"No, sir. Sorry. I'm with BSFIF. You don't have authority over me. Now, this man is coming with me to answer some questions. I'll release him when I'm satisfied. You're free to go now, Commodore." Pause. Then to Johnny, "And you better not make me angry."

Chapter Fifteen

"Oh, shit," I muttered. We could hear Johnny being manhandled and Clarke continuing to demand explanations.

We listened in rapt attention, holding our collective breaths. Before long, it appeared as though Johnny was in a small cell, waiting to answer questions. He wouldn't speak, because he knew they were watching him, either through a window, a vid screen, or a two-way mirror.

Now we had two immense problems on our hands.

I stared at Cliff. He was watching me, his eyes dark. Then I turned to Sahar. "Is this Clarke?"

Her face had paled. "It can't be. I vouched for him. He didn't do this."

"You think they caught Johnny and just won't answer to Clarke?"

She took a deep breath. Then, "Yes. That's what it has to be."

I swore.

Alyssna said, "There's more, Mac. The weapon. They've added a fusion reactor. One for the laser, one for the neutral beam."

I chewed the inside of my cheek.

"Mac, we're about to switch the real weapon for my fake one. If it only has one reactor, they'll notice pretty damn fast!"

"I know that!" I roared. Then I blew the air out of my lungs in a rush. "Shit, sorry, Doc." Then I noticed Sahar looking at me, stern. "Sorry, Sahar. Truly, I am."

"I'm upset too. I am Mayor but I have no authority over those labs. It's been frustrating for my people. We can only make requests to the BSF. They either take care of them or ignore them." She shrugged. "We have no say." Then she locked her eyes to mine. "And please don't swear around me."

Inwardly it annoyed me, but I knew better than to act childish. This was her city and her office. "I'm so sorry, Sahar."

She nodded to me.

I continued, "More likely, the BSFRL ignores what you ask. Sounds like the BSF has *zero* say over what goes on there." It was a fact that made me wonder exactly how much power the division had over what was going on in the Indian Ocean . . . or if the BSF even had any idea what was happening there. I wondered what would happen once the weapon had satisfied their administrators. I'd just assumed the BSF had known, but then again, Clarke apparently hadn't been aware. Would the Research Lab division of the BSF just hand the weapon over and then start on something else?

Sahar was staring at the team. Her face had a calm intensity, though I could tell that she was thinking about something. "Mac," she said finally, "care to go outside with me?"

I turned slowly to her. "Outside? Of the office?"

"No, for a swim." She rose to her feet. She turned to her desk, then back to me. "Please come out with me. I'll show you around."

—••—

TEN MINUTES LATER, WE WERE swimming away from the city, moving to the east, farther into the English Channel. Renée and Meg were with us; we were following Sahar.

It took Renée a minute or two to agree; her PCD was missing and was not where she had left it. But she shrugged it off and within a minute was with us and outside swimming alongside.

Sahar Noor was a powerful swimmer. She was wearing a wetsuit that had a hood and a loose material that stretched down to just past her knees. There was an inner layer, and the loose material attached there, and then the wetsuit continued to her flippers. Her strokes were powerful and her legs churned the water effortlessly. Meg and I flanked her and together we moved farther from the city. Soon the modules were lost to sight, with the exception of the bright lights at the apex of each. Above, the surface was bright. Sediment and sand swirled around us like an underwater sandstorm. The currents were strong here, but we were all efficient swimmers.

Within a few more minutes Sahar stopped and drifted to the seafloor. She checked her PCD, put it back in its sheath, and adjusted her position.

She was facing southeast.

"Pray with me," she whispered. "It's time."

I stared in shock. "We're in a bit of trouble."

"There's always time to be thankful," she said. "Look around, Mac. Meg. Look where we are."

"Johny is—"

"He's fine. He's not hurt. They're asking him questions."

In fact, I'd left Richard, Cliff, and Alyssna back to listen in, to find out what exactly was going on.

"What are you—" I started, but she cut me off again.

"Not now. Soon." She began speaking Arabic, though it was more of a song than words. A chant, a poem. It seemed mystical.

Renée, Meg and I floated there, on the bottom, watching.

"Mac," Sahar said once again. "Pray with me."

"I'm not—"

"Just go through the same motions. Look at it like meditation or yoga. Enjoy the peace."

I sighed, and my bubbles soared upward. Then I took the same position, about a meter away from her, and tried my best to follow along. Renée was on my other side, and she smiled at me for a long moment before we began to mimic Sahar's movements. I grabbed Renée's hand and squeezed.

It lasted for ten minutes, and afterward, we sat there, staring at each other. Sahar's dark eyes were behind the full facemask. They looked somber, but there was no fear or anger.

I looked around me. Visibility was low and it seemed as though we were in our own bubble with no one else nearby. It was indeed calm and peaceful. Serene. A void of quiet.

I took several more deep breaths. "Thank you," I whispered.

"You don't have to be spiritual to enjoy this," Sahar replied. "I wanted to get us away. To think about this."

"And away from prying ears and eyes?"

"Possibly." She sighed. "They took your man and not Clarke. On the surface it looks like Clarke arranged it. I promise you that can't be the case."

Meg said, "I do trust you, Sahar. But is it possible that you just aren't aware?"

There was a long pause. "It's totally possible. But it doesn't make sense. He would have had his people just arrest us all in the office and not let us get into the labs at all. Instead, we now know where the weapon is."

"Hopefully, but we're not sure," Meg said.

"It doesn't make sense to try to lure us in there," I said. "Sahar's right. They could just take us in on suspicion. The crime would be the same."

"You trust Clarke?" Meg asked.

"I trust Sahar, and her logic makes sense. The question is, what are we going to do?"

"We need to get Johnny back," Renée said. "We can't leave him."

"They might just let him go in an hour or two."

"If they don't?"

I hesitated and thought it over. "Then we rescue him when we steal the weapon and leave the decoy. We're not leaving anyone behind."

Meg's face showed horror. "But surely they'll realize we were there! The point is to be in and out without anyone knowing! That's why we picked March 17."

"I know. But maybe Clarke can redeem himself with this."

"What do you mean?"

I shrugged. "We get Johnny out. We have Clarke take responsibility for it."

"Meanwhile, we've got to get the weapon."

"Which we'll do quietly. They'll never notice, and therefore won't check the video feed. Not for a while anyway. By then, we'll have all four components."

Sahar looked confused. "Four components?"

I said, "There are four pieces to this weapon, Sahar. One is on a war-sub in the Pacific. That's the next stage in our mission. The other two are in the Indian Ocean."

"I had no idea. I thought it was just one."

"It's a challenge, for sure."

She looked away and I could see the thoughts churning through her mind. "Strange, the Indian Ocean keeps coming up."

I didn't respond to that.

Meg said, "Mac. Putting aside the problem with Johnny for a minute, what about the weapon? The additional reactor. Ours doesn't have that."

I forced a grin. "Actually, Meg, Sahar was right." I looked around. Our bubbles drifted upward, caught in the eddies and currents and twirling like waterspouts on the surface as they rose. The odd fish darted by, and the sound of the regulators was peaceful and steady. "This is calm and relaxing. And I now see a solution."

Sahar grinned behind her mask. "See? Allah will always provide a way forward, even in the most difficult of times."

—••—

BACK IN THE OFFICE, RICHARD, Cliff, and Alyssna were staring at the speaker on the low table. Voices were spitting from it. Angry voices. I tried to decipher Johnny's attempt to reply. He had an indignant tone, which absolutely fit with the situation. He was trying to explain his role on Commodore Clarke's staff, with little luck.

"Come on, now!" a voice snapped. "You were in an off-limits lab! What the hell were you thinking?"

"We're here to inspect our people. You're BSF too! What are *you* talking about?"

"I don't answer to you, Lieutenant."

"You're right about one thing there."

"What?"

"I'm your superior. And you're going to hear about this after, from Command Operations. BSFCO is not going to let insubordination go unchecked. You can bet—"

"I don't give a rat's tit about that."

Pause. "You're risking your career right now."

There was the scraping of a chair on the deck. The angry Brit said, "You're risking a hell of a lot more than that, if you don't start answering!"

"What the hell does that mean? We're both Brits, dammit. I'm doing my job."

"You weren't *doing your job!* You were off by yourself, shoving your nose where it don't belong!"

"Why?" Johnny laughed. "What are you hiding? Chunks of metal and wires lying around? I don't even care what you guys are doing."

"Good one. I almost believe it."

"I'm just doing what the Commodore asks. He gives me tasks and I make note of them. I send out his orders to the necessary—"

"Oh, *come on.*"

"—people and remind him of upcoming events. You think I enjoy this posting? I want out, chap! I want to be on a warsub somewhere. Instead, I'm picking up his dry cleaning!"

There was a hesitation at that. "Where are you from?"

"Liverpool."

"When were you born?"

"Twenty ninety-three."

"Month?"

"August."

"Day?"

"Twenty-five."

"What's your ID?"

Johnny recited a fourteen-digit number. I raised my eyebrows at the others. He made me proud. The details were correct.

"What were you doing in that lab?"

"Looking for our people. We still haven't spoken to Kitchener and Whalley. And now you've sent the Commodore away, we'll have to come back for that."

"Bugger *off.*"

"If you want. Does that mean I can leave now?"

"No! Shut your mouth!"

"How can I answer questions if—"

The chair slid aside and the hatch ground open and closed. There was distinct sound of a lock clicking.

I looked at Richard. "It's been like this since we left?"

He nodded. "What's the plan, Mac?" He glanced at Renée and back to me. "We're in a bit of a pickle right now."

"Actually, it's not too bad. We're still going ahead tomorrow with the operation, once the festivities kick into high gear."

"And Johnny?"

"We'll pull him out of there."

Cliff said, "A prison break? We can go in, get him out in just a few minutes. Disable the alarms and neutralize the guards."

Sahar bristled at the euphemism, but I raised a hand. "No, no," I said. "We have to be quiet, Cliff. We can't let them know we've been there. We'll get him out, but quietly. Without any suspicion."

Richard's eyes widened. "I like the sounds of that. But how, exactly? And what about the changes to the laser module?"

I paused and stared at the others. "We have only one option with that. We have to make sure ours has *two* reactors."

A long, pregnant pause fell over us. Richard said, "But where—"

"From *SC-1*. We have a reactor of the same size and type."

Meg said, "But that's for the SCAV drive! We can't—"

"Why not?" I watched her for a heartbeat. "We can attach it to the laser pack." I turned to Alyssna. "Can you do it?"

She frowned. "It's the same size?"

"Engineers have standardized them now. Compact, used for factories, communities, even spacecraft." I shrugged. "The decoy weapon and the SCAV drive are only a few meters apart right now." I checked the time. "We have about twenty-four hours. We go tomorrow. And we haul in a decoy with *two* reactors. Not one."

Meg was staring at me. "But Mac. We won't have the SCAV drive."

"So, it'll be a few days back to Trieste. But we can repair the drive there, then go for the next component." I shrugged again. "Hell, what choice do we have? It's either this or the entire operation is over."

"And what about Johnny?"

I replied, "The Commodore will have to come in with us. He'll have to get Johnny out."

Her eyes flashed. "Are you sure? You want to just march in with the man who may have caused this situation?"

Renée said, "If he's the cause, it'll put you at risk too, Mac."

"We've been through all this. We have to trust the man. It's either that or we have no hope."

They remained silent, simply staring at me.

—••—

SIX HOURS LATER, WE WERE back in *SC-1*, and our plan was in high gear. Meg had dismantled the fusion reactor from the SCAV compartment at the stern of the seacar, and Alyssna was creating a bracket to weld it to at the rear of the fake laser pack. Cliff was helping with the manual labor. Johnny, captive in the research lab, was quiet; the questioning had stopped an hour earlier, and he was presumably in a cell, sleeping or waiting for us to do something.

Richard and I were in the pilot's cabin, and he was asking me about Sahar and what had happened outside.

"We prayed together," I said. "It was that time of the day."

"What was it like?"

"Peaceful. Relaxing."

"You should be careful, Mac."

I blinked. "Why?"

"There have been two attempts on your life! You have to be aware of your surroundings. That was . . . dangerous."

"Oh, that."

He chuckled. "Yes, *that*. You have to be careful."

"I think it was entirely unpredictable. No one could have known I was going out there."

"There might be a team of people watching you."

"Point."

He sighed. "Do you trust the Commodore?"

I stared at him. Then I looked outside the canopy, at the docking pool and the docks surrounding us. The ceiling of the module was fifteen meters over our heads; there were a series of cranes and harnesses on railings crisscrossing the chamber. "I think so. He could have arrested us at any time. He hasn't done it."

"Maybe he wants the weapon for himself."

That made me stop. "But they're all BSF. They're the ones *creating* the damn thing."

"Still, it doesn't seem as though the BSF and the BSFRL really work well together."

I sighed. "He's helping us steal the four components. The purpose is to help defeat our enemies and form Oceania. This is the only way he can do it . . . by helping us."

"I hope you're right."

I stared at him. "So it's on me, is it?"

"What does that mean?"

"Just that everything is always on my shoulders. The decisions, the pressure, the guilt." I swore. "How much can one man take?"

His eyes grew soft, and compassion was clear in his features. "You're doing a wonderful job. Better than your dad could have done. You've brought us this far. The movement depends on you."

An overwhelming surge of anxiety flooded through me. "Way to put more pressure on me."

"I'm saying that you should be so proud of yourself. When this mission is over, you can—"

"You better not say *relax*. The Russians are ready to attack. The USSF will figure out the Germans don't have the Isomer Bomb. They'll realize it's us. China is going to figure out their colonies are declaring independence and they're not going to sit still while that happens. It's all on me, and it's coming to a head, Richard."

He watched me silently. "We just have to stay away from distractions. We need to focus and stay the path."

"You think by focusing it'll make things easier?"

"Not easier. But it'll help make things happen."

I considered that. "Sometimes it's so difficult, Richard. Dad dying really destroyed our family. Meg and I are trying to pull it back together. Thankfully I also have Renée now, too. She's really helping."

His face grew hard. "You can get through this, Mac. It's almost all over. We'll get the weapon, then we'll declare independence. We'll announce Oceania to the world. And then . . . "

"And then we'll have to fight a war," I supplied for him.

"We'll be ready though. No one will expect an underwater particle beam."

I sat back, finally feeling some measure of focus. I glanced over my shoulder at the weapon behind me, where Meg and Alyssna were working on it, then checked the time. We could get a bit of sleep, and then we'd begin.

Chapter Sixteen

IT WAS 17 MARCH. CELEBRATIONS had sparked to life all over the city. We could hear it in the corridors. The Commerce Module was one massive party. Music blared from the pubs and restaurants. Laughter and cheers echoed wherever we went. Everyone was wearing green. I was sure that divers outside the modules could hear the celebrations.

We were wearing green too, to fit in, and we explored the city to see the festivities. There was a parade at noon. It wound its way through the Living Modules, where it picked up participants—anyone who wanted to join—and it snaked its way through the travel tubes and corridors and went through the central module and toward the university, where an even larger celebration was taking place. Families with children were participating; the youngsters wore green hats and green shirts and beads and had noisemakers and trumpets—anything to signify a celebration.

Everyone was drinking, yelling, cheering. A few fights broke out here and there, but people generally stopped them from getting too bad.

Life underwater was hard, in every colony. A struggle. It was nice to blow off steam once in a while. Citizens everywhere enjoyed events like this, and I smiled as I watched. It was common to see hardworking people enjoy a small break from the rigors of everyday life.

Sahar started the parade with an announcement about celebrating cultures and embracing each other's heritage. It was a nice speech, and she had a huge smile on her face. She wore an emerald green hijab that sparkled in the light, and a traditional blue scarf to signify St. Patrick. Her eye makeup had a green tinge as well. The people loved her; all the children of the city, wearing green costume jewels and clothing, practically swarmed her along the parade route, which made her smile widen even more. It was an incredible scene: a Muslim woman in a green hijab leading an Irish parade through an underwater city.

We walked the parade with Sahar, who led the line with the other city councillors, and as the time grew close to dark, we drifted away toward *SC-1* to prepare for the moment.

We changed into our gear and prepped for the mission. We inserted receivers in our ears and attached throat mics concealed under collars. We carried guns in holsters on our right thighs, as was customary in the BSF, and knives in sheaths on our left thighs, which was traditional for almost all undersea fleet sailors.

I found Renée in the seating area, and she put her arms around me. She always worried about me just before missions.

"Did you find your PCD?" I muttered as I nuzzled her neck.

"Pardon?"

"You said you lost it."

Realization spread across her face. "It was in Sahar's office the whole time. I just misplaced it."

"Ah."

"Please be careful," she whispered into my ear.

"Always." I held her tight, but not for long.

—••—

RICHARD AND I MARCHED CONFIDENTLY to the travel tube just outside Research Module A. We were wearing dark blue BSF uniforms. Commodore Clarke met us there. I checked the time and Clarke glanced at me.

Renée piloted *SC-1* outside, where she parked near the city and waited. Sahar, Cliff, Meg, and Alyssna were on board with her.

"It'll be a skeleton crew now," he muttered. "Everyone else is out celebrating."

I nodded.

Time to go.

—••—

WE MARCHED TOWARD THE LABS. Clarke barked at the person at the desk—not one of his people—who seemed resigned to the visit and pre-occupied with his own issues. He clearly did not want to be on duty just then. Clarke signed the log and within seconds we were in. A hatch with a large BSFRL logo split down the center and sighed open.

It caught my eye. Only for an instant though, because there were more important things to do, but it was more than a sub fleet logo. There was something else on it about an "Imperial Force."

No such thing existed in the BSF.

That being said, there were obviously troops in the city representing it, and the guard who had taken Johnny had said something similar that had piqued my interest.

The labs were well-lit. The decks were steel, as in all other places, though there were no grates here. No spaces for water to drip down, which was more common in other colonies. Here it was plain steel and easier to clean, I assumed. There was equipment piled along the deck outside of hatches and labs. It was empty . . . there was no one around. I breathed a sigh of relief. I had worried that not everyone would leave for the party, but Sahar had been correct. The majority of the city was celebrating. The few guards in the labs were located at their stations, which we would avoid. We knew where they were because Sahar had already provided the map. I recognized the layout of the corridors; I just didn't know what each lab or office was used for.

Clarke intended to speak with Johnny, under the pretense of freeing him, which justified his presence.

Richard and I would take care of the rest.

Richard was in a Lieutenant's uniform. He looked official; his facial expression was serious, though it was likely to contain his nerves. He knew not to speak, for he could not emulate the accent.

My own uniform had Captain's insignia on the shoulders.

We split from Clarke with a glance. "Good luck," he mouthed. He was going to distract as many guards as possible. In fact, Johnny's detention had given us an added distraction for the theft.

There were signs on the walls and arrows on the deck. The lift was in the center of the lab, and we found it easily. We stepped on it and I pressed the button for the first level. A gate lowered, there was a thrum of power, and it started to descend. It was hydraulic and wide, meant for large equipment.

It stopped, the gate raised, and I peered at the area surrounding us.

The moonpool.

———•••———

THE LARGE DECK HATCH WAS closed, however, which Sahar had warned us of. We'd need to open it and expose the water below the module to bring the device in. I found the panel on the bulkhead and studied it.

I swore.

Richard was looking around. There was scuba gear piled against the bulkheads, as well as lockers. There were workstations for sailors and an office with a transparent partition. It was likely the guard station, but it was empty.

"Can you do it?" he asked me in a quiet voice.

There was a pressure readout on the display as well. It read 4.0. I said, "No."

"Can't hotwire it?"

I stared at the pad. It required a palm print to open the moonpool hatch. There was also a code to enter, but it was eight digits long. "Can you check the guard station? There might be a hatch override there."

Richard investigated and returned in thirty seconds. "It's the same as here. Palm recognition with a number pad."

I swore again. It required both to open. I could bypass the number code, by cross-circuiting some wires, but the palm code was another issue entirely.

There were numerous scuba tanks lying around the bulkheads and in the equipment lockers. Richard and I closed the hatches into the chamber—from the lift and offices and the corridors—and began to open the tanks, venting the air outward.

I grabbed my PCD and signalled Meg in *SC-1*. "Is Sahar there?"

"Go ahead."

"We're at the moonpool. Plan B. Please call City Control and warn them."

We'd already anticipated this. Sahar had one of her people at Pressure Control, waiting.

We hoped.

We knew the cameras were watching and recording us, but there would be no need for anyone to review the footage until much later, when they realized that there was a decoy laser pack in their labs. Then they'd see what we'd done, but it didn't matter.

By then, it'd be too late.

"There are thirty tanks in here, give or take," Richard said.

"Do them all."

We moved quickly. Ten minutes passed, and I wondered how Commodore Clarke's efforts were progressing. Hopefully he was stalling and causing a ruckus with Johnny in the cell.

The pressure was building, and we had to continually perform the *Valsalva* maneuver—squeezing our nose and forcing air into our ear canals. Normally used for popping one's ears, now it was to equalize pressure. Scuba divers did it all the time; I'd had lots of practice. Once, two years ago, I'd achieved the world record of deep dives, although no one else knew about it.

Except Kat, but she was now dead and gone.

I shivered.

The sound was shrill as the tanks continued to vent.

Richard's face was red as he struggled to keep up with the increasing pressure. "I'm not sure how much more I can handle . . ." he ground out.

On the hatch display, the pressure was at 5.7 atms.

The alarm started to flash, but there was no sound.

Sahar's person had silenced it.

Normally City Control would have noticed and sprung into action. Any pressure issues were a major danger to the city integrity.

But I knew what would happen here.

The computer would act in order to prevent the hull from rupturing *outward*.

There was a clang of equipment as a mechanism unlocked.

And the moonpool hatch slid aside.

—••—

IT WAS AN AUTOMATIC SELF-PRESERVATION system to protect the colony. Each cabin or travel tube had pressure monitors. It was important that the interior pressure perfectly matched the exterior at all times, without exception. If they matched, and the moonpool was open, then the water would not rise into the module. It was a conduit directly out into the ocean. But with the pressure increasing in the chamber, the computer recognized that the only way to equalize was to open the hatch and allow the excess air out.

As the hatch rumbled aside, the air blew outward and a flood of bubbles churned down into the water.

The pressure plunged in the moonpool chamber and our ears popped again and again until it normalized at four atms. The water in the pool churned as the air rushed out, large bubbles blew *downward* toward the seafloor—which was only five meters below the pool—and then they seemed to slither and squirm along the edge of the module as if they were organic things with minds of their own before they soared freely to the surface thirty meters above. Had someone been watching from the outside, they might have called City Control to report a pressure emergency. Still, the blue pressure lights were not flashing, and there was no alarm ringing.

I raised the PCD to my lips. "Cliff, Meg—it's time."

The dark pool slowly calmed and ceased its roiling. Then a metal spear pierced the surface and rose upward into the chamber.

SC-1.

Meg had brought it to the surface, but she wasn't going to moor the ship.

She was just *hovering* in place, just over the surface of the seafloor.

I looked up at the ceiling and located a hoist. Dangling below it was a harness sling with wide straps. "Richard, we have to find the controls to that."

"Already got them."

He was looking better already. The pressure had stabilized and he'd recovered quickly. He was at a console and was also looking at the ceiling. There was a hydraulic whine as he manipulated the crane and lowered the harness toward the pool. *SC-1* lurched in the water and then a moment later began to descend again. I could see Meg and Renée in the pilot cabin. Renée was smiling at me through the canopy.

She waved.

I risked a quick smile in return.

"Keep your mind on the job," Richard said.

"Don't worry."

"Distractions, remember . . ."

"I got it."

SC-1 disappeared, her thrusters churning the water as it descended and powered away to the west. Richard lowered the harness, and it sank below the water's surface. I stared down, trying to make something out. Then Meg turned on the powerful floodlights at the bow of the seacar, illuminating the area under Richard and me. There, on the seafloor, was a large object enclosed in a yellow waterproof tarp. A scuba diver was swimming around it, wrapping the harness around the device. He pushed the straps under it, brought them up the other side, and connected each to the harness, which was attached with a chain to the hoist.

It was Cliff Sim. His bubbles rose and broke the moonpool's surface. Eventually he backed away, looked up, and gave the thumbs-up sign.

Richard activated the hoist, and it started to whine once more, only shriller this time.

The decoy wasn't as heavy as the real thing, however. We'd have to go through the same process again, but in *reverse* as we moved the real laser module *out* to *SC-1*.

In my ear, the comm clicked. "Mac, it's Clarke."

"Go ahead." I watched as the package rose from the water. I stepped aside and pointed at the elevator lift platform. There were large yellow hatch marks and arrows on the deck—warnings to stay away while lifting heavy objects onto the lift's deck.

"There are only three guards in the lab in the upper level."

I grunted. We'd predicted that it would be a reduced complement during the festivities, but this was better than we could have hoped for. The laser was in the upper level, and the lift would take us straight there.

He continued, "I believe there are three on the lower level. No one has even spoken to me. I took a quick circuit. I'm going to see if I can get them to accompany me to see Johnny now."

"Will they release him to you?"

"I'm not sure yet. What's happening down there?"

I told him, and he remained quiet for a moment. "We're right on schedule," he eventually replied. "Good luck. I'll see if I can get these guards to come with me now."

I watched Richard as he lowered the device to the lift platform. "We'll be up there in about three minutes," I estimated.

"Got it." He clicked off.

I unhooked the harness and Richard moved the hoist back to its original position. Then we quickly unzipped the waterproof yellow tarp, bundled it up, and I threw it to the side.

Cliff surfaced in the moonpool and hauled himself up to the deck. He spit out the regulator and pushed his mask up. "Do you need help with the laser?"

"Stay here," I said. "We can't let anyone see you." I gestured at the tarp. "Get this ready to use again." I stepped onto the lift and Richard joined me. "We'll be right back."

—••—

SC-1 WAS STILL BELOW THE module, waiting. When we brought the laser pack, we'd lower it into the water and to the sandy seafloor. Then Meg and Renée would use the seacar, with its moonpool hatch open, and swallow the laser inside.

If we could get it back down to the moonpool.

The moan of the hydraulics was shrill as it pushed us to the upper deck. The gate swung upward as it came to a stop.

—••—

RICHARD AND I LOOKED ABSOLUTELY official as we marched confidently from the lift and into the corridor. I checked the PCD and noted the position of the tracker that Johnny had left in the lab. I pointed and Richard and I turned down a wide passage toward a hatch just as wide. There was a BSFRL logo again, with a stenciled ENERGY BEAM RESEARCH label under it.

We approached the hatch.

It didn't open.

"Shit," I said.

Chapter Seventeen

"WHAT NOW?" RICHARD ASKED. HE looked around. There was no keypad or handprint sensor.

We had hoped the lab would open because we'd already gained official access to the facility. I thought furiously and then signaled Clarke. It was a risk, but I had no choice. "The hatch won't open," I whispered.

He triggered his own mic on, but he was not speaking to me. "*I'm here to get my man back,*" he snapped at someone. "How can you not recognize that? He's an officer in the BSF, and he's my assistant. I am simply *not* leaving here without him."

I sighed. Then I turned to Richard. "He's busy." I pursed my lips as I stared at the hatch. "There must be a sensor of some sort. The technicians and engineers must wear a key card or an ID. As they get near, it opens."

"They might have them clipped to their uniform or wear them around their neck or something. They might leave them here when their shift is over?"

"The guards must have them on now," I said, staring at the older man.

His face went slack. "You want to steal one from a guard? *Now?*"

"We have no choice, Richard. We can't leave without the laser pack." I gestured over my shoulder. "The decoy is here. We have to make the switch or this whole enterprise ends now."

I keyed Clarke again and explained the dilemma. He was still arguing with the guards and didn't react at all. I sensed that they were closer to Johnny, however, because he was spitting questions that were not directed at the BSF sailors.

"Let's search this level," I hissed. "Quickly. Meet back here in two minutes."

—··—

Normally we'd come up with a method to blast through the hatch, but in this case, we couldn't leave evidence that we'd been there.

The only sign we'd left so far were the emptied scuba tanks.

For an instant, I wondered what they'd think when they found every single tank emptied of air. Would they assume someone just hadn't been doing their job?

I considered for a minute whether we could use the same trick on the hatch to the Energy Beam Laboratory.

But no. The corridors were too extensive, and the computer would likely open hatches into the Research Module itself to equalize pressures. We'd been able to isolate the moonpool chamber and seal it, so downward had been the only way for the computer to equalize. This was not the same situation.

There was a guard station nearby. Clarke had lured the sailor away, however, and I quickly scanned the desk. We'd discussed something like this happening, but we hadn't had a solution other than to simply *find a way in*. Find a sensor. Get a guard to do it. Hotwire the hatch.

I swore. There was nothing there.

Richard triggered the comm a moment later. "Nothing," he concurred.

I stared at a ladder that led downward to the deck below. Clarke had said there were guards there.

There might be a way.

Thoughts churned through my mind. I could incapacitate one of them. Knock him out. Steal his ID and use that. But that would leave evidence.

I could *kill* one of them, and we could just remove the body through the moonpool. Would anyone know? Would they check the video footage? Or would they just assume the guard had walked out to join the festivities in the city?

An image of Sahar flashed through my mind.

Damn it. She wouldn't approve, and a part of me didn't want to disappoint her.

I'd have to venture one deck down, and steal an ID.

I stepped onto the ladder.

—••—

"Sahar," I whispered.

"Go ahead," she responded in my ear.

"Do you have access to the video feed in this area? From City Control?"

"No. It's off limits to city personnel, including the Mayor."

I needed more intel. I didn't want to encounter a guard, and then have to explain myself.

Footsteps rang on the steel deck nearby and echoed in the corridor. I pressed myself against a hatch and tried to stay out of sight, grabbed the gun on my right thigh and prepared to draw it. Then I thought better of it and switched to the knife on my left. I drew it and tested its balance.

I crouched, ready.

The steps got louder, and within seconds a figure appeared before me. He walked past, focused on the corridor before him. He turned to the right, down another corridor.

I took a hesitant step toward him. I'd have to knock him out. Perhaps take him as a prisoner, then release him in a few weeks. I swore to myself, then checked the time. I had to be back with Richard in only thirty seconds.

I took a breath, ready to strike—

Then my comm clicked. "Mac." It was Clarke, and I pulled suddenly to a stop. "You need Johnny's fake ID. It's in his PCD. The guards took it yesterday when they detained him. It's outside his cell."

"You're sure it'll work?"

"It already did, yesterday."

"Can you get it?"

A pause. "I think so. I'm close to getting him released, but we'll have to leave the labs immediately to keep up the charade."

I moved quietly to the ladder and climbed back to the upper deck, toward the Energy Beam Lab.

A few more seconds passed. "I'll get the guards to follow us to the exit. The PCD is here, on the desk outside of the cell. I'll leave it there for you."

"Where is it?"

"East of where you are. Down the long corridor marked *Security*. But it means I'll be gone and you'll be on your own in here."

It was the best we could do; there was no other choice. "Do it."

—··—

MINUTES LATER, JOHNNY WAS OUT. I could hear Richard raging at the guards now, and he was creating quite a ruckus. His voice echoed down the corridors; it wasn't just in the comm in my ear now. Then, we heard the footsteps clanging past. Richard and I hid behind the fake laser component in the lift. Clarke kept up a running narrative as they left, which gave us an idea of their location.

We sprinted down the corridor to the east. The security annex was easy to find, and a BSFRL SEC OPS sign and logo clearly identified the office. We burst in . . .

And there, on the desk, was the PCD.

Richard grinned.

—··—

THE ENERGY BEAM LAB'S HATCH sighed open as we stepped within two meters of it, automatically triggered by the ID on Johnny's PCD. Clarke had ensured that it was absolutely authentic. A part of me realized that had we planned better, he could have arranged the same for us.

But no matter. Soon we were in the labs, and staring at the laser module in the center of the chamber.

We'd made it.

A light was glaring on it from above. It looked nearly identical to the one Alyssna had created for us. At the back, the two fusion reactors were clear, but I noticed an immediate issue. Richard did too.

"The reactor brackets are different."

"They are indeed."

"They're yellow."

"I can see."

I swore. The shape of the bracket was off too, and the steel supports for the two spheres were bright yellow.

But there was nothing we could do. We had to hope that no one would investigate, or if they noticed, that they would just assume someone else had made the changes.

The reactors looked the same though. The deuterium injectors, the radio-wave generator, the power cabling . . . it was all so similar.

I turned to Richard. "Let's get it out and the decoy in."

—••—

CLARKE HADN'T LEFT. WE COULD hear him continuing to argue with the guards on the deck below us. Soon we had brought in the decoy and moved out the real laser module. We positioned the decoy the same way, stepped back, and stared at it. The light from above shone down on it, and the displays on its side twinkled and blinked exactly as the real one. Alyssna had made sure that an installed computer made the displays respond the way the real one would, although the device would not actually function.

Richard swore and said, "It's hard to see the difference. It looks so real."

"As long as it takes them four weeks before they realize, we'll be good." I hoped they didn't notice the brackets on the back. Alyssna had claimed that they weren't actually using the laser; it was strictly being stored here to protect it.

"Let's get the real one to the moonpool."

The module was on a trolley already and there was no need to use a hoist. It was heavier—Alyssna had said five hundred pounds—and it was more of a challenge to get it into the lift, but we did it quickly. Clarke continued barking complaints and commands as we worked. Thankfully, he'd had a lifetime of experience leading others, sounding commanding, and, I had no doubt, tearing underlings apart.

In the moonpool chamber, we quickly tarped the device, attached the hoist straps, lifted it over the moonpool, and lowered it into the ocean.

I watched it disappear beneath the waves and move downward to the seafloor. *SC-1* was still there, and Meg or Renée switched the floodlights back on to illuminate the region. Cliff removed the harness, and we brought the hoist back to the ceiling.

I could see Cliff guiding *SC-1* over the laser module, using hand signals and gestures, getting ready to load it into the seacar.

—••—

A minute later, we'd sealed the moonpool hatch and removed all evidence that we'd been there.

Then we marched out the front hatch of the labs. Clarke was still screaming at the guards. His face was red, there was a throbbing vein at his temple, and his victims looked rattled as his spittle flew toward them. There were six there; he'd managed to attract the entire lab's complement with his screaming.

Johnny glanced at us, and I held his PCD out to him. "You forgot this," I said in a British accent.

"Cheers, mate."

The guards glanced at the exchange, but otherwise, didn't seem to think anything of it.

We'd entered the labs with Commodore Clarke, and we were leaving together. Nothing else was amiss. The guards in the upper level assumed we'd been in the lower level, and vice versa.

I hoped, anyway.

I swore to myself as we marched away.

We'd done it.

—••—

Ten minutes later, we were in the Docking Module, aboard *SC-1*, with the entire team. Everyone was smiling. In the centre of the seacar, filling the entire space over the moonpool hatch, was the tarped laser module.

Component One.

Alyssna had unzipped the tarp and was going over the dual-reactor setup at the rear. She swore several times as she realized that hers appeared different in a number of ways, the most obvious being the painted brackets.

She was like a Mother Hen fussing over her chicks, and I smiled at the scene. She was going to get to work on the device all she wanted, once we were back at Trieste.

Clarke and Sahar were with us, and I turned to them. "We have to get back to Trieste now. The SCAV drive doesn't work, so there's no time to waste." Then I said to the others, "But I have to do one more thing here before we leave."

There were frowns at that.

"What is it?" Renée asked.

"Something we need for the next stages. For Components Two, Three, and Four."

Then I turned to Sahar. "Thank you so much for your help. We couldn't have done it without you."

I expected Sahar to say a farewell and leave, but it didn't happen.

She glanced at Clarke, then she said to me, "There's something you don't know."

"What?"

"I've spoken to the Commodore about this. He's going with you to help with *Aurora Rex*. But I'm coming too."

—••—

I FUMBLED WITH MY WORDS as I figured out what I was going to say to that. "But Sahar," I objected, "it's going to be risky."

"I'm prepared for that."

"There might be violence."

She shrugged. "Maybe. Battles, perhaps. But I hope we can avoid death. I don't desire to participate in that."

"Then maybe you should—"

"I did not help you so you could kill people *later*, Mac."

"It's not something I *want* to do, Sahar."

"I don't mean that. But I've contributed to the theft of this component. Now there are three more to complete. The only reason we can do those three is that we did this one. If people die, then it will be on my conscience." She crossed her arms. "I can't have that."

I exhaled and considered it. "I can't promise anything."

"But you can try. If that's the best I can get, then so be it. But I will be there at your side for this. Make no mistake."

I stared at the determination in her face. Then I looked at the others, and they had curious expressions on their faces. Renée in particular looked impressed with Sahar, and that was enough for me. "Very well, Sahar. Welcome to the team."

She grinned. "I thought I was already on it."

—··—

I was back in my civilian clothing—cargo pants and a black t-shirt—and I marched through the Living Module toward the cubicle.

The partition slid aside at my knock, revealing a man rubbing his blurry eyes.

"Hello, Chalam," I said. "Are you ready for an adventure?"

The young geologist stared at me. His face showed confusion. "Pardon me?"

I paused, and then, "We're going to steal the weapon you told us about."

Chalam Kaashif immediately straightened, and his expression grew hard. "Are you serious?"

"As a heart attack."

"But how—"

"We've already started." Then I waited a moment before, "It gets better."

"I don't—"

They'd killed his brother and their two companions, so I knew this would make his decision easier. "How would you like revenge for what they did to you?"

Now his eyes turned to embers. "I would like that very much, Mac. And I'm going to kill them for what they did."

Interlude: The Mid-Atlantic Ridge

One Year Earlier

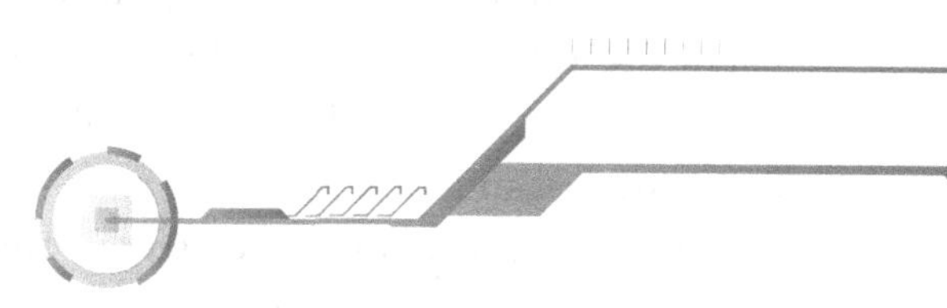

DATA PROCESSING

Interlude:	The Mid-Atlantic Ridge
Date:	March 2130 AD
Depth:	3,282 meters
Latitude:	27° 55″ 13′ S
Longitude:	17° 35″ 43′ W
Time:	2118 hours

MAC HAD GIVEN THE ORDER to attack, and Katherine Wells and her squad of armed seacars aimed down into the Rift, sighted the FSF and USSF forces, increased speed, locked onto targets, and fired. The results were instantaneous. The enemy warsubs ejected countermeasures, began to evade, and returned fire.

There were torpedoes, mines, countermeasures, and multiple smaller and faster seacars cluttering the battlefield. Large explosions overwhelmed the listening sensors, distorting and blanketing the sonar display in *SC-1*'s pilot cabin with white flashes. Their attack surprised the warsub crews, however, and many took massive impacts that exceeded their hull integrity.

Some imploded immediately.

Others ended up with gaping and jagged holes in their sides, taking on water, trailing bubbles, and spinning downward to Crush Depth. The battle was taking place at or close to that depth anyway, and one warsub after another stuttered to a stop, shuddered in its death throes, and began to descend.

The implosions further cluttered the sonar. Debris flashed across the canopy, currents of oil drifted upward, and there were even bodies floating about, explosions shoving their limbs around like rag dolls. Bedsheets and clothes and plastic and plates and equipment and pieces of paper clouded the water.

Kat veered from the enemy warsubs as their torpedoes made contact. At her side, her two companions were making a running commentary about the battle. Then the sonar alarm rang out, and Kat's eyes went wide. She slammed the throttle to full and swore.

"Mac!" she cried.

"What's wrong?" He was far below, in The Rift, on the other side of the FSF and USSF forces.

"Torpedo on my tail!" she blurted, trying to evade.

"Hit the SCAV! Get out—"

Kat swore again and said to her companions, "I'm trying my best. He forgot we don't have the SCAV." She evaded by powering dangerously close to the cliff face on the east side of the massive canyon. She pulled away—

And the torpedo detonated.

"Remember, you have no companions but your shadow."
—Genghis Khan

Part Four: Second Component

Chapter Eighteen

WE ARRIVED BACK AT TRIESTE on 22 March. The journey from Churchill had taken five days because the SCAV drive was down. In a way it was a long five days, because there was still so much to do, and spending unnecessary time traveling was tedious, but it was also a nice period to unwind and plan the upcoming operations in the South Pacific and the Indian Ocean.

I also spent time with Renée, which was a break from what we'd been through over the days leading up to the heist in Churchill. There were eight of us on board *SC-1*, along with the large laser pack just aft of the living area, and there wasn't much space. There were two recessed bunks in the bulkheads just aft of the pilot cabin, and two couches, but otherwise there wasn't a lot of room to lie down. Renée and I found time, as lovers do, and we had sex where we could. We kept quiet, however, which was difficult, but we didn't want to be disrespectful.

I'm not sure what Sahar would have thought, had she found out. Would she have understood the cultural differences and tolerated it? Or would it have made her furious?

Renée and I didn't want to find out, so we kept our lovemaking slow and quiet. That was nice, too. The orgasms were even more intense.

We had set up a space in the engineering compartment for a bit of privacy, but it didn't change the fact that things were cramped.

I was most concerned about Sahar, who deserved and needed privacy, but she endured the voyage like a trooper. In some ways, in fact, she didn't just "endure" it—she loved it. She was on the adventure of a lifetime, she'd stated, and had a smile on her face during most of the trip to Trieste. She kept up her prayers, and Meg and Renée even joined her at times, mostly to meditate and show welcoming companionship and inclusion.

Cliff, Meg, Johnny, and I spent the time piloting—our max speed was only 70 kph—and we plowed our way through the Atlantic toward the warm Gulf waters.

Chalam was intense. He was happy to be on board and embark on the mission, but he kept to himself and valued privacy. He was still processing what had happened to him. I was worried about what he'd say to Alyssna or Sahar—who didn't want to cause any death—but he avoided the others as best he could. He set up a space in the SCAV compartment, behind engineering, and mostly stayed there.

Finally, we arrived, and Sahar stared out the canopy with wide eyes at the crystal clear water and the sunlight shimmering downward, bathing the modules of the city in its glow. I'd once described the scene as an Island of Light, a description more apt at nighttime, when the floodlights around the modules illuminated the city and it glowed like a massive diamond in the darkness.

I'd seen a recent photograph of Trieste at nighttime as viewed from orbit. The glow from under the water was unmistakable. The individual modules were clear, as were the transparent travel tubes, and all around the world, the underwater colonies were growing. Politicians everywhere had planned new ones. What had once been an ambitious experiment had proven itself a thousand times over now. The resources sent topside were just too important, and while that was a positive for continued colony existence, it also sent a warning to the independence movement: Nations would fight it, more vigorously than ever before.

As for those underwater cities destroyed six months ago—Blue Downs and Seascape—engineers had rebuilt them in the same footprints; their mother nations were desperate for the influx of much-needed resources and couldn't go without for much longer. The colonizing nations were going to use both cities for farming and fishing; Seascape, which at one point had been strictly for tourists, now had a new purpose for the topsiders.

Trieste was a sight for sore eyes, and my heart pounded as it appeared from the shadow of distant waters. It was like a mirage taking solid form before our eyes. Sahar gasped and mouthed something in Arabic as she stared at the city.

"It's my home," I whispered. "I love it here."

"It's so beautiful. Look at the fish, the seacars and kelp!"

"You can really see things here in this water."

"The currents aren't as strong?"

I nodded. "Yes, and the sand doesn't get stirred up as much. That being said, high waves at the surface during storms affect us, and this region is prone to hurricanes. They don't harm us, but they do have an impact. Navigation is more difficult, divers have to stay tethered to the modules, they need to carry floodlights with them to see in serious events, and we have rescue teams on high alert."

"Are the storms bad?"

"During hurricane season, from May to December, we're in their path. Doesn't mean they hit us every year though, but the season is much longer than it used to be."

It was because of the warming waters, of course. A hurricane required warm ocean water to generate the intense energy that drove their winds and spawned tornadoes within its furious embrace. The warmer the water, the worse the storms. The latent energy from evaporation emerged in the atmosphere in the counter-clockwise churning monsters, driving faster winds and generating more precipitation. The energy released from condensation in those beasts boggled the mind.

And they'd been growing worse since the 20th Century. At first the storms had been flashing warning signs. The Galveston disaster in 1900, then Andrew and Mitch and Katrina. Cyclone Tracy in Australia destroyed an entire town—Darwin. A serious danger signal of the escalating issue were storms like Allen and Dorian. Both had exceeded the Category Five designation, prompting meteorologists to suggest adding a Category Six. Eventually that did happen, and now they were suggesting a theoretical max Cat Seven.

It made me shiver.

I was happy to live underwater.

——••——

WITHIN HOURS OF ARRIVING, CLIFF met with his investigation team, and I made sure to get an update afterward. We were in my office, just off City Control, where I'd been catching up on city business. The office was all steel with a small viewport, there was a pile of stuff to do on my desk, as well as a full inbox to deal with, but walking in put a smile on my face that no amount of work could dampen. I loved it.

"My team has looked into the carbon monoxide attack on you and Renée," Cliff said as he sat in the chair across from me. He dwarfed the chair and seemed to spill from it; the muscles on his arms rippled. He'd been working out more and more since the events at Seascape, when Zyvinski had arrested him and Meg and tortured them for weeks. They'd broken his leg, but it had since healed, and his limp was now nearly gone.

"They've reviewed the video?"

"There were a lot of people in the area. Divers were coming and going constantly over the previous days. It's difficult to make out who brought tanks in, moved them, and so on. Your masks too. The cameras weren't in positions to get a good view of your lockers. Sometimes large crowds were there. A class even had a field trip and that's where they exited and returned. It was a big crowd of people milling about. Not just kids . . . staff, teachers, and other civilian volunteers."

I grunted. The schools were located in the Living Modules. "So, no luck."

He shrugged. "I do have a list. But it's long, and not helpful."

"Did you cross check it with the people working in the mining division?" We had thought that the culprit likely had access to the blasting explosives, because the first attempt on me had been an explosion.

He blinked as if my suggestion insulted him. "Of course, Boss. Nothing really stands out."

"Really?"

"Well, nothing believable, anyway."

I sighed. "Keep at it."

"You know what will make it easier? When there's another attempt on you. Then maybe I'll get more evidence."

I stared at him. "You're being sarcastic."

"Of course. I want you to take a guard."

"I told you I'd think about it."

"Are you?"

"Yes," I lied.

"You've had days to consider it."

"I still am."

He stared at me, clearly aware that I was just putting him off.

———••———

AFTER A FEW HOURS DEALING with issues in the city—the farms need-ed more equipment, the mining division needed more prospectors, and a malfunction in a fish fence allowed a million Red Snapper to escape into the Gulf, the lucky bastards—and eventually I set things aside to get Johnny. Together we marched through the Commerce Module to a café. The atrium was nine levels—four above bedrock, five below—and lit by a skylight above which allowed natural light to flood in. Around each balcony were vines intertwined with the metal spindles, provid-ing much-needed greenery. Flowers were rare in underwater cities, though I recalled there'd been one on Sahar's desk when I first met her. Businesses and offices circled the atrium, and many of the food service ones were cafés, and pubs.

Chalam was sitting at a table, looking over the railing at the atrium.

He smiled when we arrived and gestured for us to take seats. "Mac, Johnny, nice to see you again."

"I didn't see much of you on the trip here," I said. "Strange to achieve such a feat on a small seacar."

He looked abashed. "I am still mourning my brother. Trying to pro-cess what happened."

"I understand."

"I also feel . . . guilt."

That surprised me. "But why?"

He sighed and stared down. He didn't respond for a long minute. Then he looked back up, letting the sunlight touch his face. "This is re-ally nice, Mac. The sun shining down through the module, even though we're thirty meters under water."

"Planners designed it to let light get into every business, all the way to the first level."

"It worked."

I remained quiet. He sipped his coffee, then looked down again. "I was in the seacar and the hull was shimmering. Something was eating away at it. I instinctively *knew* it was about to give way. The pressure was going to get us. I have no idea how it happened though, or what it was. You said it was some kind of weapon that vaporized the water. A welding weapon of some sort."

I remembered his story. I shuddered. It must have been terrifying. He still didn't know the terrible truth of what had killed them.

He continued. "I rushed to the airlock. Grabbed scuba gear. I was frantic. I knew we only had seconds. I called to the others—" He choked off his words, and his lips were trembling. "I—I—"

"Go on."

He stared at me. "I can't remember if I warned the others to get their scuba gear on, Mac. I pulled my mask on, and then I saw the blue lights flash. The water flooded in—" He took a deep breath and exhaled slowly. "It's the last thing I remember, before waking up in the BSF warsub."

I frowned. "You did the best you could. Manse's girlfriend was piloting. The other woman was sleeping. You had to get your mask on first before you could offer help, Chalam."

"I don't think I warned them enough," he murmured. "I—I can't remember what I said, in fact."

Johnny said, "There's nothing more you could have done."

"My brother was lying there, passed out, his stump bleeding. There was a pile of bloody liquid—liquid flesh and fat—on the deck! I needed to get a mask on him, and a tank. But I didn't."

"How could you? The ocean flooded in."

"Still," he muttered. Another long series of heartbeats. "But then something just as terrible happened. No one would listen to me. No one believed me. *Or*, they knew what had happened and they ignored me. Except Mayor Noor. She listened to me. But it didn't change anything. They're all still dead." His eyes hardened. "But you're going to help me get revenge now, Mac." A sick smile spread across his face. "I think it'll make me feel better."

"It won't, actually. Just be prepared for that."

He looked shocked. "What do you mean?"

I shrugged. "I've dealt with it a lot. It won't bring Manse back. It won't solve anything."

"It'll make the people responsible pay."

"If you say so, but they don't care. They're just doing a job for their superiors."

"And who's that, exactly?"

An image of a red and black logo flashed through my brain. "The BSFRL, I think. Or someone associated with them." At his quizzical look, I added, "The Research Lab arm of the BSF." But there was something else to this too, I thought. Something else was going on here . . .

His jaw dropped. "The BSF did this? I'm a British citizen though!"

"Yes. But they are testing their weapon. You were in the open water." I shrugged. "I think you were likely too close to their facility. They saw it as an opportunity to test The Water Pick."

He stared at me. "Water Pick?"

"It's a nickname."

"How do you know so much about it?"

I glanced at Johnny and took a deep breath. "Chalam, the inventor told me."

"And who—"

"Alyssna Sonstraal. She was on the seacar with us."

His face showed shock at first, then it slowly flattened. He was showing little emotion now, like a robot. "I met her?"

"Of course. We were all there. She's going on the mission with us."

"To get revenge?"

I shook my head. "To steal the device. That's where we're going. We need you."

He looked away, pondering that. "Why does she want it, if she invented it?"

Johnny said, "She lost access to the project. She wants to keep working on it."

I stared at him, wondering how he'd take this news. We needed his help, but couldn't afford to have his anger fester within the team. However, he also needed to know the truth.

"I'm—I'm not sure what to think," he muttered. "Her invention killed my brother." His tone had turned to ice.

"Are you still interested in helping us?" I asked.

"Can I still get revenge?"

"I told you, that won't help you. It doesn't help you deal with grief. But, I promise we are going to take the weapon from them. It'll hurt them where it counts."

He looked horrified. "That's your version of *revenge*?"

"In a way. You are your own person. You can do what you want. But we're going to steal this device from them. Take it away. Then we'll have it, and we'll use it if necessary. Are you willing to tell us where they hit your seacar? The *exact* location?"

He paused and stared at me. "I will. But not yet. Not now. When we get there."

That startled me. "You don't trust me?"

"It's not that." Pause. "I don't want to get sidelined here. I want to be a part of it. I want to be right where it happened." He hesitated again, then said, "I'll tell you when it's time. I promise. Now, answer my question."

I stared into his eyes for a long moment, then I shot a look at Johnny. "The answer is yes, if that's what you want."

"Good. Because I'm going to kill the people responsible."

Does that included Alyssna Sonstraal?, I wanted to add. *And what will Sahar say about this?* But I didn't. I rose and said, "Let's go meet someone."

—••—

CHALAM STARED OUT THE VIEWPORTS and the transparent travel tubes as we marched though the city toward the Research Module. He kept muttering under his breath, his eyes wide, and wonderment clear in his face. I understood exactly what he was feeling.

"The water is clearer here," I said.

Johnny added, "It's pretty wonderful, isn't it?"

"Mac, it's better than that." He shook his head. "All our lives, Manse and I wanted to live under the water. We chose geology so we could make an impact at Churchill Sands. But this . . ." He trailed off, staring at a seacar as it powered over the travel tube. His eyes followed it the whole way. "This is what we'd envisioned, but it's not what Churchill is like at all."

I shrugged. "We have rough weather here too, sometimes. Churns everything up."

"But the colors here . . . the fish . . . " His eyes darted about as he stared. "I could get used to this."

I smiled. "I've been here since the early 2090s."

He turned to me. "I know your history, of course. You don't have to—"

"It's okay. I won't. But I have to be honest with you." I struggled to decide how to say it. I swallowed. "I used the concept of revenge to lure you to this. But the truth is, revenge really isn't a force for healing."

He looked shocked. "But surely we're going back to the Indian Ocean, right?"

"Eventually, yes."

"What does that mean?"

I glanced around. Triestrians were wandering past us, traveling the other way in the tube, and many were waving and making comments to me. Children high-fived me. "It's not the place to explain. Wait three more minutes."

"But I'm going to get close to those responsible, right?"

"Absolutely, if all goes well. But what I'm *trying* to say is that revenge is an anchor that drags you down. It doesn't make life easier. It makes it harder. I want you to trust me when I say this. I have extensive experience."

He was still staring at me. "Because of your dad?"

I grunted. He knew history. "Yes."

"Did you and Meg eventually get revenge?"

"I forgave the killer. Meg didn't."

"And who is better off?"

I considered that. "We both have our issues. But she's been through more hardship because of it than I have."

He nodded and looked away.

———•••———

SOON WE WERE AT THE hatch and it slid aside at my request. Doctor Max Hyland was inside, at a holoscreen, dictating code to the AI. He turned to us and a huge smile split his face. He rose and practically leaped toward me to give me a huge hug.

"Mac!" he cried. Then he turned to Johnny, who got a similar greeting. Then to Chalam he said, "It's great to finally meet you, the famous geologist!"

The other looked abashed. "I don't have my PhD yet, Doctor. I'm still a student."

"You're a university professor and an instructor. That makes you a legend."

Chalam chuckled. "If you say so."

The two had already been collaborating for me on a side project that was soon to become our team's main focus. They'd been conversing via video feed, but now it was time to bring the two face to face so they could solidify our plans.

"Are you here for a while?" Max asked. He was in his forties with dark hair and dimples. His enthusiasm and good spirit were infectious. The ladies found him very attractive, as did some men, I had learned. And Max was receptive to both.

"Until we leave again, yes," I said "But I hope you'll be coming with us then."

He blinked. "Me?"

"Yes. To put into action what you two have been working on."

"I see."

"Can you fill me and Johnny in?"

He walked back to the holoscreen, motioning for us to follow. "Yes, come see." He quickly brought up a 3D projected map of the Indian Ocean. He zoomed into one area, and the joint USSF/ BSF underwater warsub base Diego Garcia centered in the image. To the east was a massive geologic feature. The isobath lines—cartographers called them *contour lines* on land, but this was underwater—identified a massive trench. They stretched north and south and were very close together, but they never crossed—one of the cardinal rules of such lines that signified elevation, or in this case, depth below sea level.

He said, "This is the Chagos Trench. Chalam has educated me about it." Max moved the image and Diego Garcia disappeared off to the edge as he brought the trench into focus.

I stared at the feature. "It's striking, that's for sure."

"And it has all three tectonic boundaries. It's unique in the world. It is part of a major region that is tectonically active." An oval shape appeared, stretching to the east and nearly touching Sumatra, part of Indonesia. An area just off Sumatra's coast flashed red. "This is the location of one of the most devastating quakes in human history. December, 2004. It was a 9.1 Richter quake on the boundary with the Sunda Plate that spawned a tsunami that killed nearly 230,000 people. One hundred and seventy thousand alone died in Sumatra. Many others were in Sri Lanka and Thailand."

"The Burma Microplate, to be precise," Chalam muttered under his breath.

"I know this disaster," Johnny said. "I've heard of it. The Boxing Day Tsunami, right?"

Chalam said, "Yes. The entire region is active. A subduction zone caused it. One section of crust sliding under another. The tension builds over time. Pretty much the entire Ring of Fire around the Pacific Ocean is one long Subduction Boundary. Eventually it gives way, and the crust moves meters in only seconds. It displaces water at the surface which spreads like ripples in a pond. They're not wind-driven waves. They're displacement waves. Unstoppable. That's the tsunami."

"Go on," I pressed.

"A section of the crust nearly 1,500 kilometers moved. Whole islands shifted. Cartographers had to redraw maps. It was a natural event, of course, but the consequences on human lives around the Indian Ocean were monstrous. Sections of the crust rose forty meters. This is what caused the water displacement. The wave that hit Indonesia was thirty meters high."

I swallowed. That height was the same depth of Trieste *under* the water. It was difficult to conceptualize a wave that high hitting a populated area.

"The last people to get hit died eight hours later, if you can believe it. Happened in South Africa."

"But how—"

"There was no tsunami warning system in the Indian Ocean." A shrug. "They simply didn't know it was coming." He paused for a moment. "There was another one in 2011 which caused the Japanese Tsunami and the resulting meltdown at Fukushima Nuclear Plant. That one was so large it shortened the length of our day. Japan moved two meters. Both of these quakes were due to Subduction Boundaries." Chalam paused and stared at the map. Then he indicated another location on the map, near to the first. Another red light flashed. "Then came this quake, here, on April 11, 2012. Very similar in size, in the same general region as the Boxing Day Quake, also just off the west coast of Sumatra. It was 8.7 on the Richter Scale. People were immediately concerned about the quake. They thought it would spawn another tsunami."

"Did it?"

He shook his head. "The wave was only thirty centimeters."

"But you said it was a quake nearly the same size and in the same location."

"That's why it caused so much interest," he said. His eyes were glowing now, he was in his element. "That's why Manse and I were there. Well, partly, anyway. There are multiple boundary types in the Chagos Trench, which is weird. Well, turns out that boundary wasn't a Subduction boundary! It was a Transform Boundary!"

Silence met his comment. Johnny and I just stared.

He continued, "One crust doesn't move under another there. Instead, they grind past each other! A Strike-Slip, like the San Andreas Fault in California."

"So, there's no tension?"

"There's a lot of tension! The crust plates get caught up with each other. Over years the tension grows, then it gives way. The crusts move relative to each other, causing the quake."

I frowned. "I don't understand. It sounds the same as—"

"Yes, but there's no displacement of the water at the surface. Well, no massive displacement, anyway. Just a bit. Everyone was expecting this massive wave that never materialized."

Max was watching the presentation. He said, "Chalam and I have been going over this area for the past week or so, Mac. I don't really know why yet, though."

I said, "Are you familiar with the area now? The trench?"

A shrug. "I'm not a geologist, but I guess so."

I glanced at Johnny, then, "We're going on a mission. You two are coming with us. We're going to steal a weapon from the British Submarine Fleet. We already have the first component. A laser pack."

Chalam's face hardened. "Is that what killed my brother?"

"Not really." I took a breath. "A ten-terawatt laser blast encloses the real weapon. It creates a vacuum channel, or pathway, through the water to the target. We stole the ten lasers five days ago in Churchill. That component was in the seacar on the way here, covered by a tarp. But now we're going for the other three components."

Max Hyland's eyebrows raised. The notion shocked him. "Where are they?"

"One is on board a BSF warsub in the South Pacific. The other two are here." I pointed at the map of the Indian Ocean.

"Is that the weapon?" Chalam growled. He'd been waiting to hear this for a while now, and I knew it was time to tell him. "You said it was something that vaporized water. A welding weapon of some sort. Well, a ten-terawatt laser pack would definitely qualify."

"That just creates the channel, or the void."

Max was a physicist, and he knew how unique this was. "A vacuum pathway, underwater? *Contained?*"

"By the lasers, as long as they're firing, yes."

"Incredible."

"What's incredible is what fires down the vacuum channel." I paused and then, "It's a neutral beam."

Max's face paled. "A neutral beam? Underwater?"

"Yes. Sustained."

He swore. "What's the range?"

"Only a few hundred meters. Two hundred at the most, I think. Doctor Sonstraal can answer that for you. It depends on—"

"Likely the temperature, salinity, suspended sediment," Max interjected.

"The weapon is dynamic apparently, altering its wavelength based on those variables. It doesn't have a great range, but it is deadly against warsubs. And more efficient and reliable than torpedoes." I watched Chalam as I said this. He was furious.

"This killed my brother. As well as Kalinda and Preet."

Max was watching the other's expression. "Are you serious?"

"It happened a few weeks ago. I want revenge against those responsible."

I sighed at that, but pressed on, "We're going to steal it. We leave in two days. But before we do, we need to lock down our plans."

"How does that involve me?" Max asked.

"And me?" Chalam said.

I turned to Max. "We need some Isomer Bombs for this mission, Max. I hope you have built a few for us." Then to Chalam, "And only you know where the base is. The modules you discovered on the seafloor, at a depth of 500 meters. That was the secret facility. That's where Doctor Sonstraal and her team were developing The Water Pick."

Max said, "You're sure it was a neutral beam?"

I said, "Absolutely. Chalam was an eyewitness. And I need both of you for this mission. Your participation is crucial. Are you with us?"

Chapter Nineteen

CHALAM'S FACE HAD PALED AND he stared at me. "So a . . . *neutral beam* vaporized the water and dissolved our hull? And melted my brother's hand?"

"The laser vaporized the water. The beam just passed through the void, straight to your seacar. And it didn't melt the hull, or your brother's hand."

Max said, "Neutrons would have knocked the protons out of atoms. Pushed molecules apart. Shoved electrons aside. Technically not melting from heat. Just . . . disassociating atoms. Dissolving them." He frowned and looked away. "Someone invented this weapon?"

"She's here, with us now," Johnny said. "She's coming with us to steal it back."

"And what happens then?"

"She's going to stay here and work with us."

"She's been here for weeks already," Johnny added. "Working with us."

"Incredible," Max breathed. Then he straightened and faced us. "Count me in. I want to be a part of this. I need to learn more. And if this weapon will help us protect Trieste, then absolutely I want to participate."

Chalam was watching the exchange. "I don't understand why we need to know about the Trench though, Mac. I've been teaching Max about it. Neither the base nor Diego Garcia are in it. They're farther to the west."

"You two are part of the plan to get the Third and Fourth Components from The Vault. We definitely need to know the geology of the area in order to steal them. But the Second Component is next, and it's on board the *Aurora Rex*."

"What are the components?" Max asked.

I thought back to Alyssna's lesson. "The Second one is the Staging System, to feed power to each part of the weapon. The Third is the Aiming Module, and the Fourth is The Accelerator."

"And these three with the ten lasers is the . . . *The Water Pick?*"

"Exactly."

Chalam said, "You don't have to ask me again." He glanced at Max. "We're both in."

—••—

Johnny and I left Chalam in the lab to continue planning with Max, who guaranteed that he'd have more Isomer Bombs ready for us. He'd have them loaded in *SC-1* and ready to go in two days. Meanwhile he was also going to keep working with Chalam on the geology of the region.

Johnny said, "The big issue at the moment is *Aurora Rex*," he said. "How are we going to locate her?"

"That's the Commodore," I replied. "He should be able to tell us where she is. We're going to go to Blue Downs in two days and launch the next operation from there."

I had planned to go meet Alyssna in her lab, just a few decks away from Hyland's. Johnny went on to his office to deal with city business, and he was also going to make sure *SC-1* was ready for the upcoming voyage.

Alyssna had already arranged for the Laser Module's transport, and sure enough, inside, I found her fawning over the weapon. She was connecting cables to sensors and computers and was running a variety of diagnostics.

"I can't believe what those morons have done here," she snapped, barely looking up at me.

"Does it work?" I asked.

"Of course, but the efficiency is down. It's not detecting the water conditions as quickly as it was before. And the wavelength transducer is off. I'm not sure why they made these changes. I have to adjust everything."

"Care to chat for a bit? I can have some coffee delivered?"

She finally looked at me, as if realizing for the first time that I was in her lab. She smiled and straightened. "I'm sorry, Mac. Of course, that would be nice."

We moved to a seating area in the corner and I called a local café. I looked around; her lab was really taking shape, especially with the massive laser pack in the center. The device seemed to pulse with power. The lasers arranged around the barrel—currently a void space waiting for The Accelerator—looked deadly. "Don't turn it on by accident," I muttered. No doubt a ten-terawatt blast would instantly melt the bulkhead to the exterior.

"It has safety measures built in."

"Good." We made small talk while waiting for the coffees. Alyssna was happy in Trieste and had already seen many improvements over her previous working situation. Here, she was her own boss. I had given her total freedom.

Coffee arrived and we sipped it, practically in the shadow of the lasers. "This would impress your dad, I think," I said. It had been a calculated comment, and sure enough, her face froze.

She stared at me. "I doubt it."

"I have had to deal with my own issues regarding our own father. Meg and I, both. He destroyed our lives." I'd already told her about it, on *SC-1*. "It was only recently that we fully reconnected."

"And restarted the independence movement."

I shook my head. "Actually, that never stopped. I didn't realize it. But when I took over Trieste City Intelligence, I had a distinct advantage over my dad."

Her eyes showed her confusion. "What?"

"The SCAV drive. Nations are desperate to get it. It gave us a major advantage in battles. That's been the impetus for independence now."

"I see."

"But your invention is going to be the next catalyst for us. And you created it, Alyssna."

"I did." She nodded. "But it wouldn't impress my dad."

"Why not?"

"For the same reason he was *never* impressed. I was born a girl."

A long silence descended over us. I had known this was a difficult topic for her. She stared at her laser for long minutes. Finally, "You want to talk to me about my dad. But I asked you a question that you ignored too, Mac. Would *you* like to talk about it now?"

That genuinely confused me. "Pardon?"

"Remember, a while back I asked you about Katherine Wells. I asked you how she died. You said you buried her at sea but wouldn't say more. *No comment*, you said."

"Ah." I leaned back. I wanted Alyssna to open up to me, to feel a part of the team. I said, "She was with us during a battle in the Mid-Atlantic Ridge. We call it the Third Battle of Trieste."

"I've never heard of it."

"It's not common knowledge. We obliterated a fleet of USSF and FSF warsubs. They were trying to locate our base there. Captain Heller of the USSF wanted to kill me."

She looked shocked. "And you won?"

"We destroyed ninety-eight USSF vessels. Killed Heller. We destroyed double that number of FSF warsubs."

"Bullshit."

"It happened, because of the SCAV drive and our deep-diving tech, called the APD. We can descend to over 6,000 meters with it. We only had some fifty armed seacars to do it."

Her eyes were wide.

"And now The Water Pick is going to add to our arsenal. We're going to be a serious power."

"I'd say you already are." Pause. "But how did Kat die?"

I sighed. "She was in *SC-1*. A torpedo detonated too close. Her control console exploded in her face. Shrapnel impaled her."

"And have you recovered?" She studied me. "You're with Renée now, so you must have."

"A part of me will always remember her." I exhaled. "It's been tough to get over. I spent a while suffering. Renée helped me, and I fell in love with her."

She nodded slightly at that.

"I don't jump from relationship to relationship," I explained. "I didn't love anyone until Kat. I was forty-four at the time. I fell hard for her."

"She was kind and loving?"

"She was. But there's more." At her raised eyebrow, I said, "She was *fierce*. Fiery. She argued with me a lot. She was hard to keep happy. She had her own plans and ideas, and I was always trying to modify mine to compromise. It bothered me at first, but I fell in love with the process, and with her. We were better as a pair than apart, I think."

"Renée is like that too, I've noticed."

I thought about the past, how Renée had spent a year trying to find and kill me. I snorted, and Alyssna raised an eyebrow again. "She is, actually. Funny that you say that."

"Thanks for telling me about Kat."

"Where's your dad now?"

She stopped suddenly, her face growing dark. But she said, "I don't know, Mac. He might be dead. When I left Zambia, I left forever. I studied at Cambridge and never looked back. I don't care, frankly, where he is. He was never a father to me."

"Maybe not in spirit, but the impact is always there."

"Meaning?" Her eyes flared.

I shrugged. "Just that those relationships—regardless of how we view them—play a role in who we are and what we become." I pointed at the laser, growling with power under the lights. "Look at that, Alyssna! It wouldn't exist if it wasn't for your dad."

"*I* did that, Mac. Not my father."

"But if your father hadn't rejected you, would it exist? Would you have built it? Would you even be an engineer?"

She stopped at that and stared at me. I couldn't tell if it was in anger, or self-realization.

She said nothing more.

—••—

I HAD A BREAK IN my schedule after visiting Alyssna, which I found shocking, because my work at Trieste never seemed to end. There were forty-five minutes before my next meeting with the City Control staff for a monthly update on procedures and to review any new issues. After taking a quick scan of the agenda, I saw that Grant Bell wanted to provide an update about the increasing traffic around Seascape, which came up nearly every meeting, Joey Zen wanted to address a pressure control issue in one of the travel tubes, Melissa Larret had an issue with the mining vehicles not following departure procedures, Germaine Kraft had an update on the city's sonar systems, and a work crew foreperson was going to update everyone on the repairs to the torpedo launcher that the explosion had damaged a few weeks earlier.

Forty-five minutes seemed an eternity for me, so I called Renée to see if she could meet at a café near City Control.

"Actually, it's time for my swim," she said over the comm on the bulkhead just outside of Alyssna's office. "Care to join me?"

"I'd love to," I said without hesitation. "Our last one didn't work out so well."

"Funny."

"Where are you?"

"The airlock near my living compartment. I'm just getting changed."

"I'll be right there." A sudden thought occurred to me, and I added, "Can I bring Sahar? I want to give her a tour outside." I recalled how the fish and colors outside had amazed her.

"Absolutely! She'll love it."

I signed off and signalled Sahar. She'd been exploring the city with Richard, and she immediately said yes, with enthusiasm.

Five minutes later we were at the Living Module airlock. There was a seating area just outside with a wall of lockers; each resident in that section had their own. I had to carry my own tank, regulator, full face mask, and wetsuit in, and Sahar had her own equipment, which she was already wearing. The hood covered her hair. She had a massive smile on her face; she couldn't wait to float among the incredible variety of wildlife she'd been watching from inside just a few minutes earlier. Perhaps she'd take the opportunity to pray.

We checked each other's tanks and equipment and moved into the airlock.

"Richard didn't want to let me go," Sahar said. "He was giving me the most wonderful tour. I just couldn't resist your offer though."

Renée asked, "What did he show you?"

"The central atrium was *magnificent*. It was simply amazing, especially with the sun overhead. We also went through some travel tubes. He even showed me the nuclear plant, which you moved underground after The Battle in 2129."

I chuckled. Leave it to Richard to tie in a tour with his view of the necessary changes for the independence movement. "He feels it's too dangerous to leave power plants exposed to attack."

"They hit it in the fighting?"

I nodded. "Targeted it to make us surrender."

"It's a good idea, actually," she replied.

"The strategy to hurt us, or the burying of the plant?"

"Both."

The inner hatch slid shut and we all locked eyes to make sure we were prepared. Going out was second nature now, but we could never let our guard down. There were still so many dangers, including the pressure, air supply, nitrogen narcosis, fast moving vehicles, marine life, and more.

We stood there waiting for the water to flood in from the deck up.

I looked down after a few seconds.

There was no water.

I heard a few clicks in the environmental equipment. "It seems to be taking longer than normal—"

Then finally water began to flood around our flippers and rise up our legs. It was warm and comforting, and Sahar smiled. "It's much different than the Channel!"

Her enthusiasm made me smile too.

The water rose to the ceiling and I faced the outer hatch, waiting.

It didn't open.

Chapter Twenty

"What's happening?" Renée asked.

It was a cramped chamber, with three of us in there, and we didn't have a lot of room to move. Normally the outer hatch would have slid aside immediately after the lock had flooded.

On the inner control pad, I hit the OPEN button, but it flashed a warning. "It says it can't open because there's no water in the lock."

"Clearly there is," she responded.

"Malfunction." I hit the button again, but still nothing happened. "I could risk trying to open the inner hatch." I looked at the others. If it worked, it meant we'd slide back *into* the corridor, swept in by the water already in the lock. Not incredibly dangerous, but I risked some contusions or bruises. I didn't especially want to do that to Renée or Sahar.

"Try it," Sahar said. "I can handle it."

They grabbed pipes welded to the bulkheads and braced themselves for the surge.

I pushed the inner hatch button, but it didn't work either. "It says it can't open because there's water in the lock." I snorted. "It can't make up its mind."

"Sounds like a minor sensor issue," Renée said.

"The problem is, we're trapped in here now." I pulled out my PCD to call Kristen and get her to send a repair crew.

Renée was staring at her communications device.

I glanced back at my comm. Kristen had responded and notified me that a crew was on their way to the exterior hatch. "They should be here in only three minutes." I glanced up at the others. "Can we survive until then?" I smiled.

"No problem at all," Sahar said. "These little accidents always happen at Churchill too."

I appreciated her minimizing the issue, but a chill traced down my spine and my blood had gone cold.

—··—

THIRTY MINUTES LATER, AFTER GIVING Sahar a whirlwind tour of the exterior, I was standing in the corridor, dripping water onto the deck grating, and speaking with Cliff Sim, who had come to investigate the issue. The work crew had freed us from the airlock, but during the rest of the time I had my guard up. The hair on my neck was standing on end, and I found it impossible to relax and enjoy the experience.

Renée and Sahar had continued the tour; I had to get to the City Control meeting. I made sure there was a security crew watching them, just in case.

"This doesn't feel like an accident," I said.

"I agree, Boss." Cliff peered into the chamber. A work crew had dismantled the panel and had attached some diagnostic readers to the wiring within. "It might have been an attempt on you again. Pin you inside, let your air run out."

I shrugged. "But it was easy to contact you. It doesn't feel like a serious attempt."

"Still, we should look into it."

"Let me know what you discover."

—··—

MY MEETING WAS ROUTINE. WE identified solutions to some of the issues, we agreed to try other strategies with some of the persistent ones, and some items were just updates for general knowledge by the team in City Control. They were the heart that kept the city running, and I appreciated the efforts that each and every one of them made.

The next thing on my agenda said, "Update on Social" and it made me smile. It meant a meeting with Richard about the mission, but Kristen knew that nothing related to TCI or independence could be on official agendas. Instead, we used a reference to the "Social Committee" or "Retirement Socials," or something similar, to indicate a strategy gathering.

I met Richard in my office and we sat together. He was looking good. He was an older man, but still in very good shape. His arms showed good tone for his age, and he held himself with a regal air.

"How are things?" I asked. "I heard you showed Sahar around."

"Yes, she loved Trieste. She left early for your swim though."

I nodded. "She enjoyed it too, once we got outside."

He looked at his notepad. "Things are moving quickly on the mission. The Commodore is going to be here in just a minute to provide an update."

I raised an eyebrow. I hadn't given much thought to Clarke. I'd handed that issue over to Johnny to deal with, and I knew that Graham Sawyer, one of the people in City Systems Control and working under Kristen Canvel, had been helping get him settled in Trieste. But Richard was absolutely correct—we needed more info from Clarke about *Aurora Rex*.

"How are plans on The Vault?" he asked, glancing up at me.

"Hyland is preparing the Isomer Bombs. He received more hafnium while we were away."

"You realize the USSF will be watching the flow of that now, to find out who has the Isomer Bomb."

"I realize it."

"How many do you think we'll need?"

"Five is what we've planned."

"And Chalam?"

"He's working with the Doctor." I sighed. "But his anger at the BSF is unrelenting."

Richard snorted. "Understandable."

"I told him what the weapon really is. It shocked him. We need to watch him on the mission. He is desperate for revenge."

"Sounds familiar."

"Yes, but we can't let it disrupt our plans. That's happened too frequently to us already." I was referring to Meg and Admiral Benning. She had murdered him without giving thought to our other plan. Then there was former TCI Operative Rico Ruiz, who had been obsessed with the German, Heinrich. He'd put the rest of our team in danger multiple times before sacrificing himself for the mission. He'd redeemed himself, but it didn't make him any less dead.

The comm beeped and Kristen's voice called out, "Mac, Commodore Clarke is here."

"You can send him in," I muttered. "Thank you."

The hatch opened and the tall man entered. "Greetings, Mayor McClusky."

"You can call me Mac," I said.

He smiled. "We've been through a lot already, I guess."

"It's only beginning," I said. "We need to find this warsub." I paused and then, "How is Trieste?"

"Wonderful, thanks. The views are really spectacular."

I marveled at the way he rolled his R's in his thick Scottish accent. "Great."

Then the creases in his forehead deepened. "The people aren't the nicest though, I'm sad to say."

I studied him as he sat before the desk. "Have you been wearing that?" I gestured at his dark blue BSF uniform.

"Yes, why?"

I shrugged. "It's because you're military. They hate the USSF, who are always here causing trouble. Other fleet sailors as well. They end up here on their leaves, and they drink and start shit with the citizens here."

"Do they spend money?"

I stared at him. "The trade-off isn't enough."

Clarke looked away and considered that. "We leave troops at Churchill and also the French cities all the time. I don't think there are the same issues."

"Think again."

"I really am sure that—"

"There have been violent assaults in the past."

That stopped him. His face paled. "You're serious?"

I snorted. "Trust me on this. It's caused a lot of problems here. Tensions with the military. It's why people bristle when they see your uniform. Try wearing something casual. You'll get a different response. And please try not to hold it against Triestrians."

He considered that. "Noted."

"Now, how do you think we can find *Aurora Rex*?"

"I've asked some of my contacts. I know some officers on board. Trained some too. I've narrowed down their AOPS and we have two options."

He was referring to the Area of Operations. "Go ahead."

"We can go to Blue Downs and wait. They leave troops there on leave. The country has rebuilt the city and things are in full swing there. They might arrive soon."

"Option two?"

Clarke frowned. "Slightly more dangerous. We go to the region and create a ruckus."

"And hope the warsub shows up to stop us?"

"Yes."

"How will they respond, exactly?"

He shrugged. "Depends on what you're doing. If you're an imminent threat, they'll shoot to kill. Otherwise they'll board you. But I do have an idea to get them to approach us, calmly."

"That's an interesting option," Richard murmured.

I turned to him. "What do you mean?"

"Consider this. They board us and find the Commodore on board. What would they do?"

"Because he's senior to them?"

"Yes. He outranks *all* of them. We come up with a story and . . ."

"And we just *walk* onto the ship and steal the Staging System?" I snorted and looked away. It wouldn't work. They wouldn't just release something that was so important to them. The BSFRL had split up the weapon components to make them difficult to steal. When we finally showed our cards, they'd notify officials at The Vault immediately. "Where is the warsub?"

"Somewhere east of New Zealand."

"Are they patrolling in relation to The Iron Plains?"

"They're monitoring tensions there between China and the US, yes."

"And now Russia, too."

"Indeed."

I made a sudden decision. "Let's load *SC-1* and gather the team. We're departing in two days. We'll use SCAV to get over to New Zealand, then we'll try to attract *Aurora*. Let's make it work."

———••———

A FEW MINUTES LATER, CLIFF was on my comm. He was looking anxious. "Mac, someone tampered with the computer at the airlock. Clearly it was another attempt. It was clumsy though—the person was not a computer expert. He or she did it through a local computer. Hacked into City Control and modified the airlock controls."

"Who did it?"

He leaned forward. "Mac, are you in your office alone right now?"

A prickle worked its way down my scalp. "Yes."

"It was Commodore Clarke."

———••———

I SWORE. "ARE YOU ABSOLUTELY sure?"

"Traced it to his guest compartment in Living Module A."

"But that—" I thought furiously. He'd been so helpful so far, despite our suspicions. Sahar vouched vociferously for him. And his actions had been clear—he wanted the weapon. How would killing me help him?

"It doesn't make sense, Cliff. He wasn't even here when the explosion at the torpedo station occurred."

"*He* wasn't. But his people might have been."

"Are you searching the records?"

He scowled at me. "*Come on*, Boss."

I couldn't help but laugh at that. "And?"

"So far, nothing. But something will pop up, I'm sure."

I sighed and pondered the dilemma. The thing was, I had been considering something about the whole situation. The division between the BSF and the BSFRL seemed odd. And those black and red patches. There was real hostility there. I'd seen it up close and personal only days ago. The guards at the Churchill labs had demonstrated real anger at Clarke. They didn't even see the Commodore as having authority over them. Then there was the mysterious branch called the "Imperial

Force," which theoretically didn't exist as far as I knew. And the British sailors in the Indian Ocean had even struck at a British civilian seacar to hide their facility. Clarke had often shown hostility for the people in the labs and the fact that he had no control over them. Did he want the weapon for himself? To pull it away from engineers in the Indian Ocean and bring it into the BSF?

Cliff said, "Are we still leaving for the South Pacific?"

"In two days."

"And Clarke? He's scheduled to come with us."

"He still is." I stared at Cliff. "Look, keep this quiet, okay? Keep searching, but don't tell anyone else. I don't want to let him know that we caught him."

Cliff eyed me. "For what purpose?"

"I want to see what he's up to. We need him, anyway, to find the warsub and Component Two. Besides, it's safer to keep enemies closer, wouldn't you agree?"

"It can be more dangerous, actually."

"Just keep looking. We're all leaving together. We'll just have to watch our backs."

Chapter Twenty-One

Soon we were soaring through the Pacific Ocean, en route to New Zealand. The trip had been uneventful. The journey through the Panama Pass Through—exclusive to submarines and seacars—was smooth and quick. It had fascinated Sahar and Alyssna, who had never seen it before. Cliff was emotionless as usual—he was keeping a close eye on Clarke. Max Hyland found it interesting as well, Chalam was there but full of anger—I saw him staring at Alyssna with hooded eyes—and Renée, Meg, and Johnny had been through it dozens of times and found the underground river passage carved through solid rock routine by now.

It meant there were eleven people on board *SC-1*, which had once again created cramped conditions. It also lowered our range, as the air would be more limited, unless we could resupply. We'd stored crates of supplies in engineering, but we had also installed bunks for the guests. It wasn't very private, but it was necessary. No one complained about it though, not even Sahar.

There were also weapons stored in the aft compartments, including machine guns, pistols, and a crate of grenades, though those were meant as a last resort. Sahar was not pleased with those items; the distaste painted her expression.

The real issue was Chalam. His rage was evident, and Alyssna had immediately sensed a need to stay clear of him. The first flareup occurred only a few hours out of Trieste.

"You created the weapon?" he practically growled. They were in the living area, both sitting on the couches. The roar of the SCAV echoed through the seacar. Meg and I were piloting; the others were somewhere in the aft, reviewing inventory and getting ready for the upcoming mission.

"I did," she answered, clearly proud.

"It's a disgusting and vile feat of engineering. You should be ashamed of yourself."

"I beg your pardon?"

I turned toward them. "Uh, Chalam, this isn't going to help—"

"It killed my brother!" he snapped.

"Alyssna didn't kill him. The BSFRL did it. We're going to deal with them now."

"If she hadn't built the thing, Mac, Manse would still be alive."

I sighed. I knew this was going to happen eventually, but still. "The good thing is that we know about it and we're going to get it for Trieste and the independence movement."

"At what expense? Because of my brother's sacrifice?"

"Alyssna didn't build it to kill your brother. Other people did that. She's helping us now." I didn't want to say *She's helping you get revenge,* because that was something I didn't want to encourage. Still, it might have worked. "Don't take your grief out on her."

Alyssna's face softened and she put her hand on his arm. "I didn't know, Chalam. I'm so sorry. I thought you were a geologist helping us on—"

"I am! And so was Manse."

"I had no idea. I can't believe they'd use the Water Pick on a crewed civilian vessel! They really did that?" Her face showed her shock.

"Don't give me that ignorant shit!" he cried. "What did you think the military would use it for? It's a goddamned particle weapon that penetrates hulls and sinks seacars! It *kills.*"

Alyssna's face hardened and she leaned toward him, her fists at her side. "That's pathetic, *weak* thinking! What would have happened had we refused to develop the Atom Bomb? The Hydrogen Fusion Bomb? The internet? The—"

"Are you crazy!?" Chalam's eyes were wild now, and the two were screaming at each other in the living compartment. They had shared the same seacar from Churchill only days earlier, and we'd successfully avoided this confrontation then, but I'd feared it was inevitable. He continued: "The Atom Bomb kills people. The Hydrogen Bomb even more!"

"If we hadn't invented it and Japan or Germany had beat the Allies, what do you think would have happened? Our lives wouldn't be better!"

"My brother would be alive!"

She frowned. "You're delusional."

"And the *internet*?" he screamed. "You think that's a weapon?"

The screaming had alerted the others, and I saw their faces peering at us from the engineering compartment where the majority of the bunks were. Sahar in particular seemed rattled.

"Of course it is! How many have died from cyber attacks? How many from digital warfare? Cyber Soldiers shut down utilities and people have died. Do you think we should still be in caves?"

Chalam seemed apoplectic now. "A ten-terawatt laser enclosing a particle-beam vacuum channel is not for the betterment of humanity!"

"It is if China had developed it first," I said into the argument. I stepped toward him. "Or if Russia did it first, or gets their hands on it before us." I grabbed him by the shoulders and he pushed me away. He was staring at Doctor Sonstraal and didn't even look at me. I pressed on, "She didn't invent it to murder your brother. She did it to protect the underwater cities. We're going to steal it for Trieste. Your brother was a casualty, Chalam, and I'm sorry about that. It happened. We're going to take it back from those people, but I can't have you risking the mission because you are angry at Alyssna. We need you on this, and we *need* you focused and calm."

Sahar stepped in from aft and placed herself between Chalam and Alyssna. "This won't bring Manse back. Will it?" Her voice was calm and soothing, her demeanor one of peace.

He tore his eyes from Alyssna and looked at her. "Of course not. I'm not stupid. But he didn't deserve that. I want revenge."

"That won't bring him back either," Sahar said quietly. "You need to accept these things, and you will, eventually, but it's still so soon after the disaster. It's natural for you to feel like this, but Alyssna is a person with real feelings and you can't actually think that she created this to kill Mahiransh Kaashif, can you?"

He hesitated for a long heartbeat. "I don't know," he snapped. "She did it though. And I watched my brother's hand dissolve. The hull failed and implosion killed the others."

"She didn't aim the weapon at your seacar. She didn't pull the trigger. But she's absolutely correct, Chalam—she invented it to maintain the balance of power. To maintain peace."

"You're saying it's a weapon of *peace*?" His disdain was clear. "I can't buy that, especially from *you* of all people. You prize peace above all else."

"It's history. Our job is to remember, yes, but move forward and try to maintain peace with each other." She stared at the scene before her. "This is not that. You're displaying fury right now. Total rage. It's not appropriate, Chalam."

"Don't lecture me!" he rasped. But his eyes lowered and his expression showed embarrassment.

"Come with me, aft-ward."

"For what?"

"Let's talk about this. I need to pray. You can join me."

"I'm Hindu, not Muslim."

Sahar smiled, then glanced at me. "I've said this before: same God, different name. We all want the same things, don't we? To coexist? To pursue happiness? Contentment?'

"Not quite." He glared at Alyssna. "I think you're referring to *Brahman*, the Supreme Being, but it's not as simple as that."

"You believe in the concept of life as a sacred thing. And yet you express extreme rage right now." She tilted her head. Her hijab was blue, her eye shadow tinted topaz, and her lashes long. I couldn't stop staring at her. "You also believe in the concept of the afterlife, and karma?"

"Of course. We believe that all people have a soul."

"So your brother persists. He continues. He *will* continue. And the evil people who did this will have to deal with the consequences in their future realities. Correct?"

"Of course."

"And yet you want to take it out on Alyssna here, in *SC-1*?"

"In a way," he said, abashed.

"Come with me. Let's talk further."

They disappeared into the aft compartments of the seacar. Max Hyland appeared at his side and left with them. As Chalam departed, he shot Alyssna one last, angry look.

RENÉE HAD BEEN THERE DURING the entire confrontation. We were steaming toward New Zealand at 450 kph, with Meg in the pilot's cabin, but she had heard it as well. We all had. No one really knew what to say.

I sat next to Renée. "This is not good. He is so damn angry."

Alyssna, standing near the moonpool hatch and staring at the hatchway through which Chalam had exited, turned to me. "I feel terrible. I didn't want that to happen."

"It's not your fault. Sahar was a hundred percent correct. I think he'll see that soon."

"You think she can talk to him for an hour and he'll just forgive and forget?"

I paused. "I think Sahar has a way about her. She has incredible influence over people. You'll see." I thought about how she had taken us outside and suggested we pray together. It had been a unique experience in my life. Not that I was going to become religious, but I saw the necessity of just separating myself from the tension and stress and taking minor breaks to decompress and collect my thoughts. Prayer was a lot like meditation. I'd thought that at the time. And didn't yoga come from Hinduism? Or at least, from being spiritual? Maybe there was something to the concept. It was a good way to live, I thought.

But sometimes it seemed like I just didn't have the time.

Renée was still sitting there quietly. I said, "Are you okay? Sorry you had to see that."

She was staring at her PCD. "It's okay. I totally understand Chalam. I felt the rage after you ruined my career. I wanted to kill you."

"I remember," I said with a chuckle.

"I got over it. Chalam will too. I just hope it doesn't endanger this entire mission."

"It won't," I said. "I think he'll see that the success of this outweighs simple revenge." I watched her for another long moment. She was still staring at her PCD. "Are you okay?" I repeated.

A sigh. "The comm function hasn't worked since the incident in the airlock. I think the water damaged it."

—••—

Within another day at the tremendous speed we were traveling, we were off the coast of New Zealand and in *Aurora Rex*'s theater of operations. Our sonar was listening to all passive signals in the immediate region, though our range was only thirty kilometers. We could send out an active pulse to try and identify it that way—that range was 100 kilometers. But it was still like finding a needle in a haystack.

But Clarke had an idea. He was in the living area with us, still wearing his BSF uniform—he'd never changed it, as I'd suggested—and studying the others with a commanding gaze. He'd listened to the argument earlier in a stoic silence, not contributing in any way, which I'd appreciated. Still, I was nervous about the man now, after what Cliff had told me about his hacking into the airlock controls. I still didn't understand his motivations.

He said, "I had suggested going to Blue Downs and waiting for *Aurora* to show up. The problem is that she's likely on a six-week rotation. Meaning it could be into May before we see her."

"We can't wait," I muttered.

"Indeed. But I do have a code that we can broadcast. An emergency signal. It'll attract BSF warsubs in the vicinity."

"And *Aurora* will come?"

He nodded. "Mandated by BSF procedures. They *have* to, if they're close. And when they do . . . " He trailed off. "We take the ship and steal the component."

"It's not that simple," Meg said.

"But we have some things going for us," I interjected. We'd spoken about this back at Trieste. "We have BSF uniforms already. I do, Johnny does, and Richard as well."

"And we have the Commodore too," Johnny added. "So, when the warsub arrives . . . "

Clarke said, "They'll board us and the four of us will be here, in uniform. I'm a Commodore. I outrank all of them. Instead of them boarding us, *we'll* board *them*. Then we go take what we need."

"They won't just let us walk in and out," Renée said.

"There might be some violence," Clarke said with a nod.

"No killing though," I said. "Try not to, anyway." *These sailors didn't deserve it.*

And besides, Sahar was completely against it. I needed to keep her on our side.

"There's another major issue that we need to be aware of." He paced before us, staring at the deck. "If I make the call, *every* BSF warsub in the region will arrive. Not just the one we want. That's a risk."

I frowned at that. "We have no other choice. We can't just wait for them to arrive at Blue Downs." I stared at the others there in the living area. All were present except for Sahar, Hyland, and Chalam. Their eyes were on me, and each nodded silently at my questioning gaze. I turned to Clarke. "Go ahead. Give the signal. The rest of you, get ready."

———•••———

Johnny, Richard, and I put on our BSF uniforms. We looked official and commanding. The others retreated to the engineering compartment and sealed the hatch. When we gave the order, they would remain absolutely quiet.

I wished we had a uniform for Cliff. We could use him on *Aurora*, but then again, he likely couldn't pull off the accent.

Clarke came into the pilot cabin and sat in the right-hand seat. He glanced at me, then clicked the comm and adjusted the settings to an all-channel broadcast. "Attention. This is a Red Waterloo. Repeat. Red Waterloo. Coordinates are—" He recited our current location while staring at the nav display between the chairs. He then recited an alphanumeric code using the NATO phonetic alphabet, which the UK had adopted. "Tango Zulu Sierra One Delta India . . ."

He repeated the call several times.

Then we waited.

I'd made our depth thirty meters and set the thrusters at station-keeping. We were neutrally buoyant and hovering in one location. The water was blue and the sunlight above filtered down through our canopy. It felt surprisingly like the Gulf. The water was a similar color and the bright fish seemed familiar and welcoming.

Then the comm crackled to life.

"Attention vessel calling *Waterloo*. Identify yourself."

Clarke glanced at me and shook his head. "We don't. We just call the emergency again." He activated the comm with the trigger on the yoke. "Red Waterloo. Repeat. Red Waterloo. Our coordinates are . . . "

I stared at the sonar display. There was a white light on it now, powering toward us. "They're moving at 77 kph. It's a *Victory* Class warsub."

"That's it."

Sure enough, the callout display indicated:

```
Registry: HMS Aurora Rex
Victory Class SSN, BSF
Depth: 203 meters
Speed: 77 kph
Bearing: 27º
Estimated Time of Intercept: 22:53 minutes
```

The ETI was counting down. The warsub had just entered our 30-kilometer sphere and was racing toward us at its maximum speed. The *Victory* Class vessel was eighty-eight meters long and had a max depth of 3,650 meters. Eight tubes, one giant thruster, with a crew of eighteen. It was meant for stealth, so it was quiet when running on reduced thrust, but it was also armed and dangerous. There were thirty-eight in the BSF fleet.

I grinned. Perfect. The warsub we'd been looking for was now coming for us. And when they arrived, they'd find four BSF officers on board.

And we were going to steal Component Two of The Water Pick.

Then another chime sounded from the sonar display, and my face paled as the information there registered.

My expression was one of horror, I was sure.

Two other warsubs had appeared at the outer edges of our detection range. One was a BSF Hunter-Killer—*Churchill* Class—and the other was a *Vanguard* Class SSBN missile warsub.

"Oh, shit."

—••—

THE *VANGUARD* WAS DUE TO arrive first. We didn't want that, so I made our course 27° to move toward *Aurora*.

The drawback was that the ETI had now shrunk considerably. It was now at fifteen minutes and counting down.

And soon after that, the two other BSF warsubs would arrive.

Chapter Twenty-Two

I MARCHED BACK TO THE engineering compartment to inform the others. I kept my voice low. Their faces showed concern, though Cliff's was like stone. "Do you need me up there?"

"No. They'll know immediately that something is off. Stay here, but be ready in case they send guards back here to investigate."

"They have that authority?" Alyssna asked.

Renée said, "Since we called an emergency, they'll see it as a tacit approval to do what they want." She shrugged. "I was in the FSF. It's what *I'd* do."

"She's right. Seal the hatch and wait it out."

"Good luck, Mac," she said.

I squeezed her arm. "We'll be fine."

—••—

RICHARD, JOHNNY, CLARKE, AND I stood in the living compartment. We faced the airlock hatch. There was a sound of screws as the warsub approached. We could hear it throttling down. There were a few *pings* as they studied the surroundings to determine our precise position. Then *Aurora* stopped moving, and there was a high-pitched whine as an umbilical extended. It *thunked* against our hull, there was a sigh as it formed a seal, and pumps removed the water. Since our two vessels were both at four atms—mandated across the oceans—there were no issues moving from one pressure to another.

They'd continued to call over the comm, but we'd ignored each one.

I took a deep breath and stared at the airlock.

Richard muttered, "Here we go."

"How's your accent?" I asked.

"Nonexistent."

I grunted.

Clarke said, "I'll do the speaking. I'm the ranking officer now, as soon as they make the connection with our seacar. They'll have to respond to me and do what I say."

Johnny said, "I hope it's that simple."

"And I hope they don't recognize me," I murmured. I locked eyes with Clarke. His motives were murky and there was much to learn about him. I still needed to know why—or *if*—he had tried to kill me in the airlock. I'd decided to keep him close and watch him, but something was about to happen from which there was no turning back. "Clarke."

"Yes?"

"Are you sure you want to do this?"

"It's a bit late now, mate."

"I mean, once they see you, your career will be over. The BSF will know about you. There's no hiding this like we did at the Churchill labs. If we get Component Two, they'll know you stole it."

His expression remained stoic. "Your dad meant a lot to me, Mac. I want independence for the undersea colonies. This is part of that."

"But what happens after this mission? When they start hunting you?"

"I guess I'll have to find a new place to live. Or hide."

"What did you have in mind?"

He shrugged. "I haven't decided yet. But I want to fight with you and Richard. I know that."

I stared at him, confused. It just didn't make sense. If what he was saying was true, then why the attempt on my life?

Then I turned back to the airlock.

It opened.

———•••———

THERE WAS A HISS AS the air from the two ships mixed. I immediately detected the aroma of the British vessel, which was distinctly different from ours. Sometimes the smells were so intense they made people sick before they grew used to it.

A man in his forties stepped from the lock and entered *SC-1*. There were three others with him. His face registered surprise at our uniforms. Then he noted Clarke's rank, and his eyes narrowed.

It was not quite the reaction I'd expected.

He stared at us intently. "What is this, exactly?"

"I'm Commodore Clarke. I'm on an Eyes-Only mission in the region." He glanced at the others in the Captain's group. "Can we go somewhere to speak privately."

There was a long, extended pause. "Certainly not."

Then I noticed the red and black patches on their shoulders. They were all wearing them.

—••—

"Who are you?" Clarke snapped.

"Captain Mantis."

A woman next to him said, "I'm the XO. Lieutenant Smith. Your call forced us here. It isn't exactly what we were expecting today."

In addition to the XO, there were flanking guards who looked intimidating and angry. They were special forces, of that I had no doubt.

"No one ever expects emergencies," Clarke said. His eyes were hard, and he was glaring at Mantis. "And you are to follow orders. Let's go speak in private."

"I said, no." He stared at us. "I want to know exactly what the emergency is. Trieste is the official port of this seacar. Why are four BSF officers on board? And why didn't you respond to our queries?"

"Part of our mission," Clarke snapped. "Which I'd be happy to tell you about if we could—"

"Sadly, we don't care about your mission, Clarke." He pinned each of us with his steely glare. "We're working with the BSFIF right now. Your mission is irrelevant."

—••—

THE *BSFIF*. HERE IT WAS, again, along with the hostility toward the regular BSF.

"We're all BSF," Clarke growled. "Our mission involves British Intelligence. Are your people cleared to hear Eyes-Only information?"

There was a long pause. He glanced at the guards. Then, "No."

"Then let's go speak where we can't reveal security secrets, shall we, *Captain*?" His inflection on the rank signified his intention to outrank the other, but it didn't seem to be working.

Mantis paused and watched Clarke in silence. Then he relented. "Very well. Perhaps on *Aurora*?"

"That would be acceptable."

"I don't have a *Pipe the Side* ceremony prepared, Commodore." He appeared to be more accepting of the other's rank. He turned to the XO. "Please call Fletcher here with the bosun's whistle."

"That won't be necessary," Clarke said.

"You're a flag officer and it's tradition to hear the twelve second boatswain's call."

"Not needed. Let's go." Clarke strode confidently through the umbilical toward *Aurora*.

Richard, Johnny, and I pushed through the others and followed him onto the BSF warsub.

I sensed their eyes on our backs. They felt like laser beams burning into us.

The pistol was on my right thigh; I sensed its weight as I marched through the airlock and stepped onto the warsub.

—••—

WE WERE ON *AURORA REX*. I couldn't quite believe it. What had started as a fantastical concept that Richard had first brought to my attention—an *underwater energy beam?*—had now culminated in a very real and deadly weapon that the BSFRL was not only developing in the Indian Ocean, but *using* against civilians. Or perhaps the mysterious BSFIF was responsible? We had now infiltrated a BSF *Victory* Class warsub, and were in foreign, hostile territory, totally and utterly surrounded.

We practically charged up the corridors toward the vessel's bow. We moved like we belonged there. Clarke was next to me, and he was urging us forward. I followed his lead, but kept a close watch on him from the corner of my eye.

Behind me, Johnny and Richard filled the corridor and prevented the others from getting past us.

The Captain, XO, and the two guards also stalked behind us. They had accepted that the Commodore knew where he was going, and they were simply following, but I heard them muttering something, and that made me worry. They would not let us just *take over*, I knew. They would get us in a cabin somewhere, and then hear us out.

—••—

COMMODORE CLARKE HAD LED US to a forward lounge near the bow. He took a seat and we followed suit. Captain Mantis appeared an instant later, staring at us with narrowed eyes. Lieutenant Smith entered and closed the hatch.

The two guards stood just outside, in the corridor.

Mantis sighed. "Now we have privacy. You have used a Red Waterloo call using your division's code sign, and I want an explanation. You've pulled us from our patrol route. Even more egregious, according to my XO, you're a Commodore in charge of the Channel and North Sea region and have absolutely no authority over us here in the South Pacific."

"I have every authority. I'm a Commodore. I'm the ranking officer here."

"This is *highly* irregular. I want an explanation."

"You'll get one. But first we have to get past the issue of insubordination."

"There *is* no such thing now. I want an answer from you, *sir*. Answer me. Now."

Clarke remained quiet and leveled his icy glare at Mantis. Their eyes locked.

XO Smith said, "I thought this was an emergency, Commodore. Instead it's turned into a pissing match between you two."

Mantis growled, "The Commodore here signaled a rarely used emergency signal. Three warsubs are now here. *What is it?*"

Clarke stared for a minute longer, then visibly deflated. "You might be right, Smith. The Captain's attitude was offensive, especially toward a ranking officer. I got my back up about it."

"What is it, exactly?" she asked. Her dark hair was pulled back under a hat and her eyes were also dark. Her skin was olive and she was very pretty, though I noticed the pistol at her side, and her right hand dangerously near it.

Clarke said, "We are on a mission to retrieve a piece of equipment from you. It's needed desperately back home, I'm afraid."

A deadly silence descended over the cabin. I kept my face stoic. Surely such a tactic wouldn't work, but I figured we could at least try. The Captain and Lieutenant looked at each other for a moment, then turned to stare at us again. "Are you serious?" he finally grated.

"Absolutely."

"And why couldn't you just signal us?"

"Too dangerous. The component is secret. I'm not even sure if Smith here has clearance to know about it."

Mantis continued to glare at us. Then, "You must have paperwork."

"I only have my verbal command."

The other tilted his head and his face flattened. "You're serious?"

"As a King's fart."

Captain Mantis snorted. "There's no way I can release what you're asking for without written authorization from BSFRL HQ."

Another silence descended. I cleared my throat to speak. I wanted answers. "We're not from the RL division."

"That I can tell," he snapped, staring at my rank. "And even if you had written authorization from BSF HQ, it wouldn't be enough."

"Why not?"

"For the precise reason you just stated. You're not BSFRL."

"We're all in the same fleet, Captain. Don't be absurd."

He tilted his head and stared at me. "What are you here for?"

"We desperately require the component in the Channel. There's an imminent threat and they need the weapon. It's needed to defend the United Kingdom. You are preventing that."

"Weapon?"

I frowned. "Surely you've heard of it. The particle beam. The Water Pick. You have a necessary component on this vessel. We're here for it.

It's so secret we couldn't broadcast a command or even bring written authorization. We can't let word of it get out."

"I have heard of it. I know it's here. And command authority ordered me not to release it to anyone but the BSFRL or the IF."

"The Commodore said it before. We're all in the BSF."

He hesitated. "And why are you in a civilian seacar?"

"Because we had to get here fast, and get the component back to the Channel just as quickly. *SC-1* has a SCAV drive. We used it the whole way here."

"Trieste let you have it?" Smith asked.

"We stole it. We're on a mission to retrieve the Staging System from you."

Clarke stood. "Come on, Mantis. This is getting ridiculous. You have authorization from *me*. I'm telling you to hand it over to us. I outrank you. Now let's just do this and we can all move on."

Mantis stared at us for a minute longer. The silence seemed absolute, despite the routine calls over the comm system, the ventilation fans, boots on the deck outside the cabin, and clicks from the pressure monitors. He lifted a comm device to his mouth. "Midshipman Pettiger."

"Aye, sir?" a voice echoed back.

"Send a crew over to the seacar and take command of it immediately."

I drew my weapon in a flash and leveled it at them. Johnny followed suit.

Mantis froze as he stared at me. Clarke muttered under his breath, "You should have listened."

The Captain continued into his comm, "Do it now, and send a—"

I stepped forward and swung the butt of my weapon at his temple. He ducked and dropped the comm. Smith jerked backward and screamed. Johnny had stepped forward and he slammed his fist on the hatch's LOCK button. The guards outside had heard, and they started to pound on the steel.

I realized we had to act before the rest of the warsub knew what was happening. We couldn't risk alerting them.

"Let them in, Johnny," I growled.

He stared at me, then understanding registered. He opened the hatch.

The guards spilled in.

And all hell broke loose.

———•••———

JOHNNY AND I WENT TO work. Richard, who had been quiet, fell back against the bulkhead, staring, as fists, elbows, and feet flew. Clarke stayed to the side as well. I couldn't risk firing and alerting the crew, so I holstered my gun and swung at Mantis. I connected cleanly with his jaw and he fell to the side, dazed. The two guards were more of a challenge, and Smith demonstrated strong skills as well.

In the back of my mind, Sahar was coaching me to not cause permanent damage here. She didn't want to kill, but things were escalating rapidly.

A guard pushed me back and approached. I turned to the side and he swung with a right cross. I blocked it easily and elbowed him across the temple. Without waiting for him to fall, I swung a left hook and then another elbow. Both cracked against his face and he slumped downward, out cold.

Johnny had dispatched the other guard, and Smith was now swinging for Johnny.

I said, "Stop." I had my weapon out again, leveled at her. "I don't want to kill you, but I will."

She pulled up short, breathing heavily, and stared at me.

I pulled out my own PCD. We had only seconds. "Meg. Seal the airlock immediately. They're on their way. Do it, now!"

"Got it," came the instant response.

Then I turned back to Smith. "What is the RL division? Why the separate authority from the BSF? And what's the BSFIF?"

She stared, her eyes wide. "Are you here for them?"

"We're here for the component. We said that. Answer me!"

"They're—"

An alarm began to pound out. The lights shifted color and a voice called an alert over the comm system. *"Intruder alert. All personnel to forward cabin 4F. Repeat, intruder alert . . ."*

Chapter Twenty-Three

I FROZE FOR A FRACTION of a second.

Their entire crew was on their way to this cabin to take us in. Captain Mantis and the two guards were unconscious. Lieutenant Smith was still standing but was also hostile.

"We're going to get the component," I snapped. "You're going to help us."

"I won't."

The alarm continued to ring.

"Where is it?"

She bared her teeth. "Fuck you."

Clarke stepped up. "It's likely in the storage compartment. Amidships. One deck down. All mechanical supplies and spare electronic equipment is there."

Things were quickly falling apart, but we had no time to waste. "Let's go," I snapped. Johnny opened the hatch and we bolted out, Clarke following.

We left Smith behind to deal with her Captain, who was unconscious and bleeding on the cold deck.

———••———

THERE WERE FEET POUNDING ON deckplates all around. It echoed everywhere. Voices were screaming. We'd successfully infiltrated the ship, but the plan had ended there. Clarke's rank hadn't been enough to convince them, and now they were hunting us.

The positive was that we were wearing BSF uniforms, and we didn't stand out. The negative was that the crew knew who belonged and who didn't, and we definitely didn't.

Outside, there were sailors to the aft, blocking the corridor, staring back with hostile expressions. Some had weapons raised.

A shot rang out.

"Shit!" Clarke cried.

We ducked through a side passage and slid down a ladder to the deck below. There were more calls, and I was sure someone was shouting our location over the PA.

We sprinted around a turn and then came up against another cluster of *Aurora* crew. They also had weapons.

"This isn't working," Johnny muttered.

Clarke swore. "Mac, they are going to kill us now. These people are not going to listen to me. And now . . . they're going to trap us and take us down."

"We could split up," Johnny hissed.

I thought furiously. The ship had a small crew, but they were all chasing us through the corridors. There were too many of them, and Sahar's request kept nagging at the back of my mind.

A shot cracked out and ricocheted down the corridor. I ducked instinctively, trying to figure out which way it had come from.

Shit. I couldn't think of a way out of this.

And then it came to me. A way to distract them *and* keep from disappointing Sahar.

I raised my PCD. "Meg, Renée. Are you there?"

"We're here," Renée replied in a hushed voice. "They tried to get onto *SC-1*. They were pounding at the hatch. Then all of a sudden they left."

"I want you to detach. Detach, drift away, and fire a torpedo at *Aurora*."

———••———

CLARKE STARED AT ME IN horror. "Are you mad? We're on board here!"

"We're only at thirty meters. It'll distract the crew. We can still try to get the component and escape."

"There are three BSF warships here!"

Another shot rang out, and we pressed ourselves against a bulkhead.

More calls came over the PA, directing crew to our position.

"We don't have a choice!" I snapped. "This isn't working and you're going to have to explain it. But first we need these crew out of here or we're all dead."

He ignored my comment.

There was an audible *clunk* and then the whine of thrusters. I recognized the sound of *SC-1*'s twin screws maneuvering away.

No doubt Cliff was angry that he was on board the seacar and not here, with us, fighting.

I raised the PCD again. "Aim for the stern. Not to kill. Just to damage."

SC-1 was pulling away. Then a new alarm belched from the address system: *"Fire Control, get back to your stations! Control crew, back to your stations! We're under attack!"*

Shouts and cries echoed down the corridors. They'd realized that although we were still a threat, the greater threat was now *SC-1*. And if we hit *Aurora*, she'd be plunging to the bottom.

They had to ignore us.

The corridor cleared within seconds.

"Torpedo shutters just opened on that seacar!" a voice called. *"Captain to the bridge! Captain to the bridge!"*

I nudged Clarke. "Get us to the storage area and Component Two. Do it, *now*."

He rose slowly from his crouch. He scanned the area. "Follow me."

Then there was a high-pitched squeal, and a surge of bubbles. We could hear it through the bulkhead; it was close.

"Torpedo in the water!" a scream rang out over the PA. "Captain to the—"

The warsub shuddered, and klaxons began to hammer through the corridors. Then the flashing alert lights turned blue.

Pressure warning.

Somewhere on the warsub, water was flooding in.

We ran with Clarke toward amidships. Richard was at my side. I breathed to him, "We're going to get wet. Are you prepared?"

"We just need the component. I can do this."

"We might have to abandon ship."

"There are two other BSF warsubs out there," Clarke growled. "We need scuba gear."

"First thing's first." The priority was the Staging System. Alyssna had told us it was a meter long and half a meter deep. It would need two people to carry.

Clarke led the way and we stumbled through the corridor. The ship was listing to the side and the stern was lower in the water. We were moving *downward*, and the angle was growing worse.

We didn't have a lot of time.

"Rear bulkhead hatches are closing!" the voice screamed. *"Get out of the aft compartments!"* Then another series of orders echoed, but they were meant for the bridge crew. *"Purge ballast, keep us neutral. What's our depth?"*

"Forty meters."

"And the bottom?"

"It's just over two hundred meters here."

"We just have to keep the water out of the old lass then."

Clarke lurched to a stop and indicated a hatch. "Here's storage. It'll be in here." He held his ID up to the reader and we held our breath—

The hatch slid aside.

We stepped in.

There were more lurches as explosions pounded the warsub. I swore. Surely Meg hadn't fired more—

Then I realized it was the other warsubs. They'd attacked *SC-1*.

We were in a long and narrow cabin with shelving on the bulkheads as well as in the center of the deck. The ceiling was low with the ship's pipes and wiring exposed. There was equipment everywhere, mostly electronic and sealed in watertight bags and plastic containers. There was also larger equipment, such as motors and valves and pieces of steel furniture and delicate electronic motherboards, stacked on the deck and bolted down with wires and nets to keep it from sliding and causing damage.

"Can you find it?" I asked Clarke, staring at the narrow aisles between shelves.

The lights hung from the ceiling, and they swung crazily as detonations shoved the warsub about. The concussions vibrated the deck plates and coursed up my legs.

I stared out the hatch into the corridor. There were screams and yells from somewhere nearby. A painted sign on the deck—a blocky yellow arrow—directed crew toward the nearest airlock.

Over my shoulder I yelled, "We need to go, now!"

"It's here!" Clarke called.

I bolted back. He was staring at a large plastic moulded crate. I swore. It was much larger than Alyssna had claimed. The lettering on the side didn't make sense to me at first, but the BSFRL logo was clear. It also said: LaWS E UNPB SS.

After a second, the "LaWS" stood out to me. The rest was unclear. Then I realized the SS stood for *Staging System*.

Richard broke the seal on the container and peeled the lid back. Inside, cushioned with spongy packing, was the device. It was exactly as Alyssna had said; the crate had simply been larger to keep it protected.

"Let's go. Bring it to the airlock," Richard hissed. His face was frantic; this was the most action he'd seen since the fighting in the Mid-Atlantic Ridge a year earlier.

"This way," I directed.

Together we hefted the crate and carried it into the corridor. It was large and difficult to move, but we managed. Inside, I was also nervous, but able to smother it. The fact was that I didn't know what we were going to do, how we were going to get out. I'd hoped we'd just be able to march with it through the umbilical.

But I reminded myself of *best laid plans*. You always needed a backup.

This time, however, we didn't really have one.

The ship was listing even more. The deck was now at a severe angle. I recognized Smith's voice over the PA; she was yelling for damage control and ordering crews to the aft compartments. Alarms were ringing out and the blue flashing warnings persisted.

We were at the airlock. There was scuba gear in a locker beside the hatch, but we didn't have time to pull wetsuits on. Instead we grabbed tanks and swung them onto our backs. The masks didn't cover the entire face, so we wouldn't be able to speak once outside.

We hauled the crate in. I knew we had to evacuate immediately and hope *SC-1* could pick us up, but wasn't sure what was going on. We could hear torpedoes churning the water and the sound of concussions. There was a nearby constant whine—countermeasures, spinning and churning and trying to lure weapons in. I wasn't sure who had dropped them, but it meant a battle raged outside.

I stared at the others with me. "Are you ready to go out?"

"Let's do it," Clarke grunted.

"What's the plan?" Richard asked.

I stared at the others in there with me. "You push the crate out. It sinks. One of you put your PCD in it to mark the location. Then float together, neutrally buoyant, and wait for the battle to end. Try to stay in the same place. Keep your PCDs active so Meg can find you."

Johnny said, "We don't really have any other options here."

We could wait in the warsub, but the crew knew about us and would take us prisoner or worse. We couldn't allow that . . . we had to get to The Vault as soon as possible.

The others prepared to go outside. Then, as the inner hatch ground shut, I stepped back into the corridor. "Wait!" Johnny yelled. "What are you—"

"Sorry, Johnny," I said. "I have to do this."

—••—

THE AIRLOCK OPENED TO THE outside and the others pulled the crate out and watched it sink into the depths. Then they swam away from the warsub and disappeared into the darkness of the Pacific Ocean.

I swallowed and shrugged off the air tank and left it on the deck, along with the mask and regulator. I turned toward the ship's bow. This had to be done. I couldn't let the crew call the BSFRL at The Vault or Diego Garcia and warn them. I needed the others outside to protect Component Two.

There was no other option.

Removing the pistol from my holster, I marched toward the bridge. I clutched the PCD and keyed Meg. "Are you there?"

"Go ahead," came the reply after a moment. She sounded stressed and physically exhausted.

"What's happening?"

"Two warsubs disabled and sinking. The third is chasing us."

"Can you activate SCAV?"

"I don't want to leave you alone."

"The others are outside, waiting. Floating. They've got a PCD. Lead the third ship away, then turn on the SCAV and get back here, *fast*."

"What are you doing?"

"I'm still on board."

There was a long pause. "*Mac*. Get out of there! What are you thinking?"

"I have to do something."

"Don't play the hero. Get out. You got the component?"

"It's on the seafloor. Tell Alyssna. You'll have to descend to get it."

"Mac! Don't—"

I thumbed the comm off and pressed forward, walking uphill toward the bow.

The stern was now tilting so badly that I had to grab handrails and haul myself forward.

There were eighteen people on the warsub, at least. And I was now the only intruder left. I had to be aggressive and do the unexpected. I couldn't hide somewhere; they'd find me. I couldn't let them contact the other warsubs to let them know what we'd done. Originally, we'd hoped they would hand over the device to a ranking officer and not think twice about it. It hadn't happened. The only other option was to damage them and get to The Vault before they could warn anybody.

But the other warsubs were now a major issue.

I couldn't let *Aurora* communicate with them.

I marched right onto the bridge, weapon drawn.

The crew were scrambling to control the ship. They were directing repairs and screaming orders. There were torpedo sounds in the water just outside the hull.

The screech of the countermeasures continued.

The alerts were pounding out, blue lights bathed everyone, and no one noticed as I stepped forward gun raised, and stood directly in front of the communications station.

I squeezed the trigger.

The bullets tore through the equipment and sparks flew. Shouts ripped out and I continued, firing, into the console. I ignored them. I switched clips and emptied the entire thing into the comm panel. It was smoking and sparking; I could hear an electrical fire beginning within. I spun and stared at the crew around me. I'd caught them off guard, and they were pressing themselves to their consoles or to the deck, waiting me out.

The exit was only a few meters away, and I lunged for it. It was downwards now, due to the warsub's list, and I practically fell toward the opening.

"*Stop!*" a voice called. "Security!"

I didn't wait to find out what they wanted.

I slid and stumbled forward, back toward amidships and the airlock where the others had evacuated. I had to hold onto the railings and bulkhead handholds to keep my balance. The tilt had grown steep. More orders pounded out over the PA system and I stared at a speaker as I lurched past it, horrified.

"*Intruder is in corridor three heading aftward. Shoot to kill. Repeat, SHOOT TO KILL!*" There was a pause, and then, "*Forget the repair efforts. We need to get this rat bastard. Go, go, go! Now!*"

Chapter Twenty-Four

I TOOK A DEEP BREATH and let myself fall. I started to slide down the corridor, on my ass.

There were some shouts behind me. Then a gunshot.

I instinctively pressed my back down to the deck, and I kept sliding. Then there were some cries *in front* of me, and I looked up in panic.

I was sliding right toward a group of three armed sailors—

Damn. I was out of bullets. Directly ahead was the airlock, but then I noticed something and my blood ran cold.

The scuba tank was gone. It had rolled away; I should have secured it. Spreading my feet to either side, I pressed my boots against the bulkheads and slowed myself. I spun to a halt right at the airlock and reached up and slammed my palm on the OPEN button.

More shots.

They were having trouble moving toward me because of the tilt, but from the bow, others were now sliding downward, toward me.

"Get the machine gun!"

I cranked my head toward the sound. A crewman stepped into view and brought a long weapon up.

The look on his face was hideous. He was determined to kill.

He fired.

I hurled myself into the airlock, swearing. The gunshots ricocheted off the bulkhead and rattled around the corridor around me. Some made their way into the airlock. I ducked instinctively. "Fuck!" I screamed. The rain of bullets continued.

"Someone get a grenade!"

I snapped my eyes up. "Are you crazy!" I cried. "It'll sink us all!"

"Do it! Do it!" the voices aftward cried.

I stared around me, frantic. There was no scuba gear in the lock. Nothing. No tank, mask, flippers.

But I had no other choice.

I pressed the CYLCLE button and stared in horror at the deck.

The inner hatch clicked shut and water started to rise up my legs.

We were at least forty meters down, and I was about to go out without any equipment.

—••—

THE WATER HIT THE CEILING and the outer hatch opened. I pushed myself out and forced my eyes open against the salt water. I figured we'd descended since the others had departed, so I picked a direction on a slight angle upward and began to swim. Buoyancy was a real issue, and within seconds I was fighting to keep from floating upward too quickly. Behind me, the warsub was descending, trailing gouts of bubbles from the stern. The massive screw blades were bent toward the bow and totally useless. The list was violent and the stern would hit bottom first. I just hoped it was moving slow when it finally impacted the seafloor.

I stared before me, trying to make out the three figures of Johnny, Richard, and Clarke. I had told them to stay in the same place, over Component Two's position on the seafloor 160 meters below. They should be there . . .

I'd taken several giant gulps of air before the water had fully engulfed me, oxygenating my blood. I had a few minutes left, but fighting the buoyancy was tiring and draining me of valuable oxygen.

The sounds of the battle continued; distant concussions and reverberations rattled my teeth and pounded my ears.

I hoped the nearby wildlife had escaped before the fighting started.

The explosions hurt my eardrums.

Aurora finally disappeared from sight in the darkness below, but the stream of bubbles continued. I hoped her crew could contain the flooding and prevent any death.

My lungs started to heave and the panic began to set in. I spun completely around, searching for the others.

My head began to pound.

Shit shit shit shit . . .

Where were they?

Surely they wouldn't have swum deeper; the mix in the tanks was only for a certain depth range. You *couldn't* go much deeper with it, otherwise you risked nitrogen narcosis.

Rapture of the deeps . . .

They had to be there.

Somewhere.

I opened my mouth and screamed, a last, desperate attempt.

To call out to Johnny.

Come get me, Johnny! Where are you!?

My vision began to darken.

I was passing out.

My vision faded completely.

Black.

I was done.

The fight was done.

Independence over.

—••—

SOMETHING JERKED MY BODY AND I felt a pull on my arms. A hand shoved a regulator in my mouth and I took a deep, rasping breath. I coughed over and over, but managed to keep the regulator clenched between my teeth. Then another breath, and another, and my vision grew lighter.

The headache began to recede.

There were three figures around me, all holding on to me, keeping me from floating upward. I had a backup regulator in my mouth; it belonged to Johnny Chang.

I grinned behind the regulator and their eyes lit with joy.

Even Clarke's.

He was either a great actor, or I'd been wrong about him.

—••—

TIME PASSED. JOHNNY'S AIR TANK depleted faster, because there were two of us drawing breath from it, but within thirty minutes *SC-1* returned. We could hear the SCAV drive in the distance as it approached. The flood of steam from its stern came into view to the south, and then the seacar churned toward us. It slowed to a stop, and the shock wave of the vessel slowing shoved us twenty meters through the water. We held onto each other to keep from separating, and then they saw us. Meg was piloting; she was visible through the cabin canopy. She waved and navigated closer, using the thruster pods. She hovered above us, and I looked up as the moonpool hatch opened. She was at thirty meters—four atms—and we kicked and rose up to the moonpool and broke the surface into *SC-1*.

I spit out the regulator and looked around at the faces staring down at me. Renée in particular caught my eye, and I grinned and hugged her from the pool. She bent down and kissed me, hard and long and deep. There were tears streaming down her face and dripping onto me.

I tried my best to soothe her.

We'd done it.

—••—

SAHAR WAS WEARING HER BURKINI and had a tank on her back. Cliff was also suited up, ready to jump in the water.

"Were you going to save me?" I muttered.

"Hell no, Boss," he answered. "We have to get the Staging System. It's on the bottom."

I snorted and then laughed out loud.

We hauled ourselves up onto the deck and the moonpool hatch closed. Meg and Renée brought the seacar to the seafloor and Sahar and Cliff went out through the airlock. They'd have to decompress after, because of the depth, but within minutes they had the crate inside the airlock.

SC-1 rose from the sandy bottom, Meg activated the SCAV drive, and we rocketed south around New Zealand and then west toward the Indian Ocean.

And The Vault.

—••—

AN HOUR LATER, I WAS sitting on the couch in dry clothes, recovering from the events. Alyssna was fussing over the component to make sure it was okay. Meg and Renée were piloting, but Renée had already been back to check on me. Richard and Clarke were on the opposite couch, and Johnny was helping Cliff go over some minor damage in engineering from a nearby concussion during the fighting.

Hyland and Chalam were checking on the five Isomer Bombs, and Sahar was with us, in the seacar's living area.

"Thanks for getting the component," I said to her.

"It was easy. No problem at all."

"It was deep."

She scoffed. "I've done better, *without* equipment, Mac. I'm a free diver, remember."

I snorted at that; I had indeed forgotten. She and Cliff had decompressed for thirty minutes in the airlock before dragging the crate in. Now she was back in her hijab and discussing the events with us.

We didn't have much time. The sunken warsubs would find a way to communicate the events to their HQs soon. We needed to be at the hidden facility before that happened.

"You go through this a lot, as Mayor of Trieste?" she asked.

I shrugged. "More as Director of TCI. But it's been an adventure. If you're joining us to get independence for Churchill, you might have more of these events too."

She smiled. "I have to say, it's not the worst."

"And no one died," I sighed. "I hope."

She lowered her head for a moment. "I do appreciate your attempts to follow my wishes."

I looked up at Clarke and Richard. They looked tired, but they'd made it through successfully.

I took a breath and decided that it was time to get some answers. "Listen to me, Clarke. Enough nonsense. It's time you explained what's going on here."

He blinked and focused on me. "What do you mean?"

I pictured the logo from the labs at Churchill. Then the red and black shoulder patches I'd seen on so many sailors recently.

Something was not right here.

Something was different about these sailors in the British Submarine Fleet.

"The BSFIF. What is it? Why is it at odds with the BSF? And who's in charge of the Research Labs now? Because there's clearly—"

"I'm not sure what you're—"

I shook my head and looked away. "Come on, Commodore. Every step of the way we've encountered friction with this mysterious group within the BSF. They don't even recognize you as having authority over them. Your BSF guards at the Churchill labs *hated* working there. They complained about the duty."

"Every duty has its—"

"No." I shook my head. "There was more to it. They didn't like the others there. Security even refused to acknowledge Johnny's higher rank. It was only when you went back when most everyone was gone that they let him go. And here on *Aurora* they wouldn't even listen to you. You're a Commodore and the rank system is ingrained in every military, *everywhere*." I took a breath and steeled myself. "Now I want to know what's going on."

There was a long silence as we waited. He was staring at me.

Eventually, he released his breath and said, "I don't have to answer to you, Mac."

"We're on this mission together. We're stuck on this ship. You are holding things back from us. We deserve to know the truth."

Sahar was watching the entire exchange with a quizzical expression on her face. She'd vouched for the Commodore, but she hadn't known about this.

He looked away. "It's top secret."

"You're throwing yourself in with the independence movement at Churchill. You're going to have to leave the BSF, Clarke, eventually."

"Not immediately though. I can help Mayor Noor more if I remain in the military."

"Until it becomes impossible."

He nodded.

"Look," I said. "We're heading for The Vault. I need to know what we're heading for. What is the BSFIF?"

He still didn't respond.

Sahar said into the silence, "Mac is right, Commodore. You can't risk this mission by withholding information. I've supported you. Don't make me regret that, and don't dare lie to me."

Her tone was hard and it had an immediate effect. Clarke's eyes turned to ice. Then he sighed and looked away again. "You're too important to disappoint, Sahar," he said.

It shocked me, because he had been so antagonistic toward her in her office, what seemed like years before.

He continued, "BSF Command knows what kind of pull you have over the people of Churchill. You have the potential to go even further, onto the mainland even. Prime Minister possibly."

She shook her head. "I'm not interested. I want to stay in the oceans. I am staying at Churchill. Now, tell us about the BSFIF."

He offered a small chuckle. "I can't say no to you." He paused for a moment longer. "It's a splinter group in the BSF. The British Submarine Fleet Imperial Force. Admiralty is embarrassed about it. They are militant. They're developing new weapons, like this particle beam, using their offshoot, the BSFRL. They don't obey BSFCO. My commanding officers have sent me to . . . "

"Yes," Sahar pressed.

He exhaled and then swore. Then he looked abashed at Sahar's look of reprimand. Then he said, "My orders are to go to their HQ in the Indian Ocean. Find them . . . find their leaders, and then blow them all to hell."

Interlude: The Mid-Atlantic Ridge
One Year Earlier

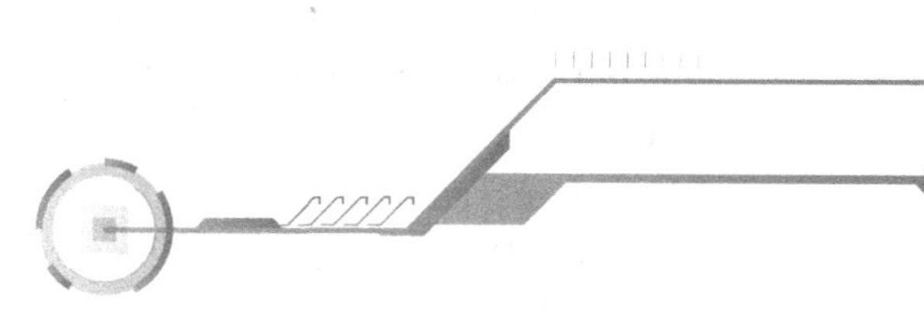

Interlude:	The Mid-Atlantic Ridge
Date:	March 2130 AD
Depth:	3,263 meters
Latitude:	27° 55″ 15′ S
Longitude:	17° 35″ 43′ W
Time:	2125 hours

THE TORPEDO HAD JUST DETONATED behind *SC-1*. Kat was struggling with the controls. Mac was shouting questions over the comm, but it was an unintelligible mess. The sonar was nearly incapable of making out vessels and torpedoes and mines due to the flood of noise in the theater of battle.

A shower of rocks cascaded over the seacar, dislodged by the detonation. Kat swore again and again. Her companion in the chair next to her had a look of horror on his face. More rocks fell on the vessel, rattling the hull, scraping across the titanium as they slid aside and fell into the depths.

Water started to jet into the seacar. She could hear it behind her, in the living space.

Then a seal cracked on the canopy, and a spray of water started shooting into the pilot cabin.

She keyed the comm to signal Mac. "More flooding! The canopy this time."

"Stay calm," came the response. "Watch where you're going."

The sonar blared and Kat snapped her gaze to it. Behind her, a series of red lights blinked into view. Small fighters, unleashed by a larger war-sub, and some were on her tail. Mac warned her.

She blurted, "I already noticed them!"

Then they fired.

The sonar *shrieked*.

Three red lines appeared on the screen.

"Oh, fuck!" Kat cried. She tried to zigzag to avoid them, keep them changing course, and keep them from hitting their top speed of eighty.

Mac was churning toward her, and he had fired at the three small vessels behind her.

But it wasn't going to be enough. They were too late, and *SC-1* was too slow to avoid three torpedoes fired simultaneously. Then one of the torpedoes hit a countermeasure, and it detonated, dangerously close to her seacar.

The explosion rattled her teeth. She clutched the yoke and swore again. The water was jetting across the cabin, and she was blinking to see through the salty and cold spray, which was coating her face and hair.

"Damn!" she cried into the mic.

"Kat, dive or go shallow!" Mac shouted back. "Get off that course, now!"

Then there was another massive detonation, and the power in the cabin flickered.

She screamed, then it went black.

KAT BLINKED FURIOUSLY AND TRIED to make out what was happening. The torpedoes had seriously damaged *SC-1*. Power was flickering, which meant there was water in the electrical system. Meanwhile they were flooding, which meant they risked descending past Crush Depth, which for *SC-1* was only 4,000 meters. She adjusted ballast and gave a quick prayer that it would work.

The sound of the pumps purging water from the tanks echoed in the seacar, and she exhaled. She made the ballast positive, understanding that with the flooding, it would eventually become neutrally buoyant.

Then negative, and they'd sink.

She'd have to get back to the base before then.

She set course for The Ridge, pushed the throttle forward, and hoped they could get back before the damage overwhelmed the ship.

Something occurred to her at that point. Something odd.

Despite the danger and the explosions and the flooding on board her vessel, there was something else that suddenly triggered a warning in the deep recesses of her brain.

The hairs on her arms stood on end.

Her two companions had left the pilot's cabin, and they were aft of her, in the living compartment, and they were arguing.

Their words were angry.

Poisonous.

A chill traced up her spine.

"A false friend and a shadow attend only while the
sun shines."
—Benjamin Franklin

Part Five: Third Component

Chapter Twenty-Five

I STARED IN HORROR AT Clarke, who was sitting across from me on the couch in *SC-1*. We were hurtling through the Pacific south of Tasmania. We'd passed the Tasman Sea, past Blue Downs, and were approaching the Indian Ocean. Then we'd alter course to a northwesterly direction toward The Vault.

Sahar was angry. She had the closest thing to a look of disgust on her face that I'd yet seen. "What do you mean, *blow them all to hell?*"

Clarke sighed. "They've turned more right wing. More militarized than the rest of the BSF. They have admirals who support them. Some warsubs are even on their side. They've taken over most of the BSFRL facilities!"

I thought about what had just happened while stealing Component Two from *Aurora Rex*. "Is that why three ships showed up when you called the emergency?"

"They were protecting each other, yes. *Aurora* is part of the splinter group. It's why the Staging System was there. The other two warsubs were there for backup."

I recalled XO Smith asking me if I was "here for them." I stared at Clarke. "Not everyone is on their side, obviously."

He nodded. "We get regular reports from sailors on their warsubs, reporting what their superiors are doing. Smith is loyal to us."

"How many warsubs do they have?"

"Forty. Not a huge number, but they're developing dangerous weaponry. The Water Pick is an example. We can't let them have it. My mission is to steal it and destroy the leadership at The Vault."

Sahar snapped, "You're betraying us?"

He looked surprised. "Not at all. I'm working with you. I'm helping to steal it."

"For us?"

"And for me. For the BSF. We'll both get it."

She looked perplexed. "Do you still support our independence?"

"Yes, of course."

I shook my head. "You can't have it both ways, Commodore. You can't give the BSF the particle beam and then declare independence for the colonies. It doesn't make sense."

He said, "The bigger threat is the BSFIF. They are a danger. We can't let them control more warsubs or develop more dangerous weapons. Every day they attract more officers."

"Under what pretense?"

He cursed under his breath. "The same bullshit, Mac. Right-wing stuff. Hating the immigration situation. Refugees due to climate change on the surface. Putting the 'Great' back in Great Britain. That sort of nonsense. It comes up again and again in history. Doesn't matter the country. I have a chance with you to stamp it out. We can do it, together."

"Why didn't you just tell us?"

"Would you have brought me?"

Silence descended, and I didn't know how to answer. I thought it over for a moment, then I made a sudden decision. "Why did you try to kill me?"

—••—

His face was blank. Then he managed: "I beg your pardon?"

"When the airlock system trapped us. Me, Renée, and Sahar. You tampered with the program. Locked us in there."

"When?" The news had flummoxed him, and if he was acting, it was a magnificent display.

"Just before we left Trieste."

He shook his head slowly; his eyes were on mine and never strayed. "Mac, I promise you, I didn't do it. Why do you think so?"

"Someone hacked the airlock from the computer in your living compartment."

"Then someone has framed me, Mac." He tilted his head. "And knowing this, you still brought me on the mission? But why?"

I shrugged. "Maybe I'm not scared of you. Or maybe I just want to keep my enemies closer."

"So you can keep watch on them." He chuckled. "A smart strategy, but it wasn't me."

I took a deep breath and mulled it over.

But Sahar was not done. "Commodore, you can't go and just kill everyone! I won't be a part of that!"

"We're going to steal the particle beam components. Then I'll help you declare independence, which I promised. But I have to give the weapon to the BSF and kill as many BSFIF leaders as I can. We have to stamp out this cancer in the BSF. Once that's done, I'm fully with you and the independence movement."

I stared at him. "We're taking the weapon to Trieste. The first component is already there, and we now have the second too."

"And of course Trieste will have it, Mac. But BSF engineers will want to get their hands on it, to make their own version."

"You think Alyssna will allow the BSF to come in and take what she knows? Or that I'll even allow that?"

His eyes flashed and his face suddenly grew hard. "Without me you wouldn't have either component! I got us in the lab at Churchill and also on board *Aurora*. Of course you'll allow it."

"Don't tell me what I'll allow."

Meg had been watching the entire exchange from the pilot's cabin. She turned the controls over to Renée and stepped toward us. "You see what I was worried about, Truman?"

"I'm not betraying you, dammit," Clarke said. "I'm still helping you steal this weapon!"

"But at the same time you're also saying you're going to take it from us." Her eyebrows raised.

"We'll work together and *share* the weapon. That's what I'm saying."

I sighed. "Why do you think we'd do that?" I stared at him for a long moment. "That's like turning it over to the enemy. We won't do that."

"But the BSF is not the enemy."

"That doesn't make sense, Clarke. You were on the side of

independence. You told Sahar you'd help her. Now you want to turn a dangerous weapon over to them."

"They already have it."

"No they don't. The BSFIF has it. You already said that. We have an opportunity now to take if from them and keep the rest of the fleet from getting it."

"I have my orders, Mac. I'm a Commodore. I'll do what's best for the BSF."

Sahar's face had gone white. She had watched the exchange in horror. "But you promised you'd help us achieve independence."

"I will. Once I finish this job." His expression was one of determination. "I'm trustworthy, Sahar. I promise you."

"But what you're saying is a total contradiction."

He frowned. "No, it's not. Turning the weapon over to the BSF is not a contradiction to declaring independence for Churchill."

"But . . . " she trailed off. "But they could threaten to use The Water Pick on us! They could threaten our people. And you want to give them this? It's . . . " She shook her head. "It just doesn't equate with what you've promised me."

"We can have both, Sahar." He watched her for a long moment. "The BSF's major threat right now is the Imperial Force splinter group. We want the weapon to use against *them*, not against Churchill."

"Until we reveal ourselves. If we tell them we want to leave and be part of Oceania!"

"I think things will be fine." He crossed his arms. "Things will work out. You'll see."

She scowled. "You promised me."

"And I'm sticking to that promise. How can you think otherwise?"

"Because you want to help the BSF!"

"They're not your enemy."

"They will be, once we declare independence. They'll occupy us." She gestured at me and Meg. "I saw what happened in Trieste after The Battle in 2129."

Clarke sighed. "I'm going to be there to help. I promise."

Sahar stared at him, fuming. Meg's face was dark, as if she was signaling, *I told you all so.*

I didn't know how to react. Cliff was watching from the engineering hatch. He must have heard the commotion and come to find out what was going on. He was staring at me, and his expression was serious. Like me, he took any threat to Trieste personally.

Clarke said, "I told you where I came from."

"The accent is hard to miss," I muttered.

"From Kilmuir on the Isle of Skye. We've dealt with oppression in the past, let me tell you. The English have oppressed Scotland since time began, almost. They stamped out our freedom. Crushed our spirit. And now climate change has obliterated my homeland. Our shores are different. The fish are no longer near Kilmuir. Most of the town is underwater. That's my history, Mac. *Underwater! Gone!* My family is living a past that no longer exists. For centuries we could trace our roots back through time. To all the major events in the history of Scotland working against *and with* the Great Kingdom! But now that's all gone, destroyed by global warming and the scourge of unrelenting water and heat. Famine. Economies everywhere are crashing. I knew it as a child, and it's worse now! And when I was a younger man, I found myself in Trieste, working with Frank McClusky. I appreciated his fierce sense of independence."

"And yet you ended up with the BSF?" I prodded.

"When the CIA killed your dad. Yes. Because I wanted to work *from within*. Until the day came that I could help."

"But now you want it both ways. You want to help *both* organizations."

He jerked to his feet and shouted, "To defeat these right-wing bastards! These people who want to establish an authoritarian regime over us. The BSFIF. They're the real threat!"

"Until they're not."

He stared at me, his face red. "What does that mean?"

I shrugged. "When they're gone, the next threat will be the big one. That'll be Oceania and Churchill. And Trieste. What will you do then?"

"What kind of threat? What do you mean?"

"Will you use your weapon against us? The Water Pick? Or worse?"

He sneered. "Or maybe you'll use your Isomer Bombs against *us*."

I feigned ignorance. "Those belong to Germany. Not us."

He swore. "And what are those bombs back there?" He gestured savagely to the aft compartments. "Your Doctor Hyland brought five on board. I know they're not nukes! And I know one blew up Seascape, the largest threat to you, last summer. Mysterious, wouldn't you say?"

"I don't know what you're talking about." I faked a half smile. "Is this something your bosses have ordered you to secure for the BSF as well?"

That stopped him, and he stood there, chest heaving. The rest of us were watching him in silence. Then he continued in a forced, pained voice, "You've baited me. Good job, Mac." He exhaled, and it was savage. Then, "That is a new technology that surprised everyone. Of course the BSF wants it."

"And you're going to try to steal that, too?"

He stared at me from a dark cloud of fury. Face red, fists clenched, veins popping on his temples. Then he visibly deflated. "Yes, Mac. They told me to find out about the Isomer Bomb too."

—••—

I LOOKED AWAY. THIS WAS a dilemma. We needed him to help infiltrate The Vault, but clearly his other motivations were going to cause enormous difficulties for Trieste. Sahar looked hurt and annoyed, and Meg was simply furious. She was shaking her head and staring at the man standing between the couches in the living area of *SC-1*.

"You're betraying us," she said in a low voice. "Did you also betray my dad? Is that how he died?"

The statement shocked Clarke. "No! We worked together, along with Richard and Jessica. The attack was maybe predictable, but when it came we had no defense. It was still too early in the movement. I left too, and vowed to prepare for another attempt, far in the future."

"Which is now, as you said," Meg snapped. "But instead, you're also helping the military which will occupy and force Churchill into submission. And you want to steal an Isomer Bomb! What do you think that's for, Clarke? To just put in a closet and never use? The BSF will want to use it against someone!"

"It's just to maintain the balance of power, which Sahar has mentioned many times before. We can't let one nation have such a weapon and not also have it. It gives others too much control over the oceans."

Meg continued to fume as she stared at the man. Then she spun on her heel and retreated to engineering, but not before fixing me with an angry glare.

I sighed. She'd been right about the man all along. I'd tried to be objective, but his motivations were cloudy and conflicted. And I still had to process the fact that he claimed innocence for the airlock attack against me in Trieste.

The Vault was 9,300 kilometers away. We'd be there in roughly twenty-one hours. And in that time we had to somehow work up a plan to steal the neutral beam and keep Clarke at arm's length. At the same time, he wanted to assassinate the BSFIF's command structure, steal the weapon from us, and learn more about the mysterious Isomer Bomb.

Or, I realized, take Max Hyland. Clarke had recognized the man's importance.

Damn.

Chapter Twenty-Six

The hours passed fitfully. I spent the first of them in the pilot chair with Renée at my side. So far, the multistage mission had been successful, but it hadn't progressed as we'd hoped. There'd been many wrenches thrown into the works, most notably Clarke and his parallel plans. Sahar would not be happy if he killed someone. We wanted to fly under the radar, so to speak, infiltrate the facility, steal the components, and leave without anyone knowing until we were gone.

That was not going to happen now.

Not as long as Clarke was on board, that is.

He seemed highly conflicted. Perhaps his history had moulded him to be this way—fiercely loyal to a place that was struggling due to climate change and environmental devastation, but at the same time beholden to an authority that at one time his people didn't even recognize. But he also claimed to be loyal to Sahar and Churchill, who wanted to split from that higher authority.

It didn't seem possible, and I was beginning to question his sanity.

Renée watched me in silence, and I flashed her a small smile. She said, "Things just got a lot more difficult."

"You could say that."

"I'm sure you'll find a way."

I started at that. "Pardon?"

"You always seem to."

"This one seems beyond solving. We almost have to just let things happen and see how it all shakes out."

She glanced behind her, then lowered her voice to a whisper. "You could just kill him."

A strobe of realization surged through me. My head felt light. Sahar was behind us, in the living area. "I know," I finally managed.

—••—

TWO HOURS LATER, WE'D GATHERED in the lounge to finalize our plans. Alyssna had worked at The Vault before, so knew some of the geography of the region, and Chalam knew the precise location. The warsub in the South Pacific—*Aurora Rex*—was on the bottom, foundering, and I had destroyed her communications to prevent a signal getting out to the BSFIF in the Indian Ocean. That wouldn't last forever, I knew. We had a very small window here and had to act as soon as possible.

"It's time to show us where exactly this is located," I said to Chalam. He had been quiet since his explosion when first departing, when he'd screamed at Alyssna about creating the neutral beam weapon. I'd hoped his silence was contrition, as he realized that he was just taking his anger and grief at his brother's death out on the only person possible.

For now, anyway.

He was yet another question mark on this mission.

He'd refused to show us the exact coordinates of the mysterious modules his equipment had detected on the ocean floor until we were nearly there.

"Do you have a map I can see?" he responded in a quiet, subdued voice.

Renée brought him a viewpad and he zoomed in on the Indian Ocean. In a minute he'd punched in a set of figures and the bathymetry of the ocean floor appeared. "This it is," Chalam whispered. "This is the location. There were several cylindrical modules on the seafloor here, at the top of this ridge." He indicated their locations, and the computer added them to the image.

Alyssna peered at it. She nodded. "It seems familiar. The engineers partly submerged the facility into that ridge using tunnels and hollows. There are some modules on the peak. But there are also listening posts located in the area."

"Can you explain?" Max Hyland asked.

"Towers. With delicate sensors to listen passively. Automated. You can't make noise, or security will be out in an instant."

I nodded. She'd already told us about this, back at Trieste. "Now that you see the map, can you locate them for us?"

She nodded and stared at the 3D image rotating in space before us, between the couches. She held her finger out. A red star flashed and remained at each point she touched. "They're here. Five of them, I believe."

Max said, "But surely there are always weird noises. The undersea environment is full of life."

"Algorithms detect the difference between mechanical and organic. Or human. Then they alert security if there's an . . . event."

"Has that ever happened?" I asked.

She shrugged. "Only false alarms, as far as I know." She shot a glance at Chalam. "Obviously that changed when your seacar came over the area."

He didn't respond, but he also didn't explode, which was a positive.

"I see," I muttered.

"And the modules are here," she noted as she pointed them out. "There are travel tubes between them, but remember, the underground facility also connects them. That's just where it pokes up above the seafloor."

I zoomed the map out so we could see Diego Garcia to the east and a massive cluster of bathymetric lines moving roughly north and south beyond the joint USSF/BSF base. "And this," I said, "is the Chagos Trench, which Chalam had been researching before they destroyed his seacar."

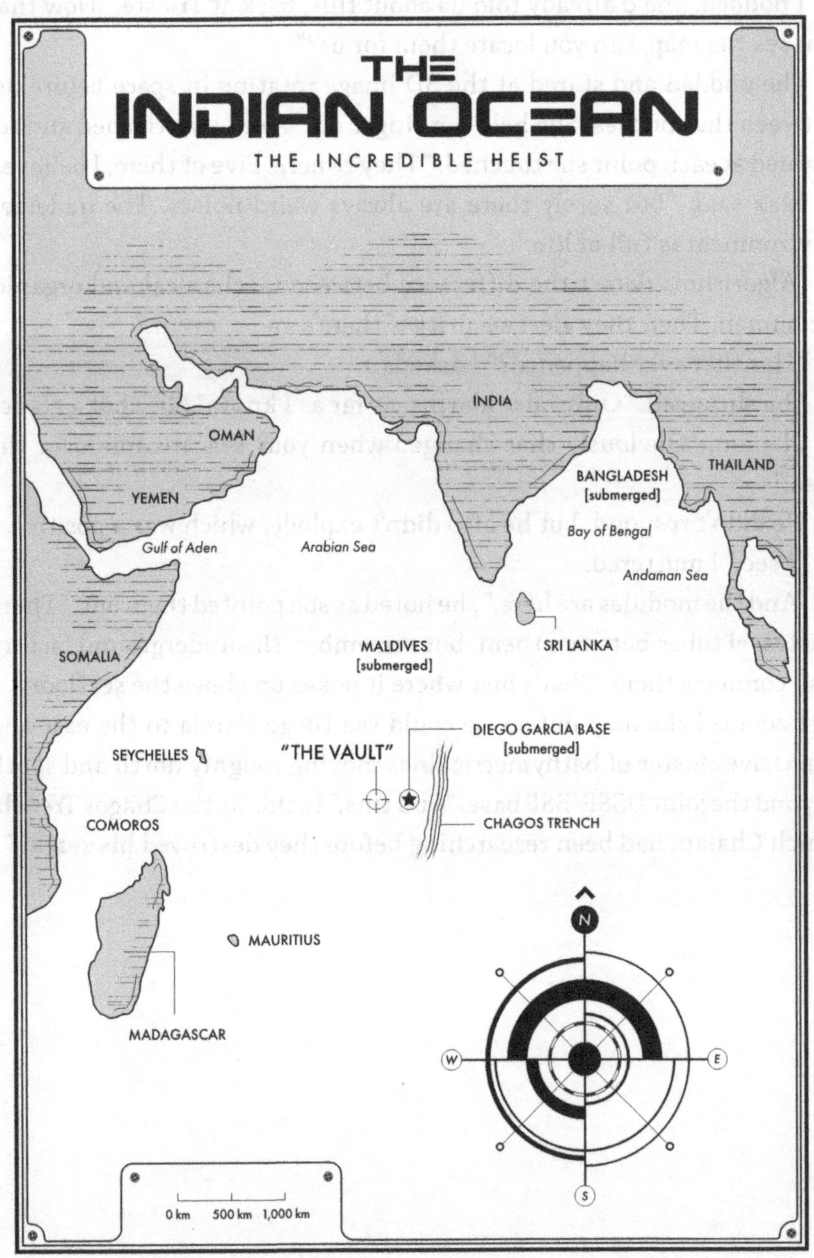

THE
INDIAN OCEAN
THE INCREDIBLE HEIST
OMAN
YEMEN
INDIA
BANGLADESH
[submerged]
THAILAND
Gulf of Aden
Arabian Sea
Bay of Bengal
Andaman Sea
SOMALIA
MALDIVES
[submerged]
SRI LANKA
SEYCHELLES
"THE VAULT"
DIEGO GARCIA BASE
[submerged]
COMOROS
CHAGOS TRENCH
MAURITIUS
MADAGASCAR
N
W
E
S
0 km   500 km   1,000 km

The young geologist nodded. "Yes. We'd been studying the tectonic plates in the region, as well as searching for magnetic sources." A shrug. "Iron ore. The world needs it right now. We had hoped to find a deposit or two for Churchill to make the trip financially worthwhile."

We stared at the region for long minutes. Then Clarke said, "So we have to get past the listening sensors and infiltrate the base. Quietly. We have to locate Component Three and Four and get out. But this—" he pointed at the nearby BSF base "—is a major problem. If a call goes out for help, they'll send everything they've got. Not to mention the security force already in The Vault. If we alert them, then it's trouble. My rank is clearly not going to be helpful here. These BSFIF bastards don't care about our military hierarchy."

"We've taken care of that," I said.

He frowned. "How?"

Alyssna also looked confused. "I beg your pardon?"

I stared at the group before me. "The most important part of any heist is getting in and out and alerting as few people as possible. The more who know what's going on, the more challenging it'll be. And if the military at Diego Garcia know what's happening, then we'll be in serious trouble. Something that Cliff suggested while stealing Component One stood out to me."

Cliff frowned. "A distraction?"

"Absolutely." I looked at the map. "And geography plays in our favor. Right here."

They peered past my outstretched finger. "The Trench?" Clarke asked.

I motioned to Max. "Care to take over?"

—••—

MAX HYLAND SAID, "THE REASON I'm here. One of the reasons Chalam is as well. We've been discussing the issue for weeks now. How to create a distraction that will pull the military's attention away from The Vault."

"While we steal the components," I interjected.

"I learned a lot about the geologic history of the region. Chalam taught me. There have been some major tectonic events here. One caused the Boxing Day Tsunami of 2004. The Vault's location gave Mac an idea. He realized we could use tectonics to our advantage."

"How?" Cliff asked.

Max stared at the group. "All military personnel are going to be on alert, but not for a theft or for intruders. Instead, they're going to be worried about an environmental threat from the other direction."

"Caused by?"

He paused and glanced at me.

I said, "Go ahead, tell them."

He grinned broadly. "I brought five bombs with me. We're going to detonate them in the trench. That's our distraction."

—••—

CLARKE WAS STARING AT THE man. I knew what was going through his head, but there was no way we could conceal it now. He growled, "What type of bombs are these?"

Max replied, "Very large ones."

"What kilotonnage?"

"Each is one megaton."

Sahar gasped. "How big was Hiroshima, Max?"

"Fifteen kilotons."

"So this is how much more powerful?"

He shrugged. "Each one is about seventy times more powerful than Hiroshima."

"And you're detonating five of them?" Her face was slack.

"In the depths of the trench, simultaneously, yes. It won't hurt anyone, and these bombs don't produce the amount of radiation a traditional bomb does."

"That is interesting," Clarke muttered, glancing at me.

I ignored him.

"That's 350 times more powerful than Hiroshima. And it'll do what, exactly?"

Chalam stepped forward. "We've been working on the possibility of using an underwater quake as an effective distraction, but we don't want to accidentally trigger a real disaster."

"But detonating five underwater bombs on a tectonic boundary might actually do that," Sahar said. "How can we guarantee that it won't happen?"

"Because history and geology have important lessons to teach about this," he replied. "Especially a quake that happened in 2012. When first detected, people worried it would spawn another tsunami because of the proximity to the Boxing Day quake's epicenter. But it didn't."

"Why not?"

"Because of the types of plate boundaries here. Some of them are divergent, meaning huge sections of the crust are pulling away from each other. Those create minor quakes, magma intrusions or extrusions, black smokers, and so on. Then there are the convergent boundaries, meaning the crust sections are moving toward each other."

Sahar looked surprised. "I had no idea it moves. How fast?"

Chalam shrugged. "It varies, depending on the location. The Pacific crust within the Ring of Fire is the fastest, at about ten centimeters per year. The Earth is a dynamic creature, always changing, always moving. Even underground, in the crust, and deep in the mantle and core."

"And the surface crust collides? It's not all one piece?"

"Not at all. It's broken into many pieces, called *plates*. There are major ones that occupy entire continents and ocean floors, and others that are much smaller. When different plates collide, only a few things can happen. They can both push each other upward, resulting in mountain ranges. The Himalayas are this type. *Or*, one can actually go *under* the other. The denser one will actually thrust downward, into the mantle. The resulting friction and rubbing of one plate under another creates great stress. It builds up over time, and the plate underneath the other, or *subducting*, can suddenly move and release great energy. The west coast of North America and Central and South America are this type. If the collision occurs underwater, and there's a quake, it can shove water upward at the surface, causing a displacement wave that spreads outward across the oceans. That's a tsunami."

Sahar had a pained look on her face. "But we don't want to create anything like that here. That's what you said."

"Exactly. But back in 2012 there was a quake in this region, which I mentioned. People were worried. But it was at a different type of boundary. It was the third type, where the plates slide past each other. They grind, they get caught up, tension builds, then they slip. They cause quakes that way. They're called Strike-Slip boundaries. The ground can move ten meters in only seconds. Sometimes buildings can't withstand it, and they collapse. Gas lines break, like in San Francisco in 1906, and huge fires result." He paused. "But underwater, they don't generate displacement. That's what we're going to do here." He checked the time. "Tomorrow, hopefully. In the Chagos Trench. We're going to generate crustal movement and a giant quake to distract the military staff in both Diego Garcia and The Vault."

Chapter Twenty-Seven

Everyone was staring at Chalam. "Is it possible?" Alyssna asked. "To cause a quake? And throw DG and The Vault into a false emergency?"

"They'll be looking to the east, waiting for a water displacement that will never come. Meanwhile, we'll be infiltrating and stealing the two components." Chalam offered a slight grin, and it was a good sign that he was moving past his anger. "We just have to place the bombs in the right places to help move things along." He shrugged. "These things are actually done fairly routinely, on the surface. Geologists attempt to relieve stress at dangerous plate boundaries to cause minor quakes every couple of years rather than experience a massive one every twenty. They do it at the San Andreas fault line. That's a Strike-Slip boundary, also called Transform. It's done in Alaska too, where seismologists once recorded the world's biggest quake in 1964. It was a 9.2 on the Richter Scale. The downtown region of Anchorage dropped almost forty feet! It destroyed the town. It was catastrophic. It caused a tsunami of over sixty meters."

"I don't want to kill people, Chalam," Sahar murmured.

"No, it won't. It'll be a big quake—we're predicting over 8.0 on the Richter Scale—but without the displacement, remember. It'll be two crusts sliding past each other and relieving stress. But the facilities won't know this. They'll detect a large quake, and hopefully all eyes will turn toward the trench. To the east."

I watched the others. "What do you think?"

Cliff said, "It sounds like an effective distraction, if it works. The facility likely already has procedures in place in case of such an event."

"How are we going to do it?" Meg asked.

"This is where it gets tricky, because we only have *SC-1* to do that job. So Chalam, Max, and a pilot will have to go without the rest of us. They'll drop the team off at The Vault, and we'll begin efforts to infiltrate it. We'll need Alyssna with us, because she's worked there and knows her way around. *SC-1* will leave for the Chagos Trench, and drop the bombs at the correct locations that Chalam and Max have worked up. Then they'll back off a bit—"

"By several kilometers!" Max said.

"—and detonate. And when the earthquake starts, we'll steal the devices."

"But Mac," Alyssna interjected, her eyes slightly wild. "I'm not familiar with the entire facility! I only know my labs and where I ate and slept."

"I understand. It's okay. We'll get you to your labs, and you point out the two components to us. The Aiming Module and The Accelerator."

"They're in two different areas."

"Show us."

She turned to the map and I zoomed it back to the facility that the rocky ridge partially enclosed. "There are four exposed modules here, on the seafloor. People refer to the entire facility as The Vault because engineers constructed it in a way that makes it difficult to crack, so to speak. It's underwater, first of all. Not deep, but still."

"How deep?" Cliff asked, staring at the isobaths.

"Five hundred meters below sea level. Secondly, the sensitive equipment is in the rock, not in those modules. Those visible structures are mostly habitat and recreation, eating and living spaces, and so on. The modules connect to the rest of the structure, underground."

"We can enter there?" I asked.

She nodded. "There are travel tubes connecting them."

"Is there security at the tubes?"

She stared at me. "First you have to get past the listening towers surrounding the facility. They'll hear *SC-1* as it nears. That's the first step, I'd say." Then she looked at the modules. "Each hatch in the tubes and the surface modules requires a pass key. We just wore them around our necks, so we never noticed the hatches opening and closing. You'll have to get one."

"Go on."

She frowned. "Well, that's just the surface modules. Under them, it's a different story. The tunnels and workplaces are carved into the bedrock. The hatches there all require the same ID, only these are more of a challenge. The surface modules are for workers, staff, and so on. The area underground is for engineers, scientists, administrators. So these IDs are not the same."

"I don't think we'll have to worry about that."

Her eyes were questioning. "But why?"

"What happens when there's a quake alert? What's the common practice?"

"The same as in any underwater facility. Evacuate to the secure shelters."

"And what happens with the hatches?"

Her face showed recognition. "They unlock, so people can escape."

I grinned. "Exactly. It's counterintuitive at a secure facility, but people *have* to be allowed to get to safety. You can't lock them in. And an earthquake emergency and imminent loss of structural integrity takes care of that."

She shook her head and muttered, "Incredible."

And they would never expect. People generally didn't have the ability to cause quakes . . . but most also didn't have access to megaton-sized bombs.

"Where is security located?" Cliff asked. "On the seafloor, or under?"

"Good question." She screwed up her face in thought. "The module farthest south is Security HQ, although I only passed through there on arrival, then on exit. Only twice."

"So, no military or security in the actual labs, underground?"

She shook her head. "I never saw them down there, though there is a docking pool there. Seacars use a tunnel to pilot in and dock. It's not connected to the labs."

"What's it connected to?"

"The security module is above."

I considered that. "So, if anyone docks, they have to go up to the seafloor level, through the security module, then they're cleared to go back below."

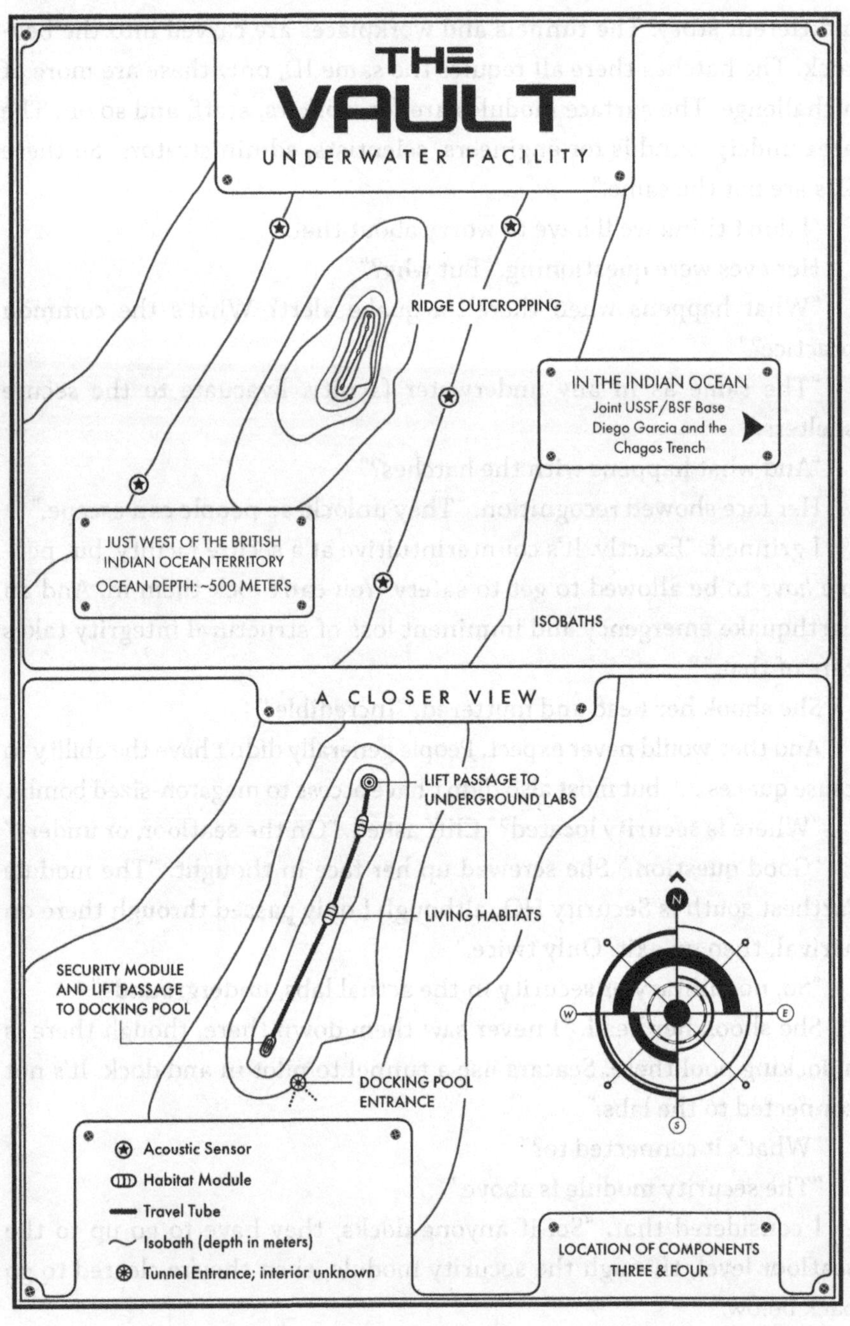
THE VAULT
UNDERWATER FACILITY
RIDGE OUTCROPPING
IN THE INDIAN OCEAN
Joint USSF/BSF Base
Diego Garcia and the
Chagos Trench
JUST WEST OF THE BRITISH
INDIAN OCEAN TERRITORY
OCEAN DEPTH: ~500 METERS
ISOBATHS
A CLOSER VIEW
LIFT PASSAGE TO
UNDERGROUND LABS
LIVING HABITATS
SECURITY MODULE
AND LIFT PASSAGE
TO DOCKING POOL
DOCKING POOL
ENTRANCE
Acoustic Sensor
Habitat Module
Travel Tube
Isobath (depth in meters)
Tunnel Entrance; interior unknown
N
W
E
S
LOCATION OF COMPONENTS
THREE & FOUR

"Yes. But at the dome, farther north."

I mulled over the situation for a while longer. "We have here a series of obstacles we have to get by, and quietly, until the bombs detonate and the earthquake scares everyone. First," I ticked each item off on my fingers, "*SC-1* has to drop us off close enough to the facility, but not *too* close or the listening sensors will pick us up. Then *SC-1* with Chalam, Hyland, and a pilot will go plant the bombs. Secondly, we'll have to disable a listening post so we can sneak past. Then we'll infiltrate the base, which is Step Three. Then we have to get past security, which is Four. Then once past it, Alyssna will have to get us to the domed module farthest north, then wait for the quake to send people to their secure shelters. That's Five. Then we move down the lift to the labs and find the two weapon components. She said they're in different locations though, so Six, we'll find the Aiming Module. Then we can get The Accelerator, which is Seven. And then Eight," I exhaled, after going over such an extensive list, "the towers in that quadrant will have to be disabled because *SC-1* will have to come back, pick us all up, with the two components."

Blank faces met my long list of things we had to accomplish.

I stared at Clarke, worried that he might totally derail the order I'd established.

"Hopefully the earthquake will distract the warsubs and military at Diego Garcia, which is only a few kilometers to the east," Cliff muttered in a gravelly voice.

"Yes, there's that." I watched the others before me. "Who wants to pilot *SC-1*?"

Meg stepped forward. "I'll do it. I think I'm the best choice, anyway. I've had a lot of experience with the seacar."

She was correct. So, Chalam, Hyland, and Meg would plant the bombs. But it still left a large number of people. "Alyssna, Cliff, Johnny, Richard—you'll infiltrate The Vault with me. The rest will stay outside, in scuba gear, and wait for *SC-1* to return. You'll have to arrange getting the weapon out." I narrowed my eyes. "Alyssna, how large is The Accelerator?"

She said, "It's a neutral beam weapon. It's big. Three meters long. One high. Very delicate too. And heavy. Several hundred pounds."

"But how did they get that in? Surely it didn't go through the surface modules and travel tubes?"

"But why—" Then she cut off her words. "Ah. I see. We can take it out the same way?"

"Exactly. Or, we can sneak *in* the same way."

She shook her head. "No. It's an airlock, but it only opens from inside. There's not even a panel on the outside. You can't see the hatch; it's hidden. We'd need an inside man, so to speak."

"Do you know anyone who could help?" But as I said it, I knew how useless the question was.

The lines in her face seemed to deepen. "No way. No one would help steal that weapon. They love working there."

I shrugged. It was worth a try. "Then once we get the equipment, we take it out through that airlock. The outside team will have to get *SC-1* there—*quietly*—once it returns."

Sahar said, "The quake might cause a lot of rumbling and noise. Water displacement too, although it won't be a huge underwater tsunami. But it might disguise us."

"While we're inside, you can work on sabotaging all the towers." I glanced at the map. "They are far apart though, which means a lot of swimming. Are you up to it?"

Sahar glanced at the others. Her face was hard and determined. "We've got it."

Clarke stepped forward. "Wait a minute. I'm not okay with this."

As I expected. I sighed. "Why not, Clarke?"

"I am not up to going out at a depth of 500 meters. That's a deadly dive! And it'll be an extended one, too! That is not okay."

"Then you can stay with the seacar—"

"No!" He thrust his chin out and stepped toward me. "I'm going to infiltrate the base with you tomorrow. We'll steal the device together, as we originally planned."

"That was before I knew about your ulterior motives."

"I told you, I am *not* betraying you!"

"No, you just have plans that don't align with ours! And we can't allow you to do what you're intending!"

Cliff said, "I take it you want to assassinate BSFIF staff, correct?"

"That's his mission," I said.

Cliff pursed his lips. Then he turned to me. "The fact is, Boss, that we could use him in The Vault. The presence of a senior BSF officer is crucial to this plan. Otherwise it's just a bunch of strangers inside the facility. But with Clarke, we'll be strangers, but with *some* legitimacy."

I stared at him. "And what about when he goes off on his own and starts killing people? We need to be quiet, remember."

Cliff stared at the BSF officer. "Simple," he said. "I'll kill him if he does anything to betray us."

—••—

THAT EVENING, PEOPLE WERE MOSTLY quiet. There was an underlying tension about what was coming. We'd reviewed the plan as much as we could, and after eyes began to grow heavy and attention began to waver, we called it quits for the time being. Cliff and Richard were in the pilot cabin, and many of the others were in the makeshift bunk section in engineering. Johnny had been training Sahar—she was going to have to help us disable the listening towers, and she needed to know how to open the panels and locate the correct wiring—and now she was praying, in the SCAV cabin. Renée and I found ourselves in the living area, sitting together before the mission got underway.

I reached down, put a finger under her chin, and tilted it up to me. I kissed her, long and deep.

"Mmm," she murmured. "That's nice."

"It's a good luck kiss." We kept kissing for a few more minutes. I was sure other people noticed, but I didn't care. The adrenaline was pumping, and I knew this was one of the more dangerous missions we'd ever been on. We were going into the unknown, without much information and without much planning, but we'd had no choice. We needed the neutral particle weapon. We were only halfway through our heist, but one way or another, it was going to end tomorrow.

She said into my neck, "Clarke has turned into a major problem."

"Cliff will take care of him if there's any trouble."

"But it could throw everyone into danger." She kissed my neck.

"We'll watch him closely. Especially now that we're aware of his other orders."

"What do you think he'll do?"

I frowned and pulled away. "He seems to think he's doing the right thing. Working to protect the BSF at the same time as preparing to help us declare independence and announce Oceania."

"The two are contradictory."

"I guess it depends on what the BSF does. There is a chance that they might support us, but I doubt it."

She snorted. "Me too."

"Chalam seems better."

"You should check in with him. Make sure he's going to go through with this."

"Oh, he will. He wants to steal the weapon."

"Still."

We disappeared into the recessed bunk at that point. We had one night left, and we weren't going to waste it.

Neither of us noticed Commodore Clarke and Chalam Kaashif speaking with each other in hushed tones in the living area after we'd left. A third person was there as well.

We wouldn't realize until it was too late.

Chapter Twenty-Eight

THE NEXT DAY, WE WOKE and brought *SCAV-1* to a stop. We were still hours from The Vault, but we decided to proceed the rest of the way with conventional thrusters—quieter than the *roaring* SCAV drive, which albeit faster, was like putting a target on ourselves in the oceans, begging the BSFIF to come straight to our location to find out just who we were and what we were doing.

We set the autopilot at a depth of 200 meters and progressed northward at a moderate velocity of only 40 kph. We ate lunch together, mostly quiet still, but there were the odd snippets of conversation. Chalam and Alyssna said a few words to each other, which was nice to hear. It was a start, at least.

Max was anxious to detonate his bombs—and not to cause death, this time—and Clarke was asking him questions about the nature of the devices. Max was glancing at me, and I shrugged. It didn't matter anymore; Commodore Clarke already suspected the truth. Eventually the world would find out, especially with the news that Russia would soon be pressing an attack.

"We're going to spread the bombs out in a precise manner," he told Clarke. "Each will be roughly two to three hundred meters apart along the fault. Chalam and I chose the locations based on the geology of the area." And since he and his brother had studied and gathered detailed surveys of the fault lines . . .

"Why do you need so many?" he asked.

"It's to make sure the crust slips."

"One won't do it?"

Max shrugged. "I don't know. It's the geologist's field, not mine. I just have to make sure they work and ensure the correct detonation size."

"Is there doubt?"

"Well, each needs an X-Ray blast first to trigger the hafnium's energy release. It's delicate, underwater. I've had to calibrate each for the depth in the Chagos Trench. But I've done a lot more testing in the past six months."

"Since Seascape's destruction?" Clarke asked, watching Hyland.

Max shot me another look. "I don't know anything about that," he said, his dimples flashing as he offered a sly smile.

Clarke chuckled. "Well, whoever invented the Isomer Bomb has triggered a new age. Forget atomics. Now we've got isomer energy."

"It's still nuclear by nature. Atomic isomers. But it's not fission or fusion. That's the difference."

"I see."

"Not that I'd know anything about it," Max said, laughing.

Clarke paused for a moment and then said, "Would three bombs work? Or four?"

"On the fault?" He shrugged again. "I have no idea. Like I said, it's Chalam's area. We picked five to make sure that there'd be no doubt."

———••———

I WENT TO TALK TO Chalam. As we sipped coffee, I said, "How are you doing?"

He looked surprised. "Better, I think, Mac. I am dealing with it. I think I'll have to settle for stealing the weapon from the bastards instead of killing everyone." He chuckled. "You're right. The guilt for that would have been way too much."

"It would have gotten all of us caught, too."

"True. But those people are just doing a job, like Alyssna said." He sighed. "I have to get over the . . . over the *incident* and just move on. Deal with my grief."

I studied him for a few moments, peering over my mug as I drank. He was staring into the distance, seemingly understanding what I'd been pushing for. Revenge was not a solution. Deal with your grief.

Things would get better.

At least, that's what I kept telling myself.

I was still waiting.

—••—

DOCTOR ALYSSNA SONSTRAAL WAS STANDING by herself—difficult in the cramped seacar—and deep in thought. I moved next to her. "Are you ready for this?"

"Mac, hi." She smiled at me. "Thanks for giving me this opportunity."

"It's dangerous." Her eyes drifted from mine and a wave of worry crossed over her features. I continued, "Are you sure you can still do it?"

"Oh yes, I want my invention back. I want to keep working on it. I can make it so much better."

I blinked. "What are you thinking?"

"Oh, better range. If we switch to tritium instead of deuterium, it'll mean way more destruction. Tritium has two neutrons in every nucleus, whereas deuterium only has one. More power. Precision aiming, and so on. I can always improve it." She exhaled. "There was a period back in the early 21st Century when the power of lasers on the surface increased dramatically. In just a few short years—"

I smiled to myself. Richard had said exactly the same thing. When a developed and wealthy nation with an advanced education system devoted to science, technology, and engineering poured their resources into a project, the rapid developments could surprise everyone. That was one example. The space race of the 1960s was another. The rapid increase of computer processing technology yet another. And now, the rapid push out into space and the solar system was beginning to grip the population. Along with ocean colonization too, of course. Things on Earth were growing dangerous, especially between nations. Many were beginning to look for other places. To the oceans, the Moon, planets, and space stations.

Richard walked past us, and he called to Meg and spoke with her in a corner. They seemed nervous, but Richard gestured to me, and my sister peered at me for a moment. I nodded at her in encouragement. Then she looked back to Richard. They continued speaking in hushed tones, about the imminent infiltration of the secure facility, no doubt.

Nerves were natural.

I said to Alyssna, "Have you considered what I said to you earlier at Trieste?"

She looked at me briefly. "You mean, about my dad?" A sigh. "Somewhat. I see what you meant, that his lack of love actually motivated me and that's why I'm where I am today. It's why I have a doctorate from Cambridge."

"That's an achievement right there."

"And I created The Water Pick. But it still hurts, Mac."

"It always will," I mumbled, almost to myself. I thought about my own dad. His actions had destroyed our family, and yet the people of Trieste *revered* him. He was a hero to them. To me and Meg, it was different. I'd wanted to avoid the path he'd been on, but then the SCAV drive ended up at my doorstep, more or less, and I'd embarked on the same path. I stared at Renée, who was chatting and laughing with the others. Meg had her arm around Renée's waist. Crinkles appeared at the corners of her eyes. I'd do anything to protect her, I realized.

She felt me watching her and glanced in my direction.

She smiled.

———••———

THE MISSION HAD BEGUN.

We were powering toward the coordinates Chalam had provided at a very low velocity. Our screws were providing five percent thrust—barely a *hum*—and we were behind a rise in the ocean floor. Then Meg powered down and *SC-1* settled to the bottom. We dared not risk the landing skids in case the hydraulics signalled our presence. *SC-1* rocked slightly to the port as we came to a rest.

Max, Chalam, and Meg were staying on board the seacar. They had arranged the bombs on the deck beside the moonpool hatch, which was shut. They'd leave and power toward the Chagos Trench. Once there, they'd plant the bombs and detonate in exactly two hours.

We put the time into our PCDs and stared at each other.

`2:00:00`

We counted to three together, and on *four*, we collectively clicked *start*, and the timer began to run.

1:59:59
1:59:58
1:59:57

I blew my breath out in a rush. I was in a wet suit, tank on my back, full facemask on. So were the others. We nodded to each other, and the airlock opened.

It was time.

—••—

SAHAR HAD A LOOK OF determination on her face. Clarke seemed nervous. Richard as well. Johnny, Cliff, and Renée were focused and zoned in. Alyssna now seemed excited to be going back to The Vault to get her invention.

There were more of us than would fit in the airlock, so we exited in two batches. The seafloor was deep there—at 515 meters—and the pressurization took a few minutes. It was tough because it was much deeper than a standard dive. But eventually we hit the correct atms, and the outer hatch opened.

It was dark outside.

A few minutes later, the rest of the team exited the seacar.

Then, with barely a whine, *SC-1* rose off the floor, pivoted to the south, and slowly moved away, her thrusters churning quietly.

We looked at each other. Our scuba on this mission had rebreathers so it didn't release bubbles; rather, the closed system recycled the exhalations and absorbed the carbon into a filter.

No noise.

We couldn't make any noise.

Renée checked a map on her PCD and pointed to the north. We began to swim over the hummock and toward The Vault.

—••—

WE MOVED SLOWLY. THERE WAS no metal on our belts or hanging downward to scrape the seafloor. We'd wrapped everything in black tape just in case. If the sensors detected something, the algorithms would consider us natural marine life, and ignore us.

We hoped.

Soon a pale glow came into view, high over the bottom. I peered at it intently, trying to make something out.

It was a tower with a light fixed to the top.

Alyssna pointed and nodded at it.

It was the first sensor.

We were in the southeast area of The Vault. The tunnel into the docking pool was on the other side of the tower, about a hundred meters farther, according to Alyssna.

She seemed to be managing well. I took a moment to study the others. The Commodore seemed fine as well, though his face was drawn and tight. The rest were focused on the tower.

We swam toward it.

I checked the time again.

1:46:28

We figured we needed to be in the facility before it hit one hour remaining, to give us enough time to prepare. We also had to decompress before we could move farther into the facility, which was at four atms. When the bombs went, we felt we could start acting more aggressively, and hope that no one would notice us as we took what we wanted. They'd be in emergency mode, preparing for a large underwater displacement to hit them.

One that would never actually come.

Within another minute we were at the base of the tower.

The water was murky from depth, pressure, and suspended sediment. The tower stretched upward and the glow was far above. The sensor equipment was at the top, raised high above the seafloor to cover a much larger area around The Vault. Along with the other four towers, the system was constantly listening to the sounds in a large radius.

I glanced at Johnny and he gave me a thumbs-up.

He adjusted his vest and began to float upward, toward the sensors at the top of the tower.

He disappeared from sight.

A second later, Sahar also rose from the seafloor and ascended, positively buoyant—but *barely*—and followed my Deputy Mayor.

I held my breath.

Around me, the silence was deafening. My blood pounded in my ears.

I breathed slowly and surely.

Johnny was hacking into the sensor and disabling it. The procedure was simple—burn some wires and sever the power source—but the effects would be dangerous: someone would surely come out soon to fix it. Repair crews inside The Vault wouldn't assume an incursion; rather, they would immediately think it was a minor mechanical issue, especially when they saw the wires *burned* rather than cut.

However, when the second sensor went, they would likely begin to think something was up, and they would step up their surveillance efforts around the facility.

A few minutes later, Johnny appeared in silhouette. He drifted to the seafloor, landed softly, and a cloud of sand billowed around his flippers. He flashed me a quick grin and another thumbs-up.

One sensor down.

Sahar landed a moment later. She'd accompanied Johnny. He had already instructed her on the procedure while on *SC-1*, but she'd now watched exactly what he'd done.

Our group checked each other over. Clarke was looking a little better—he'd relaxed a bit and his features weren't as severe—and Alyssna was still focused and intense.

I pointed at Johnny, Richard, Clarke, Alyssna, and Cliff, then gestured to the North.

Our group was going to split off and move to infiltrate The Vault.

Sahar and Renée were going to remain outside and disable the remaining sensor towers. When *SC-1* returned, Meg had to pilot close to the facility, find the exterior lab airlock, and we'd have to load the components on board.

1:33:38

We began to swim toward The Vault.

Chapter Twenty-Nine

WE LEFT THE TOWER'S ILLUMINATION behind and swam steadily. Clarke was doing fine, but I kept checking on him to be sure. Alyssna also managed well; she was an experienced swimmer and the depth wasn't affecting her negatively at all.

Johnny and I were in the lead, and Cliff brought up the rear. Before us, it seemed completely dark. We swam without truly knowing where we were headed. The light from the surface didn't reach the bottom at this depth. It was murky, thick, black water. It made me shiver as I stared around. There could be anyone nearby, and we wouldn't even know until they were right on us.

Then, a large shape appeared out of the darkness. We pulled to a stop to let our eyes adjust to better make out the structure.

The jagged ridges and peaks of the rocky outcropping loomed over us. The modules were at the peak with a travel tube connecting them. The ridge was solid rock, and there were no lights visible anywhere. It was dark seafloor, nearly impossible to make out. It was the perfect place for a research facility, I thought. There was a BSF base to the east with a large military contingent. There were acoustic sensors surrounding The Vault to listen for approaching danger. The labs were in the rock, with the only way to access it through the modules atop the ridge, one of which was the security station.

A scraping to my left caught my attention. I motioned to the others and we held still, peering into the darkness.

My guts slithered.

Then there was a *swishing* and several shadowy figures appeared.

Scuba divers, swimming to the south.

Five of them. They would pass us just meters to our left.

It was the repair team, I realized, heading out to fix the sensor we'd just put out of commission.

—••—

WE HAD A QUICK CHOICE to make. If we let them continue, it would mean that likely within thirty minutes the sensor would be working again, putting Meg's team aboard *SC-1* at risk.

I couldn't allow that, and this was something we'd already considered and had prepared for.

But I had made a promise to Sahar that I didn't want to break. We needed Churchill with us when we declared our independence to the world.

When we announced *Oceania*.

I gestured to Cliff and Johnny, and we swam after the repair team, leaving Alyssna, Richard, and the Commodore behind.

I drew my needle gun.

—••—

WITHIN MINUTES, WE WERE DIRECTLY behind the team. They were swimming for the tower, but not moving too quickly. They had tools around their belts, clanging and scraping; they obviously weren't worried about making noise.

It would make this easier.

I aimed at the legs of the one in the rear.

And fired.

—••—

THE RESULT WAS INSTANTANEOUS. HE pulled to a stop and writhed on the seafloor, reaching down to his calf to find out what had happened. He likely thought something had bit him, perhaps an eel or some other marine creature. He scrambled to find out where the blood was coming from . . .

And I was on him in a flash. I held the gun's square barrel before his mask and put my finger to my lips.

His expression froze as he stared at me in fear and realization. What they'd been preparing for, for years, was now happening, and he hadn't been ready.

And now he was 500 meters down, bleeding, and facing a hostile and armed team.

I knew he was likely not a trained soldier. He was not ready for hand-to-hand combat underwater, and that played in my favor. His comm device was a wire that trailed from his full face mask to his shoulder and down his side to the nylon belt around his waist.

I ripped it from his mask with a quick jerk.

Beside me, Johnny and Cliff were doing likewise to the rest of the repair team. They corralled them and moved them toward me. Blood from the injured man's leg clouded the area and sent a dangerous signal.

I held my finger to my mask and stared at each in turn.

I will kill you if you make a sound.

Their eyes showed terror.

None of them had weapons.

I pointed back toward The Vault, and they began to swim. Their comms wouldn't work, and they knew they couldn't get away.

We'd have to secure them somewhere, to keep them from escaping.

1:15:17
1:15:16
1:15:15

I could leave them outside perhaps, restrained and lying on the sea-floor, but eventually their air would run out. We couldn't do that to them.

Soon we met up with Richard, Clarke, and Alyssna, and we began on our way toward the ridge once again. The repair team were staring at us, eyes wild in realization of what was happening. Frantic. That was fine with me. I *wanted* them to think they were in grave danger.

It made them easier to bargain with. Easier to control.

We pulled to a stop at the ridge that rose over us. Our depth was 503 meters, but the modules were closer to 470 meters below sea level. Johnny was pointing at something, and I stared past his finger.

It was a black tunnel in the rock, just above the seafloor.

The docking pool lay beyond that opening.

Gesturing with his needle gun, Cliff indicated that he wanted the repair team to go toward the opening.

We followed them.

They led us through the tunnel to a large hatch in the rock. It was the airlock leading back to the pool. The repair team were shooting glances to each other, and I knew what they were thinking.

They were worried that we were going to use them to force our way into The Vault.

They were right.

There was a camera above the hatch, and Johnny darted forward with a fabric bag. He wrapped it around the camera and retreated, staring at it. The camera was still functioning, but security would only see *black*. When the airlock started its cycle, I hoped they'd just think someone from the repair team had returned for some reason or another.

Complacency was our weapon.

I keyed the airlock, and the large hatch opened.

We entered, the water lowered, and the decompression began.

1:12:03

"Who the hell are you?" one of the repair crew growled at me.

The decompression sequence was working to bring us down to four atms, but I'd had to adjust it because we'd been out for a long time. We had a thirty-minute wait ahead of us, and it made me sweat. Time was ticking, and it didn't give us long to locate the components.

He was an older man, East Indian perhaps, and he was scowling.

"Just shut up," I said. "You *might* survive. Take care of your friend here. He's still bleeding. Don't resist; it'll be better for you."

They stared at me, then glanced at each other. Then, collectively, they seemed to deflate.

We stripped their equipment and outer clothing off and restrained them against the bulkhead with zip ties. Alyssna wrapped a tourniquet around the injured man's leg, slowing the bleeding. He started to say thanks, then gasped when he noticed her face.

"What are you doing?" he blurted.

"Shut up," I said again.

"But—"

I swung my gun and cracked him across the scalp. He yelped and his head snapped back and hit the metal bulkhead. He was out.

But he'd recognized Alyssna.

Not that it mattered. No one would know she was living in Trieste. In fact, it might pin the blame on some other group, like the BSF.

As I thought it, Johnny, Richard, and Clarke stripped off their wetsuits, revealing their BSF uniforms.

I did the same, and the eyes facing us were incredulous.

We were four BSF officers infiltrating their base, along with a former engineer who had worked in their labs.

It made me laugh inwardly.

—••—

THE COMMODORE SUDDENLY SPOKE, AND it sent a shock through me.

"Who's in charge of this facility," he asked.

Faces stared up at the man who towered over them. One of the repair crew was a middle-aged woman, and she was shivering on the deck. A younger man replied, "I don't have to answer you."

Clarke pulled the knife from the sheath on his left thigh. "Answer or you die right now. Are you BSFIF?"

The man swallowed. My instinct was to stop this and stop it immediately—but I wanted the answer too. I needed to know exactly what was going on with Clarke and his not-so-secret mission.

The man said, "This is a BSFIF base."

Clarke knelt and held the knife to the man's throat. "Go on," he said.

Cliff and Johnny were watching, silent. Cliff's hands were twitching. He was ready to put a stop to it at a second's notice.

The man whispered, "Admiral Hitchens is CO of this base."

Clarke looked up at me. "Hitchens was stationed at Diego Garcia." Then he looked back to the prisoner. "When did he arrive, and who was in charge before him?"

The man shot a look at his companions, then jerked back at Clarke's knife in his throat. "He arrived six months ago. The previous CO was

Admiral Thompson."

"Where is she now?"

"I don't know! They took her away aboard a warsub."

Clarke said to us, "They probably took her to Diego Garcia. Removed her from duty here because she wouldn't follow the BSFIF."

"Do you know her?" I asked.

"Not personally, but she's loyal to the BSF. She likely resisted their plans and they put someone else in her place. Hitchens. We haven't received a report from her in a while."

When they started escalating their aggression, no doubt, by testing the weapon on civilians. Or speaking about taking over the BSF. "Did you know she was here?"

"No. The brass at BSFCO don't know about this facility."

I frowned. There was a lot going on here that didn't involve us.

We just needed the weapon and we needed to get out safely. That's all I cared about.

—··—

0:43:30

The decompression completed with a chime and the inner hatch opened. Cliff had removed his wetsuit and pulled on one of the repair crew's work jumpers. Alyssna had taken another. The rest of us were in BSF officers' uniforms, and we looked like we fit in.

We were strangers though, and people would know we didn't belong.

Then again, I was sure sometimes people arrived from DG—new crews rotating in, for instance—and we might get a few minutes of safety before people really began questioning us. We'd come up with a plan, and after a tumultuous couple of weeks, we were finally going to see if it worked.

There was a prep room outside the airlock where people could change, charge their tanks, store their equipment and so on. Engineers had carved it from the solid rock; the walls were basalt, sealed with a waterproof and airtight coating that gave them a shiny, wet appearance. Crystals in the rock glistened and sparkled. This was the room that all people passed through on their way into the facility. Security was the next area we'd encounter; it was up through a lift to the southernmost module at the peak of the ridge. It was one of the modules Chalam's magnetometer had detected all those weeks ago. After that, there were three more modules before we would hit the next lift going *down*, back into the solid rock to the facility's laboratories.

I put my palm on the airlock hatch, to shut the repair crew in.

"Wait," a voice hissed.

It was the younger man whom Clarke had been speaking with earlier. He had a wild look in his eyes. "What?" I asked.

"Don't do that. I promise we won't call out."

"Bullshit. I'm not dumb."

"No, don't!" he pleaded. "Listen. If the airlock cycles with us in it, it'll drown us. We don't have any equipment!"

I mulled it over. I could jam the door open so it wouldn't close—and therefore wouldn't cycle—but then the prisoners could call for help. "I'd have to gag you."

"Anything. Please. Just don't seal us in here. I don't want to die like that."

I understood his fear. Being in an airlock without the proper equipment would terrify anyone. A glance at Cliff confirmed it, and within minutes he'd gagged them. We used a zip tie to keep the hatch open; if anyone triggered it from the outside, it wouldn't cycle.

We turned back to the lift that led to security.

We entered.

Chapter Thirty

Cliff and Johnny had drawn their pistols and I put a hand on Johnny's wrist. "Only if necessary. Remember that."

He stared at me. "Mac, we're in the shit here."

"I know that."

"They'll figure out what's going on soon, maybe in *minutes*. Surely you can't keep us from—"

"Don't say it." I snapped a look at Clarke. His eyes were steel. I continued, "Look. Sahar asked us not to. I have to at least *try*. We need Churchill with Oceania."

"What if it puts this whole mission at risk?" Johnny asked.

"We try to get through this without killing."

Clarke was glaring at me. "Don't be a fool, Mac. I like her too, but this is war."

My jaw dropped. "These are *British* sailors in the BSF! How can you of all people want them dead?"

"This is a BSFIF base!" His face went red. "Splintered from the BSF! They're traitors."

"They just work here. They can't control who's in charge, for fuck's sake. It's the military! You do what your superiors say."

He snorted. "And how many USSF sailors have you sent to the bottom? How many have you killed?"

"Too many, Clarke. But they were trying to kill me. These people are just keeping their scientists safe." I stepped toward him. "And if you disobey that, then we'll leave you behind and do this ourselves."

He straightened and met my approach with one of his own. Our noses nearly touched. "Are you threatening me?"

"Not me, Clarke."

From behind him, Cliff pressed his knife into the man's back, at a kidney. "It'll be me if it happens," Cliff rasped into the man's ear.

Clarke's face went pale and he turned to look at Cliff. "You wouldn't."

"Of course I would," Cliff replied in a simple, matter-of-fact tone.

There was a deadly silence as the senior BSF officer stared at the other. Then he deflated. "Very well. We try to talk our way through."

"That's what we planned, with Alyssna's help. And if that doesn't work," I said, "then we restrain them, like we did the repair crew."

"And then?" he sneered.

"Then—and only then—we shoot to kill. Understand?"

He stared at me for a long moment, then said, "Agreed."

—••—

THE LIFT WHINED SOFTLY AS it thrust us upward. The shaft wall was also solid rock and it slid just inches past our eyes. I took several deep breaths, preparing myself. We had no idea what was before us; Alyssna had only been in this area of the complex twice before: once on arrival, and then when departing.

I glanced at her. We'd already gone over a plan while approaching the Indian Ocean, and she fixed me with a piercing look. She could tell what was going through my mind.

She said, "This is not a problem. I can do it."

"Just to distract them, remember. They'll know no ship came near. Just confuse them."

"I've got it."

The lift ground to a halt and the hatch opened.

—••—

THE AREA WAS WELL LIT. Large lights hung from the ceiling. The floor was also white, as were the bulkheads. I squinted against the brightness, then glanced around. A clearly marked path in red led the way to a desk area where sailors likely expected us to present our orders and identify ourselves. Before that was a three-meter-long and two-meter-high cylinder through which the red path led. It was a scanning device that would indicate all weapons or chemical agents.

I took a breath and walked confidently toward it. I was wearing a Captain's uniform and the Commodore was at my side. Johnny and Richard were just behind, also in BSF uniforms. And behind them, Cliff and Alyssna, in workers' jumpsuits.

One by one we passed through the scanner. It remained quiet, but I knew it was alerting the personnel in charge of our weaponry and other concealed items.

A conversation floated to my ears; there were three people speaking on the other side of a long desk that stretched from bulkhead to bulkhead.

A woman's voice: "They're not responding."

"Try again." This one was male. Young and brash.

A different man: "They couldn't have all lost communication."

"They could have if our receiver is out. The malfunction might be there, not at the towers."

"Still, that's not likely."

"The first sensor is still out. The second one has now gone black too."

"The airlock opened some time ago. They must have returned."

"They were decompressing last I checked," the younger man said.

"Should have ended by now. Check the camera again." This was the woman. She was in charge.

"It's dark, but the feeds are still streaming. It's working." Pause. "But the cycle is over. They're out now."

"I still think we should send a security team out immediately. This is not normal."

There was a pause as they realized the lift had stopped and someone had just entered the security office. The last of us stepped through the scanner and we stood staring at the three. They looked up and didn't quite know what to say. They were frowning at our uniforms.

Clarke barked into the silence, "Well? What's the procedure here? Don't just sit there."

"Sir—" the woman said. She was wearing a security insignia on her sleeve, and her blue BSF uniform was distinctive. There was a red and black BSFIF logo on her shoulder. I hoped their adherence to protocol would confuse them.

"I'm Commodore Clarke," he said. "It's been a long and terrible trip. I want to get settled promptly."

The other two men were scrabbling at computer consoles, and the woman continued staring, a look of extreme confusion on her features.

Clarke turned to Johnny. "Make sure to stow my gear safely in my quarters."

"Aye, sir," he replied in his British accent.

I belatedly realized that we were not carrying any gear with us!

Clarke pressed on in his commanding voice, "And I'll want to speak with Admiral Hitchens as soon as possible. See if you can make that happen."

"Aye."

The woman opened her mouth, then closed it again. She just stared.

"Well," Clarke spat. "We're waiting."

"I'm—I'm sorry, sir. We're just dealing with a small issue."

I said, "The airlock is buggered. The controls weren't responding. Kept us in there for far longer than we needed, and we couldn't call out."

She turned to me. "Were you outside? I don't understand. Where did you—"

"Of course we were," I snapped. "On our survey. We all were." I gestured at the others, willing Alyssna to do her bit. She hadn't said anything yet, but now was the time—

As if she could read my mind, she stepped forward and said, "Doctor Malkins in particle physics arranged it. Surely he made you aware."

The woman tilted her head and her jaw opened farther. "Doctor . . . Doctor Sonstraal? I didn't know you were still . . ." She trailed off and just stared.

The incident had completely confused her. She was off balance, off guard.

Clarke said, "I wish I could say the facility is looking great, though we couldn't really see much from outside. Just rock. We're going to inspect the labs now."

She was studying Alyssna. "I thought you departed the facility months ago."

"Just temporarily. I've been back for a few weeks."

Her mouth opened, then closed. "I—I'm sorry, I didn't realize."

Clarke said, "Let's just get cleared, all right? I have a schedule to maintain." He turned to Johnny again. "Make sure we're ready to go back to DG tomorrow."

"Aye, sir."

"What boat did you arrive on, sir?" she asked the Commodore.

"A transport from DG. It's in the docking pool."

She glanced at the security screens, no doubt wondering why it wasn't there. "And why did you come through the personnel airlock and not the one at the arrival pool?"

"We performed a visual inspection outside. I already said that." His face grew hard and he stepped forward. "What's your designation, sailor?"

"Warrant Officer Rivers, sir. Again, I'm sorry. We're experiencing some technical issues today, and we weren't aware of your arrival. There were no orders preceding it either." She frowned and glanced at the other two men with her. They were still searching their computer databases.

Alyssna said, "Surely Doctor Malkins notified his supervisor? Chief Lisbon? She should have notified you, if he didn't."

"I didn't receive anything." She was still staring at Alyssna, no doubt trying to figure out why she had no idea that a scientist who had left months ago was not only back, but supposedly had been back and working at the facility for weeks now.

Clarke said, "No matter. Let's get through this and continue on."

The woman came to a decision and in a flash her expression turned from confusion to concentration. Professionalism. "Very well. Please step forward here." She indicated a square on the white deck outlined in red. The path through the scanners led directly to it. "Step into that square while I check the scan."

She had accepted that although something odd was going on, she was going to follow procedure, at least until she could answer the question of the current malfunctions. There was a good chance that the problems had allowed a BSF transport to arrive without them realizing it; after all, two towers were currently not functioning, meaning they couldn't detect sounds in an entire quadrant of the area outside the facility.

Our plan was working.

I began to feel a thrill of success percolate through my body. Rivers was processing Clarke into the facility—

And then it all fell apart.

She'd checked his ID and had noted the weapons on his thighs, logged them into the system, but allowed him to continue carrying them, as was customary. There was a gun on his right thigh, and a knife on his left.

When Rivers went to clear me next—she was working her way downward through the ranks, the standard procedure—Clarke suddenly did something we had not prepared for.

He pointed at the younger male assistant behind the desk and barked, "You! You can escort me to see the admiral. Let's go."

And then he turned his back and continued through the chamber toward the bulkhead hatch and the travel tube beyond. It snaked along the peak of the ridge, leading toward the next structure in the chain before the final module and the lift downward to the labs.

The man shot a look at Rivers, then after a brief pause, bolted to his feet to follow the Commodore.

———••———

I WAS STRUCK BY THE simplicity of his plan. They'd cleared him first, naturally, and then he'd taken advantage of the situation.

We were left with a dilemma. If we put up a fuss, we risked the entire operation. Security was already processing us, having decided to believe our story, and we were on the verge of entering the facility. But if we prevented Clarke from leaving on his own, they'd figure out this whole situation was wrong. They were already confused, not fully understanding what was happening, and they had fallen back on the only thing they knew: military protocol.

Or, we could just continue on and let things play out. Clarke would be off doing God knew what, but the only thing we should really concern ourselves with was stealing the two components.

But of course I knew what he was doing. This base was now BSFIF, unknown to the BSF command structure, and his orders were to eliminate their leaders.

I glanced at Richard and made a sudden decision. Yelling after Clarke, I said, "Wait! Sir! Where are you—"

He looked over his shoulder and said, "I'll see you at the labs. I've got to meet with Admiral Hitchens immediately."

"But what about—"

He whirled and passed through the hatch before I could finish. The other security man followed him, scrambling to keep up.

I stopped and fixed a look at Cliff.

He was staring at the hatch where the Commodore had just disappeared.

His face was grim.

Damn.

—••—

I TOOK A BREATH AND eyed the two members of the security team. They were working to process us, one by one. They had cleared me, Johnny, and Richard, and there was still Richard and Alyssna remaining. They were behind a desk, giving us verbal commands as they stared at the scanner readouts. We weren't carrying anything that might surprise them, but then Rivers asked something that sent a shiver down my spine.

"Okay, let's see your IDs please."

I didn't have one. Nor did Richard, who was also in a uniform.

Johnny, on the other hand, stepped forward with his PCD in his hand. He held it out and it projected his ID in front of him, complete with scannable barcodes, a listing of his placements, and his current assignment. It was the one Clarke had given him back at Churchill, before we'd stolen Component One.

"Your current assignment is BSFCO." It was a statement, not really a question.

"Yes," Johnny said. "With the Commodore."

"At Churchill?"

Johnny nodded. "That's where I'm stationed."

Rivers looked at him. "But then where are the orders to Diego Garcia? And I don't see any notes of entry to the base. Commodore Clarke said you'd been there?"

Cliff was stepping to the side, so he could get a clear path to the guards.

Johnny said, "We did. It should be here." He frowned at the ID. The last entry was in Churchill, just before 17 March 2131. The fact that there was nothing since then was confusing indeed, because apparently he'd boarded a warsub for the Indian Ocean, debarked at DG, entered DG, departed DG, and headed for The Vault . . . and each step would have involved a security official examining the ID and making a note of each stage in his travel and an entry in his log.

But there was nothing.

Cliff kept moving, and I stepped to the other flank while they were talking.

My hand was on the pistol at my side.

Chapter Thirty-One

"Is the ID corrupt?" Alyssna asked. "Mine seems fine. It has my arrival logged here."

A chime sounded and the man turned from his station to look at a control panel. He said, "Another tower just went down. That makes three."

Rivers stared at him, and her face flattened as she realized the terrible truth.

This could not be a mechanical fault.

She was struggling to fight through her dependence on military protocol, I knew. She was wading through the challenge of deciphering the current problem while also following Standard Operating Procedure. Our arrival—especially Commodore Clark's—was yet another issue clouding her thought process. It had become a morass that she was fighting her way through, only things kept happening that should have sparked her senses that something was terribly awry.

And it had finally happened.

She pulled her weapon and a look of rage painted her face.

"Just hold it right—" she cried.

And Cliff moved.

He jerked forward in a flash and chopped her wrist as the weapon was rising toward me. It clattered to the floor and she clutched her arm in pain. The other guard was bringing his up, and Johnny leaped forward and his foot cracked into the man's chin. He fell back, against a chair, and then stumbled into a desk. Papers and books and a metal coffee cup skittered across the deck, rattling loudly as he rolled across the tabletop and hit the white metal in a pile, limp.

Rivers turned suddenly and lurched toward a console against the bulkhead.

There was a large red button there; she was bringing her palm down on it—

It was the base-wide alert warning.

And I jumped forward and pushed my hand over the button. Her palm slammed on my hand and I kept my fingers straightened, protecting the button. I grabbed her around the waist and pulled her back, and she fell into a fighting stance and spun toward me, her foot whirling through the air as she let out a battle cry.

I blocked the kick and pushed forward, knocking her off balance.

My gun was out in a flash and I aimed right at her. "Stop."

She was breathing heavily, sitting on the deck, staring up at me. "What the hell are you doing?"

"It's obvious, isn't it?"

She stared at Alyssna. "And what about you? You *did* leave, right? And never came back."

Alyssna didn't reply and Cliff and I rapidly secured the two guards back-to-back, hands bound together. Rivers pierced her with a look that could melt steel.

I signaled Renée and said, "We're in. Mostly safe." There was no response, and I realized that her PCD still wasn't working. I switched to Sahar's and her response came seconds later, in text format:

this is Renée . . . what does that mean

"Clarke took off," I whispered. I knew there was likely no way the sensor towers could pick up my voice in Renée's ears, but nonetheless, it was instinctive.

moving to next tower . . . three done so far

"Keep it up. How's Sahar?"

Sahar responded a minute later:

here mac

```
doing great
what's happening there
```

"We're at security. We've restrained a number of personnel. Moving farther into the facility now."

```
keep it up
but what do you mean about clarke
```

I sighed. "He has his own agenda, Sahar. He had an opportunity to get away and he did. He's following his orders."

```
must stop him
```

I paused. "I'll try my best, but that's not our priority."

```
has to be mac
we can't go around murdering innocent brits
```

"It's his mission against the BSFIF." I hesitated, then, "But I'll try my best. I promise."

Richard was staring at me. His mouth was hanging open. I gestured for him to remain silent.

I continued, "Good luck to you two. And remember, you have to be at the exterior lab hatch in—" I checked my PCD.

0:19:08

"Nineteen minutes." I swore to myself. Was that even possible? "Can you make it?"

Renée had the device again and responded:

```
frenchie here... gonna try our best
gotta focus now
good luck love
```

She clicked off.

I turned to Richard. "We can't let him go around murdering people, Richard."

"We *need* The Water Pick."

"We'll get it."

"That's our focus. No distractions, remember!" His expression was hard, and I studied him for a heartbeat.

"Yes, I know." I took a breath and stared around me. "Let's secure the hatches and move on. We can't let security get back in here. They were too complacent . . . but they'll realize something is going on, pretty damn fast."

—••—

THE TRAVEL TUBE WAS NOT exactly what I was used to, but only because its bulkhead was opaque. Its hull was solid titanium and just eight feet tall at its apex. There was also no conveyer, as would have existed in an underwater civilian colony, and we marched through as quickly as possible.

Something was beginning to tingle at the back of my mind. Something I couldn't quite put my finger on, but it was bothering me.

It didn't involve Clarke, for his agenda had already triggered my senses—it was something else entirely.

I frowned inwardly. Damn. There was a danger I was unprepared for, and I didn't like that.

Cliff interrupted my thoughts. "Boss. What should we do with Clarke?"

I sighed, because I knew what Sahar had requested. I thought I knew what to do to keep her satisfied, but I had to haul myself back to the present to deal with it. Whatever was bothering me would have to wait. "The rest of us will take care of the two components. We'll find them and get them ready to transport. You can look for Clarke once we get to the labs. Watch out for security though. Every admiral has their own—"

"I got it," he said in a severe voice. He knew what I was asking.

"But try not to kill them," I asked, shooting him a look.

He glanced at me from the corner of his eyes as we marched quickly through the tube. He did not look happy.

—••—

Minutes later, we were at the next module. The hatch slid aside for us, thanks to Johnny's ID, I assumed—and we entered a living area.

Alyssna said, "This is where we slept. There are bunks here. Recreation. We should be able to move quickly this way." She led the way and we continued marching at a rapid clip through the module.

I checked my PCD.

0:14:03

As I thought it, that feeling hit me again. Something about the time until the bomb went, or the PCD, or *SC-1* and the mission Meg was currently on.

I shook my head and pressed on.

Alyssna led us through the next travel tube.

A voice called to us from the living area. There'd been a seating area with couches, games, holoscreens, game tables, and more. The male voice said, "Alyssna! Is that you?"

The hatch closed behind us, shutting the voice down.

We continued to move.

—••—

The next travel tube was another lengthy journey. We marched quickly, quietly, and confidently. Our faces were hard, determined. We knew what we had to do.

The PA system crackled to life at that point. *"Attention, security to Lab Level Three. Repeat. Security to Lab Level Three."*

I glanced at Cliff. "Maybe Clarke made his move."

0:09:17

The next module seemed much like the previous one. There was a cafeteria and some offices off smaller corridors that branched to the side and stretched down the module's length. Other people were there, who watched our group march past with questioning looks in their eyes. Some of them stared at our uniforms. Others noticed Alyssna and called to her. We ignored it all and pressed on.

There were some potted plants along the bulkheads, with bright lights positioned directly above each. There was even artwork in this module. It was pleasant, airy, and bright, even though we were so far below the surface. No sunlight ever reached this deep. The people who lived and worked here were trying to make it feel like home, which made me feel that they stayed here for perhaps months at a time.

We passed more crew and personnel but ignored them all.

There were more calls on the PA system, and the people we passed must have thought it related to us in some way. It was logical and made sense. After all, Johnny, myself, and Richard were wearing officer BSF uniforms. Cliff and Alyssna were in work crew jumpers.

0:03:28

I keyed the PCD and signaled Renée and Sahar. "You have three and a half minutes. Get ready."

`got it`

I took a deep breath and pocketed the comm device. One more module to go.

The travel tube was identical to the others. None of us were speaking. We were pressing on, in mission mode. Even Alyssna was focused on this. Her eyes were steady, her expression fixed.

0:01:03

We were in the final travel tube just outside the last module. I peered through the hatch viewport. It was a small, circular module—a dome— and at the center was a lift leading down. There was a station next to it with two guards.

They looked nervous, staring at a control console and a holoscreen. They shared a few words, checked their own PCDs, then spoke again. I couldn't tell what they were saying, but their body language was clear.

They knew something was amiss in their facility.

0:00:28

I pulled back and looked at the others. "Are you ready? There are two in there."

There was no response. Just determined faces. Cliff was standing stock still, like an angry mule. Johnny was rigid and tense. Richard's expression was tight.

0:00:17

Richard said, "We've got this. Let's do it."

0:00:16

Cliff nodded but didn't speak.

0:00:14

Johnny glanced at me. His eyes were hard.
He was ready

0:00:10

Alyssna also looked determined. She was staring ahead at the lift and wanted to get to it. She wanted to take back what was once hers.

0:00:05
0:00:04
0:00:03
0:00:02
0:00:01
0:00:00

Almost simultaneous to the counter hitting zero, another call came over the PA system. *"Attention. Attention. We have a situation on the lab levels. Everyone go immediately to your emergency collection zone and report to your superior. Security, send a team outside now. Intruder alert. Repeat, intruder alert."*

A low rumble started to shake the module.

"Sahar and Renée," I rasped into the comm. "There's a team coming out to search for you!"

The rumble continued and I muttered, "It's happening! Get ready!"

I glanced at the bulkheads. The vibration was working its way up my legs.

The voice on the PA had stopped.

The deck plates were rattling. I wondered for a minute if we should have brought scuba gear with us, but we were far from the trench and hadn't thought the quake would be destructive.

It was just meant to cause a distraction.

But still, the rattling was growing more intense and the lights hanging from the ceiling began to swing back and forth.

"Oh, shit," I muttered.

The voice again: *"Get to your collection zone. We're experiencing a quake."*

The lights in the corridor turned yellow.

I breathed a sigh of relief; at least they weren't blue. That meant *pressure loss*, the last thing one wanted underwater in a saturation environment.

"Condition Yellow. Repeat, Condition Yellow."

Alyssna had informed us earlier that this was the quake protocol. Right now, personnel would be scrambling to get into emergency pressure cabins, just in case of bulkhead rupture. But still, they had ordered people to the collection zones *before* the quake. What was going on down there?

Gunshots pounded out from the levels below.

Their explosions floated up the lift shaft.

What the hell?

I peered through the viewport; sure enough, the two guards had left.

The labs below were empty.

The lights were flashing a weird combination of red—*emergency*—purple—*intruder alert*—and yellow—*incoming quake impact*. The lift operated normally and we stepped out into what was clearly a physics lab of some sort. There was equipment and machinery everywhere. Monitors lined the bulkheads and holoscreens displayed data and lab studies and line graphs that none of us had the time nor inclination to study. We needed the two components, and that was it.

Except, that is, for the Commodore.

I swallowed. He was down there, somewhere, and was likely near the facility's CO.

Alyssna glanced around and immediately darted off down a corridor. She glanced back and gestured to us. "This way," she hissed.

The corridor was glistening basalt, carved to smooth perfection. All the labs showed signs of the rock walls, but the deck was smooth white metal and the ceilings were drop panels with intense lighting. The entire facility was a glaring white, in fact, except for the corridors which were black rock with embedded shining crystals, glistening in the glare of the lights.

As we ran, I grabbed the PCD and rasped into it, "Renée, Sahar. Be on the lookout. They are *out* there! Watch out!"

Alyssna turned left and then right. Then we went down a steep ladder and made another turn. Then she pulled up short in front of a closed hatch. Along with the customary BSFRL logo, there was a label:

Encased Particle Beam
Neutral Physics

—

Sonar Integration

"It's the Aiming Module," she hissed. "It's in here."

Chapter Thirty-Two

I STARED AT THE HATCH. In a way, it took my breath away.

Component Three.

We'd made it.

The PCD was in my hand and I looked down at it. No communication at all.

Richard pulled up beside me, huffing from the run down the corridor. All personnel had cleared the area. A low rumble continued to rattle the base, and the warning lights kept flashing. The ceiling illumination began to flicker; it grew dim, then stronger, then dim again.

Then the PA roared to life again.

"Attention Admiral Hitchens. Please contact Control immediately. Admiral Hitchens. Sir, signal us immediately."

Then an alarm started to blare.

Alyssna looked around. "It's the collision alert."

"They're worried about a displacement wave," I said. It made me smile and I glanced at Richard. "It's working."

He stared at me, his eyes like lasers. It made me frown. "Are you listening?"

He pointed at my PCD. "Put that away and focus! Dammit, I have told you again and again about distractions."

"It's hardly a distraction," I muttered. "We have a team outside in danger."

"Let's just get this piece and then the final one." He faced the hatch as it slid aside.

I put his abrasive comment aside as we were in a stressful situation. People react differently to dangerous stimuli.

The lab was clean and sterile. Mostly white. There were computer monitors, tablet holoviewers, scanners, and more. Workstations and cubicles. In the center, studded with protruding wires and connection ports, was a device the size of a toaster. Alyssna rushed to it and started to pluck the wiring away.

The rumbling continued and vibrations grew in intensity. The quake seemed to be *growing*. Not diminishing as time progressed. "How long has it been going?" I muttered.

"Two minutes."

It was a long one, but not unprecedented. Some large ones had lasted for upwards of ten minutes.

Imagine, the stress on a building as it crawled and crunched along for a ten full minutes! It was these forces on concrete and steel that brought high rises down before building codes strengthened structures and bridges in the 20th Century. Concrete needed to sway without fracturing as the structures moved. Metal needed to be *strong*.

The walls of this facility were rock. Moving crust fractured rock easily. It made me very nervous, but this had been necessary. All the personnel had willingly left the labs because of the quake and the possible incoming wave.

We put the Aiming Module on a cart and pushed it into the hall.

The rock under our feet lurched and we stumbled to the side.

Then it lurched again.

"Oh, *shit!*" I cried.

Blue lights started to flash.

Pressure loss!

The strobing visual alarms bathed the corridor in a kaleidoscope of lights.

The audio alarms were also piercing and beginning to spike straight into my brain.

Red—Purple—Yellow—Blue.

Red—Purple—Yellow—Blue.

Red—Purple—Yellow—Blue.

Emergency—Intruder Alert—Quake—Pressure Loss!

It was a cascade of alarms.

Then a voice cried out, "Halt right there! Stop what you're doing!"

A shot rang out and a bullet ricocheted down the hall.

It was a security team. They marched straight for us. We had a choice to make and very little time. The held their weapons before them, aimed. They were ten meters down the corridor and approaching fast.

The decision shot through my mind faster than their bullet.

I pulled my gun and leveled it at them. "Stop where you are!" I shouted.

"Put the weapon down! Get on your knees!" They were still coming, and they were mad.

I continued, "We're BSF officers!"

"Bullshit!" They pressed on.

Behind me, Alyssna hissed, "Mac! The Aiming Module is in the open! Don't let it get hit!"

It was on the cart in the corridor. I stepped in front of it, shielding it.

"I said *stop!*" the security soldier screamed at me.

I held my gun out, rock steady, aimed at his face. He finally drew to a halt, five meters from me.

Cliff and Johnny were at my side. Each had their weapons out.

It was a standoff.

"Where is the Admiral?" the soldier asked.

"I have no idea. We're here from DG," I stalled. "The Commodore went ahead of us."

"Commodore?"

"Bertram Clarke. He is here somewhere. He came with us."

"When did you arrive?"

"An hour ago. We passed through security, as per procedure. And you better explain why you fired at us!" I tried to make my statement as commanding as possible.

His face showed shock. "Are you daft? Look around you! Look at the alarms!"

"There's a quake. I heard."

"*An intruder alert, donkey.*"

I pretended that it surprised me. "You think it's *us*? But we moved through security. Rivers cleared us."

He frowned and just stared. "Security is not responding right now."

Then there was a voice from behind the team of soldiers:

"*Don't move or you die.*"

The speaker had a thick Scottish accent.

—••—

"COMMODORE!" I YELLED. "DON'T—"

Shots rang out and I turned and bent over the cart, pressing the Aiming Module under my torso. There were screams and cries as multiple shots exploded against the rock walls. Pieces of shattered stone skittered across the deck.

Then there was silence.

Beside me, Cliff's face was severe but calm. Johnny's was one of shock. I straightened and looked up the corridor. The security team was gone.

Dead.

Clarke had shot them all.

In their backs.

—••—

HE'D BEEN ON A RAMPAGE down there. He'd been killing every Imperial soldier he came across.

I stared at the carnage and thought about Sahar. She had put her trust in this man. She had pleaded with us not to kill innocent Brits. She had encouraged us to include Clarke on this mission.

And he had gone rogue.

He stood over the bodies, a pistol clutched in his hand. Blood was pooling on the white deck and trickling into the collection drains at its margins. The crimson on white was stark and violent.

I walked slowly toward him. "Are you insane?" I said.

"I am doing my job. Let's finish this."

"I won't let you kill more people."

"It's not your decision," he snapped.

I stared at blood splattered across his neck and face. He had been standing too far from the sailors for the blood to have been theirs. "Where did that come from?"

He didn't answer. His eyes were lasers.

"Where's Admiral Hitchens?" I grated.

"Let's not discuss that," he said, his voice gravel. "Sahar wouldn't like it."

"You asshole."

He glared at me. "You can think what you want, Mac, but I want what's best for the undersea colonies. For Churchill."

"By assassinating BSF officers? How many have you killed here?"

"They're criminals! They committed crimes against the BSF and against our sworn oath. They broke it. BSFCO sent me to do a job, and I'm doing it."

I shook my head and stared at the blood on him. At the dead bodies on the deck at his feet.

He continued, "Don't play holier-than-thou! These men and women abandoned their duty."

"Some of them may have just been doing their duty, following orders. They're in a hidden base working for scientists! Shuffling papers and keeping the base operating. They didn't deserve to die, Clarke!"

"They were willingly working against the BSF!" He stood toe to toe with me and his hot breath was in my face. I held my ground. He practically growled, but I didn't move, didn't speak, barely breathed. "*Look at the patches on their uniforms!*"

He stepped away and marched back the way we'd come, back toward the lift.

"Where are you going?" I asked.

"Just find the neutral weapon. Take it."

I stared at his back as he stalked away.

———•••———

RICHARD APPEARED AT MY SIDE. "Mac," he hissed. "We're almost done. We need The Accelerator. Forget this. Let's go."

He'd been pushing me for weeks to focus on the job, but this was more than losing focus. Clarke was clearly a danger to our mission.

"Where is he going?" I muttered, mostly to myself.

"Does it matter? He's following his own agenda. We have to forget him."

I sighed, stepped back, and leaned against the rock wall. "One moment, Richard." I pulled out the PCD and signalled Sahar. "Are you okay out there?" I checked the time. "Meg and *SC-1* should be back soon." I knew they were traveling using the SCAV drive, but circling around Diego Garcia, who we hoped were watching the Chagos Trench closely and would avoid what was happening at The Vault.

I waited for a text message.

Nothing came.

I stared at the screen intently.

Richard was still watching me. "Mac," he rasped. "Let's get The Accelerator! The people in control here could be calling for help *right now*."

My expression must have been blank, for he was growing frantic. "What's wrong?" I asked.

"This is not the time to relax." He worked his jaw for a moment. And then, almost to himself, "We're not going to win a war by being weak. We have to be *strong*. Merciless. Heartless even. *It's the only way to win a war*."

"Renée and Sahar are outside. There's a security team outside searching for them. I'm checking—"

"There's no time! Fuck this! *Let's go*, Mac."

I watched him as a silence descended. He was correct, but Johnny and Cliff were already working on it. They were with Alyssna, searching the labs, and trying to locate any other remaining security officers.

He turned, a frustrated and angry expression clear on his features. He marched away, fuming.

I studied him, curious. We were on the verge of success, and yet he was furious with me.

Johnny called from one of the labs, "Mac! There are more dead bodies here. Security. They look like . . . they look like the Admiral's detail!"

That made me curse. Dammit. Clarke had assassinated everybody still in the open down there.

My PCD flashed, calling for attention. A message from Sahar appeared.

```
still outside
we disabled all towers
now near the airlock hatch
you have to open from the inside
no sign of troops or sc-1
```

```
we wait
```

Then my earpiece screeched and a high-pitched squeal erupted from the speaker. I yanked it from my ear, swearing. A minute later, another message appeared on the screen.

```
that was Renée's pcd
suddenly came to life?
made loud noise
security heard us
```

Then a minute later:

```
they're heading for us!
they know where we are
mac we are in serious
```

Somehow Renée's dead PCD had abruptly flared to life and given them away.

And then that feeling strobed through my brain again—*something is very wrong!* The tingling had exploded into a downright flood of awareness.

About what had been going on the whole time.

About who had been trying to assassinate me.

Chapter Thirty-Three

The tingling in my brain had taken a hold of me. I couldn't think about The Accelerator. Couldn't help Johnny, Cliff, and Alyssna as they searched the labs for the neutral beam generator. I stared at the deck, not seeing a thing.

Only images that had already happened strobed through my mind. Things that others had said, or actions I'd witnessed, or events that had seemed coincidental at first but really weren't.

They slowly solidified within me and my eyes glazed over in anger and rage.

Richard was standing in the corridor with me. Johnny was calling to me, but I couldn't answer him.

Cliff appeared at my side to tell me they had located Component Four, then he stopped as he noticed my expression.

I muttered to Cliff, while still staring at Richard, "I think we have some things to figure out."

"We have the component. We're getting it ready to move. When Meg returns with *SC-1* we can take it through the umbilical. It'll fit, but barely. We can leave the Commodore here." Then his eyes flashed. "Or, I can take care of him."

"Load the components. Leave Clarke here. He's on his own now." I was still staring at Richard.

"Got it, Boss."

"Wait."

He stopped and stood there, staring. "Everything okay?"

"No, it's not." I sighed and said, "When the bomb went off at the torpedo launcher inspection and hurt Renée, weeks ago at Trieste, what did your investigation show?"

He frowned. "Is now the time—"

"Yes!" I roared. "Answer me, Cliff!"

He stared at me for a heartbeat. Then, "A bomb. Ammonium nitrate, stolen from the Mining Division."

"That's right. And yet, when it happened, Richard said that it was likely a torpedo detonation. That's the theory that he was pushing."

Richard's face was a mask of confusion. "We all thought that. It was the likely cause." He tilted his head. "Mac, what—"

"And what did you find, Cliff?"

"There were too many suspects. It was impossible to narrow down."

"You told me that you had a list. You said there was 'nothing believable' on it. Why'd you say that?"

Cliff hesitated. "Well, maybe we shouldn't talk about it just now."

"Tell me." My voice was steel.

He hesitated and then said, "I cross-checked the people who had been near the stores of explosive with the people who had also been in the moonpool when the culprit sabotaged your tank with Carbon Monoxide."

"Go on."

"There was a name, but I didn't think it possible."

"It was Richard."

Cliff stopped and studied me. Then he glanced at Richard, then back to me. "Yes, he was near the explosive stores. He's in charge of the shelter constructions under the Living Modules. He had also swum out by the torpedo launcher days earlier."

Richard said, "But I always swim a five kilometer—"

"But it was a different route than he usually takes," Cliff continued. "And only that one day."

"Go on," I pressed.

"He was also in the moonpool in the hours before your swim outside."

"You didn't tell me."

He shrugged. "I kept it in mind, but it didn't seem possible, like I told you, Boss."

I said, "In Churchill, Renée's PCD went missing. Lost. We found it later, still in Sahar's office. It's seems hard to believe that it was in the office the whole time and she couldn't find it." I pointed at Richard.

"What were you doing to it, while the rest of us were outside Churchill?"

He just watched me and didn't speak.

I pressed on. "Later, in Trieste, there were two more attacks. The first was the Carbon Monoxide attack. We'd assumed it was against me, but it wasn't, was it, Richard? It was Renée!"

Cliff swore. "Are you—"

"You switched her tank for one contaminated with CO. The video picked you up in the moonpool. And you planted the microbombs that shorted our comms."

Richard said, "Mac, this is not the time to—"

"You sabotaged my comm not to keep me from calling for help for myself . . . but to keep me from calling for help for Renée!" I took several deep breaths. "Then the airlock attack," I spat. "You had already inserted some code into Renée's PCD. It didn't work in the airlock. *You* did that. In fact, her PCD comms stopped working entirely, and didn't again until just a few minutes ago!" I paused and took several deep breaths. "You planned to lock her in that airlock and kill her. She was unable to call out."

"Mac, I—"

"But I was with her, which you didn't expect. Sahar too." I thought back to the sequence leading up to that event. "You'd been showing Sahar around. When I called to invite her for the swim to tour the outside, you resisted. Sahar said you didn't want her to go. It's because you'd arranged the attack on Renée!"

"I—"

But I didn't let him finish. Cliff was staring at me in horror. "In fact," I snarled, "you disabled her PCD. But now, she's outside, and you just triggered it to signal their position. You just did it, from in here."

He remained silent.

Cliff said, "But Mac, this doesn't make sense. Why?"

"It's the reason you didn't pay attention to his name on your list of suspects. It's the reason he was able to do what he did without anyone suspecting. Because he's so obsessed with independence and defeating the superpowers, *no one* would ever suspect him. It's the reason we weren't able to figure it out until now."

"But we still don't know *why*. What's the motivation?"

I sighed. "Richard has said to me repeatedly to focus on the mission. To not get distracted. He's said that over and over. First on *SC-1* when returning from Churchill. He said, 'We just have to stay away from distractions. We need to focus and stay the path.' Then, back at Churchill in the BSFIF labs, while stealing Component One, he said again, 'Keep your mind on the job . . . distractions, remember . . .'" I paused and took a breath. My heart was pounding.

Cliff's face, usually so calm and serious, was now displaying a cascading series of emotions. "I had my people check your tank before your swim with Renée, Mac. I never thought to have hers checked. I'm so sorry. I didn't even consider that *she* might have been the target."

I sighed. "Each time it *could* have been me. *I* was scheduled to do the torpedo launcher inspection. *I* was out with Renée when her tank poisoned her. *I* was in the airlock with her when it malfunctioned. We just assumed . . . " I stared at Richard. "After the airlock attack, you knew we'd blamed the Commodore for it. Cliff had traced the hack back to his computer. But it's only because you were deflecting suspicion! You broke into his cabin and did it! You pinned the blame on the person we already suspected. Naturally, we'd also think it was him. But it wasn't at all. Clarke isn't a saint, but he isn't trying to kill one of our team. It was you, Richard. It was you all along!"

—••—

"In fact," I said, "this whole thing has been you. This whole mission. From the very start. You started us on this. To steal the weapon. *You* introduced us to Sahar, to Alyssna, to Chalam. *You* wanted to go get this neutral beam. You've manufactured this entire situation."

"I didn't manipulate you!" he shouted. "I presented an option and you agreed with me! Trieste needs the neutral beam!"

Behind him, Johnny and Alyssna had hauled a trolley into the corridor with the large device perched atop it. It looked deadly; a single massive barrel three meters long. The lasers we'd already stolen would enclose it. There were wires and cables spiraling around it.

All it needed now was for us to connect it to the Laser Module, the Staging System, and the Aiming Module.

And a fusion source, of course, to feed power to the weapon.

I exhaled. "Richard, you've been a long-time proponent of independence. You fought beside my father. But you've become obsessed with it. You're so focussed on it that you've resorted to killing the people I love just to keep me 'on the path,' as you say. You're sick." I clenched my teeth. Hard.

I almost tasted blood.

The rage was burning through me.

I couldn't control it.

Then I raised my pistol and pointed it directly at Richard.

His face went pale. "Mac, I only want what's best for Trieste. After they killed your dad, Jessica and I fled. For thirty years we worked at Ballard and waited for the movement to take hold again. And then you started it! With the SCAV drive, you finally had a way to achieve what your dad started. But then I saw that things distracted you. Kept you from working sometimes. Your mind started to stray."

"So what did you do?" I roared. I held my gun steady. My palm was sweating, and then the barrel started to tremble. "Did you kill her?"

The horrible truth had occurred to me. Every muscle in my body quivered.

I couldn't control it.

Cliff was watching me. "Uh, Mac. She's still alive. Renée's outside. We have to go—"

"Not her," I said. My finger twitched.

"Then who?"

"He killed her, Cliff, to keep me 'focused.' To keep me working for independence. He was telling me he was with us, working for us, fighting for independence, but at the same time he was trying to hurt me. Trying to make me angry. Trying to keep me consumed with rage."

Cliff shook his head. "I don't understand. Who are you talking—"

"Katherine Wells, Cliff. He's not just trying to kill Renée. He killed Kat, one year ago."

Interlude: The Mid-Atlantic Ridge

One Year Earlier

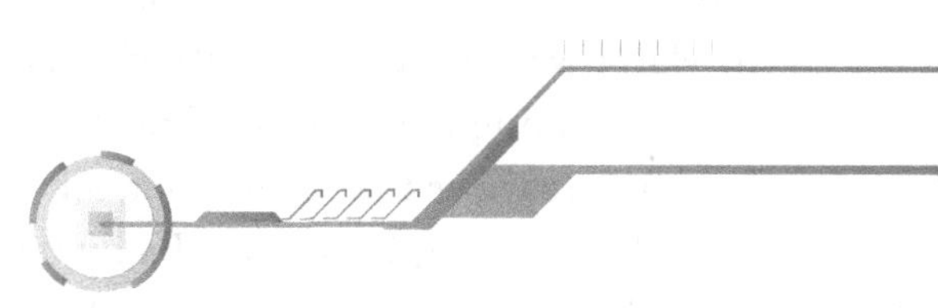

Interlude:	The Mid-Atlantic Ridge
Date:	March 2130 AD
Depth:	3,688 meters
Latitude:	27° 54″ 11′ S
Longitude:	17° 35″ 41′ W
Time:	2143 hours

KATHERINE WELLS HAD INVENTED THE SCAV drive. She had done it to fuel Trieste's fight for independence, and also for every other city in the oceans.

And it had worked. She'd just watched the defeat of the FSF and USSF forces in the Mid-Atlantic Ridge. The fighting had badly damaged her vessel, *SC-1*, which she had designed and contracted a company in Clearwater, Florida, to build for her. She loved the seacar. It was foundering, however, taking on water and struggling through the depths. Her control console had exploded in her face. It was time to get back to the base, to abandon the fight and leave Mac and the others to finish up.

Behind her, her two companions were still arguing. It sent shivers up her spine. They were angry.

"I'm sorry," she called back to the living area. "We're flooding. The canopy is cracked and water is compromising the electrical system. We have to leave!"

The arguing paused for a moment, then it picked up again. She couldn't quite make out what they were saying because the strength of the water was obscuring all other noise.

"I'm heading back to The Ridge. Back to the base. We need to get there before we've taken on too much water." Kat stared at the console before her. The explosion had badly damaged it. There were red lights everywhere. Some areas were black—no power. Pieces of the console lay strewn about. Sharp pieces of plastic and metal.

She felt a presence behind her and turned.

It was Richard Lancombe.

His face was dark.

"Did you hear me?" she asked. "We have to get back now."

"Do we have comms?" he asked after a moment. His voice did not match his expression. It was soft, sad.

Kat checked with the thumb trigger and replied, "Nothing. I can't hear anything, can't signal anyone. We have to get back." She pointed at the ballast. It was steadily filling. "We're flooding on board as well as in the tanks. We don't have much time."

"I understand."

Another voice echoed from the living area behind her. "Don't do it." It was Jessica Ng, Richard's partner. She'd essentially been along for the ride, and she'd had a front row seat to the battle.

"I'm sorry," Kat said again. "We have to get back while we still can." She was powering away from the battle to the north, hugging the cliff face to attract as little notice as possible.

"That's not what I meant," Jessica said.

Her tone was also soft, and the hair on Kat's neck spiked. She wrenched around to look behind her—

Richard was looming over her. There was a long piece of sharp plastic in his hand.

"What are you—"

He leaped at her with a growl. She let go of the yoke and put her hands on his chest, straightening her arms and keeping him far from her. He was strong though, and he slapped her face with an open palm.

Her head snapped back and hit the control panel beside her. A stream of water hit her face, and her drooping eyes snapped open.

She tried to ask again what he was thinking, but the only thing that came out was a gargling cry of fear. Then Richard was on her again in a flash. The sharp end of plastic was at her sternum, and he began to push.

She cried out.

Behind them, Jessica also screamed something, but Kat couldn't make it out.

The spear pierced her skin.

Richard screamed as he pushed.

Images of Truman McClusky flashed through Kat's mind as she realized what was happening. She had desperately wanted a life with him, to lead the people of Trieste together to a new world where the topsiders respected and appreciated the ocean colonists.

She'd loved him more than anyone else in her life.

Kat thrust her chin up and howled in pain as Richard drove the long piece of shrapnel deep into her heart.

"How can I be substantial if I do not cast a shadow?
I must have a dark side also if I am to be whole."
—Carl Jung

Part Six: Fourth Component

Chapter Thirty-Four

THE PISTOL WAS IN MY hand, aimed solidly at Richard. His face was white. His hands were out, in defence, to keep me from firing.

Cliff was next to me. "Are you sure?" he hissed.

I nodded. "He was with Kat in the seacar during the battle. The torpedo had detonated too close. There was no more communication from *SC-1* as she struggled back to our base. We only assumed the torpedo damage had done it. But during that period, Richard killed her, Cliff. To keep me *on the path*." I snorted. "You disgust me. You've murdered someone I love just to keep me working for independence. You killed Kat so I would *focus*, which you've kept telling me." I shook my head. "Haven't I done enough? Haven't I lost enough, Richard? My family is gone, except for Meg. Kat's gone. Now you're trying to kill Renée too, but none of it has anything to do with my attempts to achieve independence for Trieste! You're mad!"

He face went red. "Don't call me that. Don't say I'm insane. I'm not!"

"What other reason could there be? You're killing people to keep me full of hate. To keep me *hating* the superpowers. But don't you see, I'm fighting for independence regardless of what you do. It's the only way for Trieste to move forward. You don't have to kill the people I love to keep me doing it!" I stepped forward and thrust the gun right into his face. "Who's next, after Renée? Meg? Johnny? Cliff?"

He stepped back against the wall, but I kept the barrel pressed into his face. "Mac, I didn't want to hurt you, ever! I want to continue what your dad started!"

"By killing Kat? By trying to kill Renée?"

"Kat had contributed all she was able to. She had nothing left to give!

She was distracting you, and so—" He stopped, realizing what he'd said.

All around us, the lights were flashing their warnings.

The PA system had been quiet; there were no more verbal commands echoing through the corridors.

There were bodies on the ground, blood still trickling from them; red streams traced paths to the drains near the rock walls.

And the alarms were still piercing the corridors.

Cliff swore. "You killed Doctor Wells?"

Richard looked frantic. "I did it for the movement! I did it for Mac!"

It made me sick. I didn't know what to say.

The sound of a seacar whined past the facility. At first I assumed it was Meg in *SC-1*, but the sound of the screws was off. Then it grew more distant, until finally it disappeared altogether.

A vessel had just departed The Vault.

Then I realized what had happened, and my mouth fell open.

It was likely Commodore Clarke, leaving.

He'd escaped.

—••—

JOHNNY YELLED UP THE CORRIDOR to me. He and Alyssna had the neutral beam on a powered trolley and were maneuvering it into the hall. Alyssna was helping negotiate the corner. She pointed and he guided The Accelerator along the deck. There was an airlock somewhere here, which only opened from the inside. Its purpose was to ship larger equipment to and from The Vault. Our plan was to mate *SC-1* to The Vault via umbilical, then load the two components into the seacar.

But things had grown more complicated.

Richard was before me. His expression was pleading, and he was holding his hands out to me, as if warding me off.

Cliff was by my side; his face was a mask of confusion and anger.

It was a frozen tableau; no one was sure what to say.

My hand trembled on the gun. My finger twitched.

"Mac!" Johnny called again. "What are you doing? The personnel will be back soon. Let's go!"

He didn't realize what was happening. He was staying on mission and doing his duty without distraction. He was a good operative.

Richard took a breath. "What do you say, Mac? Are you going to kill me? Your dad and I worked—"

"Don't say that I owe you loyalty because of Dad!"

"He was one of my best friends."

"You committed murder."

"Come on. You've killed entire boat crews. What are you talking about?"

I scowled. "You looked her in the eye and stabbed her. You drove the shrapnel into her. She was innocent. How could you possibly think that was okay?"

"For the greater good." He held his chin up.

I had noted that Jessica hadn't been around lately. She'd been with him on *SC-1* at the time. Was it possible that she had played a role? "What did Jessica think?"

He hesitated. "That's not your business."

"I thought you were married."

"We are."

"Then where has she been?"

"No comment."

"Did she participate in the murder?"

This he was prepared to answer, at least. Although it might have been a lie. "We argued about it."

Cliff was shifting next to me, and I shot him a glance. He said, "Boss. What do you want me to do?"

The implication was unmistakeable. He was asking if I wanted him to kill Richard. He would have, in a second. I had no doubt; he was completely and utterly loyal. He was the CSO at Trieste, and Richard's actions had eluded him.

Johnny called again, "Mac! Come on!" He and Alyssna had disappeared around a corner.

I was staring at Richard. There was sweat on his face, dripping along his wrinkles, and his white hair was glistening.

He thought I might actually kill him.

I deflated. "Arrest him, Cliff. Restrain him. We'll take him back to Trieste."

Cliff looked shocked. "Are you sure?"

"No." But the truth was that Sahar was on my mind. She was outside, with Renée, and there was a security crew hunting them. Sahar would not want me to kill the man. For whatever reason, I had decided to take her lessons to heart. Perhaps it would help ease my own guilt, especially after what had happened in the previous years. I'd killed many people. Meg had also murdered, and we'd all dealt with the ramifications. Hell, we'd destroyed an entire USSF base during her rescue.

But Sahar had insisted on a path that didn't require excessive killing.

It seemed weird, as I stood in a hostile facility with bodies littering the deck around my feet, but I needed to keep her on my side. I couldn't let her down.

Cliff continued, "He killed Kat in cold blood. Tried to kill Renée."

"I am aware." I sighed. "But it's possible he can still help with independence. There's also Jessica to think about."

Cliff's face showed his surprise, but after a moment he stepped forward and pinned Richard's arms behind his back and restrained him with a black zip tie. He relieved him of the PCD and his two weapons.

We stepped over the bodies as we followed Johnny.

—••—

IT WAS A LARGE AIRLOCK with a circular door that swung outward on a single, massive hinge. The neutral beam was inside, and Johnny and Alyssna were standing next to it. They stared at Richard and his cuffs, and a look of astonishment flashed across their features.

"Everything okay?" Johnny asked.

"Not really." I left it at that. Looking around, I noticed something immediately. "There's no scuba equipment here."

"The airlock is just for equipment to bring in and out," he responded. "From vessels."

I pursed my lips. "You'll stay here with Alyssna and Richard. Don't let him go, whatever you do. We'll close the hatch and lock you in so the base personnel can't get in. Cliff and I will return to the docking pool. When *SC-1* arrives and connects the umbilical, get the two components on board and come get us."

His eyes were wide. "Where will you be?"

"Outside. We have to go help Renée and Sahar."

———••———

WE'D ALREADY DELAYED IT TOO long. I'd been arguing with Richard while the two outside had been in immense danger. There was no more time to waste. Cliff and I began the journey back up to the modules and through the travel tubes, back toward security and the lift down to the docking pool.

It was the same path back that Commodore Clarke had taken, so I knew we could make it. He'd likely cleared the way of any resistance, anyway.

The errant thought made me swallow past a dry throat.

He'd murdered everyone wearing a BSF uniform in those labs.

Holding the PCD to my lips, I whispered, "Renée. Sahar. We're coming out. Stay away from them if you can. We'll be there in a few minutes." I watched the screen as we moved through the first travel tube. The alarms were still ringing and the lights flashing. Our feet pounded on the white deck as we ran.

```
got it
we're just south of the facility
a ship left a few min ago
```

"It was Clarke," I hissed. "He's continuing his . . . his *mission*."

There was a long pause as they processed that. And then:

```
have to stop him
```

I swore inwardly. "I don't know what he can do. He can get to Diego Garcia and maybe enter, but he's on his own now."

```
have to try
```

The hatches opened at our approach. We were in the living and recreation module when the hair on the back of my neck stood on end. I pulled to a halt and grabbed Cliff.

He had heard it too.

People were speaking:

"There's a team of intruders here. They're in the labs."

"Somehow they planned it to occur at the same time as a quake alert, of all things!"

"You idiot. They *caused* the alert! Everyone's in their emergency collection zones. Hidden away. Meanwhile, they're causing havoc. God knows what they're doing."

There was a long pause. I peered around, but it was dark and the flashing alerts were forcing me to squint. It was difficult to make out anything.

The voice continued, "You think they caused the quake? But that's impossible."

"It was a perfect distraction. We went into lockdown and the personnel vacated the entire facility. Security is outside chasing another group. There are only a few security guards here now. It left us wide open to—"

"But what do they want?"

"Who cares?" the one replied. "Didn't you hear that? The hatch just opened! They're in the module. Come on."

Cliff and I turned and stared at three figures as they appeared from the shadows. They were walking blindly.

Then they saw us.

"Stop right there," one of them said.

I raised my weapon. "I don't want to hurt you. We're just passing through."

They continued toward us. They weren't stopping.

"Cliff," I muttered. "Don't kill them. Just knock them out."

Cliff was watching them approach. All three were large men, but security had not trained them. They were base workers, likely repair or maintenance crew.

I stepped toward them, Cliff at my side. I holstered the gun.

The first one jumped forward and took a swing.

I bobbed and blocked his punch. The other two had targeted Cliff, but he stepped back, leading the two away, as he traded blocks and punches.

Focusing on the one in front of me, I swung an elbow, followed by a series of strikes. He managed to block most of them, but one cracked against his temple and he stepped back, dazed, and went down to one knee. Then he rose again, staring at me. "Where are you from?"

I clenched my teeth and didn't respond. Instead, I swung a foot and it cracked across his head. His eyes rolled up, showing only white in the dim module. The multicolored alerts bathed his face as he fell backward, crashing onto the deck.

Cliff was working on one of the others. They'd been no match for the man. He'd been training hard since the USSF had taken him prisoner. He'd recovered from those events six months earlier, had only a slight limp remaining, but he'd increased his musculature *and* his speed, and his moves were lightning fast. He was blocking each strike easily, and between each block, throwing *three* punches or knife edge strikes. It wore his opponent down quickly, and within seconds, he'd landed four strong hits to the other man's jaw. Eventually the man fell to the deck, motionless except for his heaving chest.

Cliff straightened and looked at me. "No problem."

———••———

SOON WE WERE IN THE security module and at the lift heading down.

Something occurred to me and I marched slowly toward the desk where we'd fought Rivers and the other guard. I peered over it and to the deck on the other side.

Cliff watched, his eyes hard. "What is it?"

I swallowed past a lump in my throat. The two were dead.

———••———

"CLARKE'S TOTALLY MAD," I SNAPPED.

"He's driven. He's on a mission. He's going to do everything he can to disable or dismantle the BSFIF."

We were in the lift heading down to the docking pool.

"To kill someone who's already in submission. I—" I shook my head. "I could never do that. It's cold. It's heartless."

"He's full of anger, and in the military you don't question orders. The BSF is clearly concerned about this splinter group. They're highly motivated to eliminate them."

"I can tell."

Cliff turned to me. "He's going to do whatever it takes to kill as many of them as he can. Then he'll expect to come to Trieste and get the neutral weapon from us."

I shrugged. "I'm not sure what else he can do to the BSFIF. He doesn't really have many other options here."

But it got worse.

The repair crew we'd temporarily restrained in the airlock at the base of the lift.

They were also gone.

Tied up still, limp, in pools of their own blood.

I clenched my fists at my sides and screamed.

There were a few seacars in the docking pool, all transports. None had armaments; they were likely just for carrying replacement crews to and from DG. We boarded one, descended to the underwater airlock, and passed through the inner hatch. It pressurized to the exterior depth of 500 meters, and we piloted out, through the tunnel and into the dark water of the deep Indian Ocean.

Chapter Thirty-Five

WE POWERED OUTSIDE AND MOVED southward a few hundred meters. The vessel was small. It had two airlocks—one on each side—and a powerful single engine and screw. The sonar and other systems were basic, but I did note that the deck vibrated with power when I pushed the throttle. It likely had a high top speed, but all amenities ended there.

It would have been nice to have a few torpedoes, but no matter. We only needed to find our people and get them on board.

The vessel descended to the sandy bottom at my touch. Our headlights illuminated the area and I signaled Sahar and Renée.

There was no answer.

"Shit. Security may have caught them." I peered out the viewport. It was just too dark. The only thing we could do is wait to see if they could find us and board our airlock. They'd then have to decompress . . .

But we had to locate them first.

"Shit," I said again.

"Can we track their PCD signal?" Cliff asked.

"Give it a try."

"No luck," he said after a minute. "I'm not getting anything."

I felt helpless. There was nothing we could do for them. And if security had found them, they were not going to be considerate. Not after what Clarke had done, anyway.

We had disabled the towers to make sure they did not detect *SC-1* when it returned. In the end, however, Clarke had totally derailed our plans.

And killed a lot of people.

It would devastate Sahar.

Our comm crackled to life. *"Attention all personnel."* It was an all-call broadcast, from the same person who'd been on the PA earlier. *"This is a base emergency. The intruders have killed numerous sailors in the facility. There are some outside still. The quake compromised the lower lab levels. There was pressure loss but hatches sealed the areas quickly. Stay in your safety zones. Don't come out. We've called Diego Garcia for help and we're waiting, but the displacement wave might hit us any minute. Be prepared for more base damage."*

I stared at Cliff. "They haven't found them yet." I pushed the throttle up and began to move. "We have to show Renée where we are, before security catches them."

Cliff was peering out the viewports, squinting, trying to make something out, but it was still impossible. We were hovering just feet over the seafloor, moving slowly.

He was holding two PCDs on his lap, and I frowned. "What's that?"

"It's Richard's. I took it from him."

I stopped the seacar and thought furiously. When he'd cuffed Kat's killer, he'd taken the communication device. A prickle worked its way down my scalp . . .

It might actually give us a chance.

"What is it?" he asked.

"Richard had hacked into Renée's PCD. He'd somehow turned her comms off, then back on, and caused a loud sound to attract attention. To give their position away."

It only took him a second to realize what I was suggesting. He started pushing keys on the device. "You want me to contact her?"

"If possible. Or, just send the same signal."

He looked horrified. "It'll give them away again."

"Or, it'll help us find them first."

—••—

IT WAS THE ONLY THING we could do.

The sonar was situated between the two pilot's chairs, as was customary. I stared at the screen intently. There were a few blips in front of us, indicating some noise, but there was no way to tell who it was. I powered forward, edging toward the location.

I kept the power low. Renée and Sahar had disabled the sonar towers, so personnel in the facility's control cabin didn't know what we were doing.

"Careful," Cliff muttered. "It might not be our people."

Within minutes, a figure appeared from the darkness.

Then another.

They held needle guns in their hands, and they turned to stare at us.

"Sahar," I hissed into the comm. "I don't know if you can see or hear me, but the security team is right in front of the seacar. They're armed."

No response.

"I can go out and try to neutralize them," Cliff rumbled.

There was scuba gear on board the small vessel. It was an option.

The floodlight swung across the area; I was searching for more divers. Sure enough, there were three more nearby. All held needle guns.

"There are five of them," I said into the comm.

Cliff was still working at Richard's PCD. He was trying to decipher how the man had hacked into Renée's communication device.

There were no signs of them on the sonar. They were being absolutely quiet. The security team was still staring at us, trying to figure out who we were exactly. Then over the PA: *"Security, that seacar is not BSFIF. Repeat, that's not us, guys! Watch out!"*

The response was instant. They turned toward us and began swimming.

I knew there wasn't much they could do. They couldn't board us, because they'd have to decompress. But they could damage us. Get on our hull, sabotage the thrusters perhaps. Or if they had an explosive, they could implode the seacar. I increased thrust and backed off a bit, but kept the divers in view.

"Got it," Cliff said. "What should I—"

"Send the same signal as before." I kept my eyes on the sonar, waiting . . .

And a white star flared on the sonar screen. It was to the starboard, about twenty meters away. They were close.

I hauled the ship around and pointed the stern toward the divers. "Hold on!" I snapped as I slammed the thrust to full. The screws turned instantly, cavitating and throwing bubbles upward. The water behind us grew instantly turbulent and a river churned *away* from the seacar. It picked the divers up and hurled them backward, away from us. There were a few angry snaps of noise as needles ricocheted off our hull, then the figures disappeared into the darkness behind us, twirling and spinning like rag dolls as our thrusters pushed them.

I'd kept my eyes on the white star flashing on the screen.

Renée's PCD.

Soon we were over it, and I hissed, "It's us, Renée. Get on board, now!"

Within minutes the airlock outer hatch opened.

I stared at the speaker, willing it alive. Within moments, pumps had purged water from the lock. A voice said from the comm, "Mac! It's us, we're in the airlock. We're decompressing."

I sat back in the chair and deflated, spent and exhausted. Renée and Sahar were alive.

—••—

THEY HAD A LENGTHY PERIOD of decompression ahead of them. Cliff and I brought the seacar to the outer airlock hatch at the labs—where inside, Johnny and Alyssna waited with the neutral beam.

I stared at the clock.

Time was ticking slowly.

So slowly.

Where the hell was *SC-1?*

Then my PCD came to life. "Mac?"

"Meg! Finally."

"We're a few minutes away. What's happening there?"

"It's gone to hell, unfortunately, but we got Components Three and Four."

I told her where we were and directed her into the waters around The Vault. I wasn't worried about security intercepting our transmission, because I was using my own PCD and not a common channel. She said, "We're about ten minutes from you. Everything worked fine. Chalam and Max came through. The quake worked beautifully."

"No displacement wave?"

"Just a tiny one. It was a large quake—Chalam thinks about 8.3—but the crust moved laterally, not vertically, which is what you wanted."

"Any warsub movement out there?"

"Diego Garcia went into lockdown. We heard the alarms. They'll figure out there's no displacement wave very soon, if they haven't already."

Which meant they'd be coming, and likely very soon.

Then she said something that absolutely froze the blood in my veins.

"We transferred the last bomb to the Commodore. He's got it now."

Chapter Thirty-Six

"Meg." I paused for a long series of heartbeats before I continued. "What are you talking about?"

"We mated *SC-1* with the Commodore's seacar a few minutes ago. The fifth bomb. We moved it over—"

"Why did you do that?"

She sensed the intensity in my tone. "What's wrong? Richard told us that we were only to use four bombs for the quake. He told me in *SC-1* just before you left. You saw us speaking . . . I thought you told him. You nodded at me. Chalam confirmed it . . . said we didn't need five."

"What did Max say about that?" I asked.

"He let Chalam decide. He's the geologist, after all. We moved the bomb over to Clarke's seacar and he left, just a few minutes ago."

I clutched the PCD in my hand.

Holy.

Shit.

My knuckles were white.

Beside me, Cliff's usually stoic face was one of shock.

"Meg," I rasped. "Listen to me. Those weren't my orders. Watch out for Chalam. He's working with Clarke and Richard." Chalam was on board *SC-1* with her.

There was a long, terrible break. When she spoke again, her voice was a whisper. "What the hell are you talking about?"

I explained what Richard and Clarke had done. She swore repeatedly as I spoke. I had tied in the airlock with my broadcast, so Renée and Sahar could hear what I was saying.

Meg said, "Richard told me that you wanted one of the bombs after we were done. He told me on the seacar. You *saw* us speaking . . . I assumed you'd sent him over to tell me!"

Part of me was shocked that she'd trusted Clarke, but we had been through so much already, and I belatedly realized the irony of what I'd done.

I'd implored her to *trust* the man.

And then he'd betrayed us, after all.

I recalled what he'd said on board *SC-1*, before we infiltrated The Vault: *My orders are to go to their HQ in the Indian Ocean. Find them . . . find their leaders, and then blow them all to hell.*

Blow them all to hell.

"Listen carefully," I said. "He's got an Isomer Bomb, and he's going to use it. He's going to achieve what the BSF ordered, and Chalam's going to get his revenge."

"He was headed east," she said. "He's not on my sonar anymore, but I can send an active pulse—"

"No! Don't." That would give away her position to every BSFIF warsub in the region. "Come get us first. Then we'll deal with it."

"But Mac," Sahar cried from our airlock. Her voice echoed in the small enclosure. "What's Clarke doing?"

It seemed obvious, after his previous actions. "He killed many at The Vault, Sahar. Now he's going to use the Isomer Bomb at Diego Garcia. He's going to destroy the entire base, and kill everyone there."

—••—

SAHAR HAD GONE QUIET. RENÉE was full of questions about Richard and what exactly was going on. I tried my best to answer everything while *SC-1* maneuvered in and the umbilical connected with the base airlock. Inside, Johnny and Alyssna opened the hatch and began to load the weapon into *SC-1*.

I'd warned Johnny about Richard and Chalam, and he was prepared for it. He secured Richard inside our seacar, and Chalam was sitting quietly, on the couch, not speaking.

Within a few minutes, Cliff and I had mated with *SC-1* and also transferred over, along with Renée and Sahar, although they had to remain in the airlock to decompress.

Within thirty minutes, we were ready to depart.

We had the Aiming Module and The Accelerator. The neutral beam was large, and we secured it to the deck over the moonpool hatch.

Then, in the Pilot's Cabin, I pushed the throttle to full and set course for the joint USSF/BSF base, to the east. We had no time to waste; we needed to catch up to Clarke.

The fusion reactor was rumbling and vaporizing seawater. Eventually the bubble began to grow from our bow back to stern. I called to Max, and he appeared at my side. "What happened?"

He looked contrite. "Mac, I'm sorry! Right before we dropped you here at The Vault, Richard told me that you'd changed your mind. He said to only use four bombs. I didn't think anything of it, because Chalam told me earlier that only four were needed to cause the quake we needed! The two comments matched, and since you trust Richard so much . . . " He trailed off and watched my eyes.

"They tricked you," I muttered. "They're working together. And with Clarke." It had been totally unexpected. I'd known Clarke was a question mark. I'd known that Chalam wanted revenge, but he had seemed better earlier. It had been a ruse though. But the real surprise had been Richard.

"What are they planning?"

It seemed clear that Commodore Clarke had sensed an opportunity and had taken it. We'd had five nuclear-sized bombs on board *SC-1* and he'd realized that Chalam's anger at the BSF had been an opportunity. He'd manipulated the situation, used Richard to back him up, and had taken a bomb and was on his way to DG. It was a hundred kilometers to the east, only two hours travel time, but he'd left almost an hour earlier. He'd be arriving there in about fifty minutes, assuming a speed of 60 kph, and only our SCAV drive could get us close in time.

I slammed the throttle all the way forward, and the acceleration pushed me back into the seat. Within seconds, our velocity was 450 kph.

We couldn't let him do it.

Sahar and Renée were still in the airlock, decompressing. It was a miserable environment for divers. To just sit and wait to exhale excess nitrogen from your body. If you didn't, however, then when the pressure dropped back to normal, the gases would bubble from your tissues and stay lodged *within* bloodstreams. They'd clog joints, organs, veins, and arteries.

One can't survive with bubbles in your vessels and brain.

Sahar had signaled me over the comm, and once we were on a path to DG, I accepted the call. Her face appeared on the screen before me.

"Mac!" she cried. "You can't let him do this!"

"We're en route to intercept him," I said. "I'll try my best."

Her face went immediately dark. "What happened in The Vault?"

I looked down. "I'm sorry to say he broke away from us and went on a rampage. He took advantage of the situation. We put too much trust in him, Sahar."

She muttered something under her breath. "*How many?* I want to know, Mac."

I stared into her dark, pleading eyes. I sighed. "I'm guessing fifteen. Maybe more."

Beside her, Renée was watching the conversation. Sahar had gone quiet and was staring at the deck. I had predicted earlier that she would have to deal with death and the ensuing guilt during our quest for independence, but this was not what I'd anticipated. That had been an expectation of battles against superpowers, submarine warfare, espionage, and so on. I'd been dealing with this guilt already and had been for years. But Sahar had vouched for Commodore Clarke, and he'd not just betrayed her, he had *killed* people.

It could consume her, if given a chance to root and fester.

Renée stepped toward the camera. She'd pulled off her equipment; her hair was soaked and she looked exhausted from the ordeal outside, but she was still a sight. She looked radiant and beautiful, but her eyes were sad, and her mouth turned down.

"What's wrong, Renée?"

That startled her. "Truman, we just found out that Richard killed Kat last year. Are *you* okay? That's more important right now."

I sighed and looked away. "I don't know what to think. I have to process it. I had a chance to kill him, but didn't do it."

"Where is he now?"

"In the seacar. In cuffs. He'll come back to Trieste with us, if we make it through this." I cringed when I thought about the fleet at Diego Garcia. They could easily overwhelm us within the next hour.

"I'm so, so sorry, Tru," she said again.

"Renée, I'm . . . " I trailed off. "The truth is that I still have to come to terms with this. With what happened." A dark cloud was swirling within me.

I hadn't been with her.

If I had . . .

I pushed those thoughts aside.

Later.

I'd deal with it later.

Then I thought of Meg, and how she had tried to teach me not to bury my feelings, but to bring them to the surface and really deal with them. Accept them and embrace them.

But this was a lot to take, all at once.

I pressed on. "I'll always miss her. She's been gone for a year. I love you now, Renée. I want to spend our lives together. I don't want to dwell on the past. But this . . . " I felt my eyes well up, and I looked away. The truth was, I *wanted* to kill Richard. He meant to help us achieve independence and freedom for Trieste and the underwater colonies, but his tactics were twisted and dark. There's no way a sane person would think to do such things.

A collection of radicals seemed to surround us.

Is that what we were?

Is that who *I* was?

I knew I was fighting for my people, for the citizens of Trieste. For all ocean colonists, to bring us into a new balance with the land superpowers.

To *be* a superpower in our own right, in the oceans.

But was I as bad as Clarke? As Richard?

—— •• ——

I LEFT JOHNNY PILOTING *SC-1* and moved back to find Chalam. He was aft of the living area, next to the moonpool hatch, sitting on the deck with zip tie cuffs around his wrists. Next to him was Richard, similarly restrained. Max Hyland was standing over Chalam, his expression one of fury, and Richard was staring at the deck, seemingly in humiliation.

Beside them, the neutral beam was secured via cable to bolts in the bulkheads on either side. It looked absolutely devastating, and I took a minute to study it before I tore my eyes away. The barrel was twelve inches in diameter. It would fit *within* the ten laser emitters we'd already stolen. At one end of the barrel was the accelerator, which generated the particles and blasted them down the barrel, aimed and directed by Component Three. It was a violent spear of pain and death, meant to hurl waves of deuterons into the enemy, to tear apart molecules and atoms and dissolve flesh. To shatter hulls, implode seacars, melt victims, and obliterate the enemy.

Chalam glanced at me, then at the weapon. "It looks scary, doesn't it?"

"It does."

"It killed my brother. And Preet and Kalinda."

"I know."

"And we stole it."

"Thanks to your knowledge of the Chagos Trench. And Max Hyland's Isomer Bombs." I paused. "But our mission ends there, Chalam. We got revenge. We don't need to kill more people."

He shrugged. "If you say so."

"Clarke already shot fifteen people in cold blood. We didn't want to do that. He's on his own mission, and he's roped you into it. He's on his way to DG with the bomb. He's going to destroy the entire base. There are people there who have nothing to do with The Vault, the neutral beam, your brother. How can you do this?"

"They killed Manse, Mac. We'd done nothing wrong. They were just testing their stupid weapon." He took a breath and exhaled slowly. He couldn't meet my eyes. "Back in Trieste, you promised me revenge. You said it to get me to agree to go on the mission with you, right?"

I shifted my feet. "You're right. I was hoping you would change your mind. Or something would help you change your mind."

"You mean Sahar?"

"Maybe. Or maybe I could do it. I tried. We got back at them. Isn't that enough?"

He shook his head. "They killed my brother. Do you know what it feels like? You have a sister. What would you do if someone hurt her? Well, Manse was like my twin. People thought we were, you know. Twins. We'd spent our whole lives together, basically. Even school and work.

And we were going to spend our lives together, in Churchill, working for the undersea colonies. But then this happened, and it's derailed my life." Then he lifted his head and stared at me. His eyes were piercing. "And I want revenge for that. I'll do anything to get revenge."

His words stopped me in my tracks. I had no response. He was absolutely correct, and it shook me to the core.

Six months ago, they'd taken Meg. And I'd done everything possible to rescue her. I'd waged war to get her back.

And in the end, we'd detonated an Isomer Bomb at Seascape to get her.

Destroying the entire base.

I opened my mouth but nothing came out. Inside, I was quivering.

I turned and walked away.

—••—

I SETTLED BACK INTO THE pilot chair and stared at the sonar. Clarke's seacar was on the screen in front of us.

He had an Isomer Bomb in there.

Chapter Thirty-Seven

On our sonar screen, approaching from the joint USSF/BSF base, were clusters of stars.

Ships from the base.

They were moving to intercept at 70 kph, likely on course for The Vault following the calls for assistance. I wondered if Clarke had called ahead and informed them of his identity. He was probably trying to bypass them, to get close to DG.

I wondered if they'd just let him in.

If they did, they'd pay a terrible price.

Johnny, at my side, said, "What are you going to do?"

I tried to speak, but nothing came out. Chalam's words had rattled me. Then I managed, "We can warn them. Tell them what's on the way."

"Mac," he replied in a soft tone. "They'll sink him."

I stared at my Deputy Mayor. "Yes, they will."

"Can we disable his seacar maybe? Prevent him from getting closer?"

I checked the torpedo complement. Meg has used some while we were on board *Aurora*, stealing the second component. She'd been engaged in battle against two other BSF warsubs.

We had only two torpedoes remaining.

"Let's do both," I said. The BSF warsubs were still a few minutes away. We had some time.

"They'll think we're attacking a senior officer in the BSF, Mac. They'll attack us too."

I snorted. "I guess we'll find out in a minute if they believe us." I steeled myself. "Prepare a torpedo." I triggered the comm and set it to the common frequency that all subs and underwater traffic monitored.

I made sure to disguise my voice using a simple software application, though they'd eventually figure out that we were in *SC-1* and were from Trieste. Sadly, we had no other options here. "Attention BSF warsubs approaching from Diego Garcia. The seacar you're nearing has an Isomer Bomb. Commodore Clarke is on board. His intention is to destroy your base. Do not let him approach. *Our* goal is to damage him, to stop him. Repeat, *he has a nuclear-sized Isomer Bomb* on board."

A minute passed with no response.

We were closing on the seacar and had him in our sights. We had dropped from SCAV, and were ready to fire.

Then came the response, "Attention traffic approaching from the west. You are to stop immediately. *Both* of you. Do not approach. We'll fire on you."

My comm squawked and I stared at it. It was a private signal from Clarke's transport. "Commodore!" I said between clenched teeth. "Don't do it! You can't get close to the base. We've warned them."

"Don't stop me, Mac," came his angry voice. "I'm getting this bomb close to the base. You can't fire on me, or they'll destroy you. You have to get the neutral beam accelerator back to Trieste. Assemble that weapon and declare independence!"

I shook my head. "Clarke, don't do this. You'll kill thousands. You'll die too. You've already killed people at The Vault. You'll have to live with that for—"

"I was following orders!"

"You can tell yourself that, but you can't live like that. The guilt will crush you."

"The British Submarine Fleet will not stand by as right-wing splinter factions try to dissolve our forces. I'm going to put an end to it now."

"You'll die, Clarke. Do you want that?"

"I'll do what I have to. You just get the weapon back home."

"You're forcing me to fire on you, Clarke."

"Don't you dare!" he growled. "You know this is the right thing to do. You know we have to weaken the superpowers to really gain a foothold in the oceans."

"No," I snapped. "There will be battles, but I want to do it with economics too! I want to forge treaties, to prove that we're essential to their existence on land. To show that we are self-sufficient."

He laughed. "You're dreaming. They won't just *let* you have independence, Mac. You have to *fight* for it! You have to *kill* for it! That's what your dad taught you. Hell, that's what you've been doing for the past two years! That's what you did at Seascape. That's what I'm doing here. Don't stop me!"

"We don't need all-out war! We can try with treaties first."

"War leads to treaties, not the other way around, Mac."

"Listen to me, Clarke. You promised us. We trusted you. You can't do this."

That stopped him, and there was a long, long break. I approached his stern; his single large screw was churning the water savagely before us. Johnny had targeted it, and our torpedo was ready in the tube. The shutter was open, and his finger was poised just over the red FIRE button. Then Clarke said, his voice a husk, "Mac. Tell Sahar I'm sorry. I didn't want to disappoint her, but I had to."

"You don't have to—"

"Tell her I said I'm sorry. I didn't mean to do this. Orders, you know, old chap. Tell her to declare independence. For Churchill and her people. Tell her that this wasn't her fault. The guilt is mine, not hers."

I decided to try one last thing.

Pushing a button, I looped Sahar into the conversation.

"Tell her yourself, Clarke," I said. "You can't detonate that bomb."

I suddenly noticed that Max Hyland was over my shoulder. He said, "But Mac—"

I hushed him with a gesture.

Sahar was on the line. "Commodore, please don't continue this. Please don't kill anyone else."

His voice was barely a whisper. "Sahar. Mayor. I'm so sorry, but I had to do this. Please don't hold it against me, and don't feel guilt. This was my doing, not yours. Command gave me orders, and I'm carrying them out. But you can declare independence and take Churchill into the future."

I shook my head at that. He was a conflicted man, fighting both his history *and* his future. He wanted independence *from* the BSF, but at the same time he was following their orders. But what he said next clarified things, but not much.

"This splinter faction will be worse than the BSF, Sahar. They won't tolerate *anyone* breaking away. They'll come down on you harder than you can imagine. We can't let that happen. The BSF will be tough, but the BSFIF will be a monster that you don't want to face. I'm going to deal with them now. I took care of Hitchens at The Vault, but the real threat is at Garcia."

"Mac," I heard from behind me.

I turned. It was Max again. "I can't right now, Doc. We're in the middle of—"

"He can't detonate that bomb."

"I know! That's what we're trying to avoid!"

"No, that's not what I—" Hyland paused to gather his thoughts. His hair was disheveled and he looked exhausted. "Well, I mean, he *can* detonate it, but—"

Johnny called out, "Mac! It's Clarke! He's diving!"

We had a clear shot and only two torpedoes. I swallowed, knowing we wouldn't have a better opportunity. "Go," I said.

Johnny pushed the button.

There was a whine and *whoosh* as the torpedo shot from our bow tube. It soared straight for Clarke's seacar . . .

On the sonar screen, the torpedo showed as a line arrowing forward . . .

I pulled back on the throttle and backed off.

The comm blared. "Attention *SC-1!* You did not have permission to fire on that seacar!"

"Calm down," I muttered. "We're saving your lives, dammit."

"But Mac!" Max blurted from behind me.

The torpedo hit the seacar. The churning screws sliced the water directly in its path. The torpedo's onboard systems detected the impact, and performed its single purpose.

It detonated.

The blast flared around the transport's stern. Bubbles exploded outward, enclosing a red flame and rapidly vaporizing water. The blades bent forward instantly, the engines stopped turning, and the vessel shuddered to an immediate stop. It started listing, stern down, and began to descend.

I checked the depth.

Only 783 meters here; not Crush Depth, thankfully for Commodore Clarke.

A flood of bubbles was soaring toward the surface. It was not a small leak. The entire aft compartment of the vessel was flooding.

"Close the airtight hatches," I said. "Come on, man."

The ship kept sinking.

Alarms started blaring from the sonar console. I jerked my gaze to it. The BSF warsubs were on approach but were still a few minutes from the area. They had opened their torpedo shutters, and our sonar had recognized it.

Johnny said, "Mac. We need to get out of here. *Now.*"

I glanced at him. "We can save him, maybe. We can—"

He grabbed my arm. "Mac. No. We can't. You know what he's going to do. Think about it."

I paused and stared at the sonar. The warsubs were approaching. There were several clusters of them—twenty-nine in total. Clarke's vessel was about to hit bottom. The bubbles were continuing, but it was a trickle now, and not a stream. I considered the situation.

Then I nodded. He was right. When the warsubs arrived, he'd detonate the weapon, taking as many of them as he could. He wouldn't allow them to capture him. And he wouldn't be able to talk his way out of it, at least not after they found out what he'd done at The Vault.

He wouldn't allow them to take him.

"You're right," I hissed. I turned the seacar to the south and pushed the fusion reactor button. The SCAV engine roared to life, thrusting us through the water. "Max, what's the blast radius?"

"Of these weapons, ten kilometers on the surface. But underwater, the blast wave will be much larger. But Mac, that's not what I mean. It won't be that big here! Not now!"

I stared back at him. "Max, what the hell are you talking about?"

He took a breath and grabbed my shoulder. "The bomb is a two-stage weapon. Remember? The first blast is the X-Ray trigger. It's the X-Rays hitting the hafnium that releases the real energy."

"Yeah, I remember. Back at Seascape, we used two torpedoes."

"But these bombs have both blasts enclosed in the shell. But the X-Rays here won't trigger the hafnium! His bomb isn't going to work."

Max looked frantic. There were bags under his eyes, his hair was a mess, and he was having a hard time speaking.

"Take a deep breath," I said. "Again." He did, each time. "Now, get it out."

"Mac," he said, putting his hands on the seat backs, looming over me and Johnny. "The bomb's X-Ray trigger needs to be calibrated for the exterior environment. Remember I said that? I calibrated these for the bottom of the Chagos Trench, at the slip fault. For *that* environment! Just over 2,000 meters, submerged in salt water."

"What's your point, Max?"

"The density, salinity, and temperature of the water determines how the X-Rays travel. I had to calibrate the bomb so they would hit the hafnium at that depth and trigger the nucleons back down to ground state in an instant—"

"Max! What the hell are you—"

"He's going to detonate in his seacar at only four atms pressure! In air. The X-Rays aren't calibrated correctly for that."

I hesitated, pondering that. "What do you mean?"

"The first blast will go, but it won't activate the hafnium. No Isomer explosion."

I stared at his blue eyes. "It won't kill?"

"Oh, it'll kill Clarke all right. Obliterate his seacar. The concussion might damage those BSF warsubs too. But it won't be a megaton, not even close. It'll just kill him, that's it."

Chapter Thirty-Eight

I stared at Hyland in horror. Then I turned back to the controls and studied the sonar. The BSFIF warsubs were only a few kilometers from Clarke. I had the opportunity to warn them to stay away, to try and save their crews.

I could also warn Clarke, plead with him not to do it because it wouldn't have the effect he wanted anyway.

Or . . .

Johnny was watching me. He could tell what was going through my mind.

We could show Clarke how to modify the bombs so they would detonate successfully, and take the enemy warsubs with him when the hafnium blew.

"What should we do?" he whispered.

"I don't know." We had five minutes before the warsubs set upon Clarke. They might try to take him prisoner, or they might just shoot him without questions, hoping to disable his weapon and avoid a catastrophic detonation.

I pressed a button and the fusion reactor powered down. We fell from SCAV and stopped suddenly as friction with the water took hold. The straps held us to our chairs, but the others had to grab whatever they could to keep from slamming forward.

"Clarke," I said into the comm. "You can't do it."

—••—

SAHAR WAS ON MY MIND. Even though she was in the airlock and decompressing from her lengthy swim outside disabling the sonar arrays, I knew what advice she would give. Her words were in my ears. Taking life needlessly was pointless. These warsubs hadn't played a role in this. Clarke's vendetta was against the leadership structure of the BSFIF, *not* the crews on those vessels. And Clarke was not going to be able to get close to Diego Garcia now.

Sahar would not want me to do it, and I desperately wanted to keep her happy, especially after what had happened at The Vault. I needed her on my side for the upcoming struggle. We were going to declare independence, and she had enormous sway over people. They adored her. They followed her. She could help me bring the ocean colonies into the future. To a time when we worked together for each other, and not to serve topsiders who only used us for our resources. To a time when we traded with each other for everyone's benefit, and formed a military partnership among the cities to protect one another in case of aggression by any other nation.

Sahar could do that with me.

People would follow her. Even topsiders would support her, and we needed their voice in the upcoming governmental debates and discussions, before nations chose military aggression as their only option.

Which was inevitable.

Johnny was still eyeing me. I turned to him. "What do you think, Johnny?"

"We need to warn him."

"Do you think he'll still detonate?"

He paused, but only for a brief moment. "Yes. He'll take his chances. He'll never know what happened, but he'll do it."

"It might be our chance to prove ourselves to them."

His eyes showed his shock. "We just stole their weapon, Mac. They're not going to trust us ever again."

I snorted. "Good point." I pressed the comm toggle again and said, "Clarke."

The Commodore's voice crackled from the speaker. "Don't try to stop this, Mac. Get away. You need to be farther."

"It's not going to work. It's not calibrated correctly for your depth. It won't detonate."

There was a long break. "Bullshit. I know you're trying to keep me from blowing it up."

"Listen to me. Hyland had to calibrate the weapons for the salinity, pressure, temperature, and other variables. The bomb isn't in the Trench right now, so it won't blow. I'm trying to protect you now. Don't die in vain."

"Then show me how to calibrate it, so I *can* detonate successfully."

"I won't do that. You can't destroy those warsubs."

He laughed, and it sounded maniacal. "Because they're innocent, right? Is that what you're about to say? Come on, Mac—how are you going to lead the independence movement if you can't make those tough decisions? You have to be willing to do what it takes!"

It sounded awfully familiar. I glanced over my shoulder; Richard was sitting on the deck, looking miserable. He'd preached the same philosophy. So had Dad. And I'd embraced it too, at times. I'd sunk vessels and entire crews.

But only because they'd been trying to kill me.

And what about the dreadnought? The thought hit me in the gut. The Russian warsub had had a crew of over 600, and we'd sent it to the bottom after triggering a meltdown in its fission core. I'd killed them all.

To protect Trieste! I screamed inwardly. They were going to destroy the city and kill hundreds of thousands of citizens, including children. They'd destroyed Blue Downs. You didn't murder needlessly, I told myself.

You don't murder in cold blood.

I said, "Clarke. We're not going to show you how to make it work. You can't do it. Those people weren't trying to kill anyone."

"They're traitors. They killed Chalam's family. They will do far, far worse if I don't stop them."

"The BSF doesn't know that. They're just trying to punish a splinter group. But you don't know—"

"We can't allow them to proceed!" he screamed. "They're traitors!"

"He's losing it," Johnny whispered.

"I'm signing off, Mac. Get out of here and do what I said. And Mac . . ."

"What?" I asked in a quiet voice.

"Good luck to you in the future. You have what it takes. Be tough. Don't ever be weak."

He clicked off, and I snorted to myself. He sounded so much like my dad.

And my dad had destroyed my family when I'd only been fourteen years old.

I stared at the sonar. The warsubs were slowing now. They'd formed a perimeter around Clarke's seacar.

And then the screen flared white.

"Oh my god," Meg hissed over my shoulder.

Max was also there, staring at the screen. The white glow had obscured everything, but it was spreading outward like one massive ripple in a pond. "Hang on everyone!" he shouted.

The shock wave was spreading toward us quickly. I maneuvered to keep our stern to it, to try and ride it out. The seacar shuddered and rattled viciously. The vibration coursed up our feet, and my body shook violently. I clutched the yoke and kept us pointing south.

Red lights flickered on the forward panel.

Hyland was grabbing the back of my chair, and he was studying the sonar. "It's a big blast," he whispered. "Bigger than the trigger alone."

"Did the hafnium go? An isomer blast?"

He winced. "I think some of it did. But it wasn't a megaton."

"How's that possible?"

He thought for a moment, looking away and considering the situation. "His seacar was flooding. It's *possible* that water had submerged the bomb and it was *close* to the environment at the bottom of the Chagos Trench. The X-Rays may have triggered some of the hafnium . . . " he trailed off.

We stared at the stars marking the locations of the subs surrounding Point Zero, the focus of the explosion. They had fallen silent. Then, one by one, they started to flare.

"Bulkheads collapsing," Max said. "Succumbing to the pressure wave. Imploding."

I counted the stars. More than fifteen were pulsing as they released loud, crunching sounds. The algorithms would have detected anything from rushing water to wrenching steel to crewmembers screaming in fear and frustration and calling for help, and converted it to pulsing lights on the sonar display.

Clarke hadn't triggered the full blast, but he'd managed a small piece of one.

And he'd taken some of the subs with him.

"Damn him," I said. "I can't believe he still went ahead and did it."

"He wasn't going to let them take him alive," Johnny replied.

Sahar's voice floated to me from the comm. "Mac, what happened? What was that shaking?"

I exhaled savagely. "Clarke detonated the bomb. He sank some of the subs. But he didn't get close to the base. Didn't hurt Diego Garcia."

"How many warsubs?"

"Fifteen or more are sinking to the bottom. It's shallow there though—only 700 meters. There might be some survivors. Other warsubs are approaching."

Silence met my statement.

Max continued staring at the sonar. He was plugging figures into his PCD. Then he said, "About 100 kilotons. It was big, but only a tenth of what it might have been." He shook his head. "But those warsubs were way too close. They didn't listen to the warnings, Mac, and they paid a price."

"I tried to tell them," I whispered.

On the screen between Johnny and I, the stars winked out, one by one.

Chapter Thirty-Nine

W E'D SUSTAINED MODERATE DAMAGE TO minor systems, but nothing severe enough to prevent us from entering SCAV and getting back home. As I powered up the fusion reactor and began accelerating, the mood shifted from worry and fear to one of realization at what we'd achieved.

On board *SC-1*, we had Components Two, Three, and Four. The ten-terawatt lasers were at Trieste in Alyssna's lab. We had all the pieces of the weapon now. We just had to get her back to Trieste so she could assemble them and use it to defend the colony against upcoming threats in the Gulf.

In the back, I hugged Alyssna and Meg. Renée and Sahar emerged from the airlock following decompression and Renée and I kissed deeply. Sahar seemed sad at what Clarke had done, but she recognized our success and smiled slightly at the burgeoning celebration on board. Music started and there was even laughter. There wasn't a lot of space because of the particle accelerator, but we pressed beside it and chatted about what had transpired over the past few weeks.

It was a deadly and dangerous weapon, and we were standing around it smiling and celebrating. It was a vicious counterpoint.

Sahar disappeared into the back to pray, and Renée and I talked for a bit before settling in to celebrate with the others.

"It's not your fault," Renée told me. "Clarke did it. He was acting on his own. He and Chalam did it."

"We should have known—"

Her eyes flashed. "Don't go there! We have to trust the people who are helping us. If they betray us . . . " She shook her head. "We have to always be on the lookout, but they weren't trying to hurt us. They just did what they thought was best."

"It could have ended our mission. It could have killed us all."

Renée gestured around us. "We're still here, Mac. We did it!"

—••—

MEG WAS IN THE PILOT chair up front. The rest of us were celebrating and going over the events. Chalam and Richard were quiet and still restrained on the deck beside the couches, but I knew they likely felt some happiness over what had occurred. The mission had been a success for them too, more or less. There was music playing and we were shouting to hear each other.

Within minutes we were dancing and holding each other tight. There were hugs, laughter, and people were telling stories of their adventures. Sahar reappeared after her prayers and was talking about evading the security squad outside The Vault, and how they'd had to hide behind a hummock at one point, the armed guards only meters beside them. Johnny was talking about navigating the security module in The Vault and trying to blend in as a BSF officer. He'd spent the night in a cell in Churchill Sands, and told us, with a broad grin, how he'd had to keep up the false accent while guards had screamed, their mouths only an inch away from his face. Their spittle had struck him at times. That brought groans of disgust from the rest of us, and slowly, the levity grew on board *SCAV-1*. The music rolled on. The volume increased. There was no alcohol, but we opened fruit drinks and laughed and spoke about the adventure and all the new stories we had.

Renée and I were holding hands, and I pulled her close. I was suppressing my true emotions, for the new information about Kat's death was sending tremors through my body, but it was something I'd deal with later. I knew I had to put a lid on it and cope with it when I had time. It wasn't what Meg would shave wanted, but she wasn't the best at dealing with emotions either.

An understatement, for sure.

For now, I just wanted to enjoy the end of the mission.

The ship tore through the Indian Ocean, southward, as we celebrated into the evening. More music played. People were singing. Even Sahar joined in; she was joyous and happy and reveling in the experience. The adrenaline must have been a rush for her. She would have to come to terms with what Clarke had done to our team, but I knew she would likely do that in private, alone, during prayers, or with the people she loved back at Churchill.

I realized I didn't know much about her family there, and decided to ask when I had a chance.

After a while, I realized that Meg was calling to me from the pilot cabin, and one by one people stopped talking to try and hear what she was saying.

I couldn't make it out at first. Hyland pointed and I stopped talking about events at The Vault and turned to look.

Her mouth was moving but I still couldn't hear. "What?" I screamed.

The others finally stopped talking, the music paused, and her words floated to me.

"There's a weird alert up here!" she was saying.

"Damage from the explosion?" I asked.

She shook her head, staring at the sonar.

Her face went white.

SC-1 fell from SCAV and we slammed forward into a wall of water. Those standing lurched forward and frantically reached out to grab a support to keep from crashing into the deck. Renée stumbled to her knees, and Alyssna barely managed to keep from falling by grabbing the large particle accelerator, which she'd barely moved away from during the past hour.

Then I heard the alarm.

It was an alert signaling a nearby contact.

I was on all fours; I'd scraped my face against the rough deck. I absently noticed blood trickle down my chin. I said, "What is it? And why'd we drop from SCAV?"

Meg turned to me. There was a look of absolute horror splashed across her face. "Mac. The sonar is displaying a message."

"Well, what—"

"A nearby noise." She was practically screaming now. "Within a hundred meters of us! It's saying *Fish farms*."

It took a moment, but in a flash of fear and terror, realization exploded through me like an atom bomb.

Fish farms.

There was a vessel nearby, and it had just destroyed our ability to stay in SCAV drive.

Chalam blurted a single swear word, his voice a strangled gasp, and he tried to say something else but only a choking jumble of words came out. His expression was one of pure panic and terror.

A cold chill fell over us in *SC-1*.

Nearby, an enemy vessel had the weapon.

The Water Pick.

A laser-encased neutral beam, aimed right at us, firing even as I thought it. They had melted our bow and destroyed our ability to stay in SCAV drive while traveling at 300 kph; knocked us into conventional drive with a sudden blast of deuterons. The aiming system was astonishing.

And forward, in our pilot cabin, the sonar alarm rang over and over.

Fish farms.

Fish farms.

Fish farms.

Interlude: The Mid-Atlantic Ridge

One Year Earlier

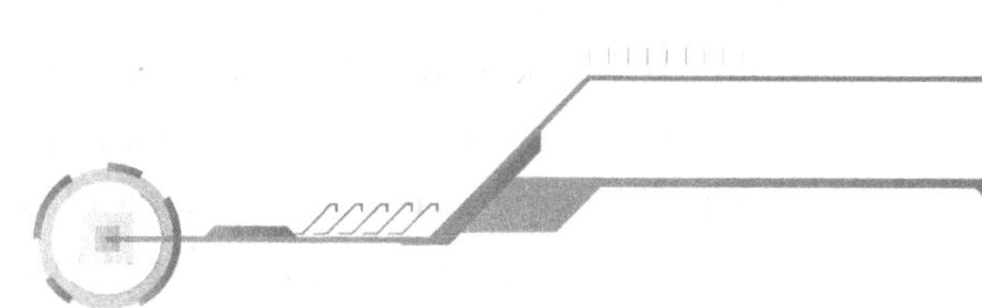

Interlude:	The Mid-Atlantic Ridge
Date:	March 2130 AD
Depth:	3,699 meters
Latitude:	27º 54" 09' S
Longitude:	17º 35" 41' W
Time:	2248 hours

RICHARD LANCOMBE AND JESSICA NG stared down at the body.

Doctor Katherine Wells was in the pilot's chair, pinned to it by a large piece of shrapnel that entered her chest just at her heart. Her face was slack, blood trickled from her mouth, there were bruises and other lacerations on her cheeks and forehead, but there was still an expression burned into her features.

It was of surprise and fear and horror.

She'd realized at the last minute what was happening, what Richard was doing, and she'd been scared.

And it showed in her face.

Jessica couldn't believe what she'd witnessed. She'd known Richard for decades. The two had fought for independence alongside Frank McClusky—Mac's Dad—back in the 2090s. She'd been proud of what Mac had accomplished in the past year. How he'd taken the mantle of leadership during the mayoral race following The Battle in 2129, assumed the position of Director of Trieste City Intelligence, and had begun a struggle for independence using the SCAV drive to convince other cities to join with them. Now he had encouraged other great minds to build more amazing weapons and technology, and they had just defeated a hostile force in battle in the Mid-Atlantic Ridge. It had been a huge success.

But for some reason, her husband, who had been by her side for so many years now, had just murdered one of the principals in the fight.

"What the hell did you just do?" she whispered, staring at the body.

Richard turned to her. "We had to do it."

"What?" Her voice was hollow; she could barely speak.

"Mac is the one to succeed at this. His father failed, but Mac has the potential. The people love him. They follow him. He can lead this battle, Jessica."

"I agree, but *why* did you just—"

"He needs to focus on this journey. He can't do it while distracted."

"And you think Kat was . . . was a *distraction* to him? They loved each other, Richard! How could you do this?"

"Listen to me!" he snapped. "This will galvanize him. Push him. Force him to continue moving forward. He needs to be angry. He needs to feel frustration and rage. I can't let him feel comfortable, ever, or he'll stop fighting."

"He's been fighting for a year now, and he's done just fine without your *motivation*," she growled. "He doesn't need this." She pointed at the body. "You just *murdered* her!"

He stepped toward Jessica, and in an instant, she felt fear swell through her body.

She took a hesitant step back.

Richard noticed and stopped. "I could never hurt you, Jess."

"You . . . you . . . " She didn't know how respond. "What's happened to you? After so long, waiting for the fight to begin. Planning and preparing while in Ballard. Waiting for someone to step up and lead. Mac finally did, and we're a part of it. And now you want to throw it all away?"

"I don't want to throw it away. I'm pushing us forward! This will help! Trust me on this."

She stared at the man she loved.

Only she didn't feel love anymore.

She felt fear.

Richard scared her.

A part of her knew that she couldn't say that. If she did, she might be next. She had to make him feel like she believed him. She'd spend months acting normal, doing what she'd always done. She'd make him feel comfortable and let time pass.

But now she knew the truth.

He was a monster.

She'd escape him, eventually. Get away from him. Distance herself from him. "Are you sure?" she finally managed, her voice a husk.

"Of course! He'll be angry, but he'll be in the fight more than ever.

He'll want revenge. He'll push like he's never pushed."

Jessica Ng steeled herself and forced her face to show calm and determination. "I see what you're saying. It might work."

His face brightened. "You agree with me?"

She hesitated. She knew she had to make it look like a struggle to consider things before accepting. "Yes, but you should have asked me before you did it."

He frowned. "I didn't know we'd be in this situation, Jess. I tried to talk to you—"

"Next time, we need to speak for longer before you make a snap decision like this."

He looked abashed. "Okay. I can do that. But the opportunity just appeared."

She peered at him. "How long have you been thinking about this?"

"For a while. I saw how he was feeling about her. But he needs to focus," he said again. "Just stay the course."

"How are you ever going to move forward after this?" The real question she wanted to ask was, *How can you live with the guilt after committing murder, you sick prick*, but she knew she couldn't.

Otherwise, she might end up dead too.

Richard turned and stared out the canopy. They were moving slowly through the rift, creeping back toward base. "I'll make it up to him sometime. I'll do my best to ensure the independence movement continues, with him in charge. He'll forgive me for this. I'll do whatever it takes."

"All the beauty of life is made up of light and shadow."
—Leo Tolstoy

Part Seven: Trafalgar

Chapter Forty

Part Seven: Trafalgar

FISH FARMS.

Fish farms.

Fish farms.

The alarm was calling for attention, and the realization of what had happened to our SCAV drive seared through me with a shock I'd never before experienced. Chalam had already realized, but he was having a hard time vocalizing the danger. A neutral beam had melted—or deformed—our bow and had changed the shape meant to create the low-pressure zone and generate the bubble of air that enveloped our seacar. As a result, we'd crashed out of SCAV and were now in conventional drive.

We hadn't lost hull integrity, though that likely wasn't far away.

I screamed to Meg, "Change course! Full power to the screws! Zigzag! Zigzag!"

Their targeting system was phenomenally accurate. They'd pinned us while at an incredible velocity and had held the beam on us long enough to haul us from supercavitation.

Some of the others still hadn't yet figured it out, though Alyssna knew already too. The irony of the situation hit her and her jaw had fallen slack. She stared around her, searching the bulkheads for evidence of attack.

A flickering, glittering light caught my eye out the starboard viewport. A series of shadows fell across the living area as the light shimmered outside. I thought at first it was the sunlight piercing the water, then I realized it was nighttime far above.

The laser was vaporizing water.

"It's on the starboard!" I yelled as I pushed through the crowd of people toward the pilot cabin. "Veer away!"

The sonar was showing the *fish farms* warning and a light was flashing angrily on the middle console. I stabbed at the ACTIVE PULSE button and our system broadcast a lone, explosive *ping*. The screen flashed in concert with the noise, and a single white blob appeared, along with an odd, narrow, straight line that pierced straight toward the green avatar at the center of the display.

The green shape was us.

The white line was the LaWs E UNPB.

Laser Weapon System Encased Underwater Neutral Particle Beam.

It had zeroed in on us, painting us with deadly high energy particles. Each hit our hull, knocked protons from atoms, pulled apart molecules, and dissolved our hull.

Bit by bit.

We couldn't let them focus on us for a sustained period. If we did, we'd lose hull integrity.

It was inevitable.

Johnny was next to me in the chairs. Meg was now over my shoulder. "What can we do?" she hissed.

Chalam yelled from the back, finally able to speak, "Get shallow, Mac! Less pressure! And everyone, get away from the bulkheads!"

The group moved as best they could to the center of the seacar. I aimed upward; our thrust was already at full power—70 kph—though the particle beam was moving nearly at the speed of light through a vacuum channel in the water; we'd never be able to avoid it.

We had only one torpedo.

I realized with dread that we weren't actually at 70 kph; we weren't even close. The damage to our bow had increased friction, and the seacar was shaking madly.

A callout label had appeared above the white dot on the sonar.

Registry: HMS *Trafalgar*
Spitfire Class SSN, BSF
Depth: 756 meters V
Speed: 70 kph

"It's *Trafalgar*," I yelled. I'd heard that name before. I searched my memory. "*Spitfire* Class."

Chalam said, "That's the ship that rescued me!"

After the weapon had destroyed his rented seacar, weeks ago and also in the Indian Ocean near Diego Garcia, he'd ended up unconscious in the water in scuba gear. The same vessel had rescued him.

The one with the neutral weapon.

And now they were going to obliterate us to get the components back.

And they were *highly* motivated.

The depth in the region was only 818 meters. They were hugging the bottom, firing *upward* at us. I stared at the image projected on the canopy. The vessel was 108 meters long. They had ten tubes, four thrusters, a max speed of seventy-three kph, and a Crush Depth of 3,100 meters. There was a bulge on the top of the hull, at amidships, from which the white beam with a flood of bubbles arced upward.

"They're staying deep," Johnny mumbled.

I kept turning the ship as we ascended, to keep our hull difficult to lock to. "The beam is coming from the top of its hull. If they were shallower, we could get below them. They're not going to let that happen."

And this area was not deep enough for us.

I searched the map frantically, looking for a trench, a crevasse, a crack or fracture.

Anything.

But no luck.

Alarms were still sounding.

Fish farms.

"Dammit!" I cried. They were matching every move we made. They were larger and less maneuverable, but they were faster and could fire at us from below.

"What's the range on this?" I screamed. "Two hundred?"

Alyssna was behind me. "To be effective, yes."

Our depth was now a hundred meters. It meant they were seven hundred meters away. The beam would not be destructive at that range.

Sure enough, Johnny said, "They're coming shallow!"

Registry: HMS *Trafalgar*
Spitfire Class SSN, BSF
Depth: 623 meters ∧
Speed: 73 kph

"Any ideas?" *Trafalgar* had increased speed to their max and were blowing ballast. They were trying to lower the range, to get the weapon closer.

Alyssna said, "You have to get below them if possible. They can't shoot downward with that configuration." She was peering at the image on the canopy, projected by the VID system.

"We have one torpedo." I thought furiously. We couldn't waste it. "Is there any way to disrupt the beam?"

"Distance," she said. "Put more distance between us."

I swore. "They have a faster top speed." I cranked my head around and searched for Meg. "Is the bow screwed? Can you check?" As I said it, I pushed the SCAV throttle forward. The ship started to rattle. The reactor was still generating steam—flash boiling seawater—but the engineered shape at the bow had changed. It was generating a lot of friction, and not the large bubble that we needed. The vibrations increased and *SC-1* started to moan.

Meg was at my back and she was peering out the canopy. Then there was a particularly loud groan—angry and sepulchral—and she snapped her head around to search it out. "Stop, Mac! That was a structural noise. The SCAV, we can't push it."

I pulled back on the throttle. So, we could use it for lower speed—which would create a lot of noise and bubbles—but we couldn't go fast.

The Water Pick neutral beam had really damaged our structural integrity.

The alarm started screaming again.

Torpedo in the water!

Chapter Forty-One

THE ALARM BLARED THREE MORE times.

There were *four* weapons in the water headed for us.

And a stream of bubbles shooting upward from the turret at the top of the *Spitfire* Class warsub, *Trafalgar*, as the particle beam continued to fire, aiming at us.

It was not going to stop.

The bubbles diminished at just over 200 meters from the warsub, but it was still firing.

I almost laughed at the name of the ship's class; it was so appropriate, I thought.

"Johnny," I snapped. "We've only got a few seconds here. Target the turret on that ship and fire our torpedo when we get close."

He eyed me. "If you get closer, the beam gets stronger."

"I know, but we don't have a choice. We have to damage it."

SC-1 heeled to the port as the torpedoes grew closer. I dropped countermeasures, then arrowed down, away from them, headed back into the deeps—

And the concussion ripped out into the ocean.

All four torpedoes exploded.

The impact of the shock wave shoved the seacar to the side. The safety straps dug into my side and shoulders as we moved. I groaned against the stress. Behind me, people slammed into the bulkheads. They were getting shoved around like rag dolls.

The seacar shook and rattled, and a stream of water shot into the pilot cabin from the canopy seal.

"Shit!" I cried. "We're taking on water!"

But it was just a bit, at that point. The pumps would easily be able to keep up with it, but water and electronics didn't mix.

I held the yoke tight in my hands. *Trafalgar* was just below us and 350 meters to our starboard. I pointed the bow toward it, but the beam was slicing straight for us.

I swore. It was no use. We couldn't get close.

"Fire," I said. It was a last resort.

Our final torpedo launched and headed straight for the BSF warsub. I pulled up and away from it, leading the beam on an angle away from the torpedo, to create a clear path for our weapon.

The warsub launched countermeasures and turned from the missile . . .

But they were already right at the bottom, and the places they could run were limited.

I held my breath.

Our weapon continued on and disappeared into the bubbling mass of countermeasures . . .

And exploded.

The concussion echoed in our seacar, and I stared at *Trafalgar*. It was a huge ship, and the chances of us doing a lot of damage with only one torpedo were limited. They had four thrusters, and even if we damaged one of them, they'd still be able to pursue and fire at us.

The concussion wave hit the warsub and the beam flickered. The bubbles stopped.

I released my breath, staring at the enemy ship, willing it to sink downward and hit bottom.

But no luck. We just didn't have the firepower to hurt it.

And we didn't have the speed to escape.

Then it started to blow ballast and rise.

The turret turned toward us, and the beam started again.

They were over 300 meters away, but they were coming.

And the neutral beam was going to slice us to pieces.

Chapter Forty-Two

I MADE OUR DEPTH THIRTY meters and stared at the screen. They were below but rising, and had matched our speed and course. We were taking on water and had no other torpedoes, but they didn't know that.

Clicking the comm, I said, "Attention *Trafalgar*."

Johnny stared at me.

I said, "We have to stall." Then I turned and yelled behind me. "Get the grenades!"

Meg was at my back in an instant. "What do we do, Tru?" Her eyes were wild.

"We don't have much hope here. But we have grenades stored on board." They were for our mission to *Aurora*, but we hadn't used them. "Listen, we can tie them into a bundle. Drop them on the ship. Like a mine." That ship was below us. We could hope that our makeshift bomb would hit it . . .

It seemed laughable though.

They were rising still, the beam was coming toward us . . .

"What are your intentions?" I asked the BSFIF warsub. "You've attacked us without provocation."

A voice crackled back, "You raided our base and killed multiple officers! What are you talking about?" The tone was dark.

"I'm sorry?" I said. "I'm not sure what you're talking about."

"Don't lie to us. You're going to die."

They were still coming, so I changed tack. "Don't get close to us," I snapped. "We have a nuclear bomb on board. We'll detonate it."

"Bullshit."

And yet the ship's approach slowed. The lie had had an effect, although small. It was still coming . . . but more hesitant than before.

I pressed on, and made my voice ice: "You noted the detonation near Diego Garcia a few minutes ago, correct? Don't come closer or you risk the same." I studied the sonar return. They were likely attempting to mollify us . . . but were still moving slowly into the 200-meter range.

"Get ready to drop the grenades," I said.

Sahar entered the living area from the engineering compartment. The concussion had battered her; her face was bloody and bruised, but her eyes were sharp. "Listen," she cried. "That's like throwing a dart and hoping it hits a marble in mid-air. It's not accurate."

"What else can we—"

"I can take it down, Mac." Her eyes were fierce. "Remember, I was a free diver? I can swim it down to them. Secure it to the hull. Then pull the pin."

—••—

Trafalgar was coming toward us.

We didn't have a lot of time.

I stared at her. "Are you sure, Sahar? It means possibly hurting—"

"We don't have a choice right now!" she snapped. "We have to get the weapon back to Trieste."

"But the mix isn't right!" I cried. "You'll get a dozen meters down and start feeling narcosis! It's too—"

"I'll change the mix as I go. I'll try my best. It's all we've got!"

She was already sprinting back to the airlock to grab her equipment. I said to Meg, "Get the package ready."

She was watching Sahar as she ran from us. Then she turned back to me. "Are you sure?"

I had to admire the British Mayor. She was going to sacrifice herself for us, perhaps because of what Clarke had done. Because she'd vouched for the man, who'd then gone off on his own mission. I said in a soft voice, "She can go out the moonpool. We'll try to stay stationary for her. Not much other choice."

Richard, who'd been quiet, yelled at us. "Mac! Let me help. Cut these restraints. I'm not a threat to you. I can help with the grenades."

Cliff was at my side in a flash. "I'll watch him. We need the help."

They also had to prepare Sahar's equipment for a nightmare dive.

I stared into Richard's pleading eyes. "Okay," I said.

Within seconds, Richard was helping Meg frantically put the grenades together, his hands steady and sure. Cliff was helping Sahar, who was sitting on the edge of the moonpool, getting ready to go into the water.

Trafalgar was below us, rising, but still 250 meters away.

The beam was slicing upward.

Something suddenly occurred to me. "Sahar! If you go straight down, the neutral beam will hit you."

"I'll go around. The bubbles are obvious. Try to lead the vessel away a bit." She glanced at me. "But don't go too far. I have to get back."

Alyssna had been watching the preparations, her eyes full of terror. She couldn't believe what we were doing. "Listen, Mac. Bubbles will obscure the beam a bit. Cause more blooming of the lasers. It'll lower the range. It'll give us a few seconds, maybe."

"Bubbles." It was a statement.

"Yes. Anything to obscure the water."

I stared at the console. We still had a lot of countermeasures remaining. I pushed the release button and dropped five. They descended a hundred meters then stopped, churning the water and bubbling like mad, between us and the approaching warsub.

"You'll have to get past those," I said to Sahar.

"No problem," she said.

Richard handed her a mesh bag, bulging with soup can-sized cylinders. He pointed at a strap. "Pull this. Then get out." He shook his head. "You'll have five seconds."

I cursed inwardly. It wasn't a lot of time, especially underwater, which would magnify the explosion.

"Where do I put it?"

"At the turret on the top," I yelled. "At the neutral beam. We have to stop that weapon."

She glanced at me and managed to flash a quick smile. "It's been fun, Mac."

Then she slipped under Component Four, hung out over the moonpool for just an instant, and disappeared into the dark waters of the Indian Ocean.

—••—

SHE'D BARELY SPLASHED AS SHE arrowed down into the water.

Richard stared into the moonpool as she swam downward. She had a tank, but the mix was a problem. As the pressure grew, more nitrogen would dissolve into her blood.

Cliff swore under his breath. His eyes were fixed on the pool. Then he turned and stared at me in amazement.

The act of heroism impressed even him.

I swallowed.

We were stationary in the water, hovering at thirty meters. Our moonpool was open, and the neutral weapon we'd stolen was dangling over the water precipitously.

Something exploded into my consciousness.

Holy shit!

I jerked upward and bolted from my chair. I said, "Everyone, come here, now. We need all hands!"

The others gathered in the living area. Below us, Sahar was swimming down—straight down—toward the rising warsub. When it came within 200 meters, we were dead. The countermeasures would give us a bit of time, but not much.

We had no more torpedoes, and Sahar had taken all the grenades.

The faces that looked back at me were despondent. Morose. Some were frantic.

Cliff's expression was once again stony, but even he had a drawn expression that he was trying to hide.

But we couldn't give in.

There was always a chance.

"Everyone," I said. "We have a hope, but only one. Sahar can disable *Trafalgar*'s Water Pick. But we have no other torpedoes, and we can't beat their speed."

Meg said, "Then what—"

I pointed at the neutral weapon. Component Four. "But we have that. It's a working high energy particle beam."

Alyssna's face paled. "But Mac, there's no power, there's no laser casement, there's no—"

"*There's no option!*" I cried. "We have a fusion reactor. We have to get the weapon back to the SCAV compartment. Hotwire the reactor to it. Then fire *through our own hull* and hit that bastard.

"It's our only hope now."

Chapter Forty-Three

Blank faces met my comment. I had already started to loosen the cables that secured the device. It was large, and heavy, and we'd need everyone. "Let Chalam go," I said. "Everyone, lift with me."

Within a minute the restraints were off—from Chalam and the weapon—and we were lugging the neutral beam aft-ward into the SCAV chamber. As we lifted, I was giving commands. "Meg, you'll connect the fusion power to it. SCAV is down anyway, so don't worry about causing damage. Alyssna, you get it powered up. Aim out the port hull." We were in engineering now, and grunting as we lifted the weapon, dragging it at times, one foot at a time. "Richard and Cliff, the beam is going to dissolve our own hull, so get the pumps ready. They've got to keep up with the flooding. We have to pump water out *faster* than it spills in."

"How fast will it get in?"

"Fast."

Alyssna said, "The beam will vaporize some of it, but around the edges of the rupture it's going to flood in. Dozens of liters a second likely." She looked at me, veins visible in her forehead as she strained with the weight. "But Mac, there's no laser meant to vaporize the water and create a vacuum channel. The range will be minuscule."

"How miniscule?"

She shrugged, which was difficult while lifting. "Ten meters maybe? Nothing, really."

"It'll have to do. I'll just have to get us close."

"But the water will drown the weapon! If it gets wet, then it'll stop working. And water is going to be flooding into the chamber!"

"Leave that to me," Richard said. He was staring at me, his eyes soft.

"Listen Mac, I know you don't agree with what I did—"

"Shut up," I panted. "Save it. There's no excuse for what you did."

"I know you feel that, but—"

"Shut it," I snapped. "Just do your job!" Eventually we were in the SCAV cabin, and we positioned the large weapon on the deck, facing to the port.

"Get the barrel right against the hull," Alyssna said.

We hauled it to the bulkhead. Cliff's muscles bulged as he strained. The barrel was two meters long and the support and control console at its rear made it unwieldy and heavy. It'd been difficult to get it through the hatches, but we'd managed to squeak it by. In the control cabin at the front, Johnny was prepping the pumps for the imminent onslaught of water. Each area of the seacar had automatic pumps ready to kick into high gear if needed. We also had extras that we could move around to danger areas, and Richard was scrambling to get extra pumps in the chamber, connected to pipes that led to the ballast, where we could pump out the water.

Meg worked frantically, making connections with thick cables running directly from the fusion reactor.

Alyssna had powered up the weapon already and was staring at the computer display on its side.

Johnny was yelling at us over the comm, "*Trafalgar* is closing! Their beam is on full, right at us!

"Any sign of Sahar?"

"None."

"All of you, get out," Richard snapped. "Out now. Alyssna, just show me how to start the beam."

The weapon was facing the port bulkhead. It would fire only ten meters, and our chances were minimal at best.

But *Trafalgar* wouldn't expect it.

It was the *last* thing they'd expect.

And it was the only thing we had going for us.

I stared at Richard. "What are you doing?"

"The only thing possible, Mac. For you and the independence movement. I'll stay in here and keep the pumps running. We can't let the water rise more than a meter in here. If it does, the beam will stop."

"But you—"

"Get out." He shoved me toward the hatch. "Leave, now. Get us back to Trieste when this is over."

He sounded a lot like Clarke, I thought. All he cared about was getting the weapon back home safely, so we could defend the city. I turned to Meg. "Get some scuba gear for him."

She left and returned an instant later, with a tank, regulator and mask.

Alyssna had pointed at a single large button on the device, and Richard shoved us out.

The hatch closed behind us.

Chapter Forty-Four

I WAS BACK IN THE control cabin. Below us, the warsub had hit the countermeasure bubbles and had blown right through them.

The beam was cutting through the water, straight for us.

Bubbles were soaring upward in an upside-down waterfall, hitting *SC-1* and obscuring our view out the ports. The moonpool was churning as the bubbles tore up the surface and blew upward into our seacar.

I had to resist every temptation to leave. To push the throttle forward and try to get away.

But that would be a losing battle. They had a higher top speed, more torpedoes, and The Water Pick.

It would only delay the inevitable.

This was our only chance.

The roaring of vaporizing bubbles echoed in the seacar. The temperature started to fall.

Our breath started to mist.

"Oh my god," Meg hissed from behind me.

Chalam was frantic. "Mac, we have to maneuver!"

"Give Sahar a chance," I muttered. "She can do it." She was still out there, but couldn't speak to us. If she did, she risked discovery. I glanced behind me. "Close the moonpool hatch, but open the outer airlock hatch. She can get in that way."

As I stared backward, something caught my eye and my breath stopped in my throat. I grunted in realization. The deck was shimmering. It was pulsating through the darker wavelengths. Glittering almost.

Tendrils of frost spread outward, growing, as if alive and searching for . . .

For *something.*

Then there was a loud *groaning.* The hull was about to give way.

The exterior water pressure was about to blast through our bulkheads.

"Get away from that deck!" I screamed.

Come on, Sahar! You got this!

And then the sonar flared white. There was a small blast below us, and abruptly the *fish farms* alarm stopped chiming.

She'd done it.

I slammed the ballast to negative and we plunged downward. I maneuvered to the side and we descended next to *Trafalgar,* which had only been about a hundred meters below us.

It appeared in our canopy, to the port. I used the maneuvering thrusters to push us closer . . .

And I yelled into the comm, *"Now Richard! Do it!"*

—••—

AN INSTANT LATER, OUR LIGHTS flickered. Richard had slammed his palm on the INITIATE BEAM button.

Within the device, charged deuterium atoms were accelerated in a coil to incredible velocities. Magnets manipulated them until they reached the threshold speed just under the speed of light, then pointed them at the emitter. As the onboard computer recognized it, the stream passed through a thin gas which stripped the extra electron away, rendering them neutral. They then shot down the barrel and at our own hull.

There was no aiming.

There was no input from the sonar system.

This was not a delicate, precision process. We'd hotwired it, flooded it with power, and pushed the button.

We'd fired blindly, but it was like putting a shotgun against the barn and pulling the trigger.

There was nowhere else for the beam to go.

An instant later, a hole twelve inches across was vapor and the particle beam was firing into the ocean.

And into the vessel directly next to us: *Trafalgar.*

The sonar blared again, and it was another *fish farms* warning.

I made our buoyancy neutral, then slowly moved us forward along the *Spitfire* Class's hull.

Trafalgar was now taking a direct hit from a neutral beam, at a range of only a few meters.

And we were slicing into her hull, dissolving metal, and tearing the BSF warsub apart. It hit anyone standing near the bulkhead, dissolving and melting flesh in an instant.

Chalam peered out the viewport at the ship just beside us. He was staring at the stream of bubbles that churned upward from the beam.

Johnny said, "She's taking on ballast, Mac. They know what's happening!"

"We'll stay with her," I cried. "As close as possible!" We didn't have the ten-terawatt laser module to create the vacuum channel, so we needed to keep the beam at point blank range. I pushed the ballast controls to negative to keep up with the vessel.

Alarms started ringing in the control cabin.

Blue lights flashed.

Pressure alerts.

We were flooding.

—••—

THE BEAM HAD CUT THROUGH our own hull. The SCAV compartment hatch kept the flooding confined, and our pumps had kicked into action. Richard called over the comm, "The water's rising quickly! I've got the portable pumps working!" Pause. "The water is spilling in through the hull around the beam. The weapon is pulsing with energy! The bulkhead is glowing and water is steaming around the edges!" We could hear him huffing as he lugged the pumps around and adjusted the thick, black, flexible pipes. "The water is nearly at the weapon. Mac, the deeper we go, the more pressure! The water is shooting in across the entire chamber!"

There was a roar behind his voice, like a waterfall.

"It's lapping at the bottom of the energy beam! There's only a few seconds left!" he cried.

"Meg!" I screamed behind me. "Increase pressure to the SCAV

compartment!" If we could increase the air pressure in that chamber to six or eight atms—or more—it would slow the water flooding in. There was a panel in the engineering compartment that had valves which could divert air to other areas of the seacar. It might give us a few more seconds of firing time. "Richard!" I called to him. "Get ready!"

I stared at the warsub next to us. They were scrambling to escape, but multiple areas of its hull were leaking; bubbles streamed upward from the slices.

It was working!

"Mac!" he cried. "I'm sorry! I did it for the movement! I did it for independence!"

I struggled with the yoke. The warsub was trying desperately to move away from us, and it was difficult to stay next to it.

The alarms were screaming now. Flooding in the SCAV compartment!

Blue lights flashed angrily.

I thought of Sahar, and what she had done for us, to disable the warsub's weapon.

I thought of Kat, my lover, and how Richard had murdered her for his own twisted motives.

I thought of Clarke, and how he had blown himself up just to take a few British Imperial Force warsubs with him.

Then the sonar screen flared white, and *Trafalgar* heaved as water imploded her aft compartments.

I could hear the alarms from the warsub crying out just next to us in the water. It was an absolute cacophony of noise as the particle beam vaporized water, compartments imploded, people screamed, alarms cried for attention, and water cascaded into our own seacar.

Trafalgar shuddered in the water as it plunged downward, trailing a stream of bubbles and blood.

"... they can only come to morning through
the shadows."
—J.R.R. Tolkien, *The Two Towers*

Epilogue: Trieste City

Epilogue

IT WAS A BEAUTIFUL APRIL day in the underwater colony, Trieste. In the world above, countries were beginning their Spring season. In the past, that meant rain, new growth, flowers sprouting, warmer temperatures, and pollen on the winds. Now, however, it was just more of the same: high temperatures, crops that continued to wither and die, and water that lapped at coastal cities and flooded crane facilities. Another one had just gone dark on the west coast—*failed*, because trucks could no longer negotiate the inundated streets—and the US economy took one more hit in a series of body blows and big uppercuts.

Trieste and cities like us seemed to be the only bright spots in the world. A colony thriving on the shallow seafloor, mining and harvesting resources by the boatload, and shipping them to the mainland each and every day.

I wondered again, for the millionth time, if the US would ever really let us strike out on our own. If we'd ever truly be independent.

We'd find out, very soon.

The atrium in Trieste was bright. Sunlight sliced down from above and filtered through the nine-level commercial and office area in the central module. I was at a café with Renée, enjoying a morning coffee. We were against the vine-covered railing, looking down several stories at the levels below. People were moving about on each deck, shopping, enjoying the morning, going to work, or coming back from a tough shift and getting ready to hit the sack.

These periods where we could relax and take a breath were nice, but they were few and far between. I wanted to enjoy it while I could.

I knew this one would not last long.

Renée said, "How's the progress on the weapon?"

I closed my eyes and turned my face up to the sun. "Alyssna has the components connected. It's ready."

"Where did you decide to put it?"

I eyed her. She was smiling at me, her eyes crinkling at their corners. "It needs to be mobile because the range is so low. An attack will come from the Atlantic direction. So . . ."

"It'll be in a sub? Patrolling?"

"That's a nice idea, but it's a bit dangerous. If the sub gets hit, the weapon is useless. I think we can come up with something else." A silence stretched between us. I continued, "Maybe a ring around the city—a tube—and the weapon could be within. It'll be able to move through the ring, on a rail maybe, and prevent warsubs or torpedoes from getting close." I shrugged. "It's a thought. Alyssna and Hyland pitched it."

Renée checked the time. "And what about Richard?"

The truth was, that was a much more difficult decision. He had admitted to murdering Katherine Wells a year earlier. He'd geared his motives toward ensuring I lived a miserable life. He was motivated to achieve greatness for Trieste, but his methods were . . .

I cringed. There was no good description for what he'd done, and why.

"I'm going to speak with him after this. I'll decide then. But I'm . . ." I trailed off.

"Go on."

"I wasn't with her when it happened. When Richard did it. I'm feeling guilt over that. If I'd been there, I could have stopped it."

She frowned. "I don't want you to feel this is just a line, but people always say that when others close to them die. There are always 'what ifs,' Mac."

I remained quiet and felt the guilt coiling through me. It would always be there, I thought. I'd have to just get used to it. "He tried to kill you too, Renée. Multiple times. I was there for two of them and managed to help. But for the first and last ones, I'm lucky you survived."

"I'm tough, Mac." She was smiling. "But you know, when the carbon monoxide nearly killed me, we should have realized something was off earlier. My PCD wasn't working. I didn't tell you. I put it away when we were out. When we returned, it had started up again. It didn't occur to me because we assumed you were the target. My comm wasn't working in my mask either. We should have realized that I was the target."

I nodded. We had to be more vigilant.

Renée was still watching me.

"What?" I asked. She tilted her head and I sighed. "I miss Kat, you know that. But she's been gone a while now. *Frenchie*," I added with a smile.

"There's something else bothering you though, Mac. Not just Richard."

I frowned. "Something Chalam said to me back after The Vault really made me think. When we found out that he'd stolen a bomb for Clarke to use against the Imperial Force. He told me he had only done it because of what they'd done to his brother. He told me that had the same thing happened to Meg, then I would have responded in the exact same way."

"And?"

I snorted. "He was absolutely right. A hundred percent. It's what I had already done, and he had no idea. I went on a rampage, all to protect my sister." I took a deep breath and let it out slowly. "He was only doing what I myself did, Renée, six months ago, at Seascape. He was acting *human*. It was a natural instinct."

"What's going to happen to him?"

"He's going to stay."

Her eyes widened. "But I thought he loved Churchill? He wanted to work as a geologist there."

"Until his brother died. Now that city reminds him of Manse. He realizes that he needs a new start." I'd had a long talk with him, on our way back from the Indian Ocean—which had taken a *long* time because our SCAV hadn't been operational—and he'd come to see that he needed a fresh start. A new beginning. "Maybe he'll move back there in a year, when he begins to feel better, but for now he's going to work here, in our Mining Division. Prospecting for us."

"What do we need now?" she asked, her eyes glinting.

"More hafnium, actually."

"Oh." She shook her head. "For more bombs."

"A few more." I rose and gave her a kiss. "I have to go now. See you later?"

"I wouldn't miss it for the world."

—••—

WE'D CONFINED RICHARD TO HIS cubicle in Trieste. He'd survived the *Trafalgar* attack, but just barely. If he'd died, it would have made things easier, but that was a morbid thought and I'd shoved it aside as soon as it had occurred to me. Inside the SCAV chamber, he'd had the foresight to alter the particle beam's path to cut a larger hole in our hull. As the rising water shorted the weapon's electronics, he'd already been in scuba gear and able to swim out the hole. He'd entered our airlock with a smile on his face, and told us about the experience. The steam had churned outward from the hole the beam had created, the hull had dissolved quickly under the onslaught, and the water had shot in from the perimeter of the opening. When we'd gone deeper, the spray had arrowed across the entire chamber, hitting SCAV electronics in bulkhead consoles. Increasing atmospheric pressure had helped, but only for a bit. Eventually the beam had ceased entirely, and Richard—while fully submerged and *outside* in the water—had watched the *Spitfire* Class BSF vessel plunging downward toward the ocean bottom.

Once back in *SC-1*, he'd willingly allowed us to restrain him again, and he endured the trip like that patiently.

Now, back in the city, he was staring at me, in his cramped compartment, sitting on his bunk, meek. "I'll understand Mac. Whatever you do. I'll take it. I'm just happy we got the weapon back here, safe and sound."

"You arranged the entire mission. From start to finish." In fact, Richard had played a role in every event, including the final attack. "I hadn't expected to find out that you murdered Kat."

"I have my motives." His voice was soft, but not remorseful. It was more *accepting* than anything, meaning it was something he felt he'd had to do.

I frowned. "You tried to kill Renée as well. Just to keep me, what? *Focused?*"

"On the path forward, yes."

"You don't think I deserve human interaction. I can only do what *you* want?" My blood was beginning to boil.

"You have Meg. She is distraction enough. Look what happened when the USSF took her. It led us off mission for months."

"Until you feel Meg is distracting me *too* much, right? But we ended up pulling New Berlin in to Oceania," I snapped. "Things worked out."

He shrugged. "We just have a different way of looking at things, I guess."

"Yours involves murdering your friend's lovers!"

He took a breath. "I'm just trying to—"

"Save it. Renée doesn't deserve it. Kat certainly didn't."

"What are you hoping for here?"

"I was hoping to see a bit of remorse, maybe. Some contrition."

"Mac." He stopped and stared at the bulkhead before him. "In war, if you want to win, you have to be willing to do what it takes. *Whatever* it takes. You have to be willing to make the hard decisions. To kill. You *know* that."

"I don't."

"You sank the USSF warsubs in the Mid-Atlantic Ridge after the battle last year. You *knew* we couldn't allow them to leave. The location of our secret base was on the line. You kept it hidden by sinking those warsubs."

"I had to . . . " I trailed off.

"It was a tough decision, but you made it. It was necessary. Sometimes these things are hard, but war is hell, as they say. You can't just win the hearts and minds of the undersea dwellers. You have to be so tough, so hard, so *heartless* that the enemy will freeze at the mention of your name, at the sounds of our ships. They need to be scared. We have to keep them scared." He clenched a fist. "The Russians knew this back in World War II. They were merciless, because they had to be. Their homeland was on the line. They were fighting the worst enemy they'd faced—the Nazis. After the Soviets won the Battle of Stalingrad, they took over 90,000 prisoners. Almost all of them died. The Soviets killed them. There was no mercy, Mac. Germany knew it, after that. When the Soviets arrived, there was no hope."

I cringed at his words. Using the Russians as an example, especially after their history in Eastern Europe . . .

"Doesn't that make it harder to fight a war? When the enemy will fight to the death rather than surrender?"

"No!" he shouted. "It means we need the superpowers to fear us! We need their submarine fleets to run from us, to give up, to not fight at all! To back down before it comes to war! That's what we need to do! They'll be launching three dreadnoughts to take us down, any day now! We have to fight harder than them. They won't show us mercy. We can't show them any either."

"And you killed Kat for that? And tried to kill Renée? That's sick and twisted, Richard."

"We're in a war!" he yelled. "We need to win! To win, you must do the unthinkable. I know it's hard, and it might not be in our nature, but war is different. You can't be yourself. Countries have lost wars because they don't have what it takes." He snorted. "Taking prisoners. Keeping them comfortable. Caring for them." He slammed his fist on a knee. "It's ridiculous! You kill! You press forward, always, and make the enemy fear you! It's the only way!"

I stared at the veins on his forehead. "You've gone too far. *I'm* not the enemy."

"You need to learn! You need to know how to fight! You're weak!"

"I've been called a lot of things. Weak isn't one of them." I sighed. "There's nothing wrong with wanting to have a family. To have people who love you, support you, protect you."

"You have Meg. You don't need anyone else."

"I do. My dad is gone. My mom is gone. You killed Kat. I need people in my life. I thought you were one . . . "

"I still am!"

"No. You're not. Not anymore. You're not remorseful at all."

"What are you going to do?"

"We have a few options. Prison is one." The irony was obvious. He was telling me *not* to take prisoners, and yet I was offering it.

He remained silent and stared at the deck. "I saved us. I saved the ship. We got the weapon back because of it."

"Maybe. It took the whole team. Sahar may have saved us all." I thought about how she'd jumped into the moonpool and swam hundreds of meters, straight down, to plant the grenades at the neutral beam emitter. I remembered watching her disappear into the shadows. *That* had been bravery. What Richard had done was downright evil. "Where's Jessica?" I asked him.

His expression changed immediately. "She's avoiding me. She's pulled away. I haven't spoken to her in weeks." He shrugged. "She can't take my tactics either, I guess."

"You call them 'tactics.' Others call it murder, Richard. It's sick."

"It's war. You have done terrible things too, in TCI."

"Not to my friends!" I snapped.

"I did it for Oceania." His voice was deliberately calm. Smooth. "We're back, and we're safe."

"Kat's not back. Renée almost died four times!"

He looked up at me. "I won't apologize for it."

I turned my back on him. "Goodbye, Richard. I guess you'll read about us in the news."

"What do you mean?" His tone had finally changed; there was a sliver of panic there.

"I'm kicking you out. You can't stay here anymore. Leave. Don't come back."

He paled. We had once done the same thing to my former Deputy Mayor, Robert Butte. "Trieste? Mac, you wouldn't—"

"And Ballard. I spoke to Grace Winton. Seascape too. You won't be welcome there either." He wouldn't be able to live in any US colony. I opened the sliding partition and stepped into the corridor. "Find a new home. According to your philosophy, I should just kill you right here and now, but I won't do it. I want to show mercy too. I won't win like that. I've said it to you before—we have to make the superpowers see that there's no other option. Letting us work the oceans is the *best* way for their futures too. I can't win and then have them hate us. We need to work with them after we declare Oceania."

"Don't do it! Don't—"

His voice was still calling to me as I marched down the corridor.

———••———

I CALLED JESSICA NG NEXT. I had to fill her in on what had happened with Richard. Her face clouded over when I mentioned what he'd done. She'd known my father as well; she'd fought by his side in the 2090s before his death. She'd ended up running to Ballard with Richard, and had been with him since.

She'd been with him when he'd killed Kat, and I needed to speak with her about it.

"Mac, I'm so sorry I didn't tell you after it happened. I was so scared."

"Of Richard?"

"Yes. I was worried that he'd hurt me. So I stayed with him for a while longer, and slowly distanced myself. I've left him permanently now."

"You saw him kill Kat?" I watched her eyes.

"I did, Mac. It was terrible."

"Tell me."

She paused. Then she looked away and began the entire story. About the attack in the Rift, the FSF and USSF forces, Kat in *SC-1*, and finally, the murder. She cried as she spoke, and as I watched, I realized that she'd been living a nightmare for months now. Maybe years.

"I sent him away, Jess. Banished him. He's not allowed back, and he can't go to Ballard or Seascape either."

"It's probably for the best." She hesitated then looked me square in the eye. "It's maybe worse than killing him. He'll take it hard. I'm sorry, Mac. I didn't warn you."

"He almost killed Renée too."

"I should have told you."

"He might even kill Meg, if I let him stay. Do you think he's a danger to us still? Now that he's leaving?"

She pondered that. "He'll find a way to help, if anything. He'll fight for independence for the colonies. Maybe he'll end up at Blue Downs, or Churchill Sands. Or New Berlin. Whatever happens, and wherever he goes, he'll fight for the cause. He'll never stop. We'll likely hear from him again."

—••—

I WAS BACK IN MY office, expecting my next visitor. I sat at the desk, staring at the mounds of work waiting for me. My inbox was in a similar state: lots to do, and not enough time to do it. The pressures were immense. People *wanted* to work and needed to be free to do it. Sometimes they needed more things from me, and I had to make sure they had the necessary resources.

The comm buzzed and Kristen said, "Your guest is here, Mac."

"Thank you."

The hatch slid aside, and she walked in.

Sahar Noor.

—·•·—

SHE WAS IN AN AQUAMARINE hijab and a shimmering, iridescent green scarf. Her eye makeup was dark, her lashes long, and she was grinning at me. The bruises had faded, and she had fully recovered from the adventure. I rose to greet her, and we sat together, in the small chamber.

"Do you still want this for Churchill?" I asked, without waiting.

She pursed her lips. "It's a tough decision, Mac. It means struggle, fighting, hardship."

"War, maybe."

She shrugged. "I'm hoping we can avoid it."

"When someone attacks, you have to defend yourself. It may involve shooting. You'll have to be prepared."

"I understand."

"Thanks again for helping us steal the neutral beam. Alyssna is going to make more. We'll make sure you've got one too, for your city. We'll also give you some of our SCAV ships—*Swords*. They have the superfast drive, as well as the deep diving tech you were asking about. To go below six kilometers."

She nodded but didn't speak.

I continued, "You know, this wasn't easy. It was one of the more difficult missions. They won't all be this hard."

"Clarke made it a lot harder."

"He betrayed us, but he didn't turn us over. He was trying to achieve two different objectives at the same time."

He'd managed to sink multiple Imperial Force warsubs in the Indian Ocean. It had given the BSF reason to crack down on the splinter group. They'd sailed there, en masse, and arrested hundreds of sailors and officers. They'd claimed that the Isomer Bomb had been a danger to the surrounding nations, and they had to stop officials at Diego Garcia. It was embarrassing for the BSF to admit it, but the massive detonation had given them a useful excuse. The world didn't want to see another colony destroyed—like Seascape—and allowed the BSF to deal with their internal issues without interference.

There were more questions about the Isomer Bomb; nations were still wondering who had invented it. They still didn't know it was Doctor Max Hyland at Trieste, but they'd realize soon. There had now been three detonations in the past six months, including those in the Chagos Trench.

And Clarke got what he wanted in the end, but he'd killed people, which Sahar had been against.

A shadow fell across her face. I said, "What's wrong?"

"When I planted the bomb, it was to take out their neutral beam."

"Go on."

"But it let you sink their ship, Mac. People died."

"You saved our lives. Don't ever forget that." Still, I knew what she was feeling. I felt it too, on a daily basis. And after my conversation with Richard . . . "I've been thinking about it a lot lately. About what it'll take to achieve Oceania. Sometimes we have to do things we don't want. There's a darkness that we need. In a way, Richard was correct."

She looked shocked. "But we can't focus on that!"

"No, but we may have to embrace it, at times. We all have a side that we want to avoid, but it's part of who we are. Richard embraced his a little too much." I snorted at the understatement. "He went way too far. But sometimes, for the greater good, you may have to do things that are . . . *questionable.*"

"I'm going to do this the *right* way, Mac. I'll stick to my morals." She paused and a stillness seemed to settle over her. "Allah says that 'Whosoever kills an innocent human being it shall be as if he has killed all mankind.'"

"I know that quote. The Quran also states that if you save the life of one, you've saved all lives." I shrugged. "Or something to that effect, correct?"

"Absolutely."

"You saved us all out there, Sahar. If you hadn't sacrificed yourself with that final dive . . . "

She processed my statement in silence.

I continued: "You saved many lives. Not just on our seacar, but possibly all of Trieste. Do you see that?"

She pursed her lips, but didn't reply.

I smiled. "I'm happy to be with you on this, Sahar. I can't wait to work with you."

Finally she said, "I am going to go outside to pray soon." She sighed, but I wasn't sure if she was still internalizing what I'd said, or if she already agreed with me. "I just love the water here. It helps see things clearly, don't you think? Care to join me?"

I smiled broadly. "I'd love to, although I'll just meditate."

"Fair enough."

Then I leaned back and studied the ceiling.

"What are you looking at?"

"We're so fragile here. The slightest attack could end it all in an instant. Russia is sending three dreadnoughts for us. We don't have much time to prepare. To get The Water Pick up and running. To get more Isomer Bombs ready." I snorted. "We have civilians here, and I've brought this on them. An implosion means those fragile ceilings could crash down in an instant. Crush everyone."

"It's the same at Churchill. The only reason I'm involved is because they elected me, and it's what *they* want. I have to follow their wishes. But here, your people *want* you to do this too. They want you to lead. Otherwise they'd have left months ago, Mac. Or elected someone else."

Still, the feeling was rattling in my brain. There was a dread surging within me. We were going to declare independence soon, and every superpower in the world would declare war on us.

They were coming.

A Note from the Author

ANY ERRORS IN REGARDS TO the physics of cavitation and supercavitation, the effects of water pressure, plate tectonics, neutral and particle beams, energy weapons, and SCUBA diving are mine alone.

Thanks to Cheyney Steadman for creating the diagrams in this book. She did a wonderful job, once again.

I decided to include a strong Muslim woman in this book to increase inclusivity in my writing. I also wanted to dispel the myths and generalizations about the culture and religion, particularly about the women. However, it was a fine line I had to thread, and I hope I succeeded. I didn't want Sahar Noor to come off as being too strong, and I also didn't want her to come off as too weak and therefore pointless to the narrative. She had to be determined with a solid moral compass, a great companion to Mac and his team, and a very capable and magnetic leader. I relied on my friend Fatima Hamou to help me along in the process. Thank you, Fatima, for putting up with my stream of questions.

I researched a great deal for the weapon in this novel. I had been mulling over the idea of an energy beam, because they have so many benefits. The LaWS weapon is a great example. Each shot costs less than a dollar in energy, whereas a disposable missile might cost hundreds of thousands of dollars. The statistics I provided in Chapter Five about the recent rapid advancements in laser weapon deterrents to incoming missiles, drones, and aircraft are real. The problem is that there are numerous issues to overcome underwater, the largest of which is disbelief. I gave Mac a healthy dose of that in *The Shadow of War*, and I also created an interesting invention that involved two different types of energy weapons to make it more plausible, as well as a very limited range. I hope you enjoyed The Water Pick.

The Neutral Beam is a real weapon. The BEAR project really happened. The US government was indeed investing money into a space-based neutral particle beam. In fact, there were plans to launch such a weapon and have it operating in Earth orbit by 2023. However, in September, 2019, this initiative was canceled as it was viewed as not "near-term" enough. The accelerated hydrogen atoms—either hydrogen, deuterium, or tritium—move at nearly light speed through a vacuum. When they collide with an object, their destructive power is immense. I did make one intentional mistake in the narrative: As the beam penetrates a target, atoms are disassociated, protons are shoved away, and electrons scattered, and the result would be *heat*, which would contribute to the melting of the material and can even cause volatile materials to explode, like rocket fuel. In this book, I made the process *cold* instead. The reason was to create more drama of impending doom, and it was an intentional alteration on my part. My apologies to those physicists out there who might criticize a "mistake" such as this, but tension is sometimes more important in a work of fiction.

Regarding the Boxing Day 2004 earthquake and tsunami, it killed a confirmed 130,000 in Indonesia, but estimates of actual deaths range upward to 170,000. This is the figure I used in the book.

In Chapter Eighteen, there's a discussion of an earthquake being so large that it's capable of changing the length of our day. The Japan quake of 2011 shortened our day by 1.6 microseconds. The reason is that it occurred at a subduction boundary, where one denser crustal ocean plate is moving under a less dense continental plate. As a result, the earth actual *shrunk* following the quake. It's akin to a figure skater who draws their arms in while rotating. The speed of rotation increased as our diameter decreased—albeit sightly—hence our day length shortened. The earth is dynamic and changing due to tectonics, caused by our hot inner core and mantle. Climate change is another issue entirely, caused by natural as well as human-made variables.

The theme of light and dark has permeated the last two books in this series. *An Island of Light* and *The Shadow of War* delve into the concepts of revenge, trauma, guilt, family, and in this novel, the darker side of war and what must be done to win. For this, I introduced Sahar

Noor, a moral compass for Mac, and someone to help keep him from succumbing to total darkness. Yes, there was still death and destruction, but it was not at Mac's hands, and for this we must thank Sahar. In my mind's eye, I know that Mac needs to feel that he can emerge from his struggle still able to function and live a relatively ordinary life. It must be a challenge for soldiers, who have truly dealt with real death and destruction, to sink back into a "normal" life after a war. *The Man in the Gray Flannel Suit*, a novel by Sloan Wilson and a movie starring Gregory Peck, examined this concept, and a running theme of *The Shadow of War* threads a line of violence and peace, and how to achieve independence without causing *too* much death and violence. Richard Lancombe and Commodore Clarke represent the darker side of conflict. The things they do are reprehensible, and yet they were motivated and not acting blindly. There were reasons for their actions. Richard's comment about countries losing wars because they weren't merciless enough is up for debate, but an argument can be made for it. Sahar Noor is clearly the other side, the light side, influenced by her culture and religion. She is not naïve, however; she knows that bad things will eventually happen when all is said and done. She's just trying to keep the violence to a minimum.

Populism is on the rise around the world right now. Much of the right-wing tendencies seem to be driven by a xenophobia and a fear of refugees and immigrants. This seems bizarre to me, as multicultural nations are stronger because of the drive to succeed and prosper. When people come from areas that are less prosperous, or regions suffering from war or famine, they are universally highly motivated to work hard and succeed. The United States was a beacon for immigration in the late 1800s and the 1900s, and the influx of a powerful and motivated workforce still resonates today. It surprises me when people reject this notion. In many ways the undersea colonies in this series are the "New World" for refugees and immigrants running from rampant climate change. Their drive and motivation will help new colonies succeed where land nations become complacent and fail.

In the United Kingdom, in the 1990s, there was a right-wing movement that included politician John Tyndall, leader of the British National Party. He had a negative view of immigration, even saying he wanted to "help the immigrants return home." His intent was to "Put the *Great* back into Britain." The movement was xenophobic. Followers wanted stronger borders and more rigorous restrictions on immigration. Does that sound familiar? The similarities to Trumpism are unmistakeable. In many ways the BSFIF in this book represents this offshoot of populism, a right-wing dynamic in a world suffering from economic disaster, rampant immigration due to climate change, and millions of refugees flooding across Europe because of rising waters. It's based on history, although I didn't devote a great deal of time to the philosophy of the movement, because at its core this book is about a heist and not an investigation of current political events—it was only partly inspired by them. Nevertheless, poor economies and environmental disasters historically trigger right-wing extremism, particularly among the jobless and uneducated, and good people need to remain clear headed and vigilant against them.

In Chapter Seven there is a mention of the discovery of exploding kelp forests in the Arctic Ocean. This is true. Researchers have indeed recently discovered a proliferation of kelp, however, they have also noted a reduction in some traditional areas of growth, such as off the Western coast of Australia.

The Rise of Oceania has involved numerous antagonists and multiple superpowers: China, the United States, France, Russia, Germany, and the United Kingdom. I have now set the table . . . and it's time for the big finish.

Mac will be back in The Rise of Oceania Book Six: *A Blanket of Steel*.

Please visit me at Facebook @TSJAuthor and Twitter @TSJ_Author. Also visit www.timothysjohnston.com to receive updates and learn about new and upcoming thrillers, and also to register for news alerts.

My futuristic murder mysteries include *The Furnace* (2013), *The Freezer* (2014), and *The Void* (2015), all published by Carina Press.

Thanks again for investing your time in this novel. Do let me know what you think of my thrillers.

Timothy S. Johnston
tsj@timothysjohnston.com
31 May 2022

A
BLANKET
OF
STEEL

The Thrilling Conclusion to *The Rise of Oceania*

Coming Soon from Timothy S. Johnston and
Fitzhenry & Whiteside Limited